STORY AND ART BY
NORIYUKI KONISHI

ORIGINAL CONCEPT AND SUPERVISED BY LEVEL-5 INC.

YO-KAI WATCH™
Volume 22
VIZ Media Edition

Story and Art by Noriyuki Konishi
Original Concept and Supervised by LEVEL-5 Inc.

Translation/Tetsuichiro Miyaki
English Adaptation/Aubrey Sitterson
Lettering/John Hunt
Design/Kam Li
Editor/Megan Bates

YO-KAI WATCH Vol. 22
by Noriyuki KONISHI
© 2013 Noriyuki KONISHI
©LEVEL-5 Inc.
Original Concept and Supervised by LEVEL-5 Inc.
All rights reserved.
Original Japanese edition published by SHOGAKUKAN.
English translation rights in the United States of America,
Canada, the United Kingdom, Ireland, Australia and New Zealand
arranged with SHOGAKUKAN.

Printed in the U.S.A.

Published by VIZ Media, LLC
P.O. Box 77010
San Francisco, CA 94107

10 9 8 7 6 5 4 3 2 1
First printing, January 2024

22

STORY AND ART BY
NORIYUKI KONISHI

ORIGINAL CONCEPT AND SUPERVISED BY LEVEL-5 INC.

CHARACTER INTRODUCTION

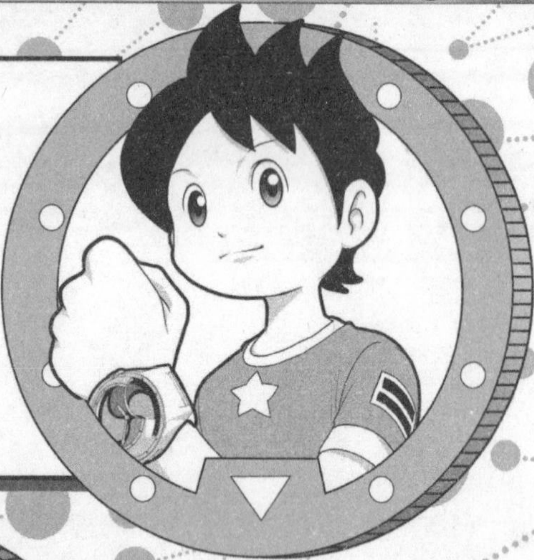

NATE ADAMS

AN ORDINARY ELEMENTARY SCHOOL STUDENT UNTIL WHISPER GAVE HIM THE YO-KAI WATCH. HE'S USED IT TO MAKE A BUNCH OF YO-KAI FRIENDS!

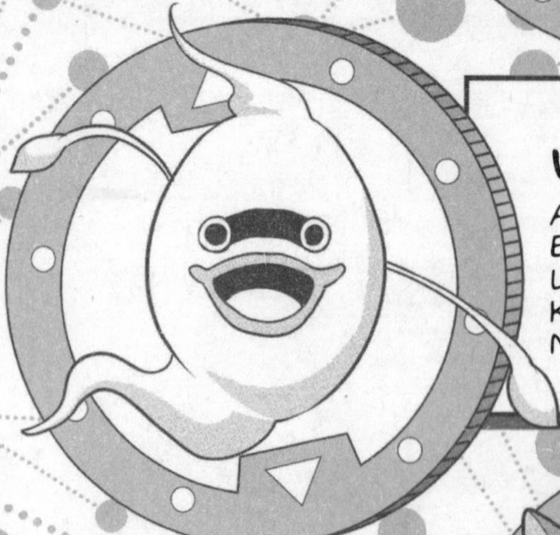

WHISPER

A YO-KAI BUTLER FREED BY NATE, WHISPER USES HIS EXTENSIVE KNOWLEDGE TO TEACH NATE ALL ABOUT YO-KAI!

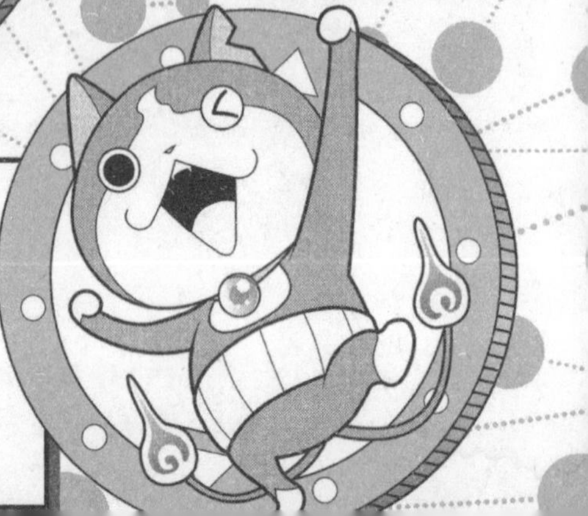

JIBANYAN

A CAT WHO BECAME A YO-KAI WHEN HE PASSED AWAY. FRIENDLY AND CAREFREE, HE'S THE FIRST YO-KAI THAT NATE BEFRIENDED. HE'S BEEN TRYING TO FIGHT TRUCKS, BUT HE ALWAYS LOSES.

BARNABY BERNSTEIN

NATE'S CLASSMATE.
NICKNAME: BEAR.
CAN BE MISCHIEVOUS.

EDWARD ARCHER

NATE'S CLASSMATE.
NICKNAME: EDDIE.
HE ALWAYS WEARS
HEAPHONES.

KATIE FORESTER

THE MOST POPULAR GIRL IN
NATE'S CLASS.

HAILEY ANNE THOMAS

THE OTHER YO-KAI WATCH
HOLDER. A SELF-PRO-
CLAIMED FAN OF ALIENS
AND SAILOR CUTIES.

USAPYON

A RABBITLIKE YO-KAI WEARING
A SPACE SUIT. HE'S SEARCHING
FOR SOMEONE.

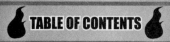

TABLE OF CONTENTS

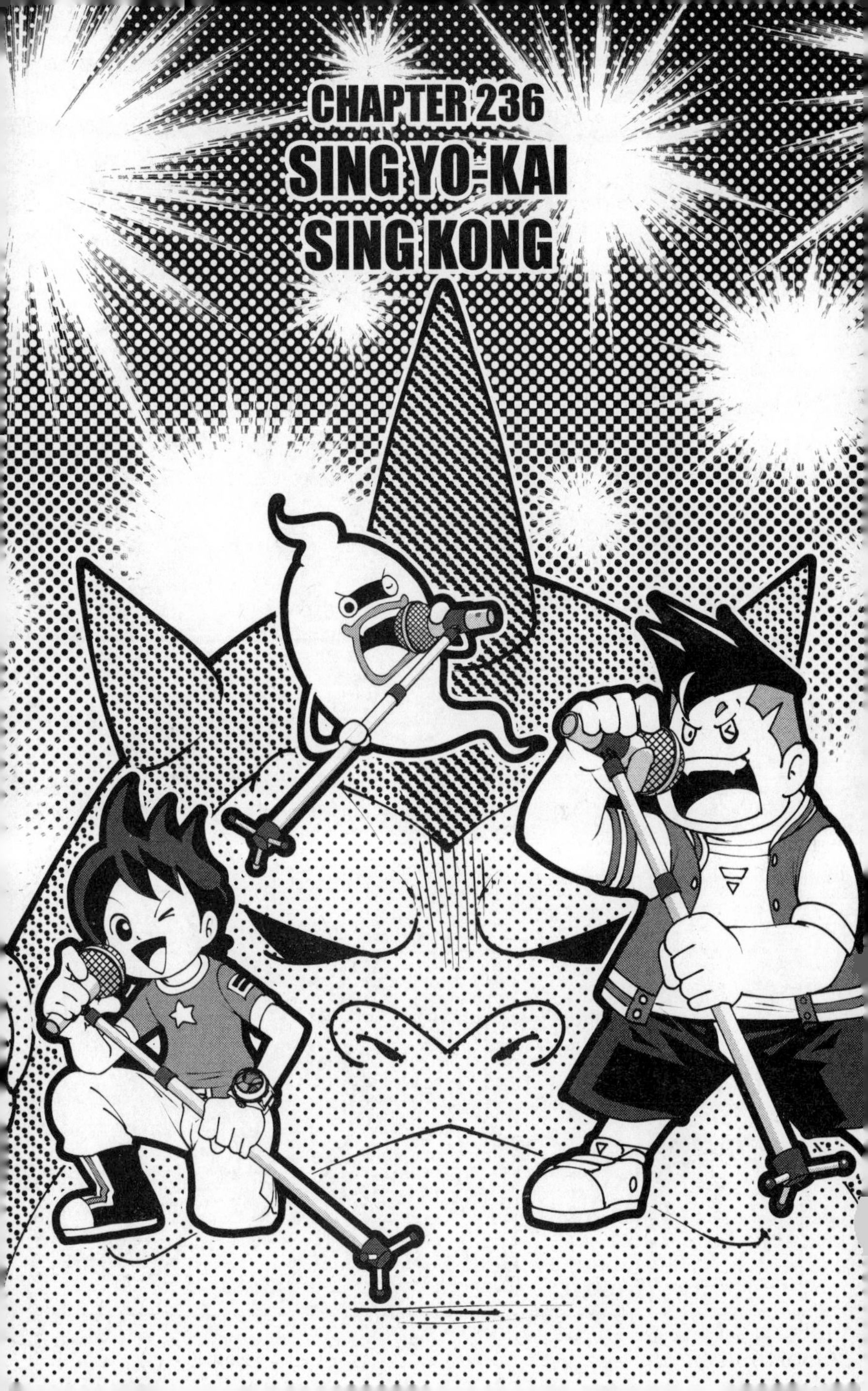
CHAPTER 236
SING YO-KAI SING KONG

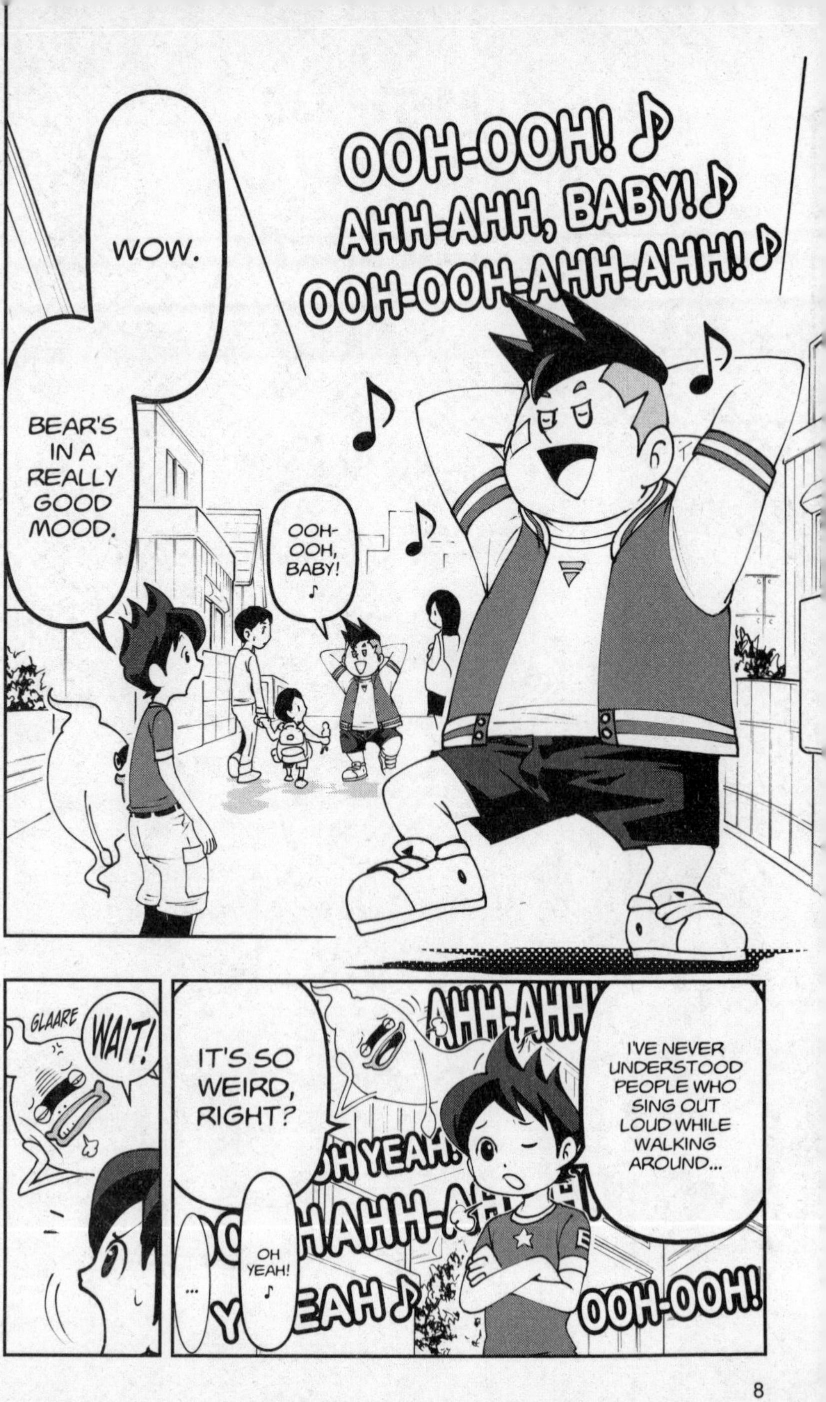
OOH-OOH! ♪
AHH-AHH, BABY! ♪
OOH-OOH-AHH-AHH! ♪
WOW.
BEAR'S IN A REALLY GOOD MOOD.
OOH-OOH, BABY! ♪
AHH-AHH
I'VE NEVER UNDERSTOOD PEOPLE WHO SING OUT LOUD WHILE WALKING AROUND...
IT'S SO WEIRD, RIGHT?
OOH-OOH!
OH YEAH! ♪
...
GLAARE
WAIT!

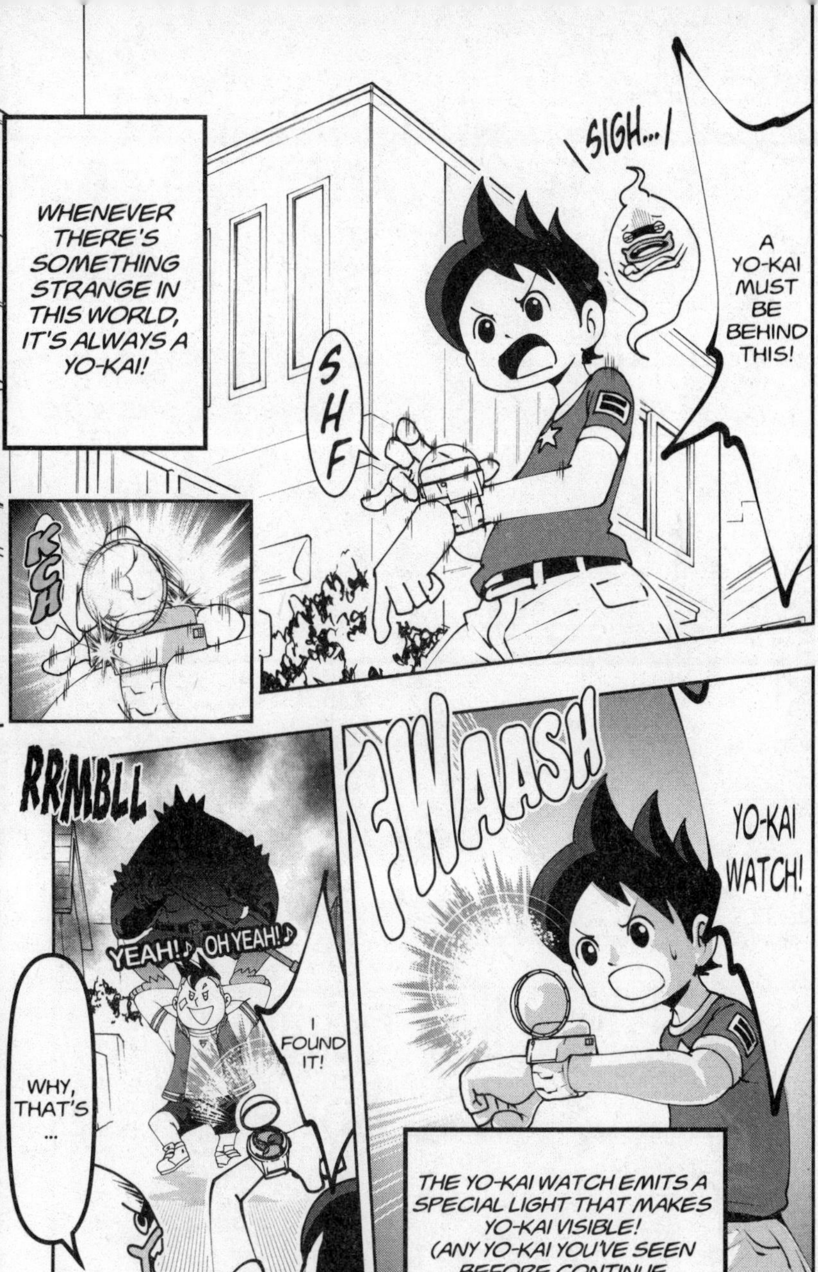
SIGH...
A YO-KAI MUST BE BEHIND THIS!
WHENEVER THERE'S SOMETHING STRANGE IN THIS WORLD, IT'S ALWAYS A YO-KAI!
SHF
KCH
FWAASH
YO-KAI WATCH!
THE YO-KAI WATCH EMITS A SPECIAL LIGHT THAT MAKES YO-KAI VISIBLE! (ANY YO-KAI YOU'VE SEEN BEFORE CONTINUE TO BE VISIBLE.)
RRMBLL
I FOUND IT!
OH YEAH!♪
YEAH!♪
WHY, THAT'S ...

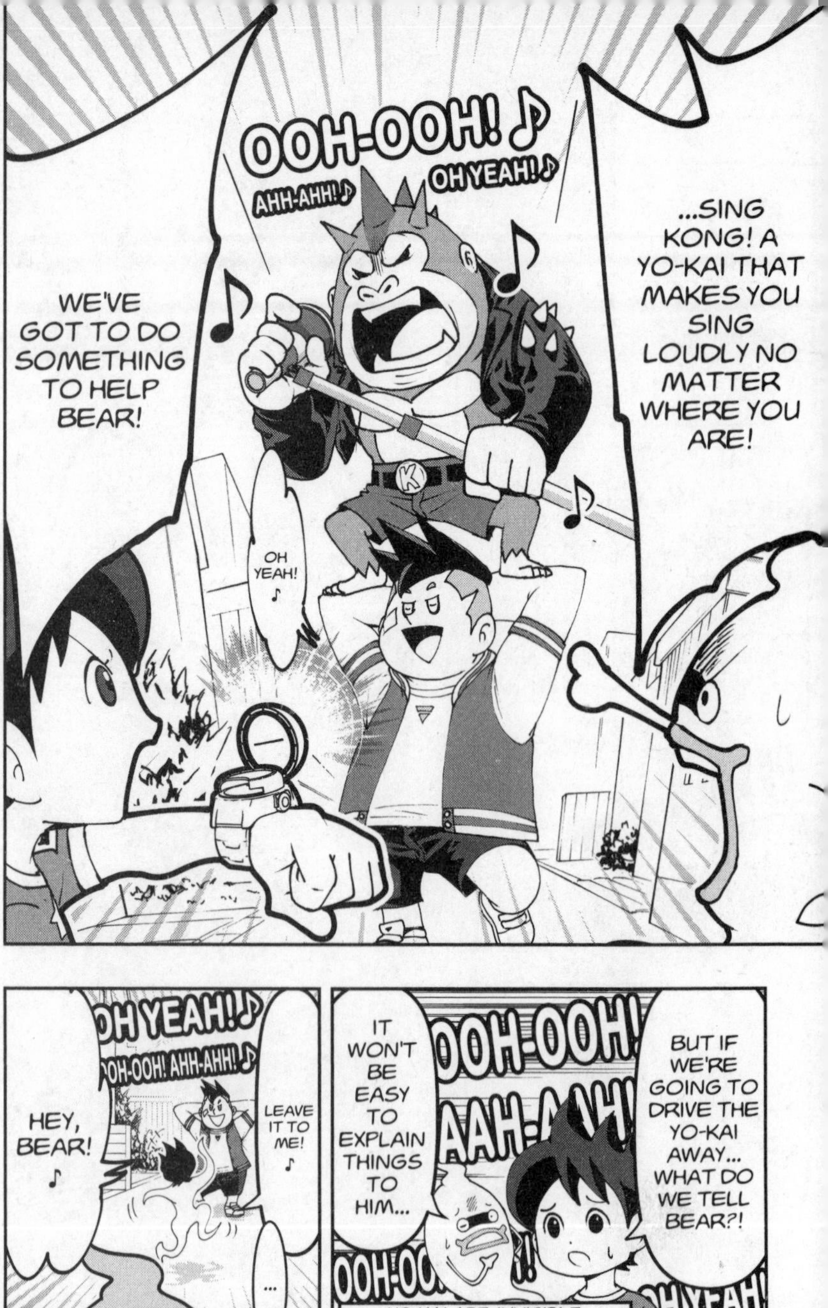
...SING KONG! A YO-KAI THAT MAKES YOU SING LOUDLY NO MATTER WHERE YOU ARE!
OOH-OOH! ♪
OH YEAH! ♪
AHH-AHH! ♪
WE'VE GOT TO DO SOMETHING TO HELP BEAR!
OH YEAH! ♪
BUT IF WE'RE GOING TO DRIVE THE YO-KAI AWAY... WHAT DO WE TELL BEAR?!
OOH-OOH!
IT WON'T BE EASY TO EXPLAIN THINGS TO HIM...
YO-KAI ARE INVISIBLE TO THE HUMAN EYE.
OH YEAH! ♪
OOH-OOH! AHH-AHH! ♪
LEAVE IT TO ME! ♪
HEY, BEAR! ♪
...

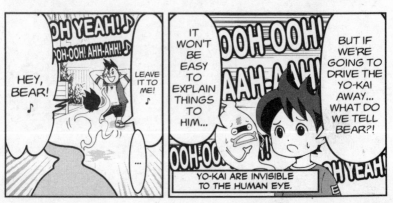

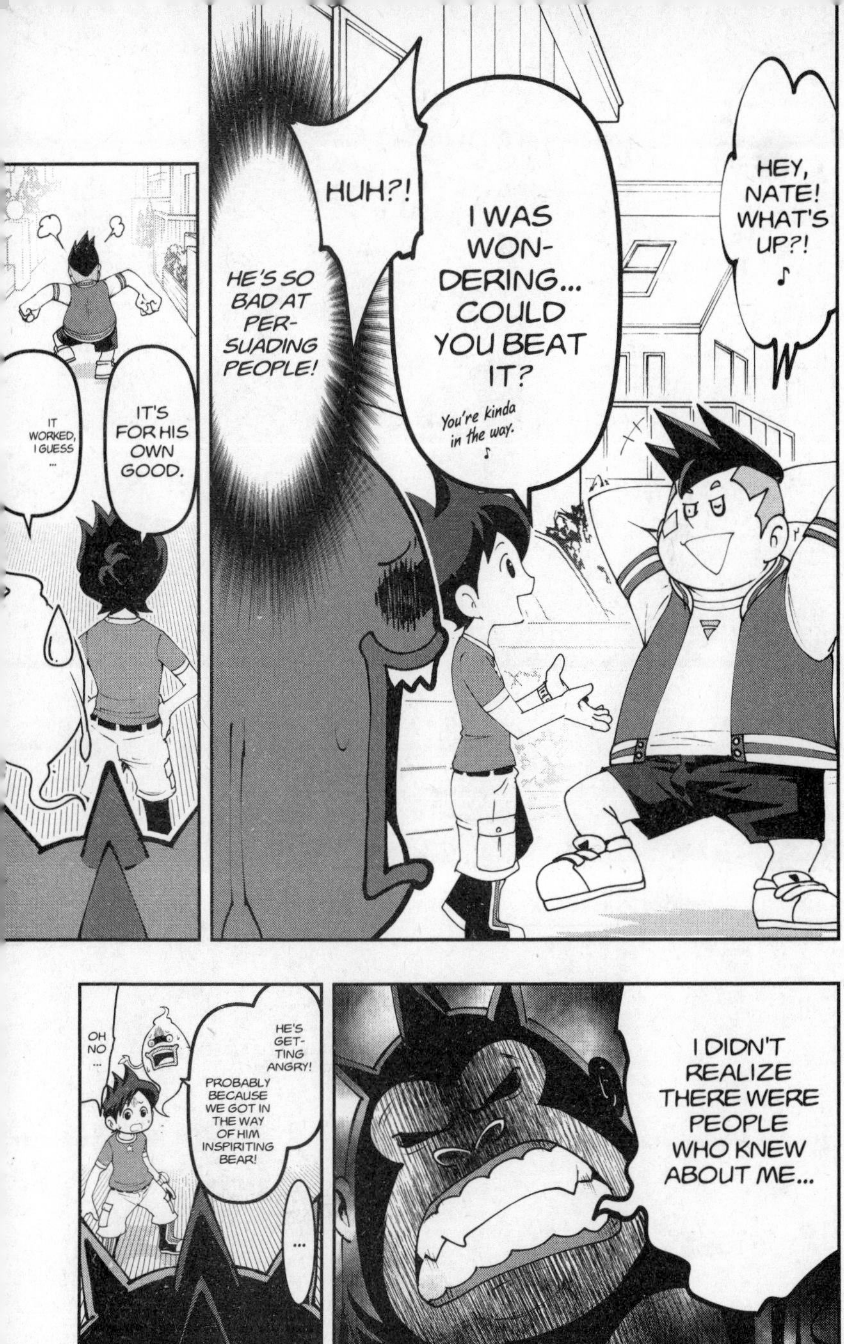
HEY, NATE! WHAT'S UP?! ♪
I WAS WONDERING... COULD YOU BEAT IT?
You're kinda in the way. ♪
HUH?!
HE'S SO BAD AT PERSUADING PEOPLE!
IT'S FOR HIS OWN GOOD.
IT WORKED, I GUESS...
I DIDN'T REALIZE THERE WERE PEOPLE WHO KNEW ABOUT ME...
HE'S GETTING ANGRY!
PROBABLY BECAUSE WE GOT IN THE WAY OF HIM INSPIRITING BEAR!
...
OH NO ...

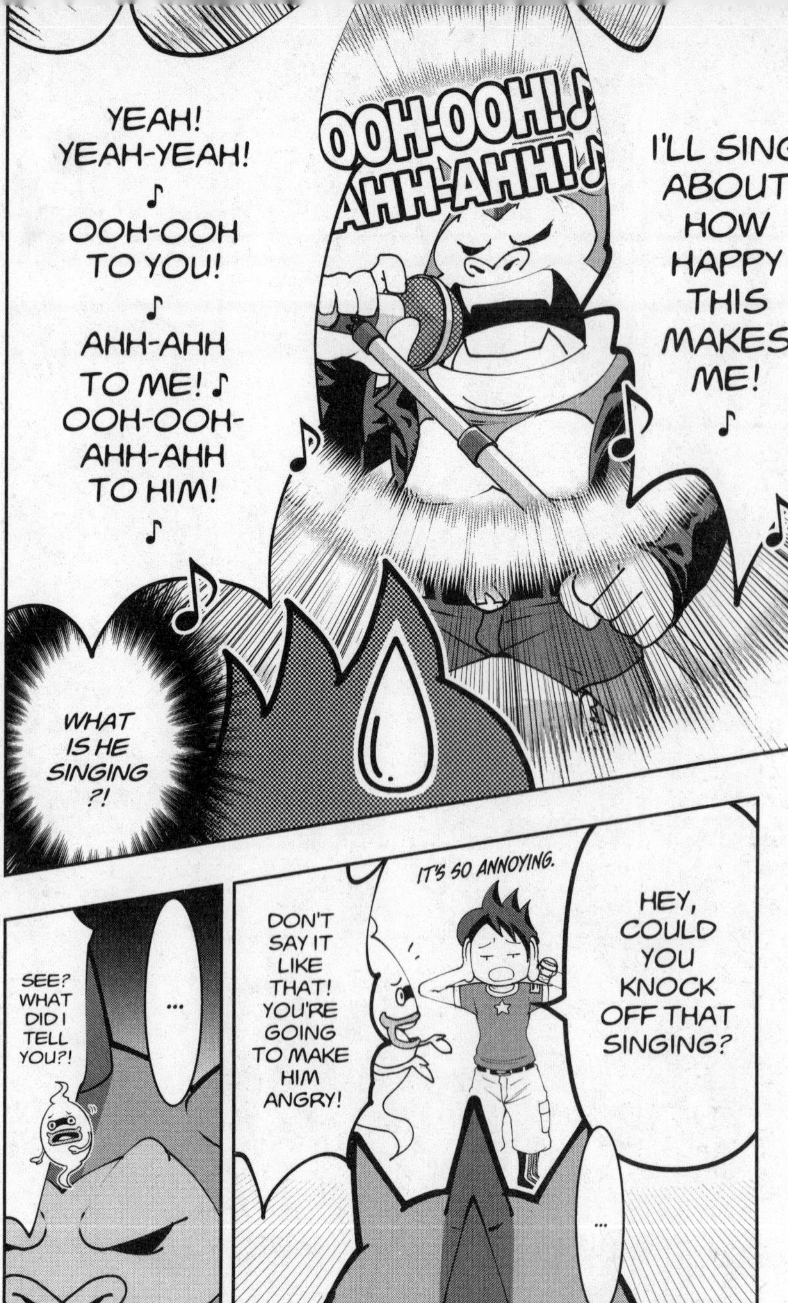
I'LL SING ABOUT HOW HAPPY THIS MAKES ME! ♪
OOH-OOH!♪ AHH-AHH!♪
YEAH! YEAH-YEAH! ♪ OOH-OOH TO YOU! ♪ AHH-AHH TO ME! ♪ OOH-OOH-AHH-AHH TO HIM! ♪
WHAT IS HE SINGING?!
HEY, COULD YOU KNOCK OFF THAT SINGING?
IT'S SO ANNOYING.
DON'T SAY IT LIKE THAT! YOU'RE GOING TO MAKE HIM ANGRY!
...
...
SEE? WHAT DID I TELL YOU?!

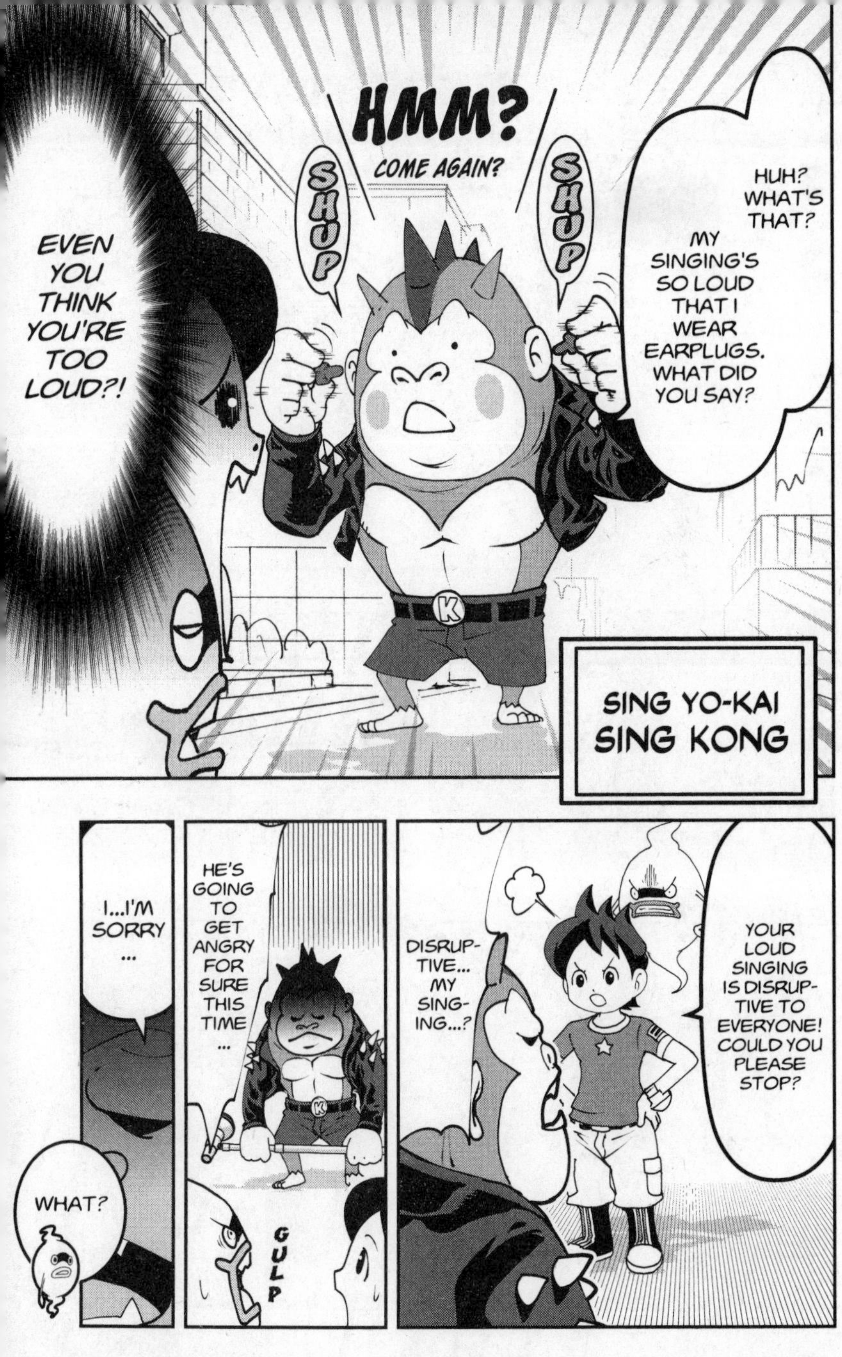
HMM?
COME AGAIN?
SHUP
SHUP
HUH? WHAT'S THAT? MY SINGING'S SO LOUD THAT I WEAR EARPLUGS. WHAT DID YOU SAY?
EVEN YOU THINK YOU'RE TOO LOUD?!
SING YO-KAI SING KONG
YOUR LOUD SINGING IS DISRUPTIVE TO EVERYONE! COULD YOU PLEASE STOP?
DISRUPTIVE... MY SINGING...?
HE'S GOING TO GET ANGRY FOR SURE THIS TIME ...
GULP
I...I'M SORRY ...
WHAT?

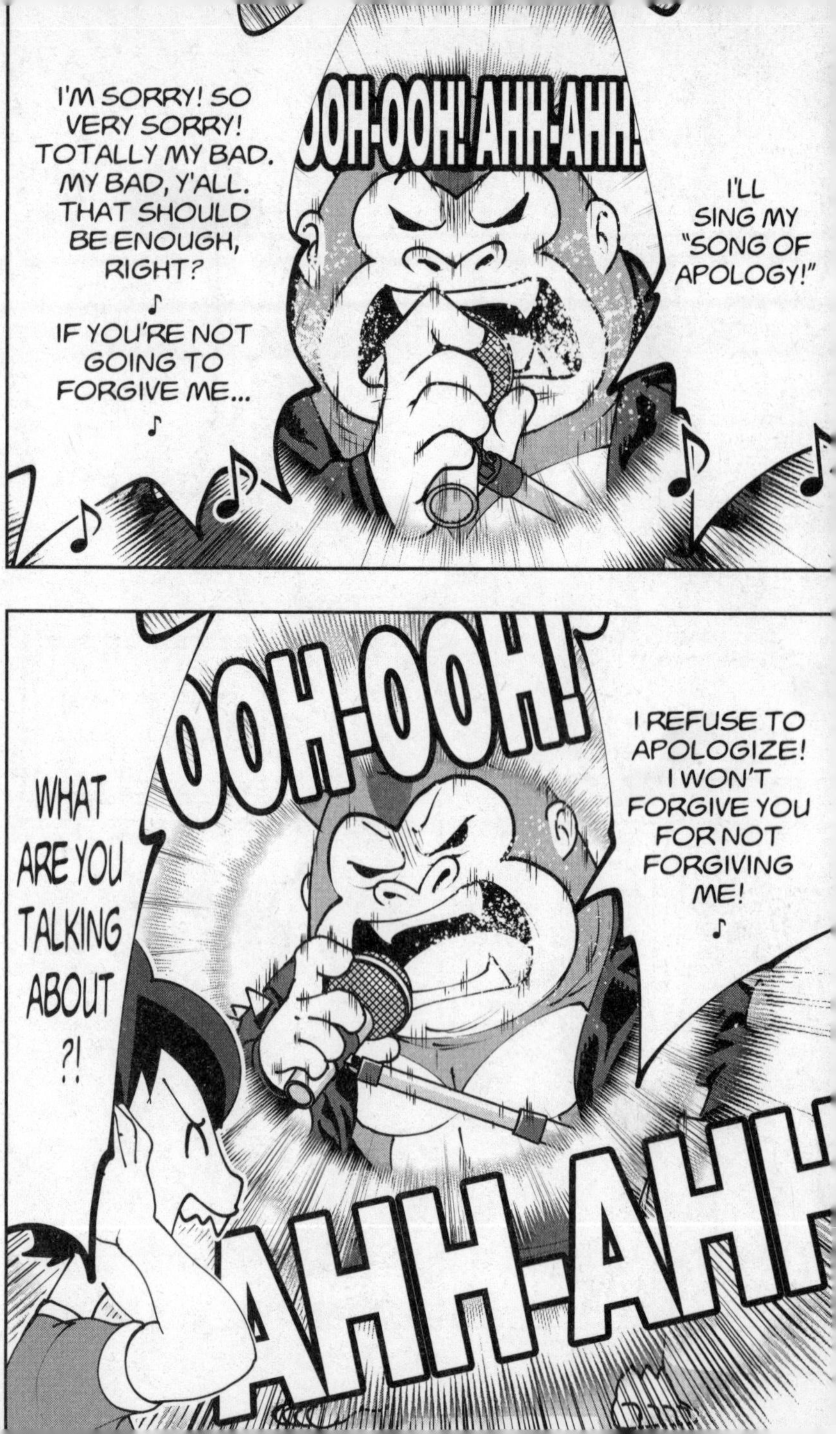
I'LL SING MY "SONG OF APOLOGY!"
OOH-OOH! AHH-AHH!
I'M SORRY! SO VERY SORRY! TOTALLY MY BAD. MY BAD, Y'ALL. THAT SHOULD BE ENOUGH, RIGHT? ♪ IF YOU'RE NOT GOING TO FORGIVE ME... ♪
OOH-OOH!
I REFUSE TO APOLOGIZE! I WON'T FORGIVE YOU FOR NOT FORGIVING ME! ♪
WHAT ARE YOU TALKING ABOUT ?!
AHH-AHH

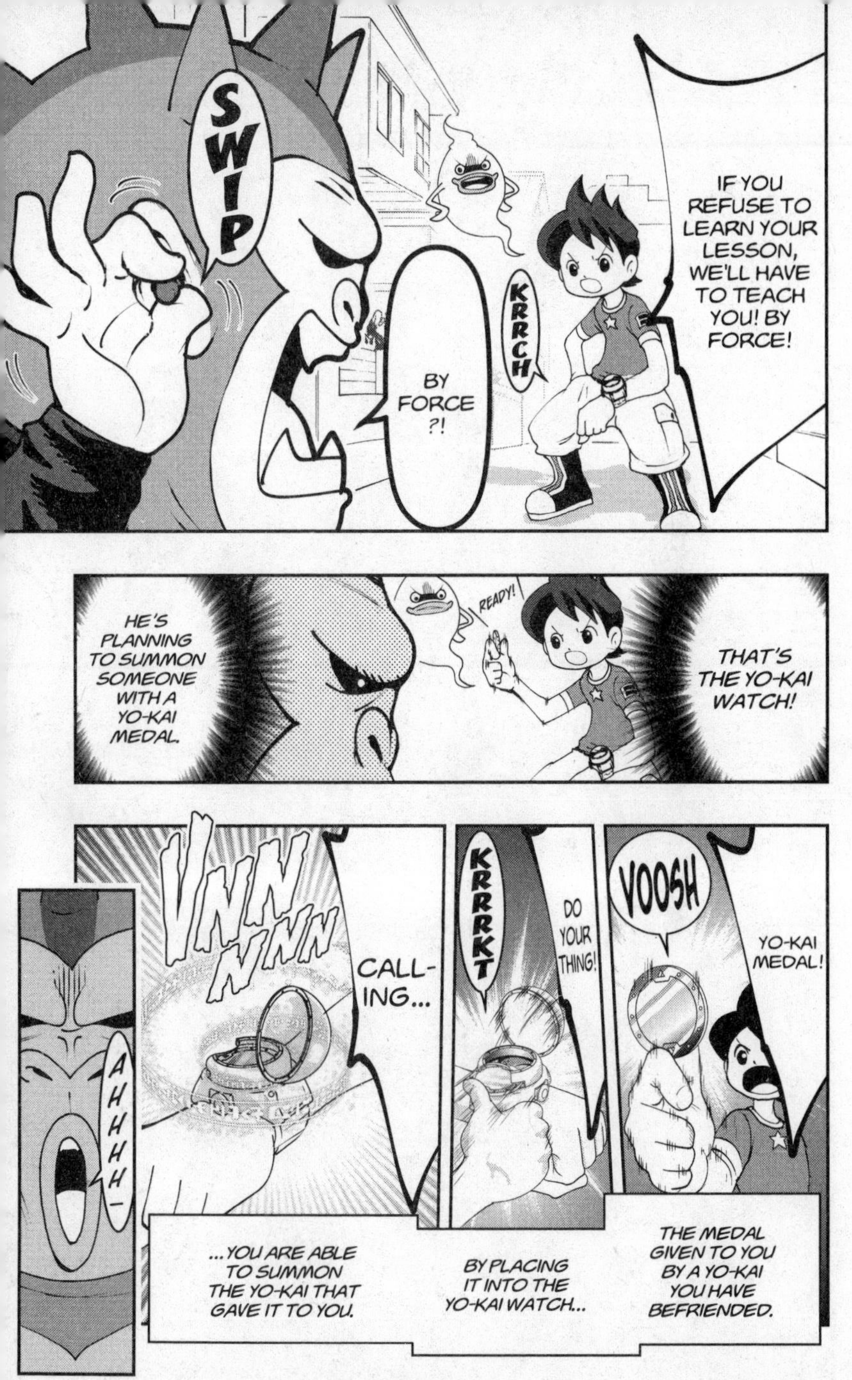
IF YOU REFUSE TO LEARN YOUR LESSON, WE'LL HAVE TO TEACH YOU! BY FORCE!
KRRCH
BY FORCE?!
SWIP
THAT'S THE YO-KAI WATCH!
READY!
HE'S PLANNING TO SUMMON SOMEONE WITH A YO-KAI MEDAL.
VOOSH
YO-KAI MEDAL!
KRRRKT
DO YOUR THING!
VNN NNN
CALLING...
AHHHH—
THE MEDAL GIVEN TO YOU BY A YO-KAI YOU HAVE BEFRIENDED.
BY PLACING IT INTO THE YO-KAI WATCH...
...YOU ARE ABLE TO SUMMON THE YO-KAI THAT GAVE IT TO YOU.

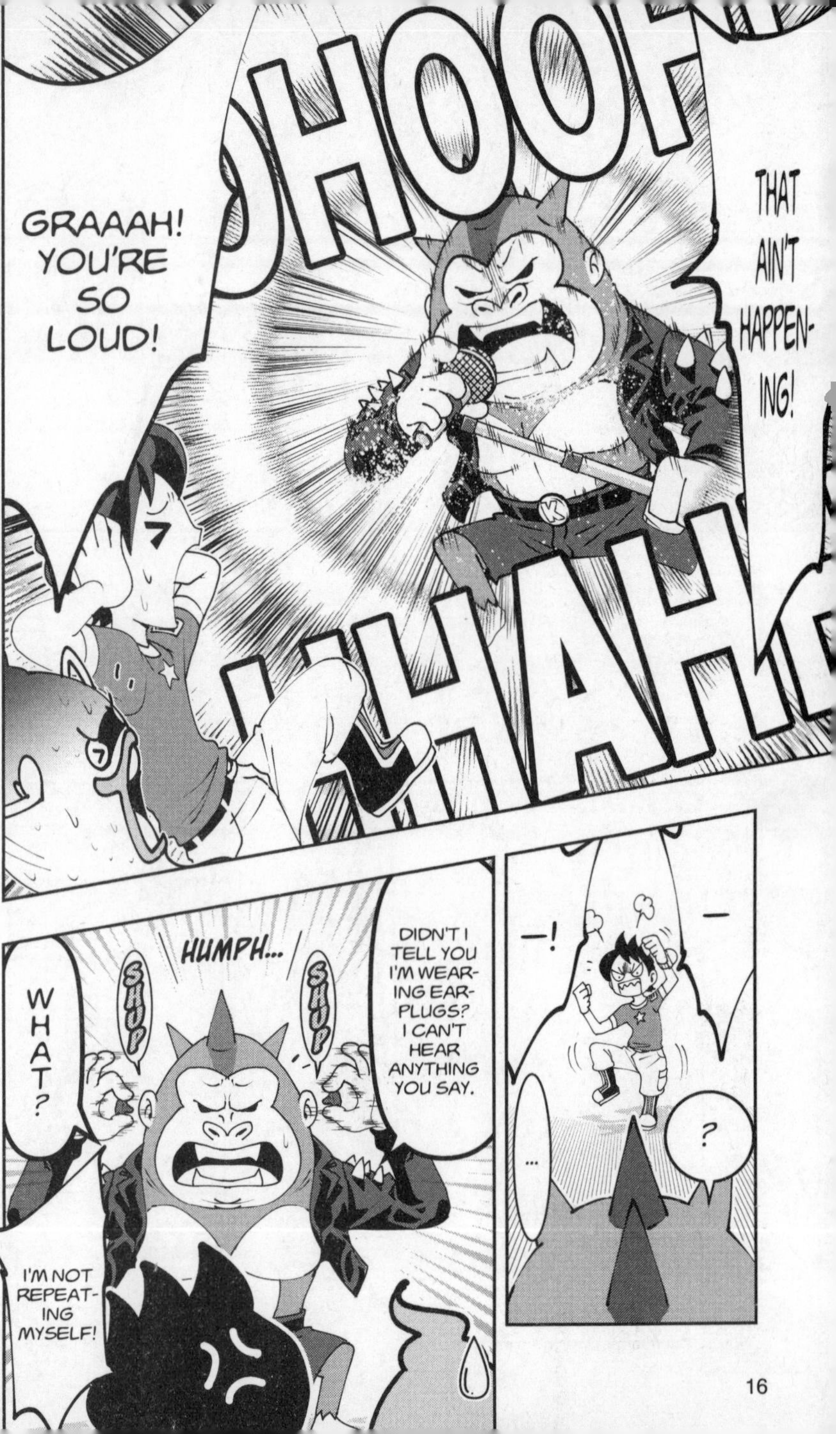
THAT AIN'T HAPPEN-ING!
GRAAAH! YOU'RE SO LOUD!
—
—!
?
...
DIDN'T I TELL YOU I'M WEAR-ING EAR-PLUGS? I CAN'T HEAR ANYTHING YOU SAY.
HUMPH...
SHUP
SHUP
WHAT?
I'M NOT REPEAT-ING MYSELF!

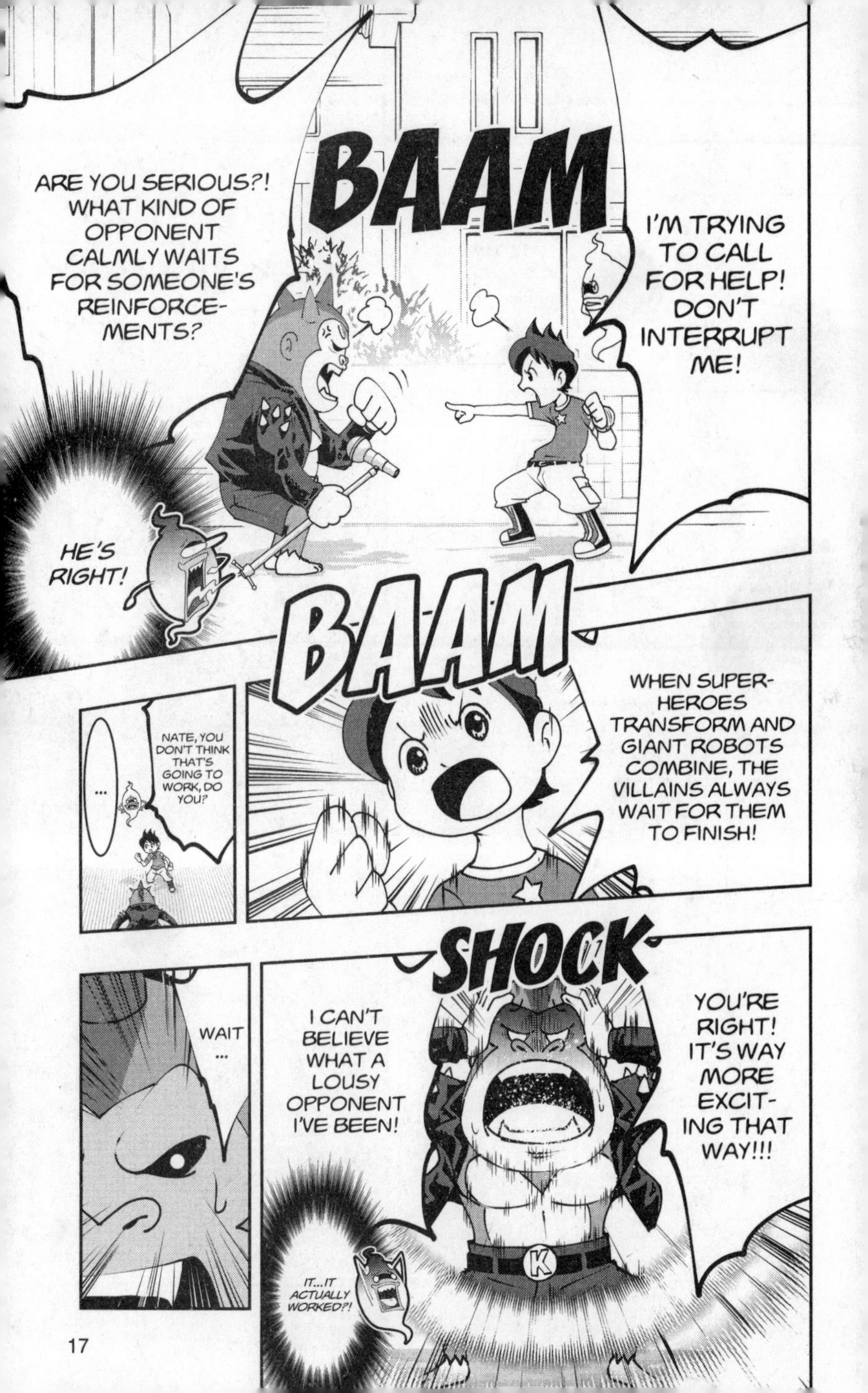

I'M TRYING TO CALL FOR HELP! DON'T INTERRUPT ME!
BAAM
ARE YOU SERIOUS?! WHAT KIND OF OPPONENT CALMLY WAITS FOR SOMEONE'S REINFORCE-MENTS?
HE'S RIGHT!
BAAM
WHEN SUPER-HEROES TRANSFORM AND GIANT ROBOTS COMBINE, THE VILLAINS ALWAYS WAIT FOR THEM TO FINISH!
NATE, YOU DON'T THINK THAT'S GOING TO WORK, DO YOU?
...
SHOCK
YOU'RE RIGHT! IT'S WAY MORE EXCIT-ING THAT WAY!!!
I CAN'T BELIEVE WHAT A LOUSY OPPONENT I'VE BEEN!
IT...IT ACTUALLY WORKED?!
WAIT ...

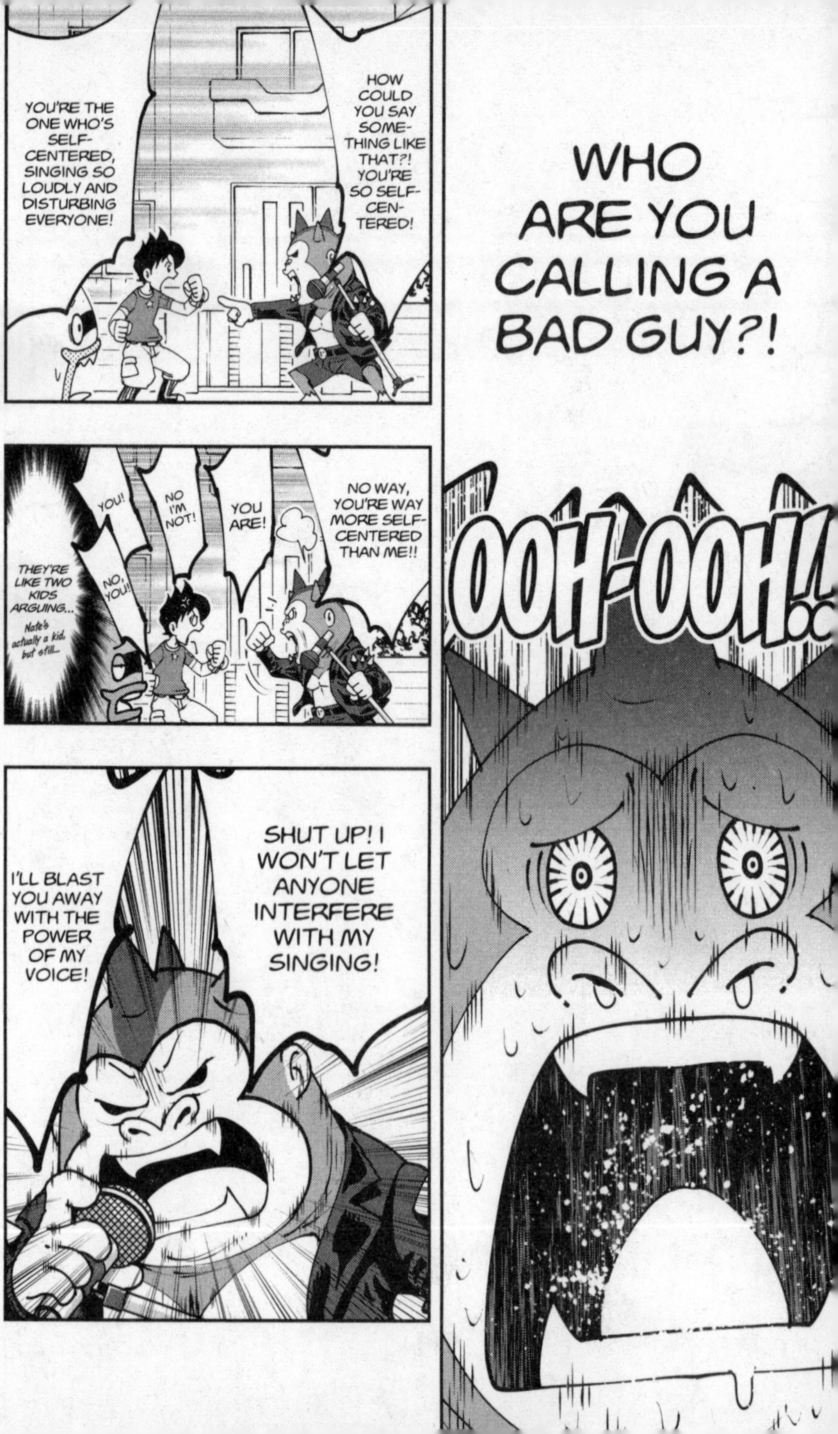
WHO ARE YOU CALLING A BAD GUY?!
OOH-OOH!!
HOW COULD YOU SAY SOME-THING LIKE THAT?! YOU'RE SO SELF-CEN-TERED!
YOU'RE THE ONE WHO'S SELF-CENTERED, SINGING SO LOUDLY AND DISTURBING EVERYONE!
NO WAY, YOU'RE WAY MORE SELF-CENTERED THAN ME!!
YOU ARE!
NO I'M NOT!
YOU!
NO, YOU!
THEY'RE LIKE TWO KIDS ARGUING...
Nate's actually a kid, but still...
SHUT UP! I WON'T LET ANYONE INTERFERE WITH MY SINGING!
I'LL BLAST YOU AWAY WITH THE POWER OF MY VOICE!

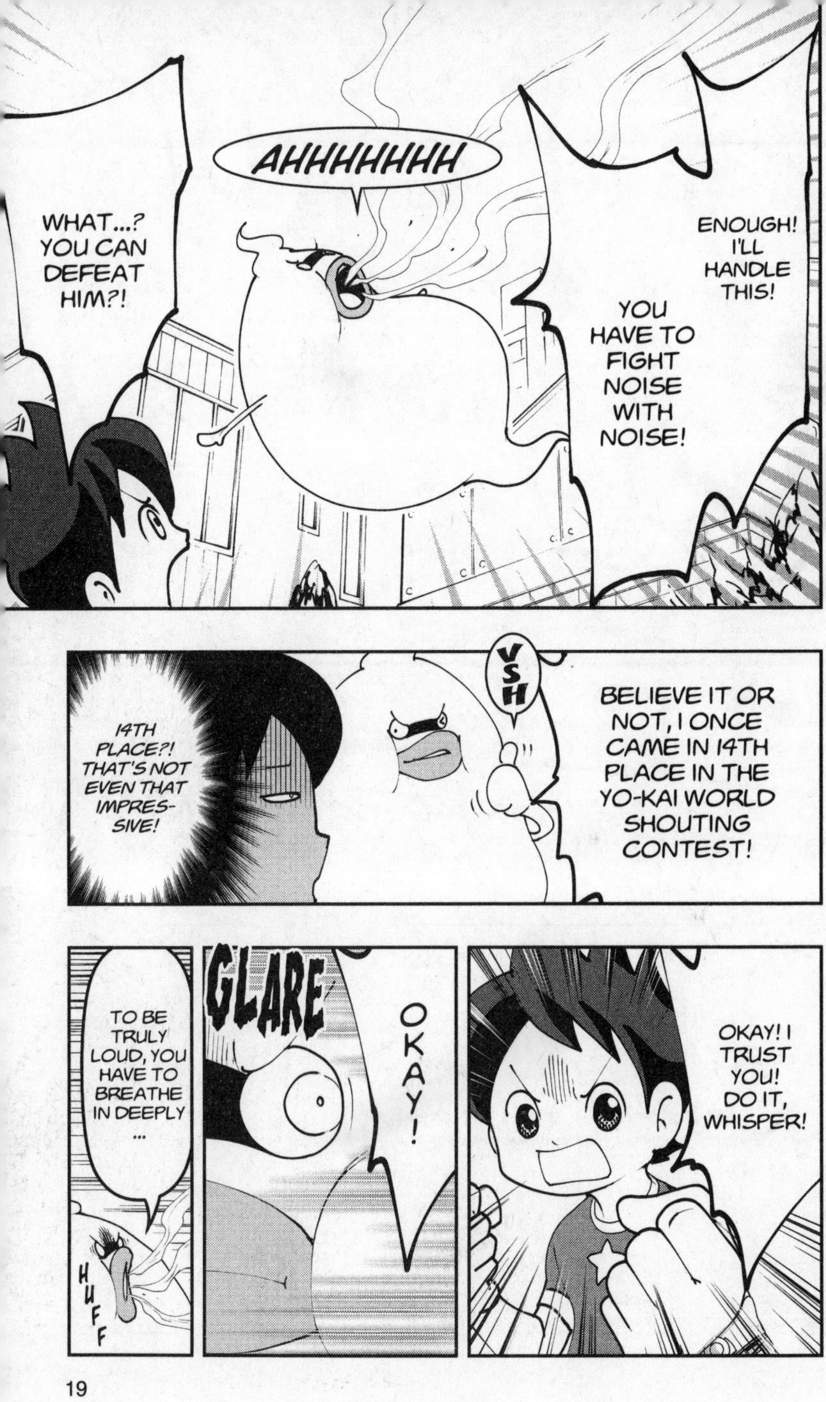
ENOUGH! I'LL HANDLE THIS!
YOU HAVE TO FIGHT NOISE WITH NOISE!
AHHHHHHH
WHAT...? YOU CAN DEFEAT HIM?!
BELIEVE IT OR NOT, I ONCE CAME IN 14TH PLACE IN THE YO-KAI WORLD SHOUTING CONTEST!
VSH
14TH PLACE?! THAT'S NOT EVEN THAT IMPRES-SIVE!
OKAY! I TRUST YOU! DO IT, WHISPER!
OKAY!
GLARE
TO BE TRULY LOUD, YOU HAVE TO BREATHE IN DEEPLY ...
HUFF

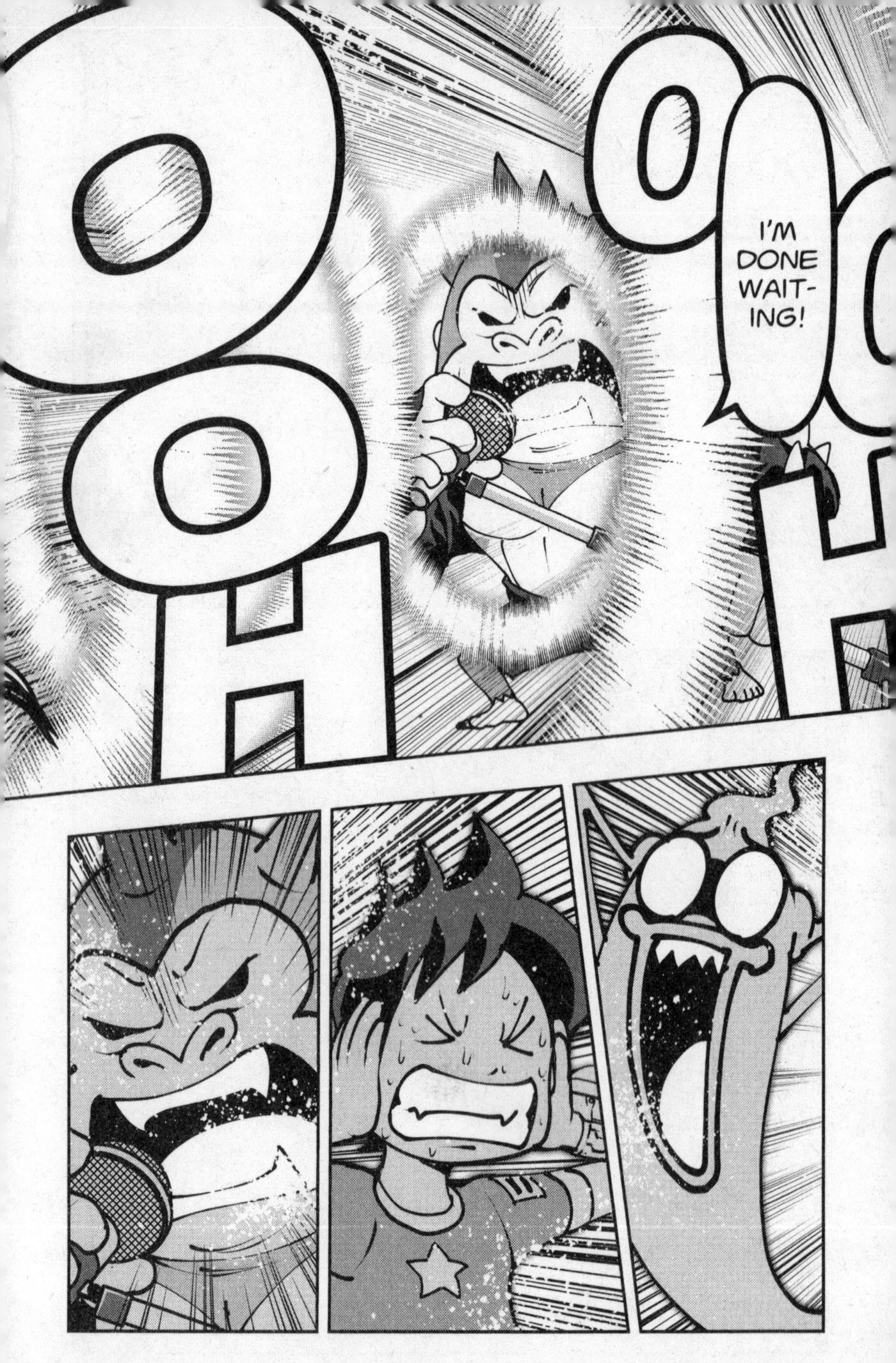
I'M DONE WAIT-ING!
OOOH

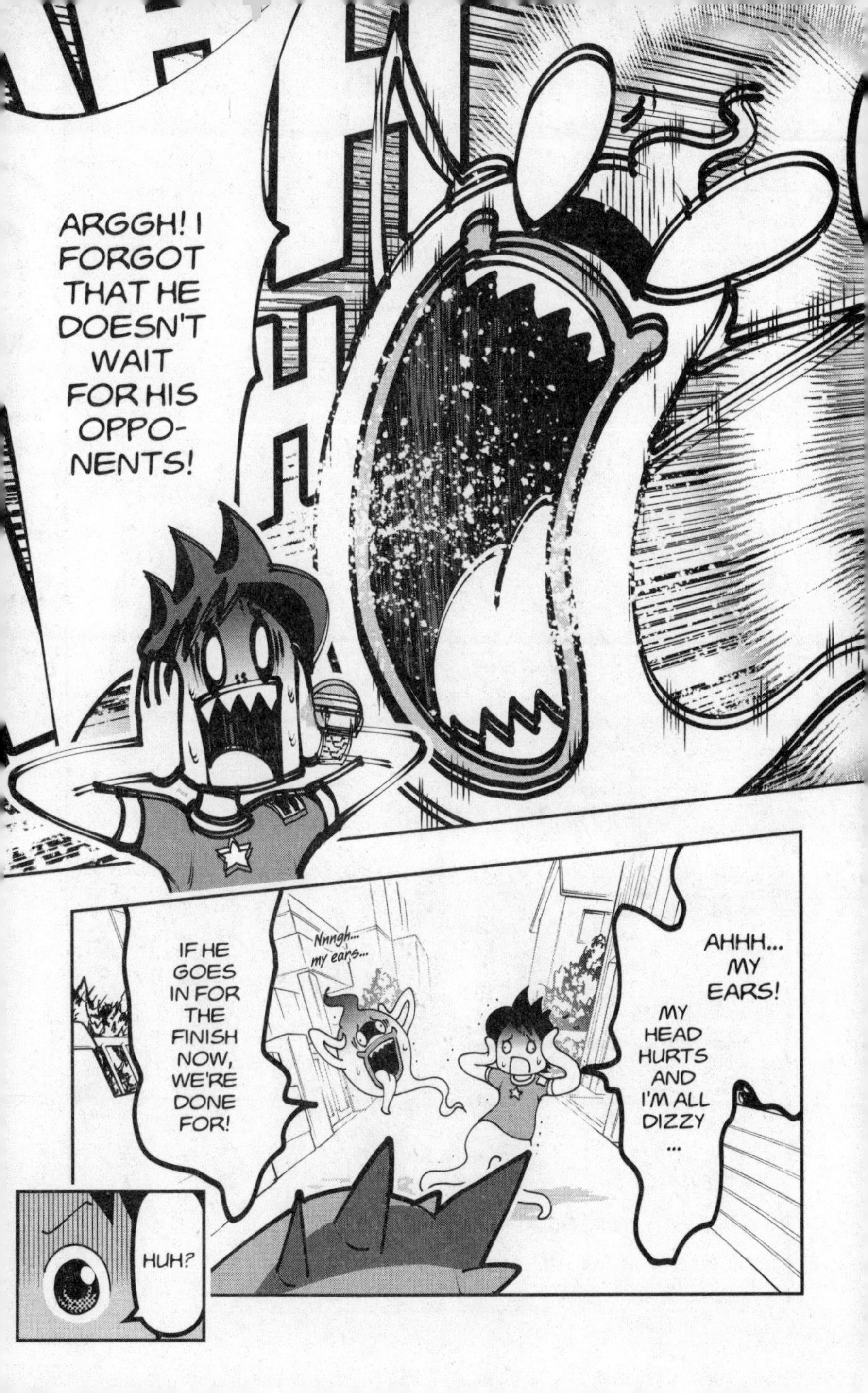
ARGGH! I FORGOT THAT HE DOESN'T WAIT FOR HIS OPPO-NENTS!
AHHH... MY EARS!
MY HEAD HURTS AND I'M ALL DIZZY ...
Nnngh... my ears...
IF HE GOES IN FOR THE FINISH NOW, WE'RE DONE FOR!
HUH?

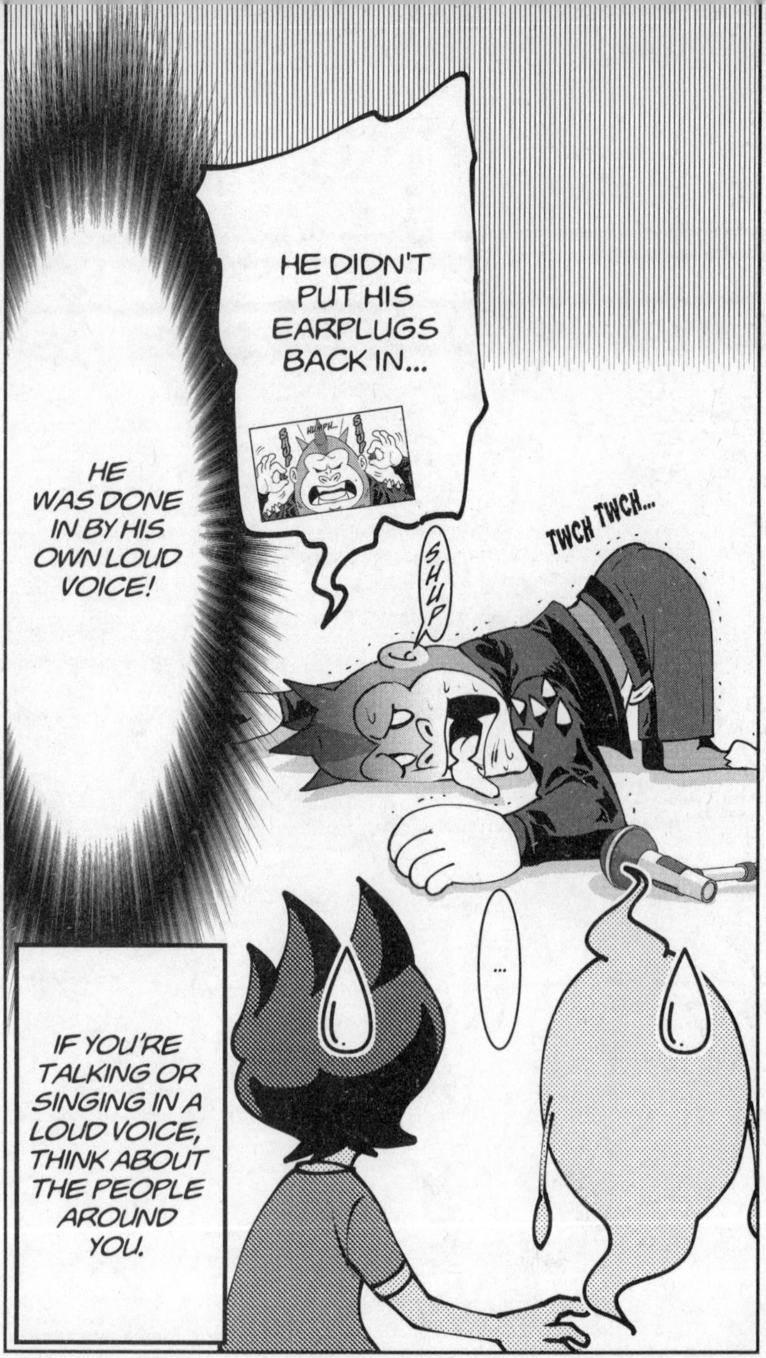
HE DIDN'T PUT HIS EARPLUGS BACK IN...
HUMPH...
SHUP
SHUP
HE WAS DONE IN BY HIS OWN LOUD VOICE!
TWCH TWCH...
SHUP
...
IF YOU'RE TALKING OR SINGING IN A LOUD VOICE, THINK ABOUT THE PEOPLE AROUND YOU.

CHAPTER 237
FRUIT YO-KAI MELONYAN

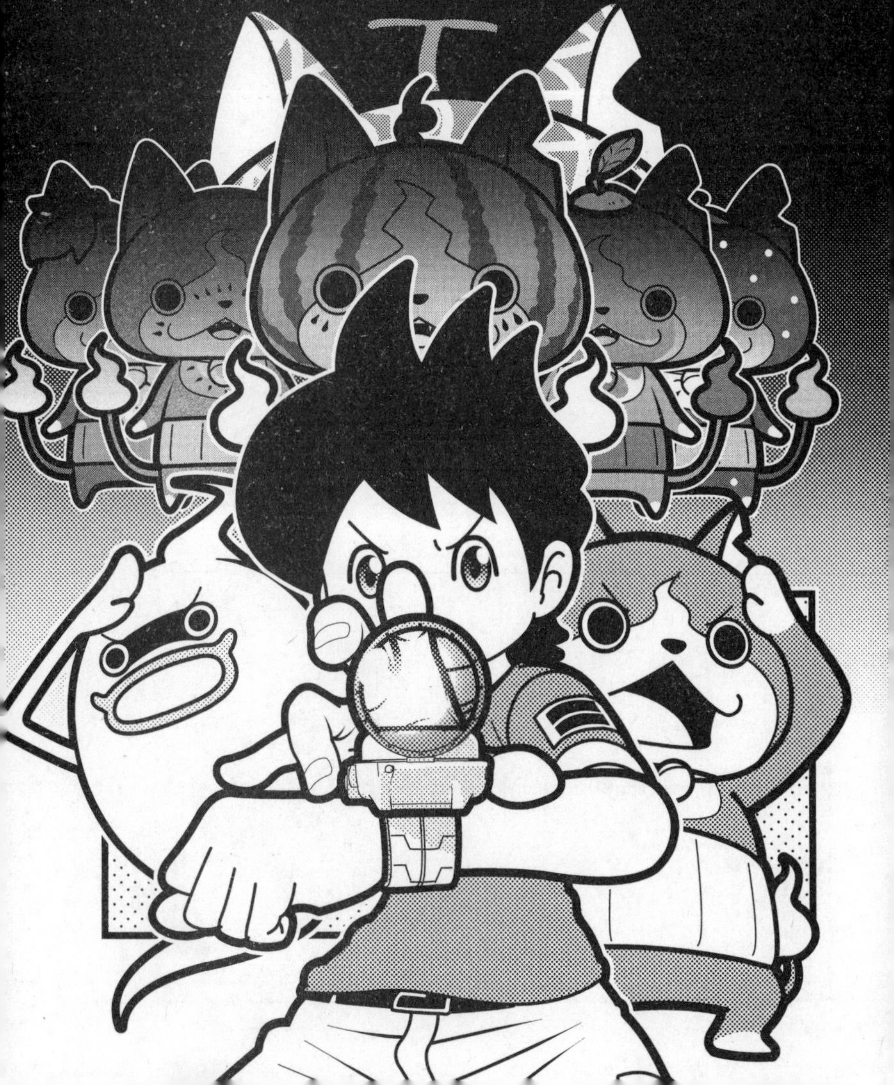

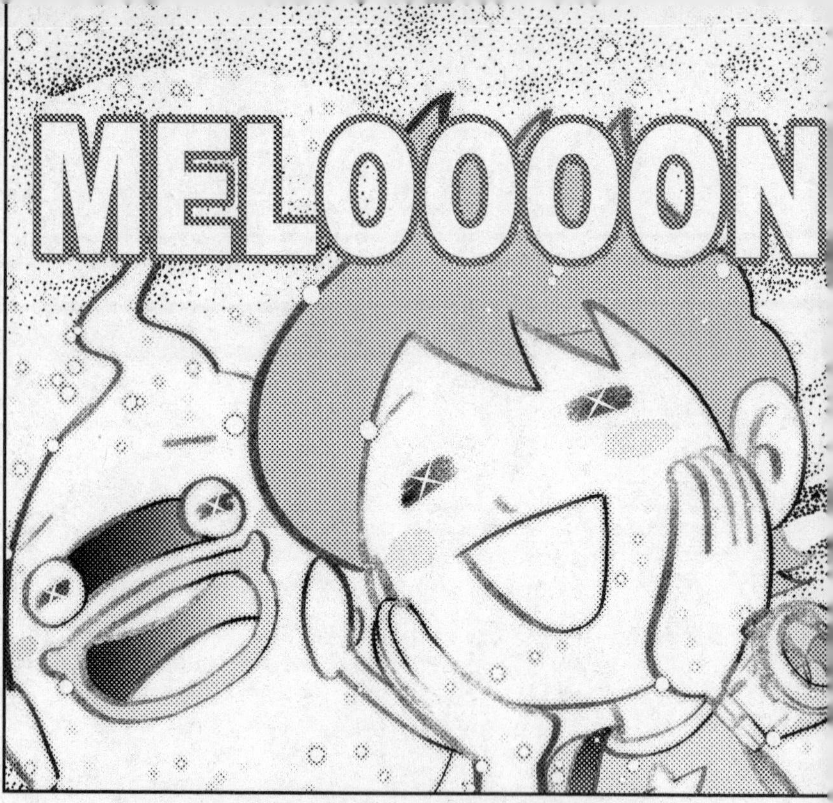
MELOOOON

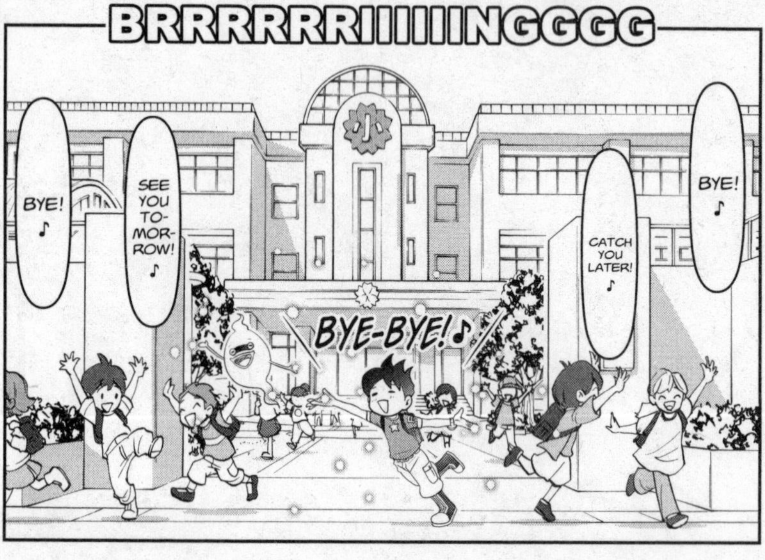
BRRRRRRIIIIIINGGGG
BYE! ♪
CATCH YOU LATER! ♪
BYE-BYE! ♪
SEE YOU TO-MOR-ROW! ♪
BYE! ♪

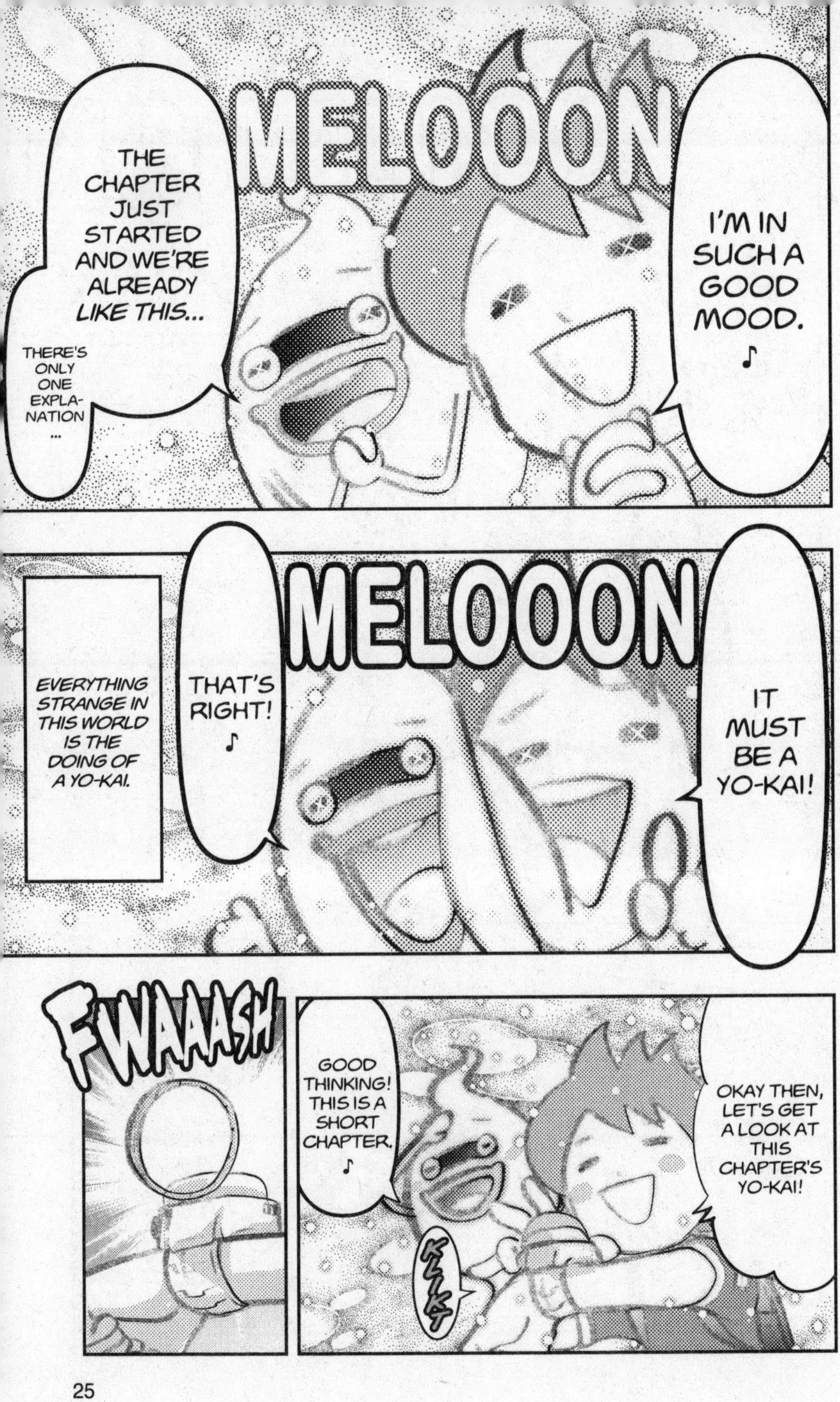
I'M IN SUCH A GOOD MOOD. ♪
MELOOON
THE CHAPTER JUST STARTED AND WE'RE ALREADY LIKE THIS...
THERE'S ONLY ONE EXPLANATION ...
IT MUST BE A YO-KAI!
MELOOON
THAT'S RIGHT! ♪
EVERYTHING STRANGE IN THIS WORLD IS THE DOING OF A YO-KAI.
OKAY THEN, LET'S GET A LOOK AT THIS CHAPTER'S YO-KAI!
GOOD THINKING! THIS IS A SHORT CHAPTER. ♪
KLIKT
FWAAASH

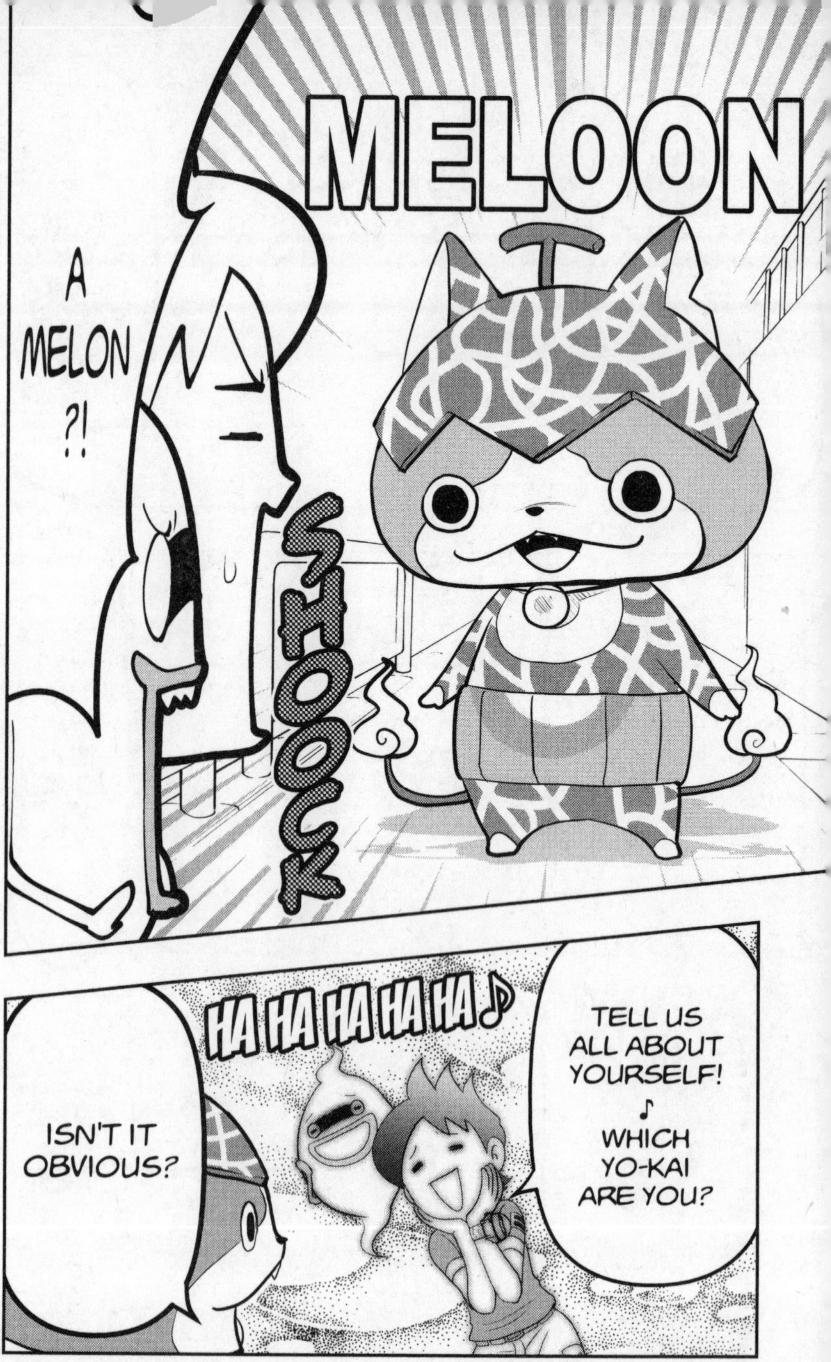
MELOON
A MELON ?!
SHOCK
TELL US ALL ABOUT YOURSELF! ♪ WHICH YO-KAI ARE YOU?
HA HA HA HA HA♪
ISN'T IT OBVIOUS?

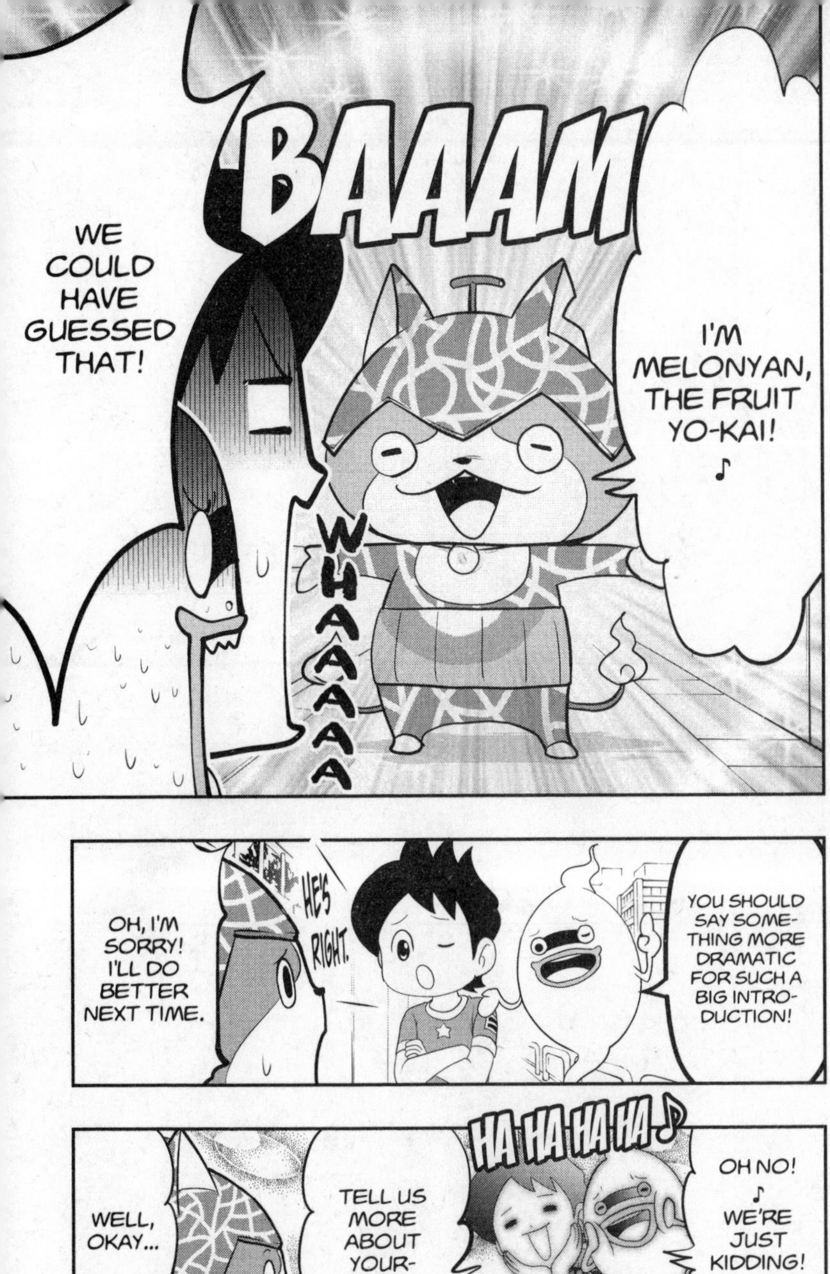
I'M MELONYAN, THE FRUIT YO-KAI! ♪
BAAAM
WHAAAAAAA
WE COULD HAVE GUESSED THAT!
YOU SHOULD SAY SOME-THING MORE DRAMATIC FOR SUCH A BIG INTRO-DUCTION!
HE'S RIGHT.
OH, I'M SORRY! I'LL DO BETTER NEXT TIME.
OH NO! ♪ WE'RE JUST KIDDING! ♪
HA HA HA HA ♪
TELL US MORE ABOUT YOUR-SELF!
WELL, OKAY...

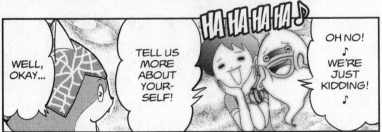

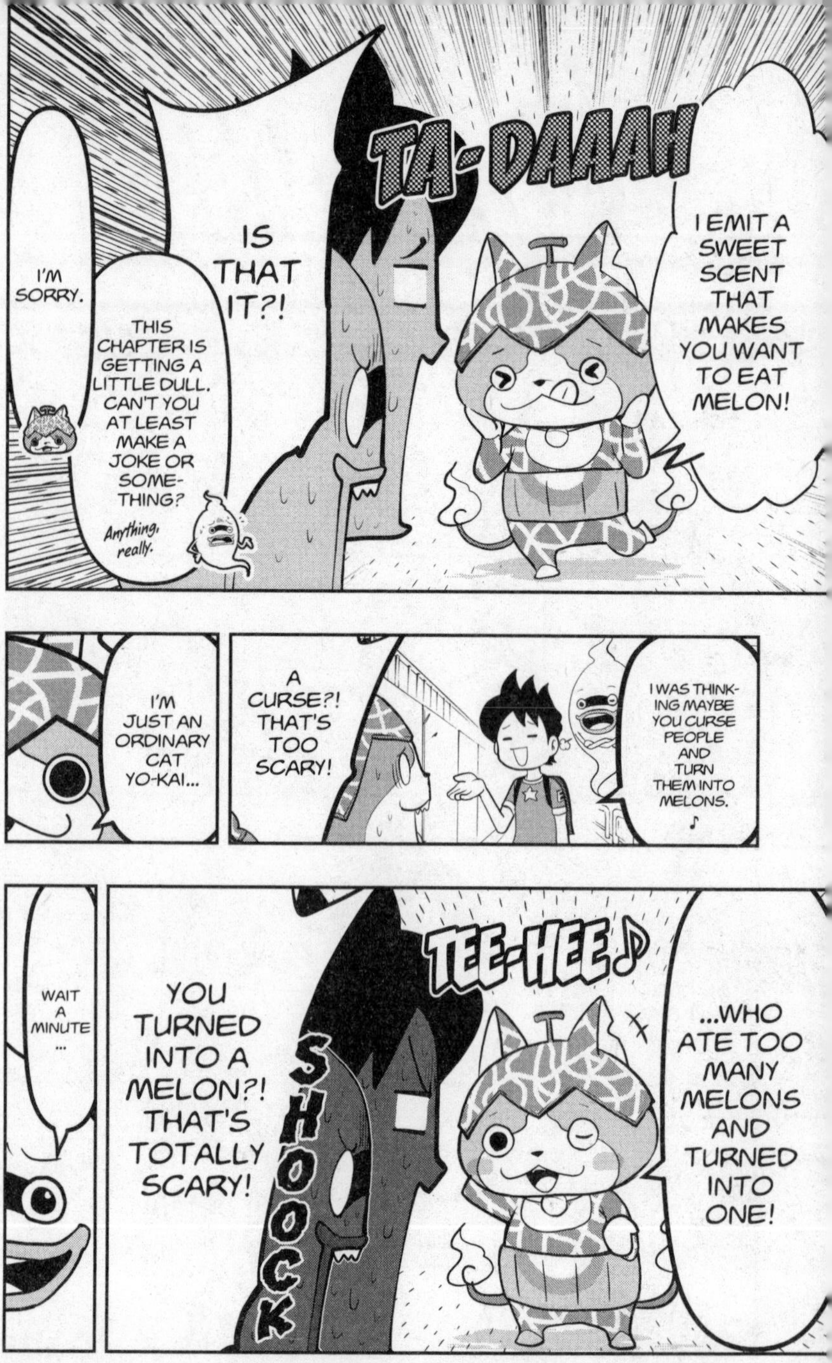
TA-DAAAH
I EMIT A SWEET SCENT THAT MAKES YOU WANT TO EAT MELON!
IS THAT IT?!
THIS CHAPTER IS GETTING A LITTLE DULL. CAN'T YOU AT LEAST MAKE A JOKE OR SOME-THING?
Anything, really.
I'M SORRY.
I WAS THINK-ING MAYBE YOU CURSE PEOPLE AND TURN THEM INTO MELONS. ♪
A CURSE?! THAT'S TOO SCARY!
I'M JUST AN ORDINARY CAT YO-KAI...
...WHO ATE TOO MANY MELONS AND TURNED INTO ONE!
TEE-HEE♪
SHOOCK
YOU TURNED INTO A MELON?! THAT'S TOTALLY SCARY!
WAIT A MINUTE ...

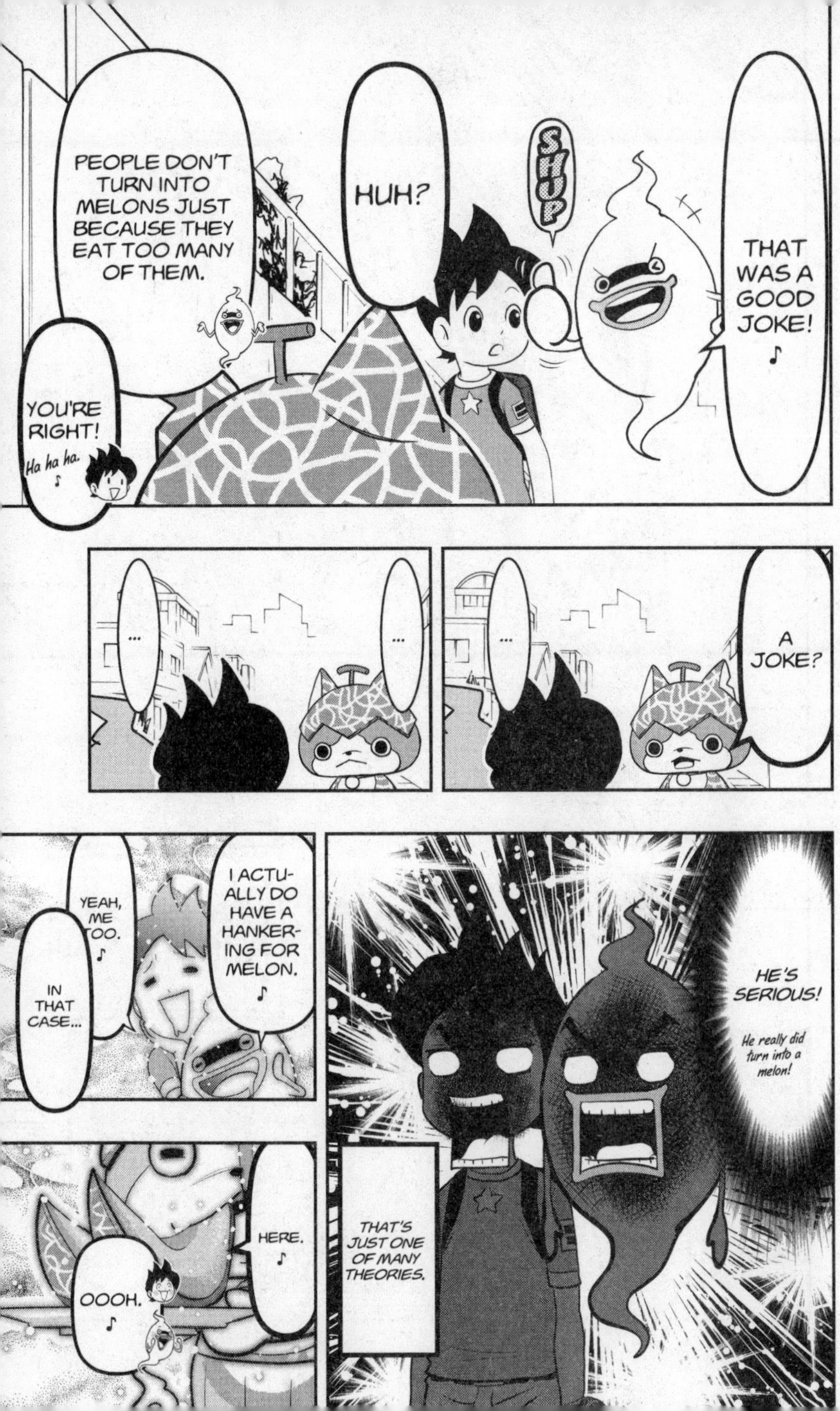
THAT WAS A GOOD JOKE! ♪
SHUP
HUH?
PEOPLE DON'T TURN INTO MELONS JUST BECAUSE THEY EAT TOO MANY OF THEM.
YOU'RE RIGHT!
Ha ha ha. ♪
A JOKE?
...
...
...
HE'S SERIOUS!
He really did turn into a melon!
THAT'S JUST ONE OF MANY THEORIES.
I ACTU-ALLY DO HAVE A HANKER-ING FOR MELON. ♪
YEAH, ME TOO. ♪
IN THAT CASE...
HERE. ♪
OOOH. ♪

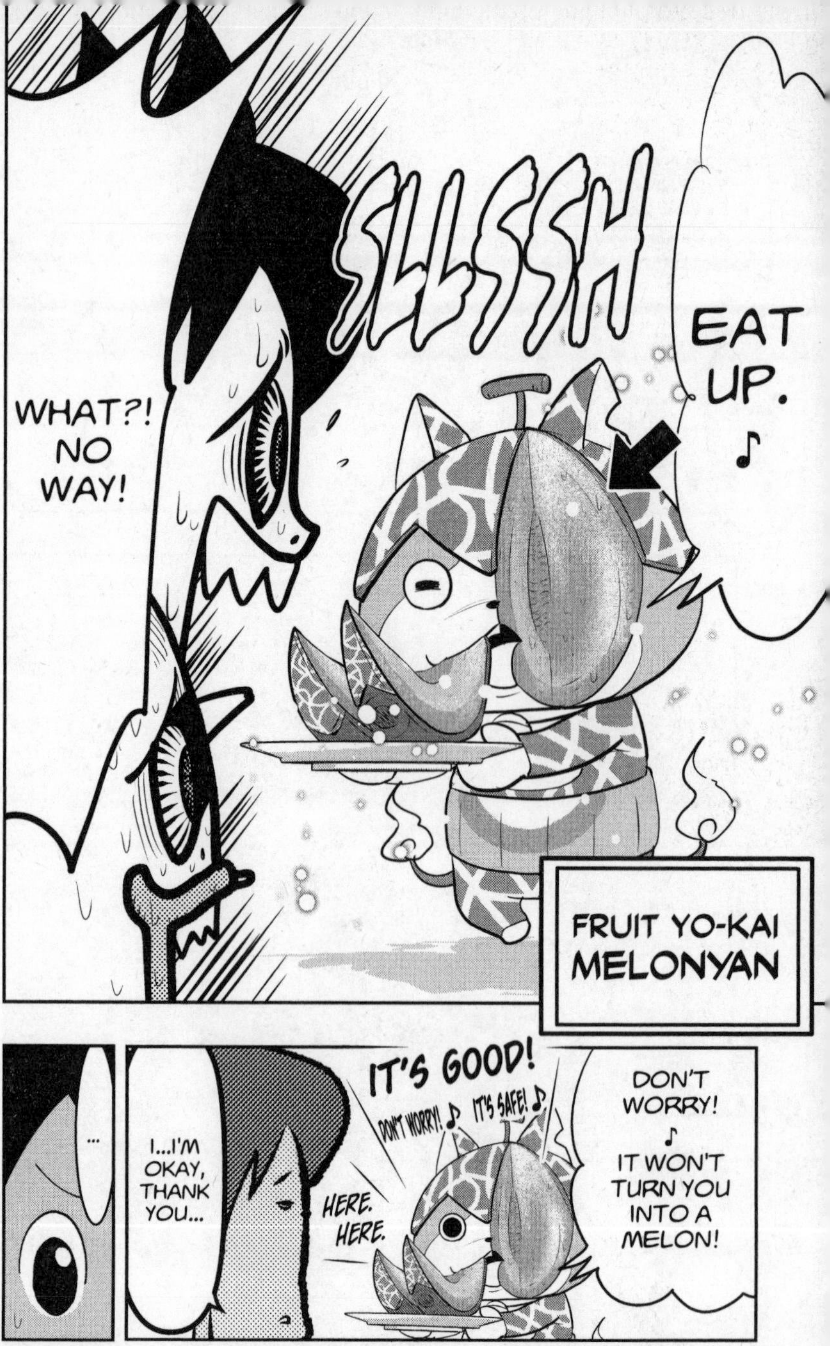
EAT UP. ♪
SLLSSH
WHAT?! NO WAY!
FRUIT YO-KAI MELONYAN
DON'T WORRY! ♪ IT WON'T TURN YOU INTO A MELON!
IT'S GOOD!
IT'S SAFE! ♪
DON'T WORRY! ♪
HERE. HERE.
I...I'M OKAY, THANK YOU...
...

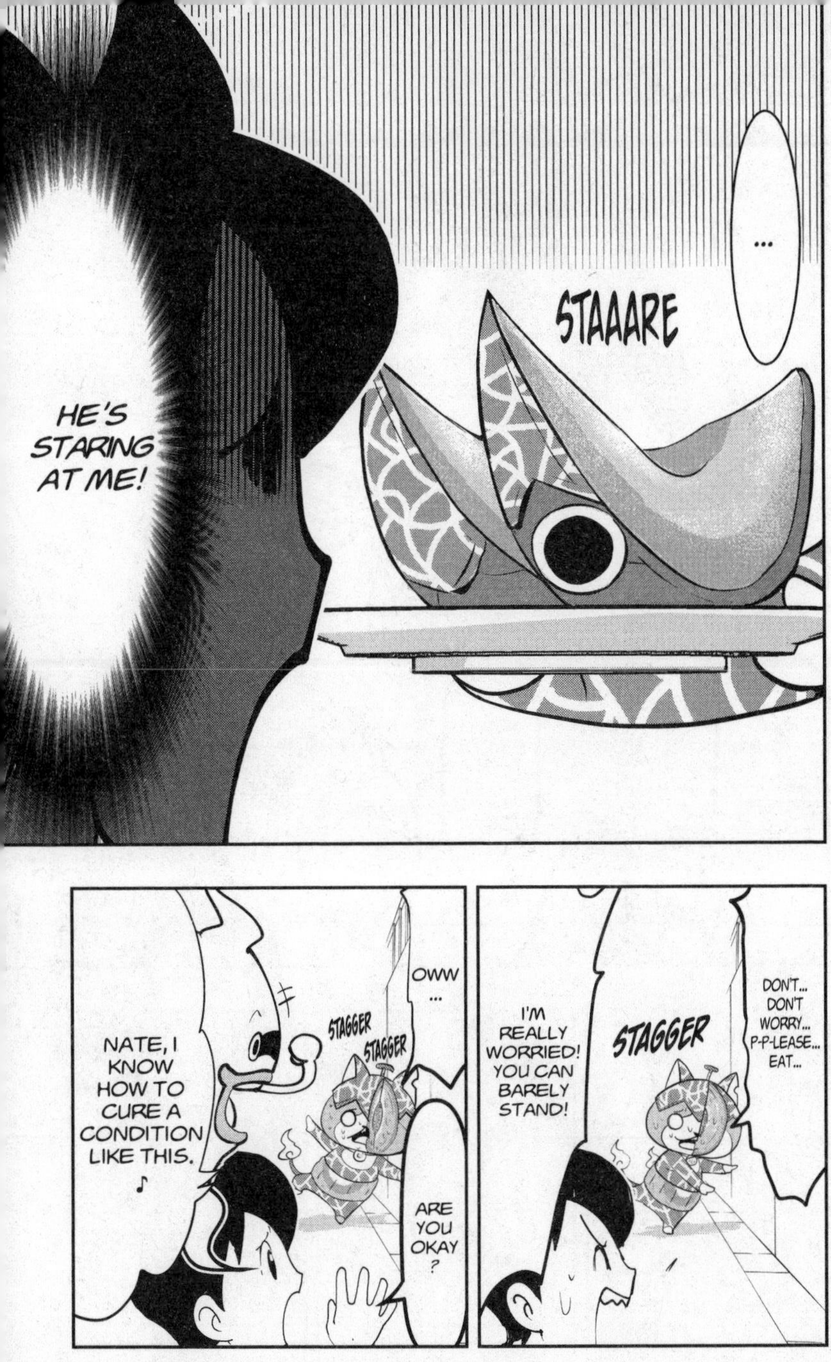
...
STAAARE
HE'S STARING AT ME!
DON'T... DON'T WORRY... P-P-LEASE... EAT...
STAGGER
I'M REALLY WORRIED! YOU CAN BARELY STAND!
OWW ...
STAGGER STAGGER
ARE YOU OKAY?
NATE, I KNOW HOW TO CURE A CONDITION LIKE THIS. ♪

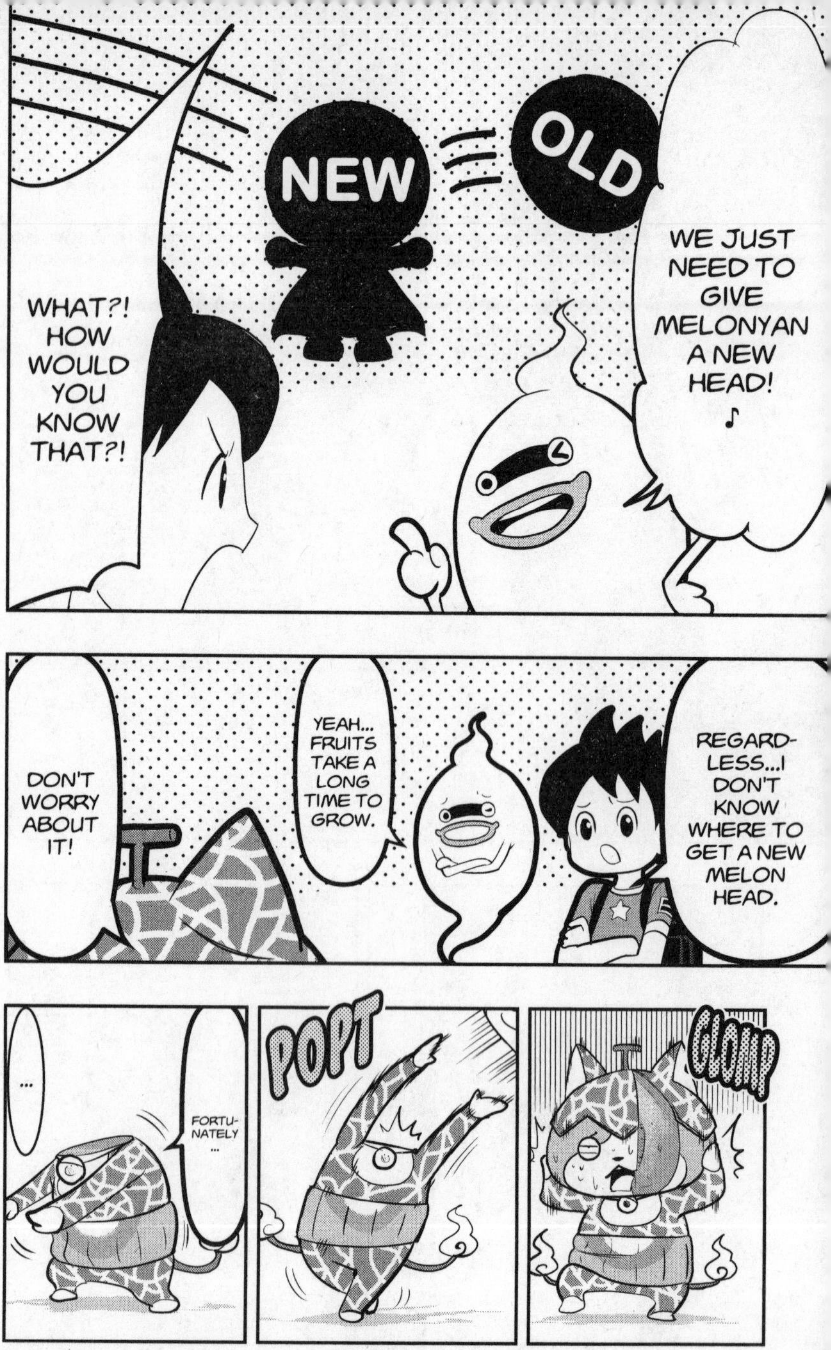
WE JUST NEED TO GIVE MELONYAN A NEW HEAD! ♪
OLD
NEW
WHAT?! HOW WOULD YOU KNOW THAT?!
REGARD-LESS...I DON'T KNOW WHERE TO GET A NEW MELON HEAD.
YEAH... FRUITS TAKE A LONG TIME TO GROW.
DON'T WORRY ABOUT IT!
GLOMP
POPT
FORTU-NATELY ...
...

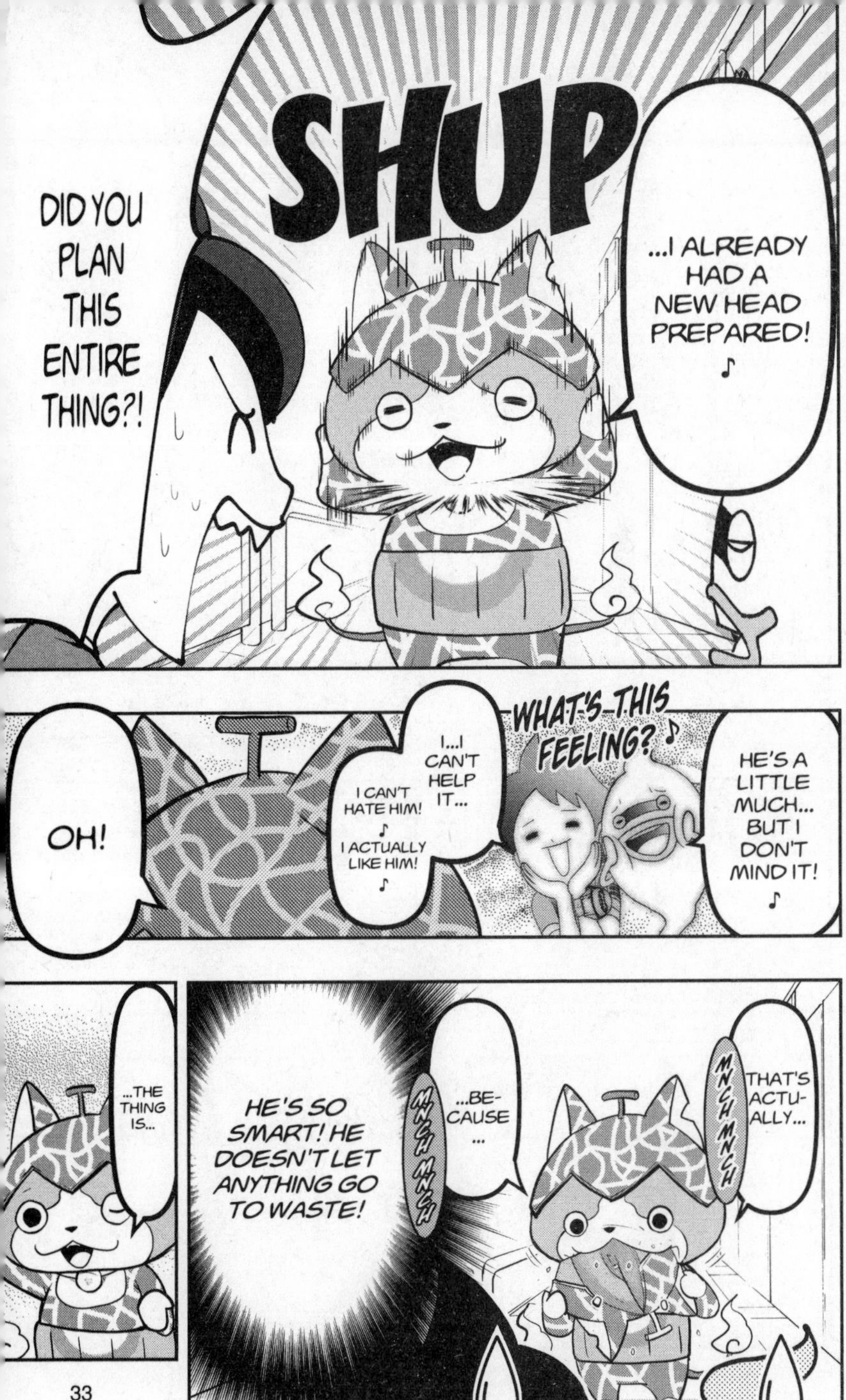
SHUP
...I ALREADY HAD A NEW HEAD PREPARED! ♪
DID YOU PLAN THIS ENTIRE THING?!
HE'S A LITTLE MUCH... BUT I DON'T MIND IT! ♪
WHAT'S THIS FEELING? ♪
I...I CAN'T HELP IT...
I CAN'T HATE HIM! ♪ I ACTUALLY LIKE HIM! ♪
OH!
MNCH MNCH
THAT'S ACTUALLY...
...BECAUSE...
MNCH MNCH
HE'S SO SMART! HE DOESN'T LET ANYTHING GO TO WASTE!
...THE THING IS...

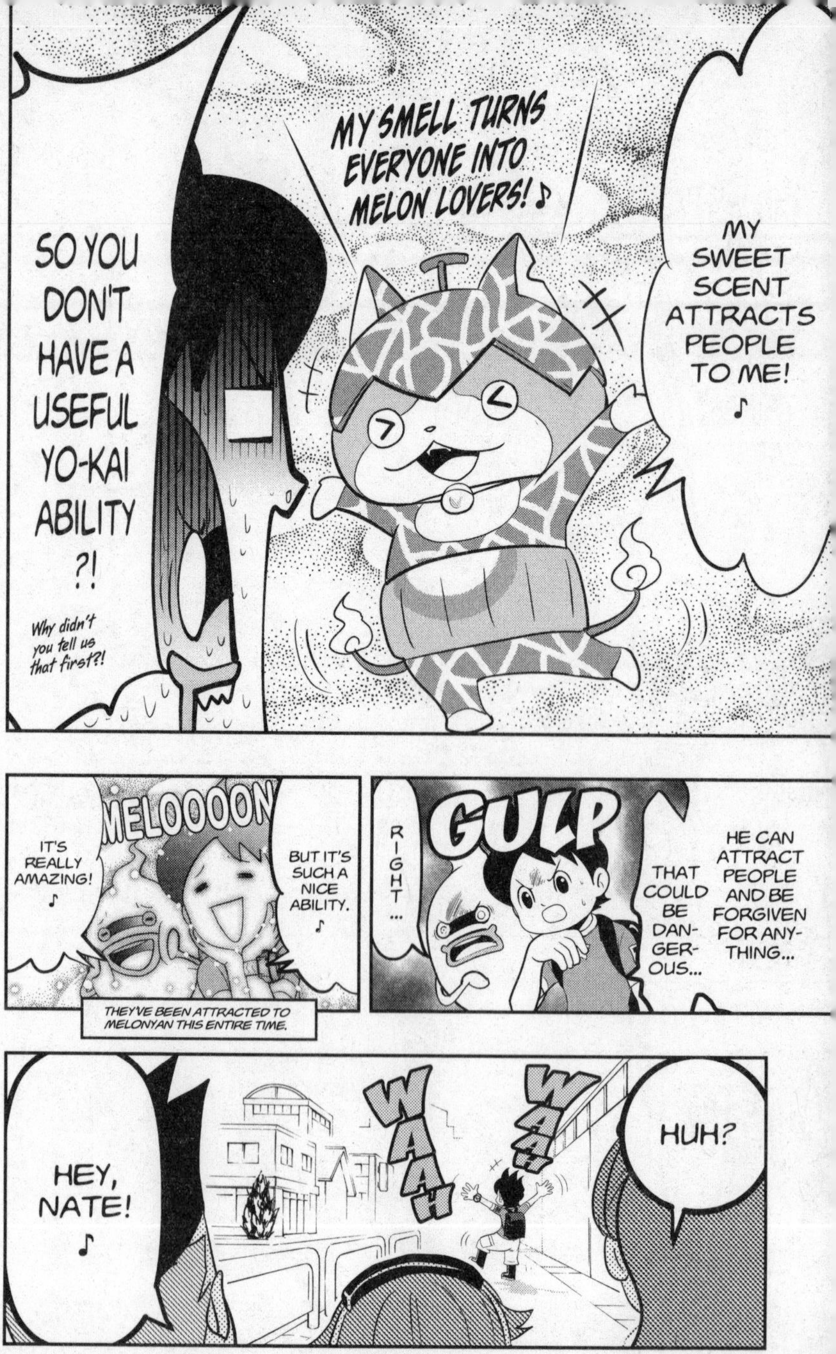
MY SWEET SCENT ATTRACTS PEOPLE TO ME! ♪
MY SMELL TURNS EVERYONE INTO MELON LOVERS! ♪
SO YOU DON'T HAVE A USEFUL YO-KAI ABILITY ?!
Why didn't you tell us that first?!
HE CAN ATTRACT PEOPLE AND BE FORGIVEN FOR ANY-THING...
THAT COULD BE DAN-GER-OUS...
GULP
RIGHT...
BUT IT'S SUCH A NICE ABILITY. ♪
MELOOOON
IT'S REALLY AMAZING! ♪
THEY'VE BEEN ATTRACTED TO MELONYAN THIS ENTIRE TIME.
HUH?
WAAH
WAAH
HEY, NATE! ♪

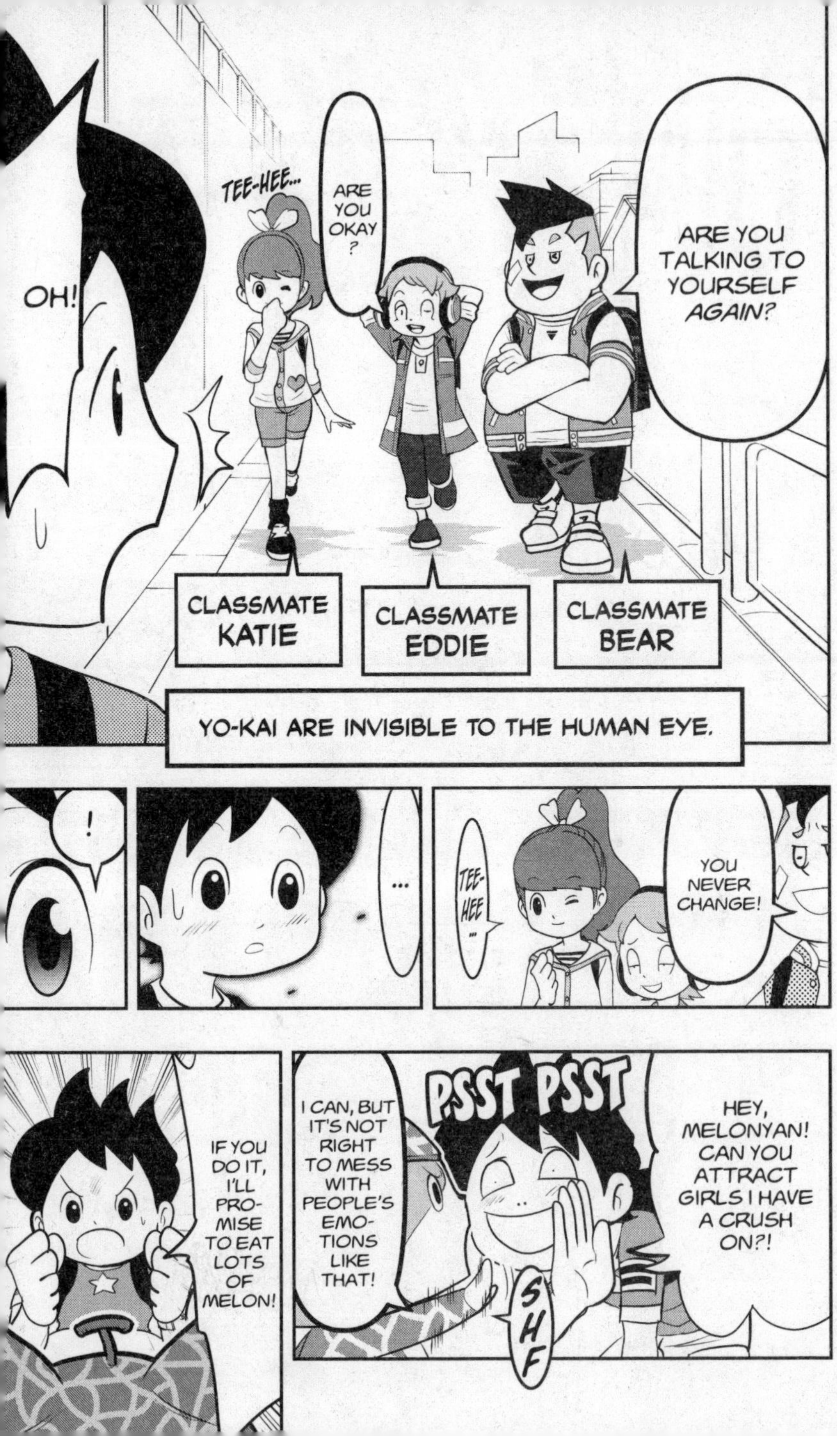
ARE YOU TALKING TO YOURSELF AGAIN?
ARE YOU OKAY?
TEE-HEE...
OH!
CLASSMATE BEAR
CLASSMATE EDDIE
CLASSMATE KATIE
YO-KAI ARE INVISIBLE TO THE HUMAN EYE.
YOU NEVER CHANGE!
TEE-HEE...
...
!
HEY, MELONYAN! CAN YOU ATTRACT GIRLS I HAVE A CRUSH ON?!
PSST PSST
SHF
I CAN, BUT IT'S NOT RIGHT TO MESS WITH PEOPLE'S EMO-TIONS LIKE THAT!
IF YOU DO IT, I'LL PRO-MISE TO EAT LOTS OF MELON!

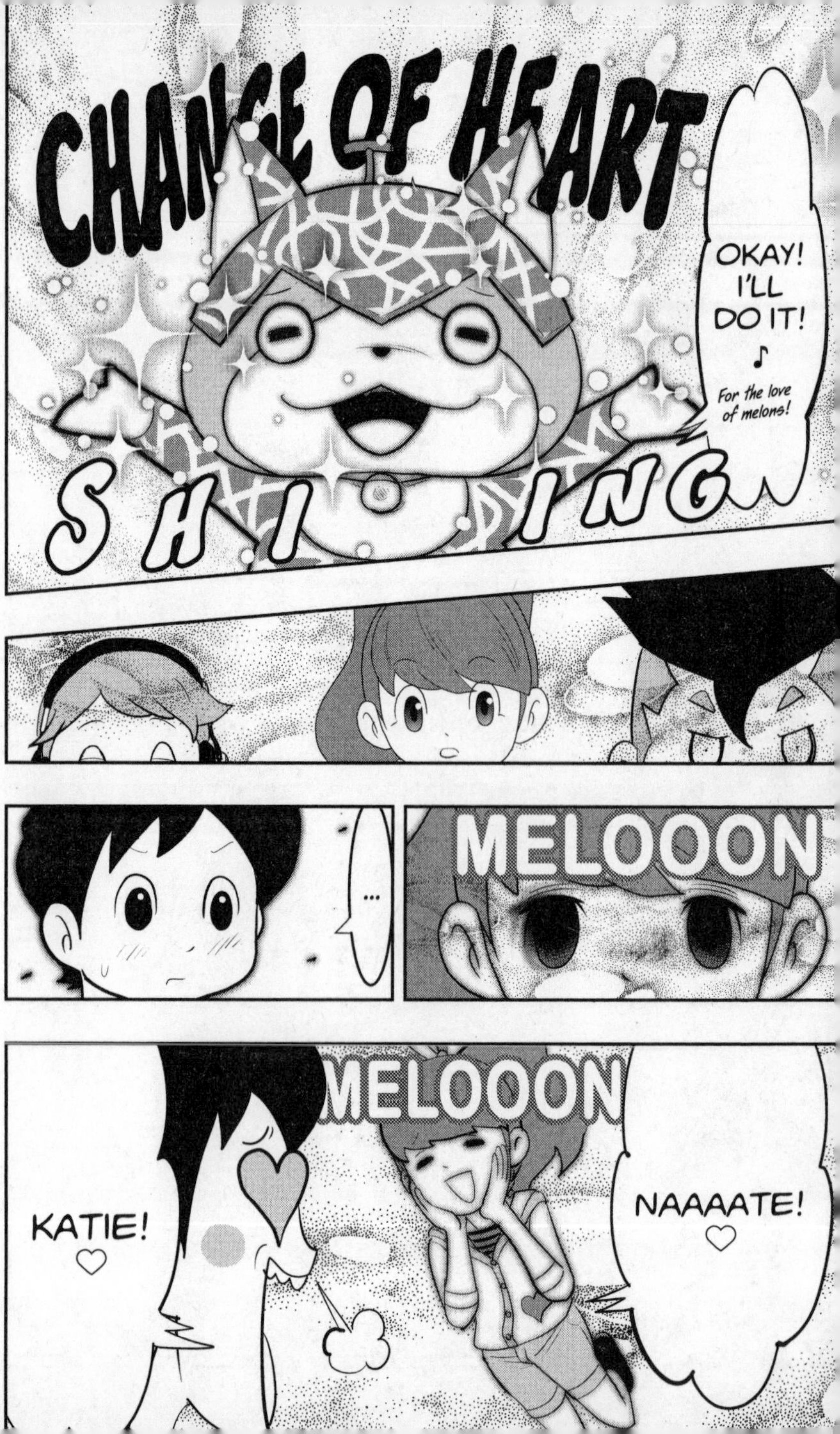

OKAY! I'LL DO IT! ♪
For the love of melons!
CHANGE OF HEART
SHI ING
MELOOON
...
MELOOON
NAAAATE! ♡
KATIE! ♡

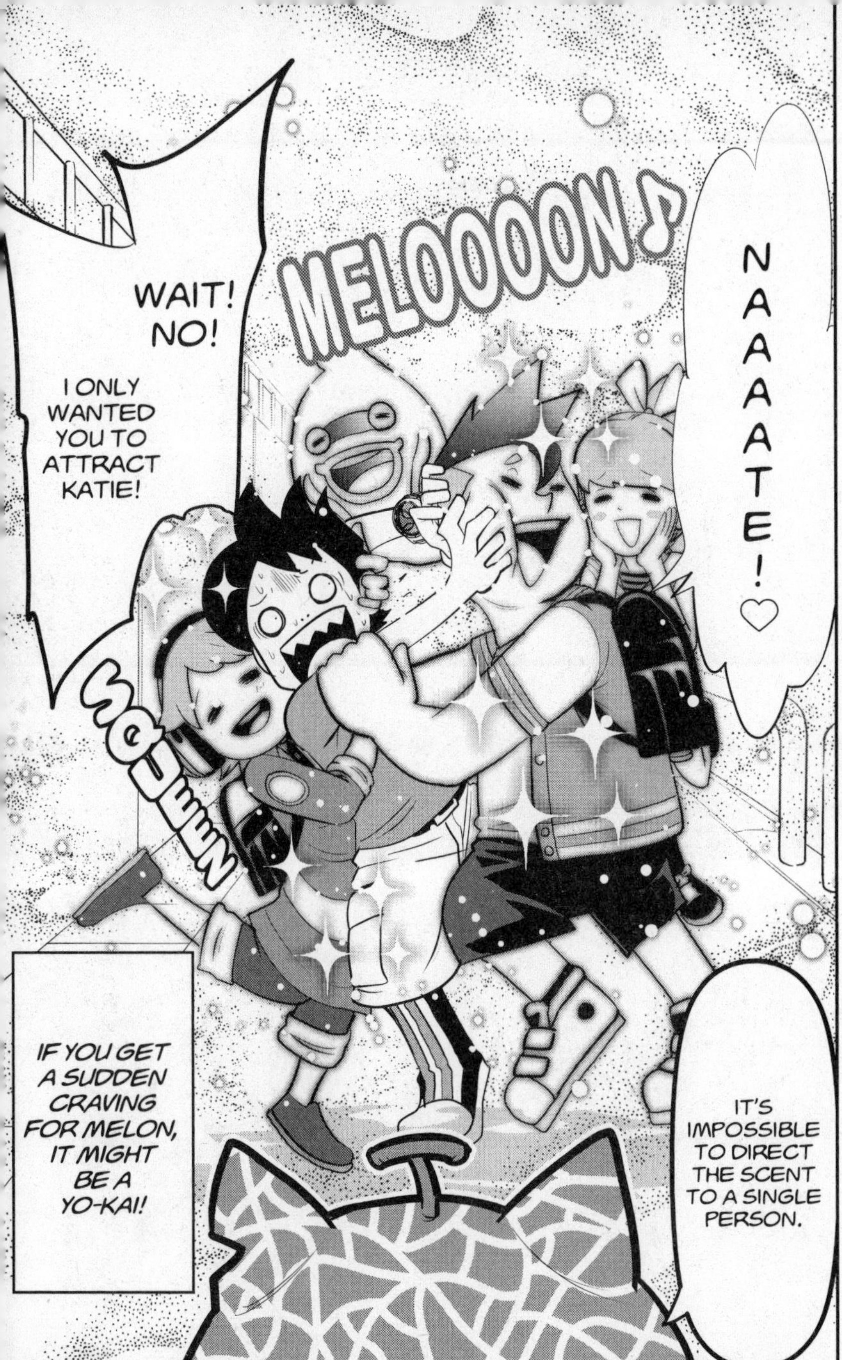
NAAAAATE!♡
MELOOOON♪
WAIT! NO!
I ONLY WANTED YOU TO ATTRACT KATIE!
IT'S IMPOSSIBLE TO DIRECT THE SCENT TO A SINGLE PERSON.
IF YOU GET A SUDDEN CRAVING FOR MELON, IT MIGHT BE A YO-KAI!

CHAPTER 238
NAUSEOUS YO-KAI SPEWART

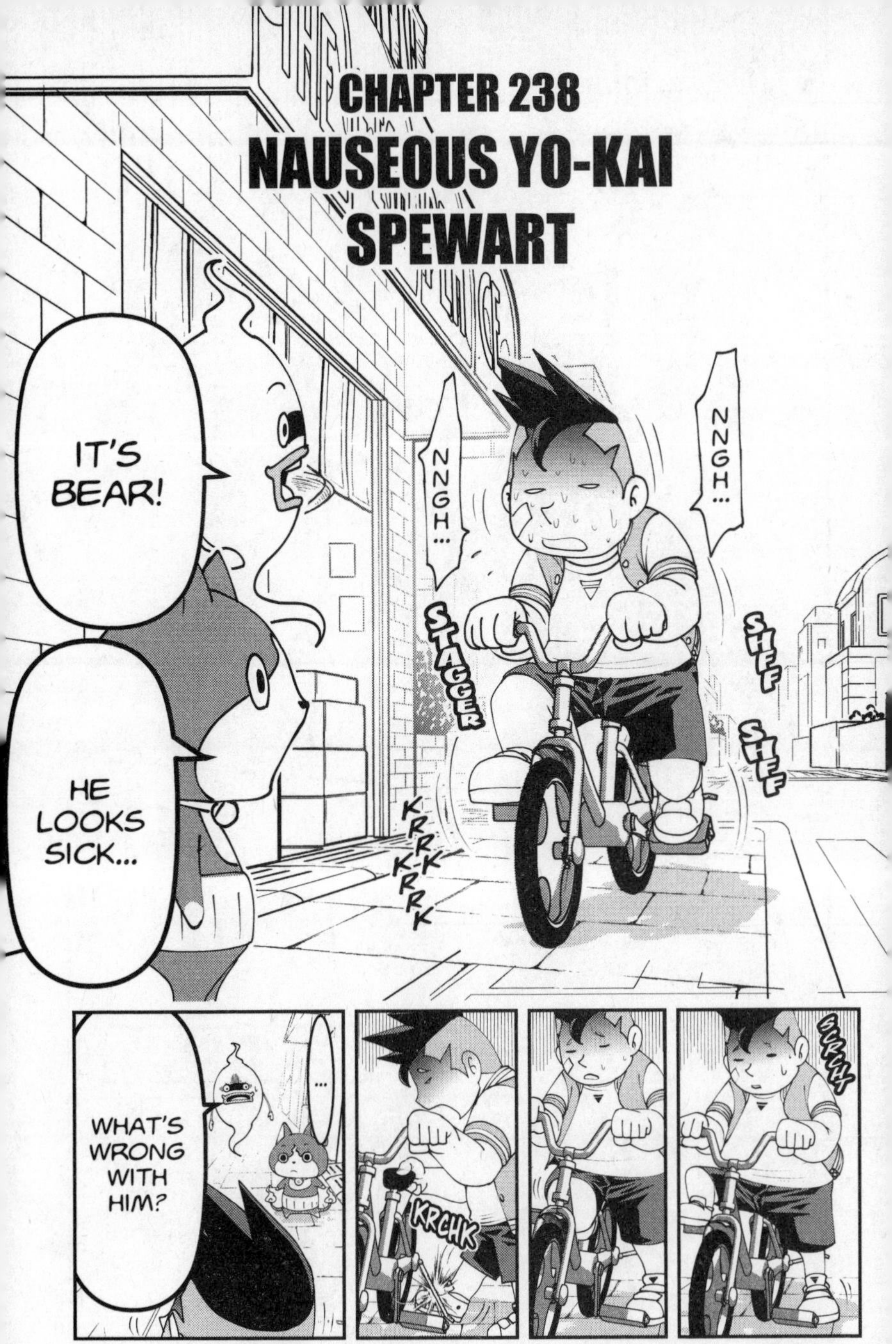
NNGH...
SHEF
SHEF
NNGH...
STAGGER
KRRK-KRRK-KRRK
IT'S BEAR!
HE LOOKS SICK...
SCRCH
KRCHK
...
WHAT'S WRONG WITH HIM?

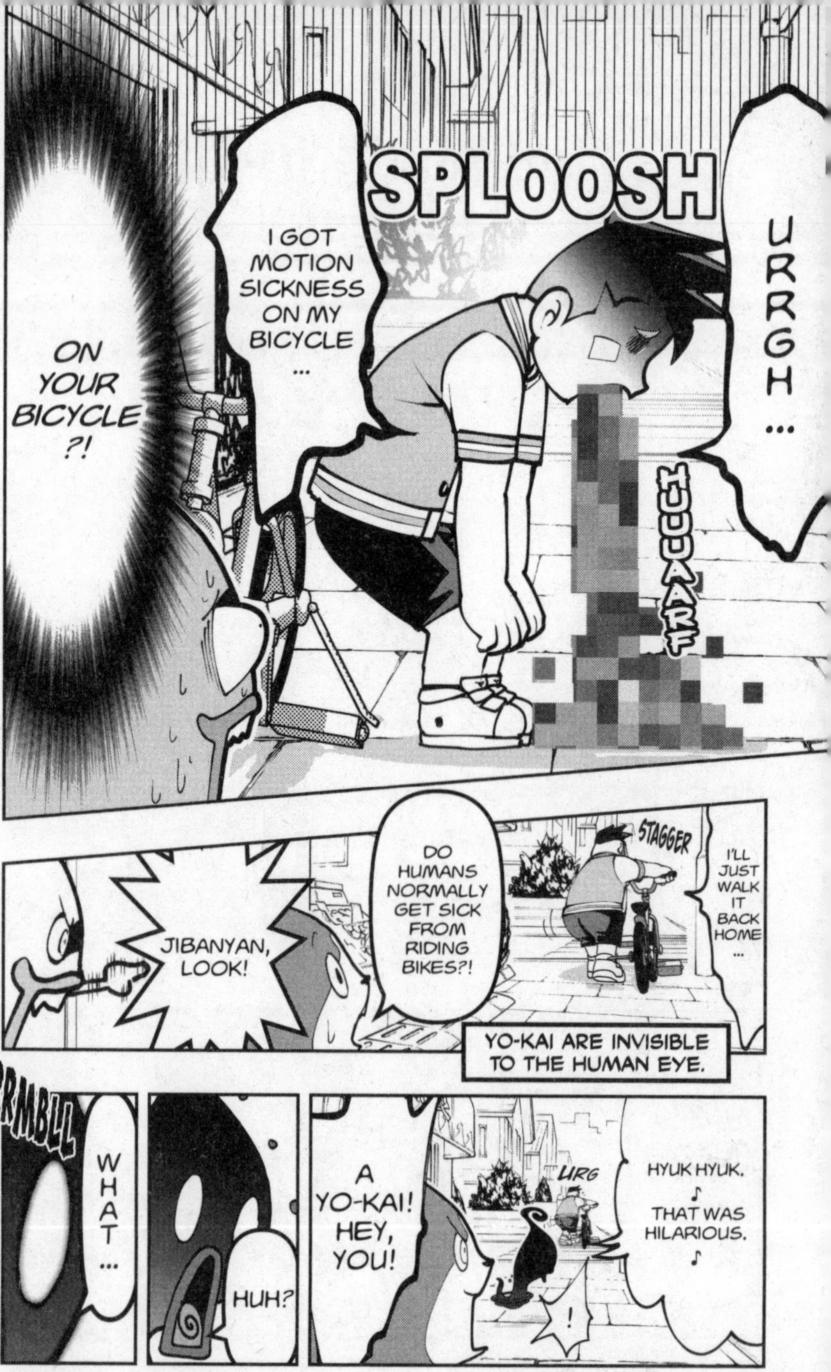
SPLOOSH
URRGH ...
I GOT MOTION SICKNESS ON MY BICYCLE ...
HUUUAARF
ON YOUR BICYCLE ?!
STAGGER
I'LL JUST WALK IT BACK HOME ...
DO HUMANS NORMALLY GET SICK FROM RIDING BIKES?!
YO-KAI ARE INVISIBLE TO THE HUMAN EYE.
JIBANYAN, LOOK!
HYUK HYUK. ♪ THAT WAS HILARIOUS. ♪
URG
!
A YO-KAI! HEY, YOU!
HUH?
RRMBLL
WHAT ...

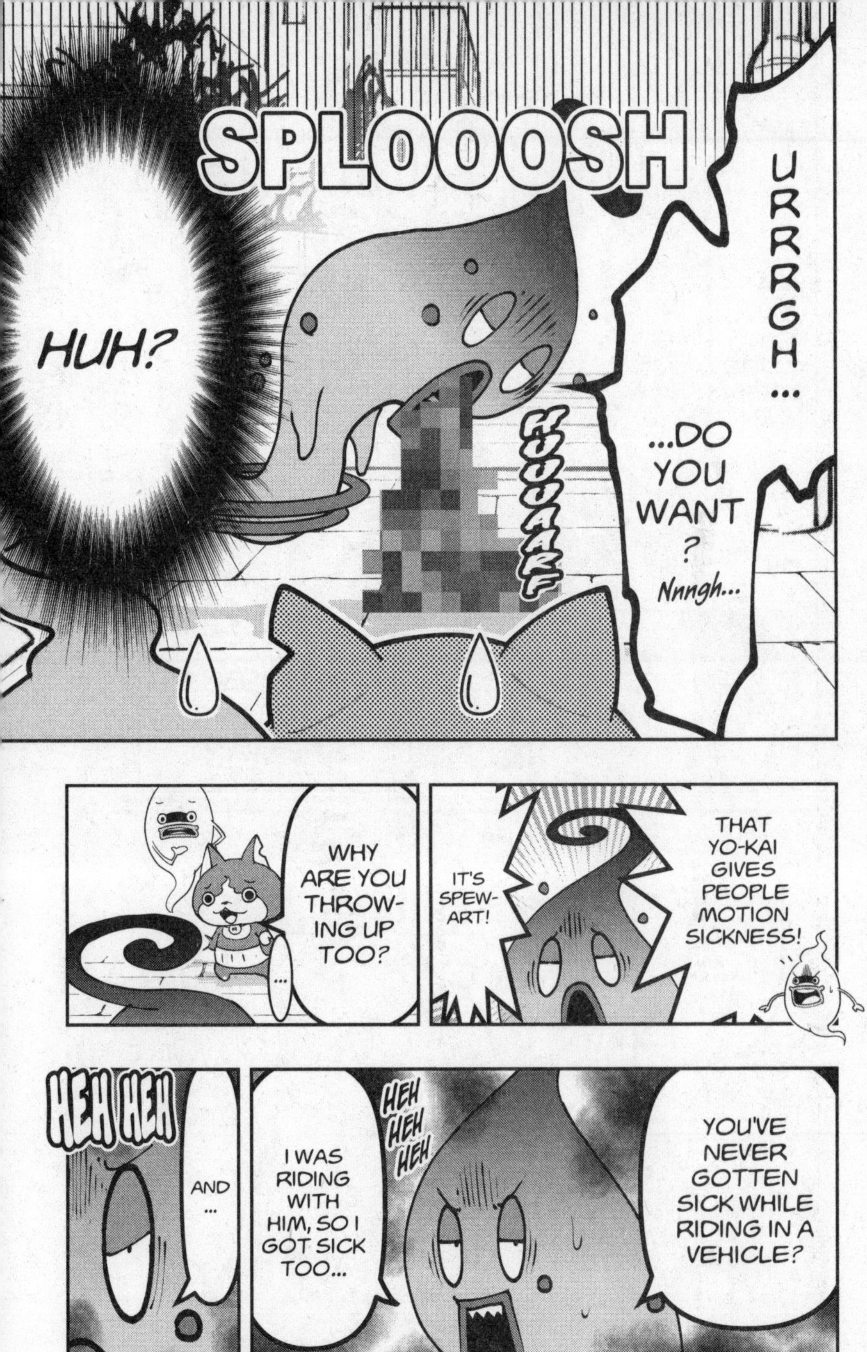
URRRGH...
...DO YOU WANT? Nnngh...
HUUUAARF
SPLOOOSH
HUH?
THAT YO-KAI GIVES PEOPLE MOTION SICKNESS!
IT'S SPEW-ART!
WHY ARE YOU THROWING UP TOO?
...
YOU'VE NEVER GOTTEN SICK WHILE RIDING IN A VEHICLE?
HEH HEH HEH
I WAS RIDING WITH HIM, SO I GOT SICK TOO...
AND ...
HEH HEH

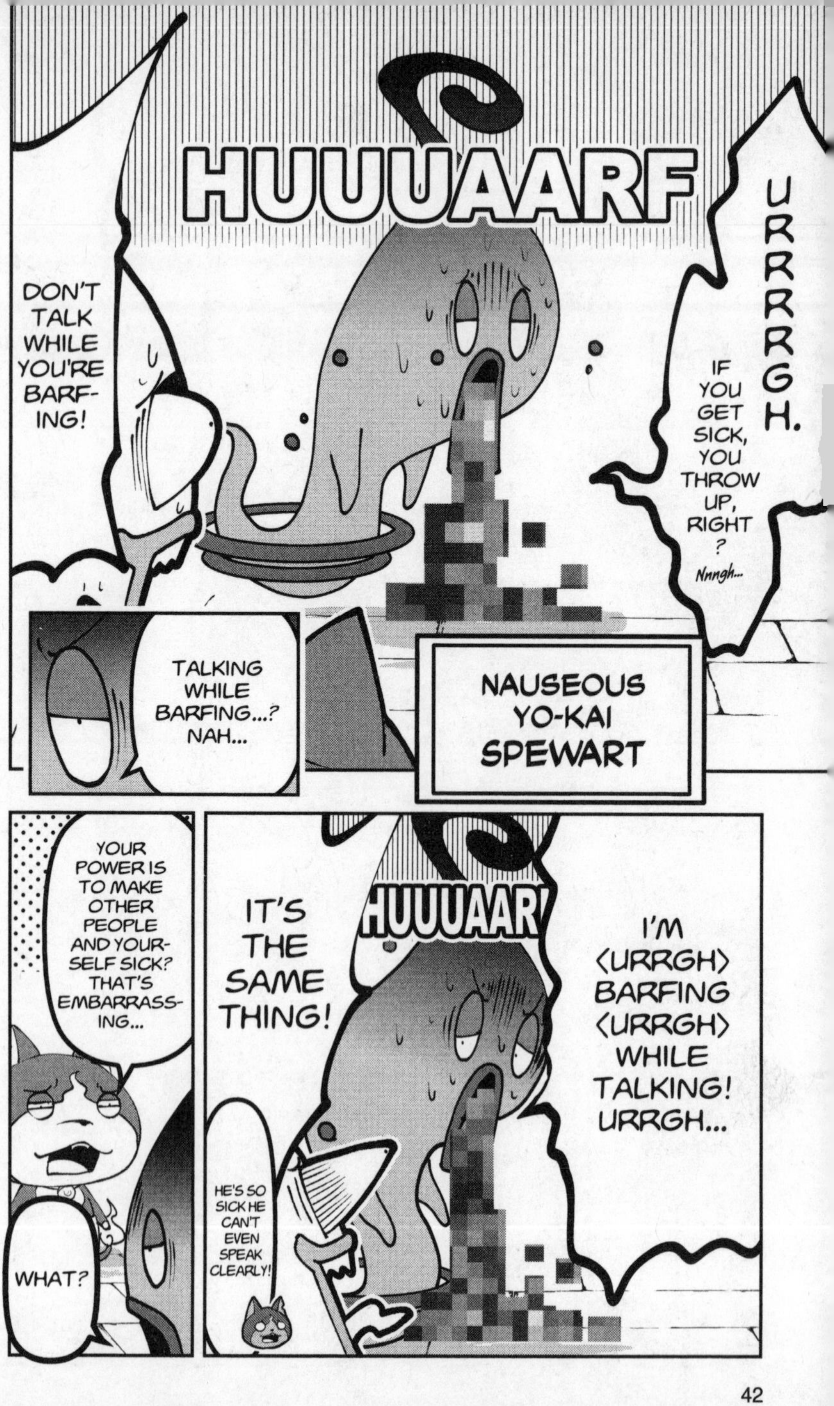
HUUUAARF
URRRRGH.
IF YOU GET SICK, YOU THROW UP, RIGHT?
Nnngh...
DON'T TALK WHILE YOU'RE BARF-ING!
NAUSEOUS YO-KAI SPEWART
TALKING WHILE BARFING...? NAH...
HUUUAAR
I'M 〈URRGH〉 BARFING 〈URRGH〉 WHILE TALKING! URRGH...
IT'S THE SAME THING!
HE'S SO SICK HE CAN'T EVEN SPEAK CLEARLY!
YOUR POWER IS TO MAKE OTHER PEOPLE AND YOUR-SELF SICK? THAT'S EMBARRASS-ING...
WHAT?

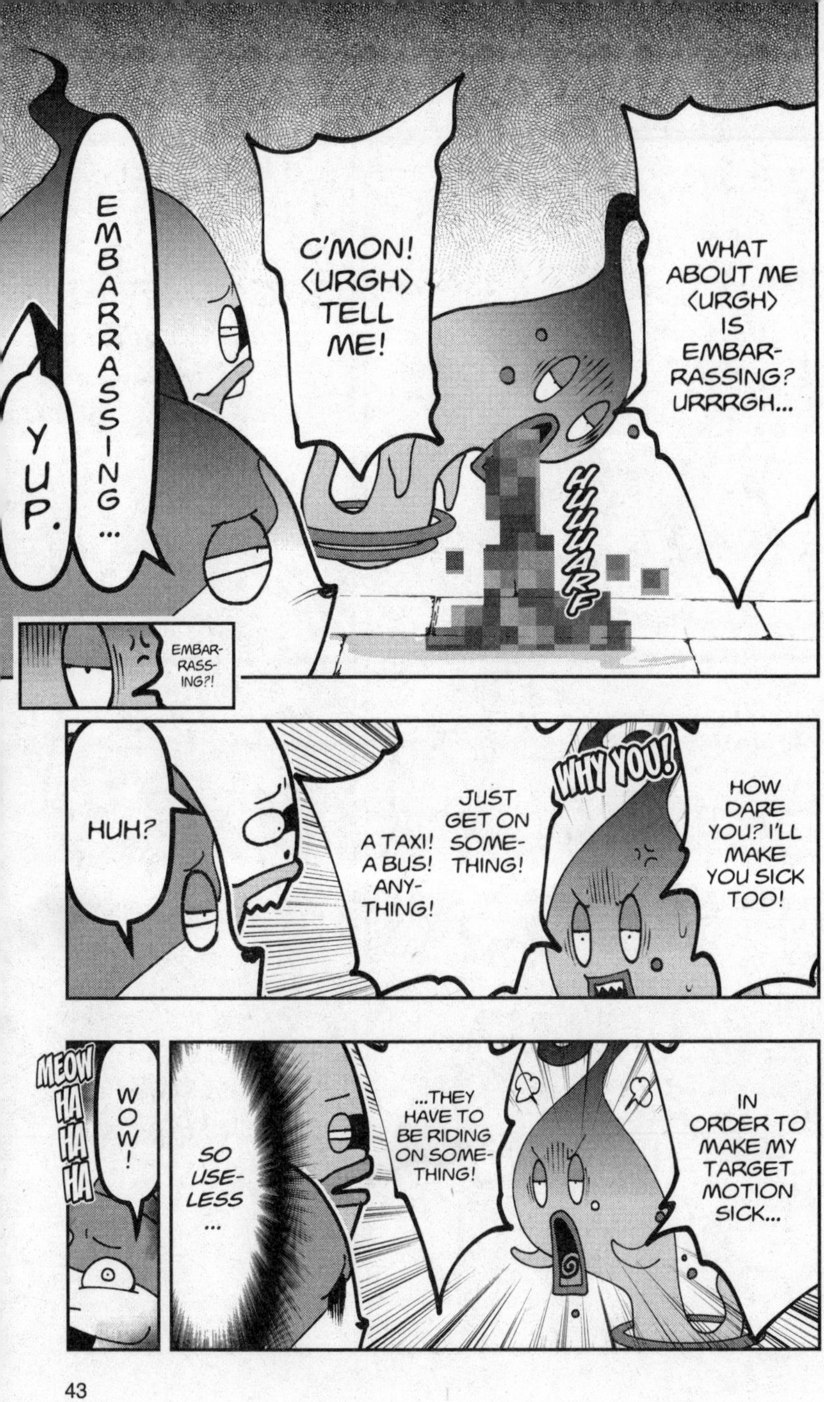
WHAT ABOUT ME ⟨URGH⟩ IS EMBARRASSING? URRRGH...
HUUUARF
C'MON! ⟨URGH⟩ TELL ME!
EMBARRASSING...
YUP.
EMBARRASSING?!
HOW DARE YOU? I'LL MAKE YOU SICK TOO!
WHY YOU!
JUST GET ON SOMETHING!
A TAXI! A BUS! ANYTHING!
HUH?
IN ORDER TO MAKE MY TARGET MOTION SICK...
...THEY HAVE TO BE RIDING ON SOMETHING!
SO USELESS...
WOW!
MEOW HA HA HA

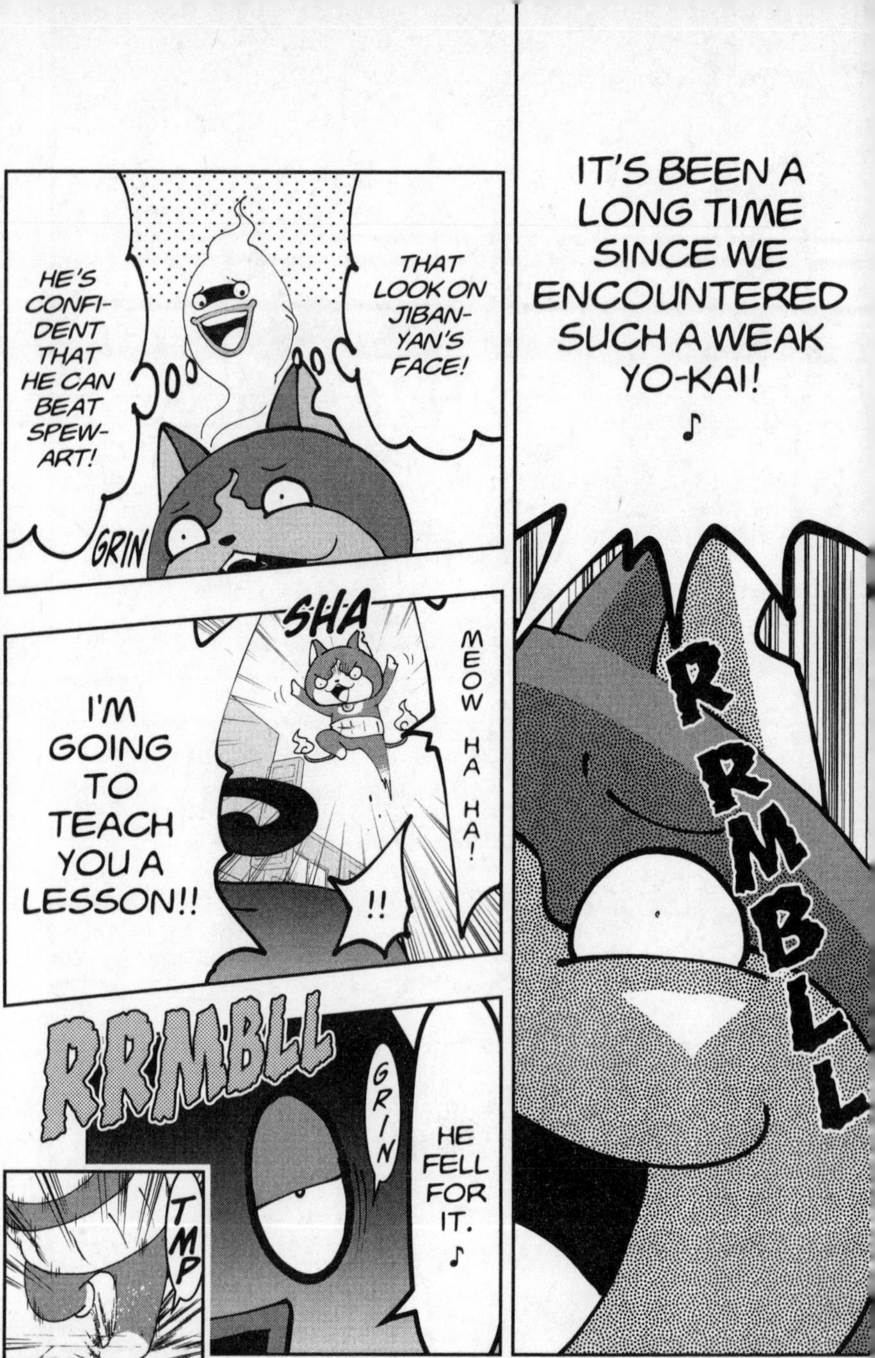
IT'S BEEN A LONG TIME SINCE WE ENCOUNTERED SUCH A WEAK YO-KAI! ♪
RRMBLL
THAT LOOK ON JIBAN-YAN'S FACE!
HE'S CONFI-DENT THAT HE CAN BEAT SPEW-ART!
GRIN
SHA
MEOW HA HA!
I'M GOING TO TEACH YOU A LESSON!!
!!
RRMBLL
HE FELL FOR IT. ♪
GRIN
TMP

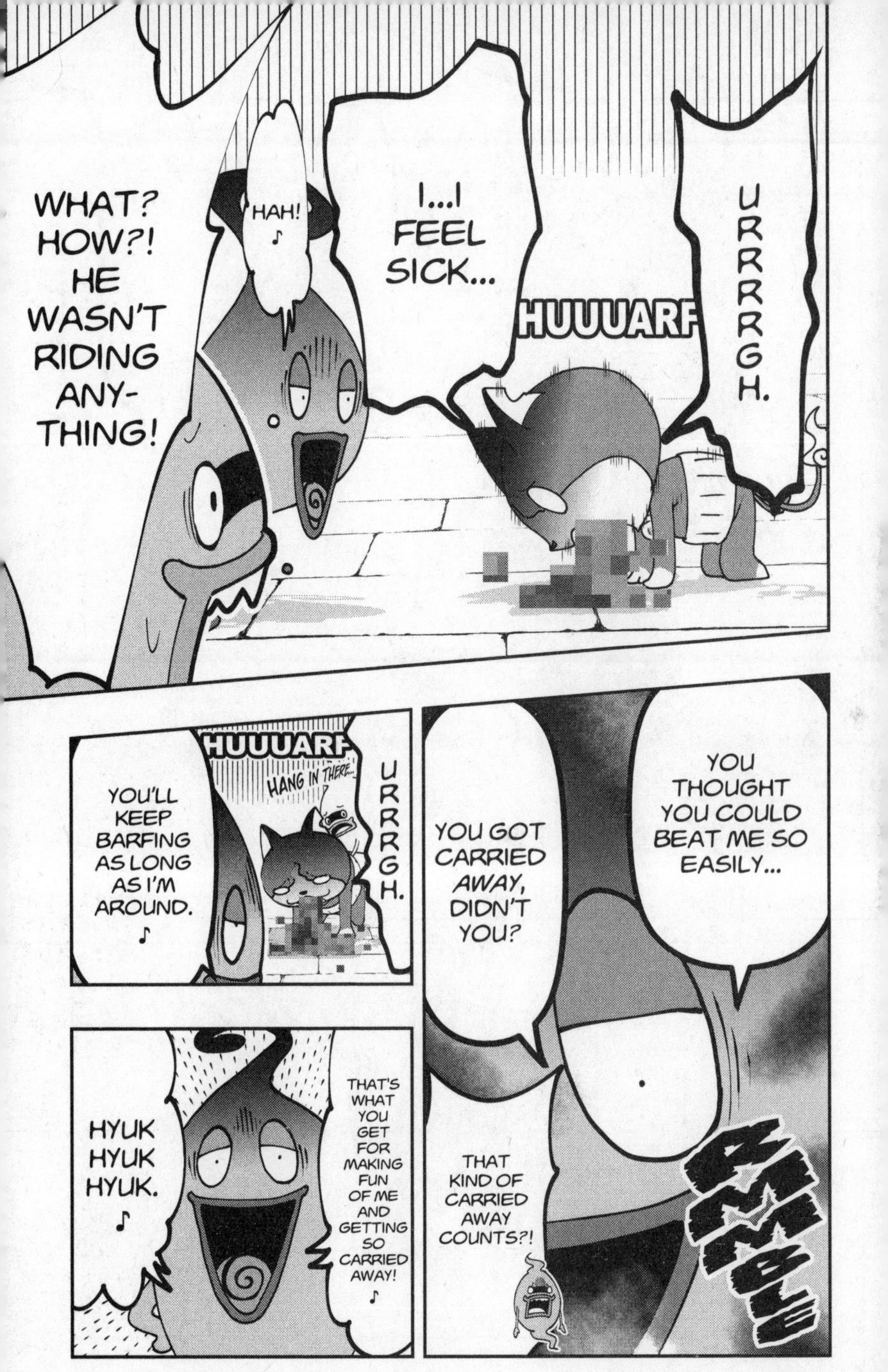
URRRRGH.
HUUUARF
I...I FEEL SICK...
HAH! ♪
WHAT? HOW?! HE WASN'T RIDING ANY-THING!
YOU THOUGHT YOU COULD BEAT ME SO EASILY...
YOU GOT CARRIED AWAY, DIDN'T YOU?
THAT KIND OF CARRIED AWAY COUNTS?!
URRRGH.
HUUUARF
HANG IN THERE...
YOU'LL KEEP BARFING AS LONG AS I'M AROUND. ♪
THAT'S WHAT YOU GET FOR MAKING FUN OF ME AND GETTING SO CARRIED AWAY! ♪
HYUK HYUK HYUK. ♪

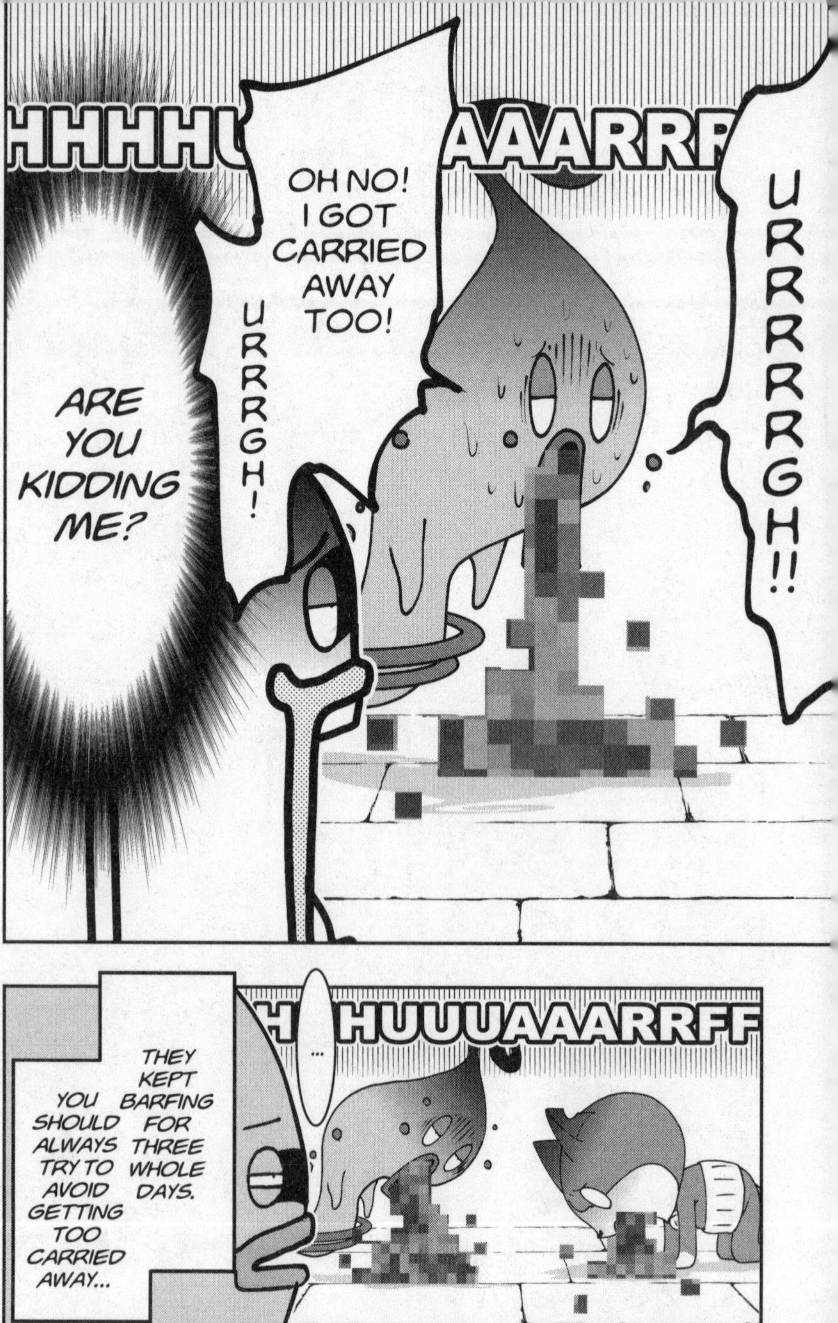
HHHHU
AAARRR
URRRRRGH!!
OH NO! I GOT CARRIED AWAY TOO!
URRRGH!
ARE YOU KIDDING ME?
HUUUAAARRFF
...
THEY KEPT BARFING FOR THREE WHOLE DAYS.
YOU SHOULD ALWAYS TRY TO AVOID GETTING TOO CARRIED AWAY...

CHAPTER 239
WEIRD ACTING YO-KAI LORD SHRILLINGTON

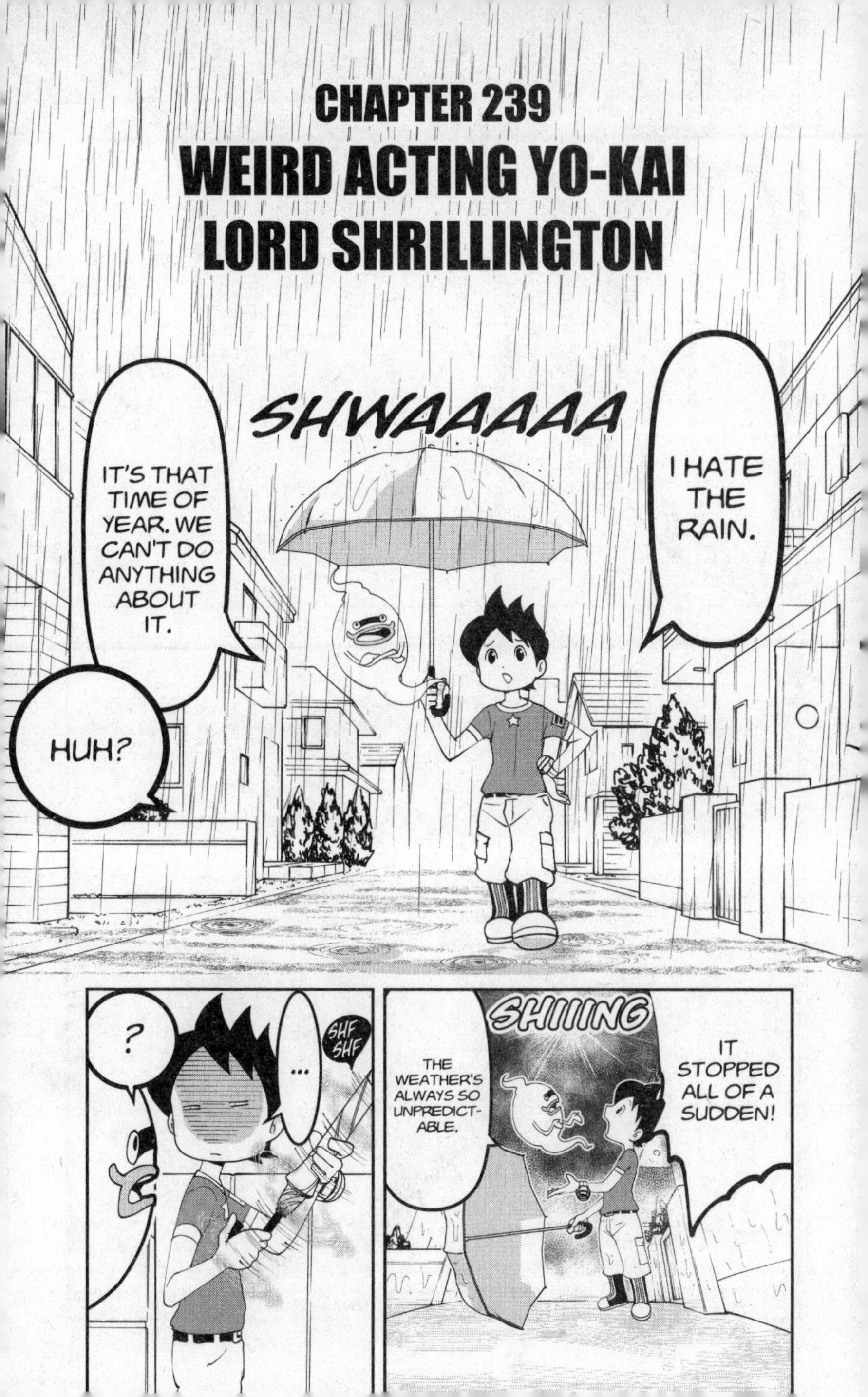
SHWAAAAA
I HATE THE RAIN.
IT'S THAT TIME OF YEAR. WE CAN'T DO ANYTHING ABOUT IT.
HUH?
SHIIING
IT STOPPED ALL OF A SUDDEN!
THE WEATHER'S ALWAYS SO UNPREDICT-ABLE.
SHF SHF
...
?

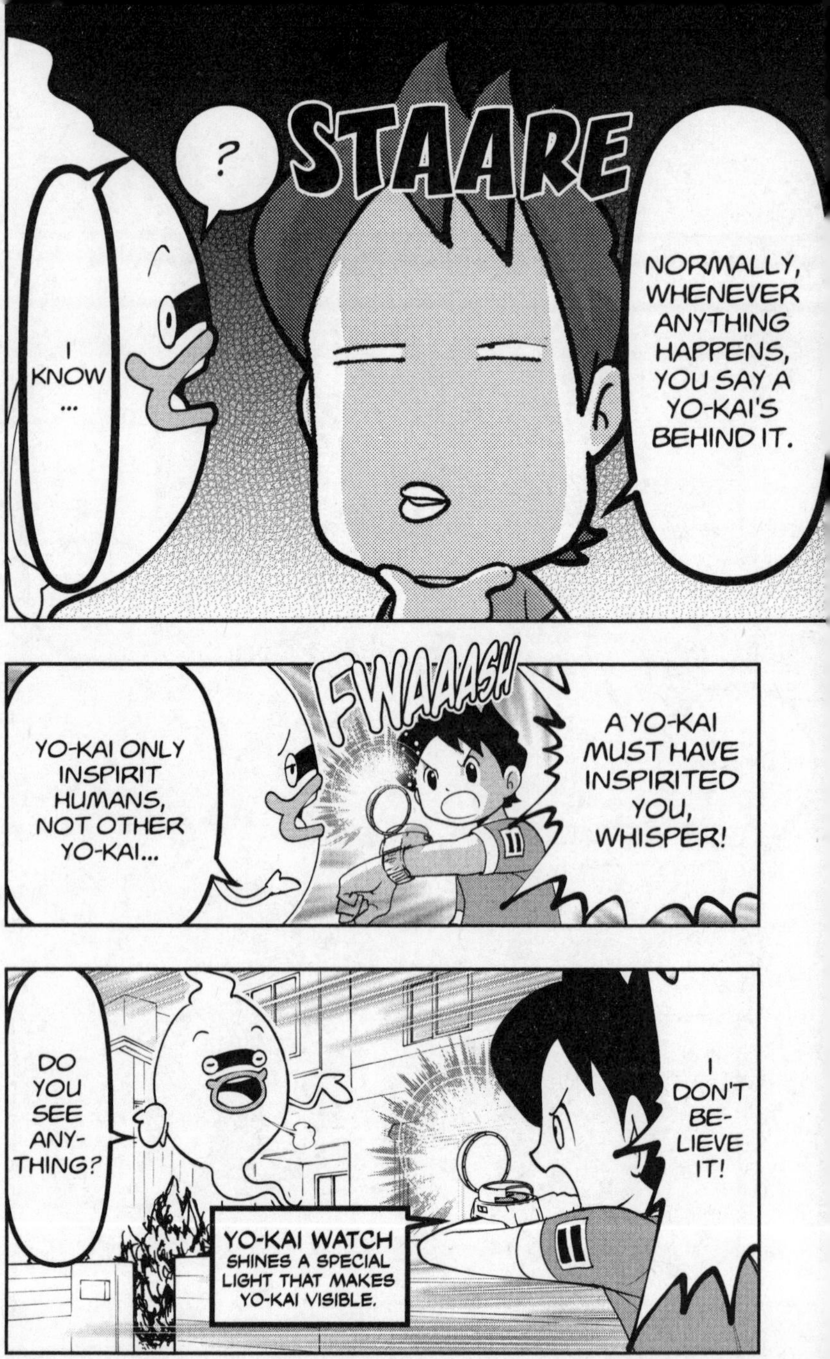
NORMALLY, WHENEVER ANYTHING HAPPENS, YOU SAY A YO-KAI'S BEHIND IT.
STAARE
?
I KNOW ...
A YO-KAI MUST HAVE INSPIRITED YOU, WHISPER!
FWAAASH
YO-KAI ONLY INSPIRIT HUMANS, NOT OTHER YO-KAI...
I DON'T BE-LIEVE IT!
DO YOU SEE ANY-THING?
YO-KAI WATCH SHINES A SPECIAL LIGHT THAT MAKES YO-KAI VISIBLE.

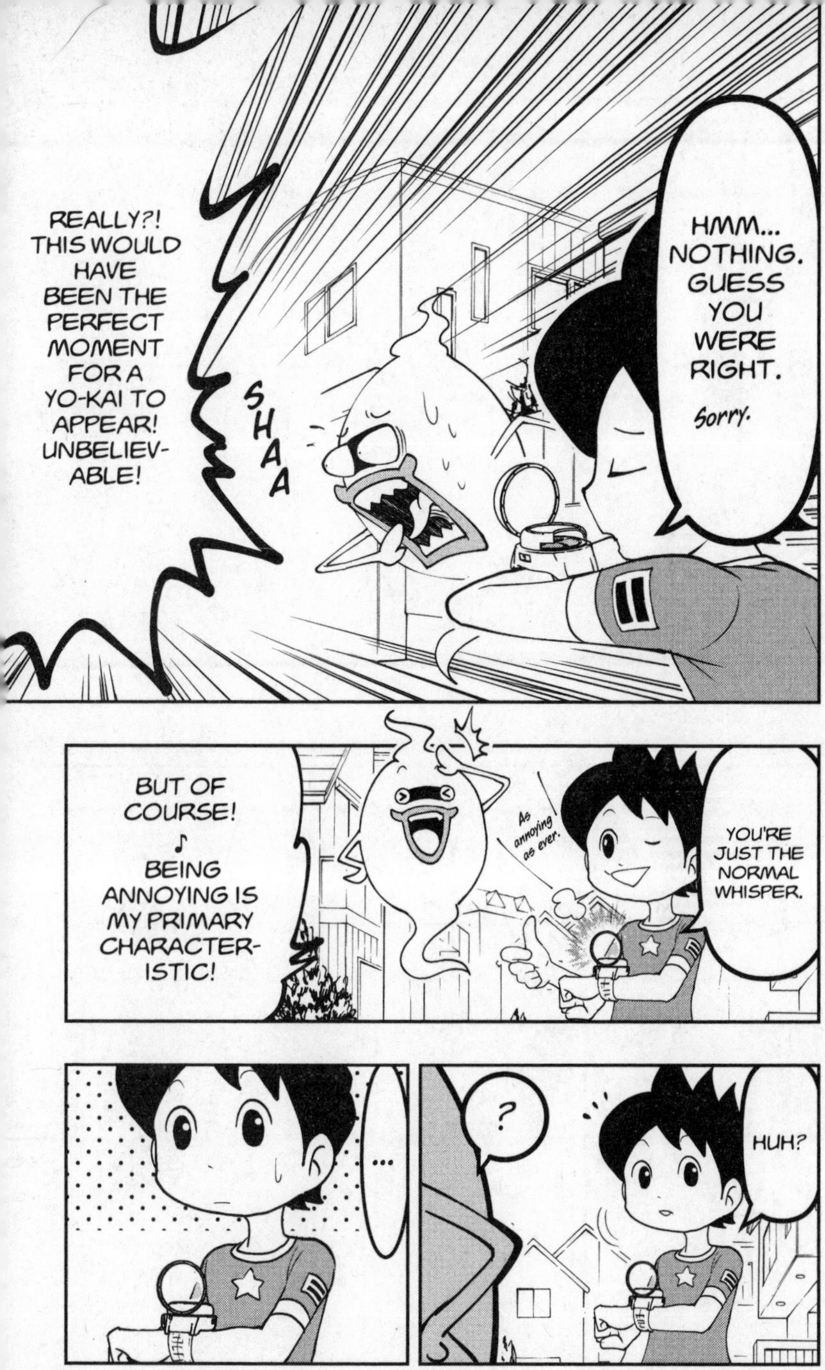
HMM... NOTHING. GUESS YOU WERE RIGHT.
Sorry.
SHAA
REALLY?! THIS WOULD HAVE BEEN THE PERFECT MOMENT FOR A YO-KAI TO APPEAR! UNBELIEV-ABLE!
YOU'RE JUST THE NORMAL WHISPER.
As annoying as ever.
BUT OF COURSE! ♪
BEING ANNOYING IS MY PRIMARY CHARACTER-ISTIC!
HUH?
?
...

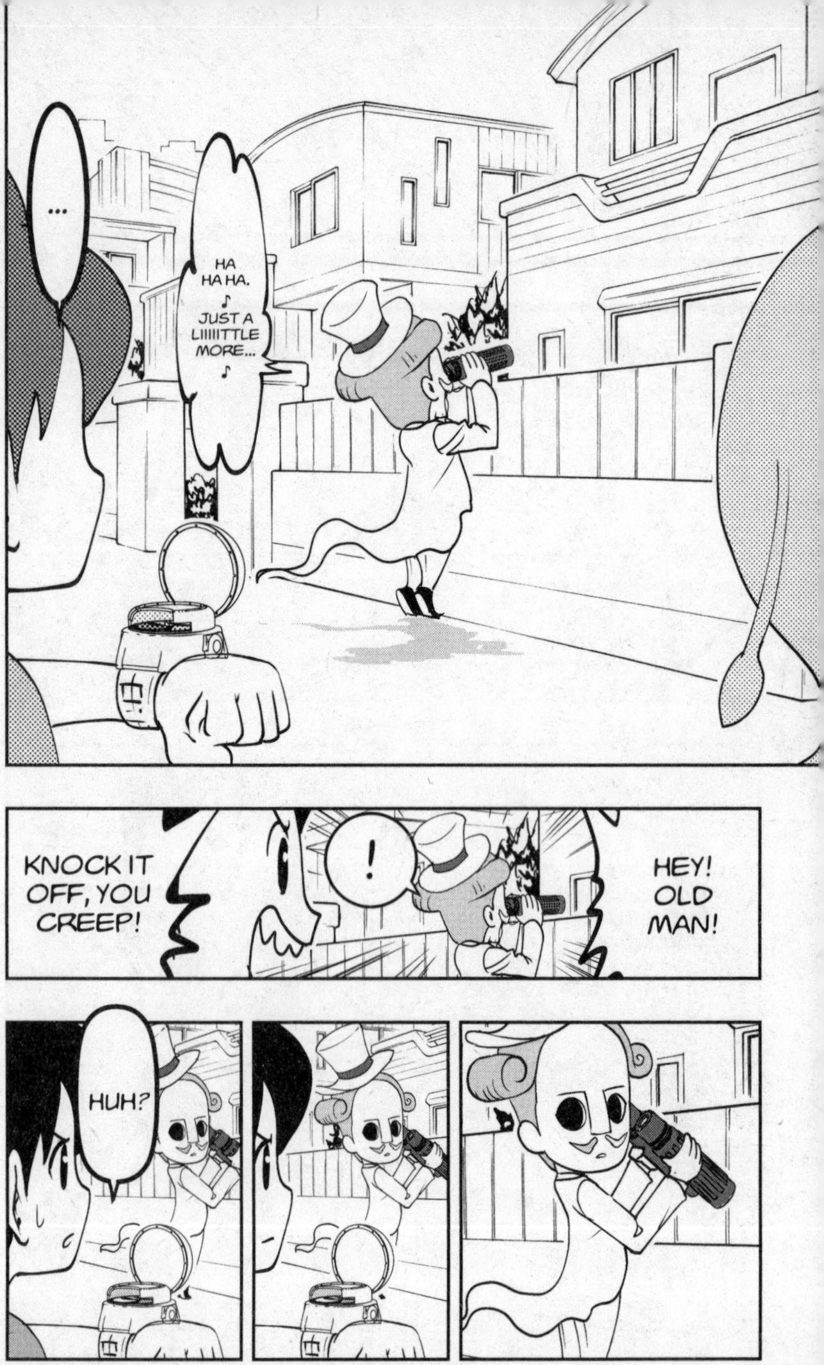
HA HA HA. ♪ JUST A LIIIIITTLE MORE... ♪
...
HEY! OLD MAN!
!
KNOCK IT OFF, YOU CREEP!
HUH?

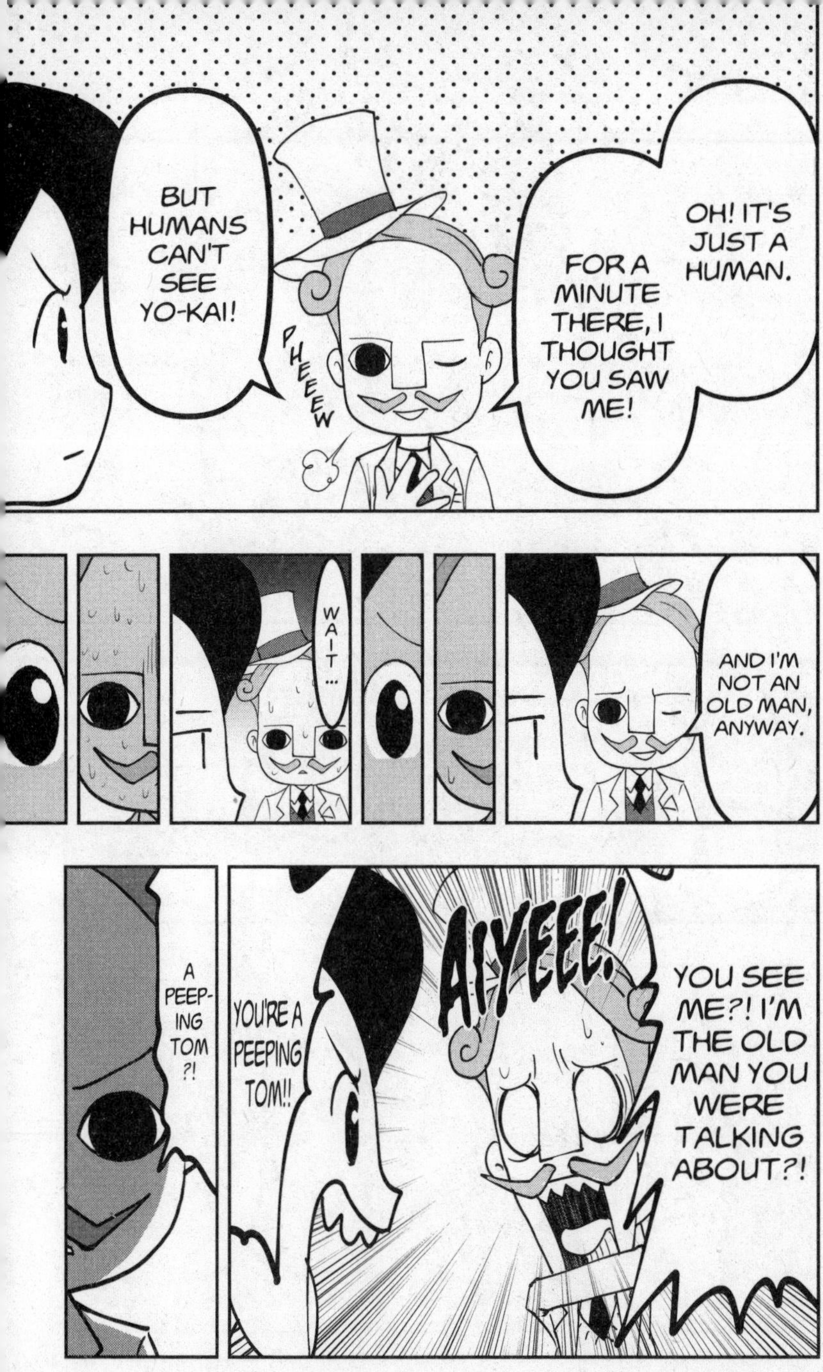
OH! IT'S JUST A HUMAN.
FOR A MINUTE THERE, I THOUGHT YOU SAW ME!
PHEEEW
BUT HUMANS CAN'T SEE YO-KAI!
AND I'M NOT AN OLD MAN, ANYWAY.
WAIT...
YOU SEE ME?! I'M THE OLD MAN YOU WERE TALKING ABOUT?!
AIYEEE!
YOU'RE A PEEPING TOM!!
A PEEP-ING TOM ?!

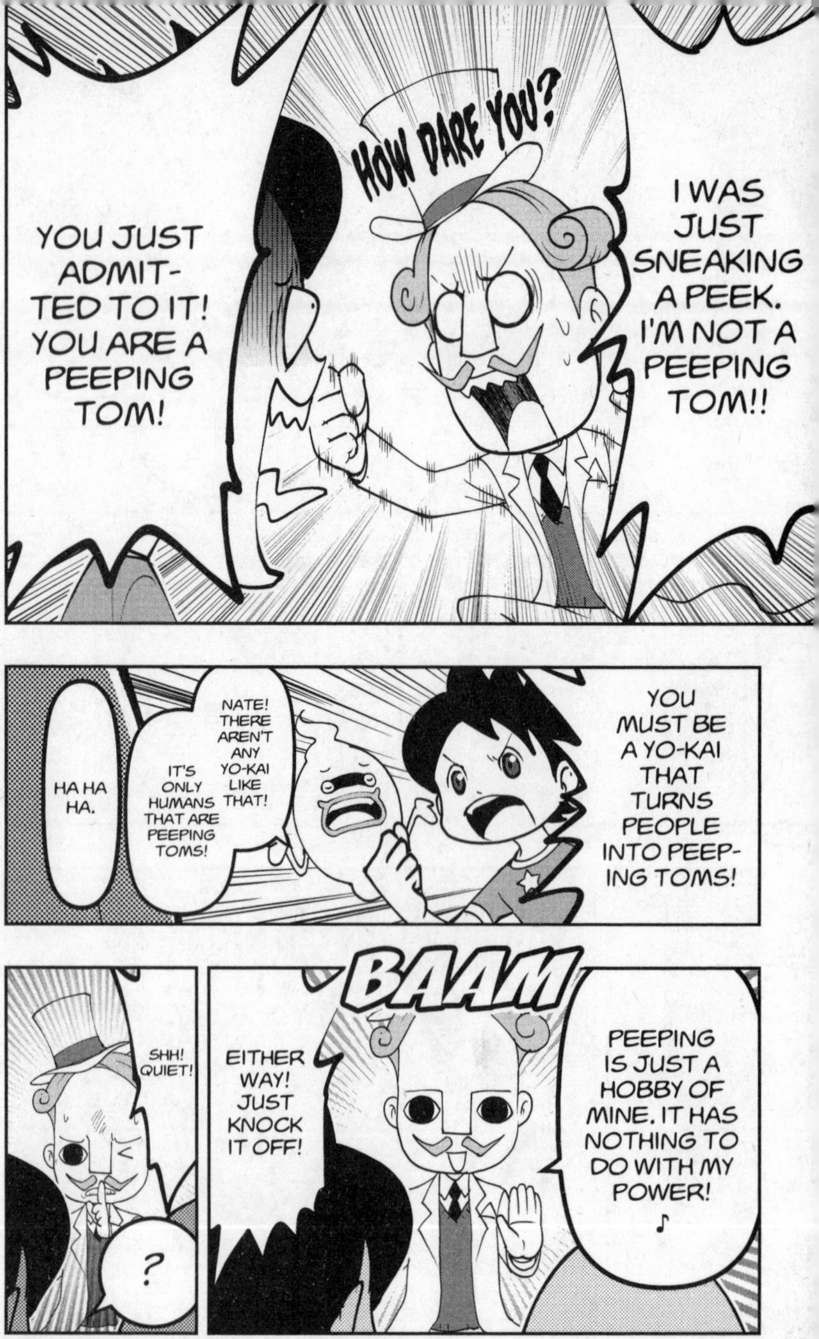
I WAS JUST SNEAKING A PEEK. I'M NOT A PEEPING TOM!!
YOU JUST ADMIT-TED TO IT! YOU ARE A PEEPING TOM!
HOW DARE YOU?
YOU MUST BE A YO-KAI THAT TURNS PEOPLE INTO PEEP-ING TOMS!
NATE! THERE AREN'T ANY YO-KAI LIKE THAT!
IT'S ONLY HUMANS THAT ARE PEEPING TOMS!
HA HA HA.
PEEPING IS JUST A HOBBY OF MINE. IT HAS NOTHING TO DO WITH MY POWER! ♪
BAAM
EITHER WAY! JUST KNOCK IT OFF!
SHH! QUIET!
?

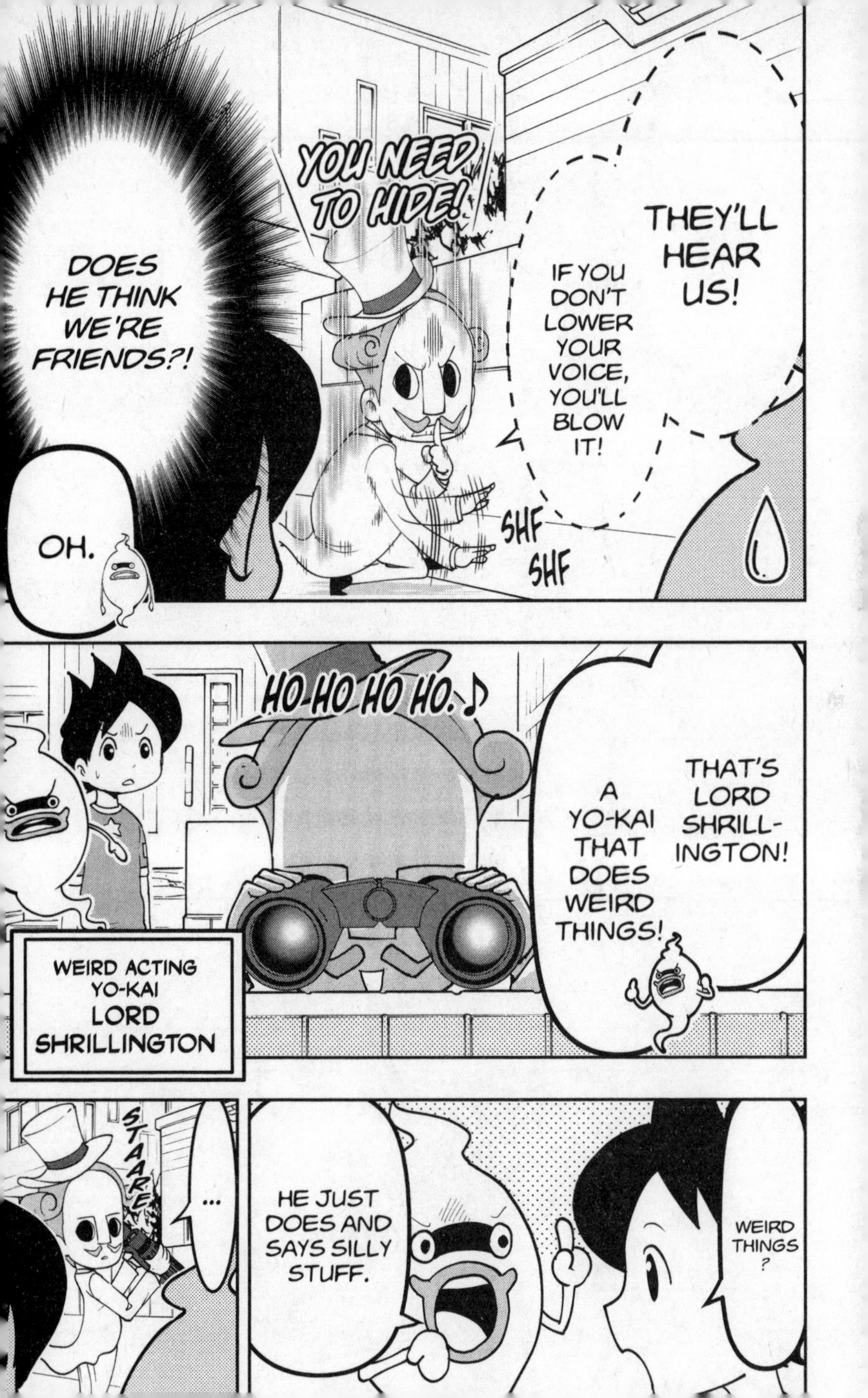
THEY'LL HEAR US!
IF YOU DON'T LOWER YOUR VOICE, YOU'LL BLOW IT!
YOU NEED TO HIDE!
SHF SHF
DOES HE THINK WE'RE FRIENDS?!
OH.
THAT'S LORD SHRILL-INGTON!
A YO-KAI THAT DOES WEIRD THINGS!
HO-HO HO HO. ♪
WEIRD ACTING YO-KAI LORD SHRILLINGTON
WEIRD THINGS?
HE JUST DOES AND SAYS SILLY STUFF.
...
STAARE

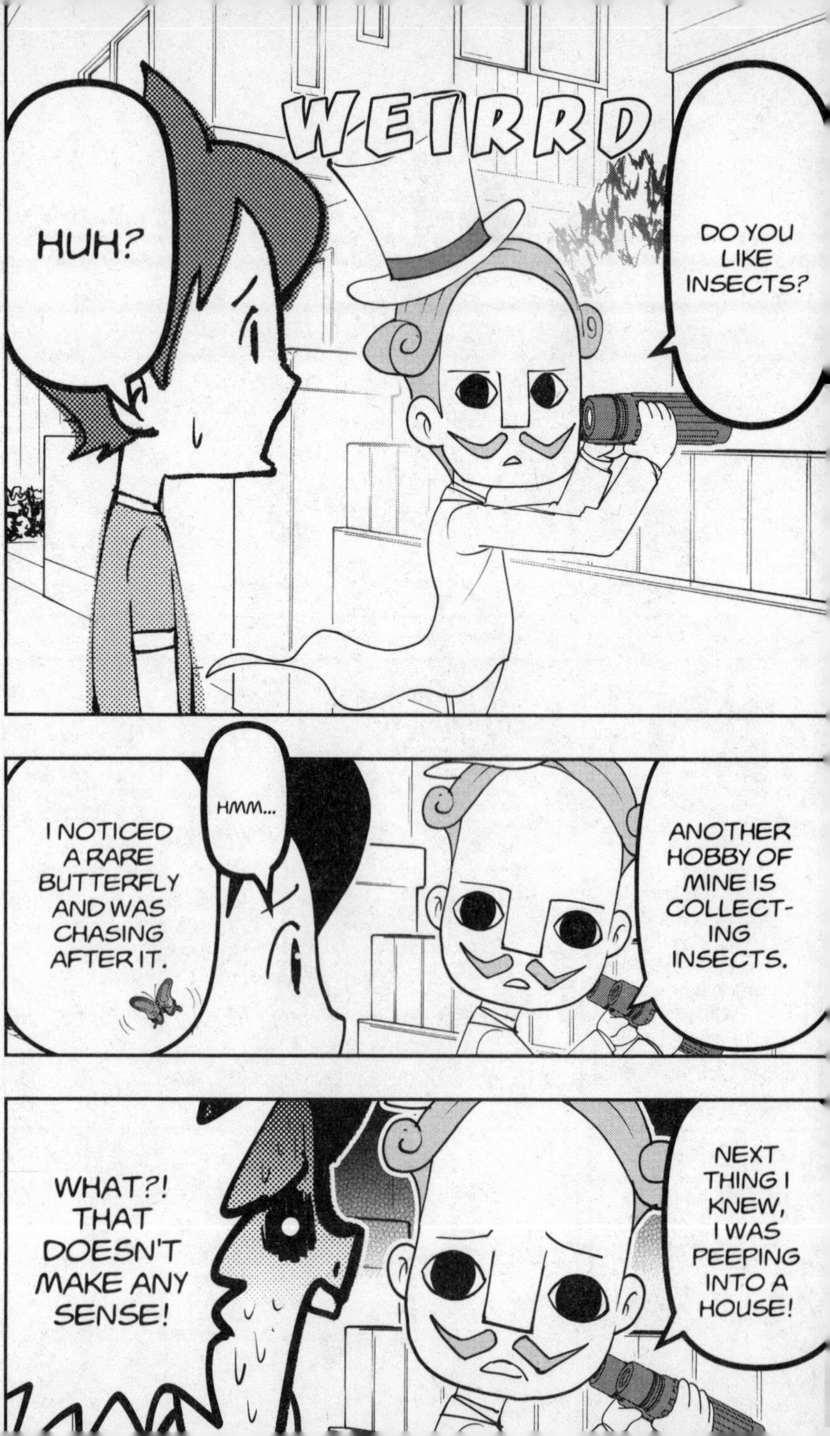
DO YOU LIKE INSECTS?
WEIRRD
HUH?
ANOTHER HOBBY OF MINE IS COLLECT-ING INSECTS.
HMM...
I NOTICED A RARE BUTTERFLY AND WAS CHASING AFTER IT.
NEXT THING I KNEW, I WAS PEEPING INTO A HOUSE!
WHAT?! THAT DOESN'T MAKE ANY SENSE!

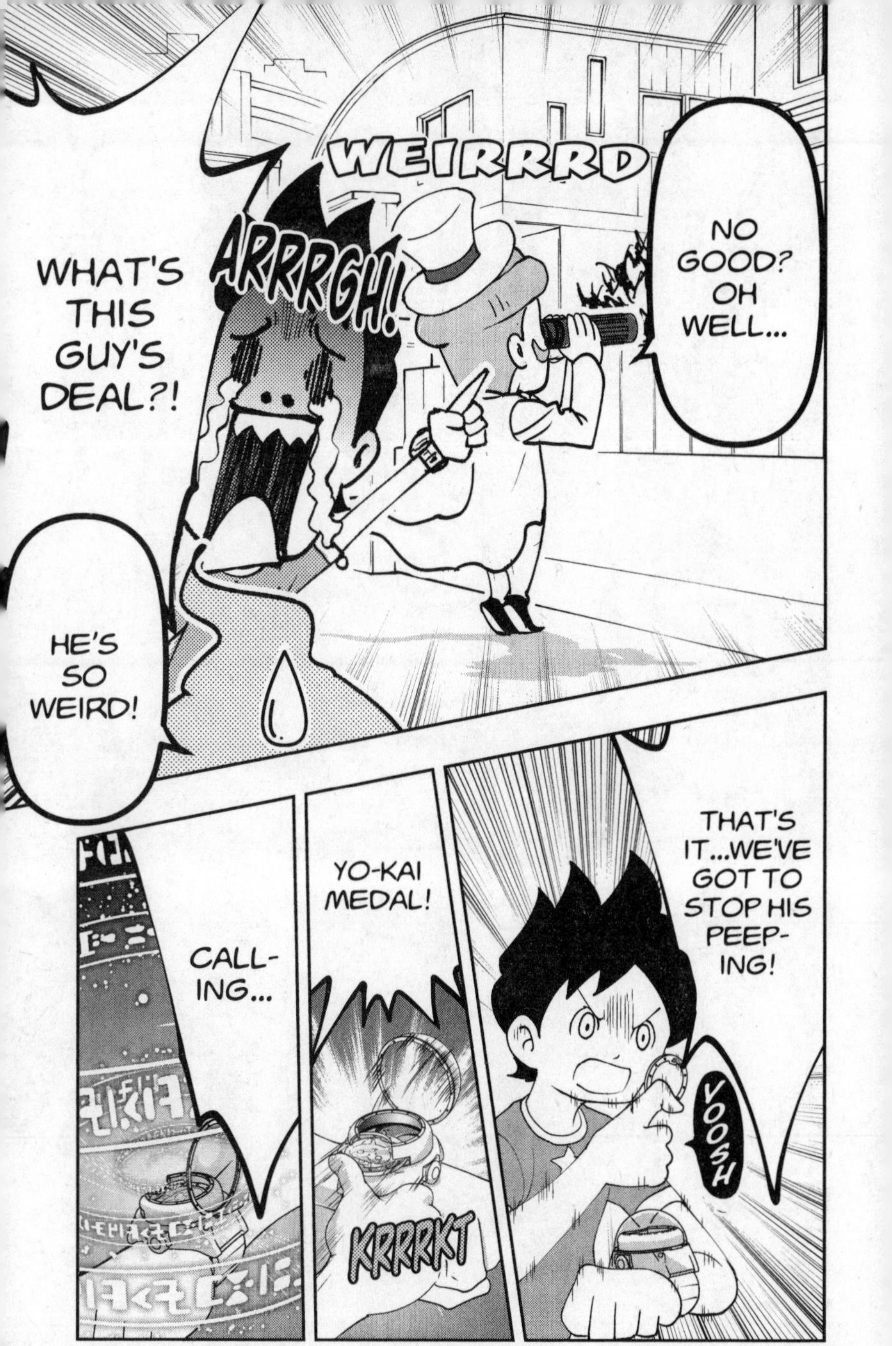
NO GOOD? OH WELL...
WEIRRRD
ARRRGH!
WHAT'S THIS GUY'S DEAL?!
HE'S SO WEIRD!
THAT'S IT...WE'VE GOT TO STOP HIS PEEPING!
VOOSH
YO-KAI MEDAL!
KRRRKT
CALLING...

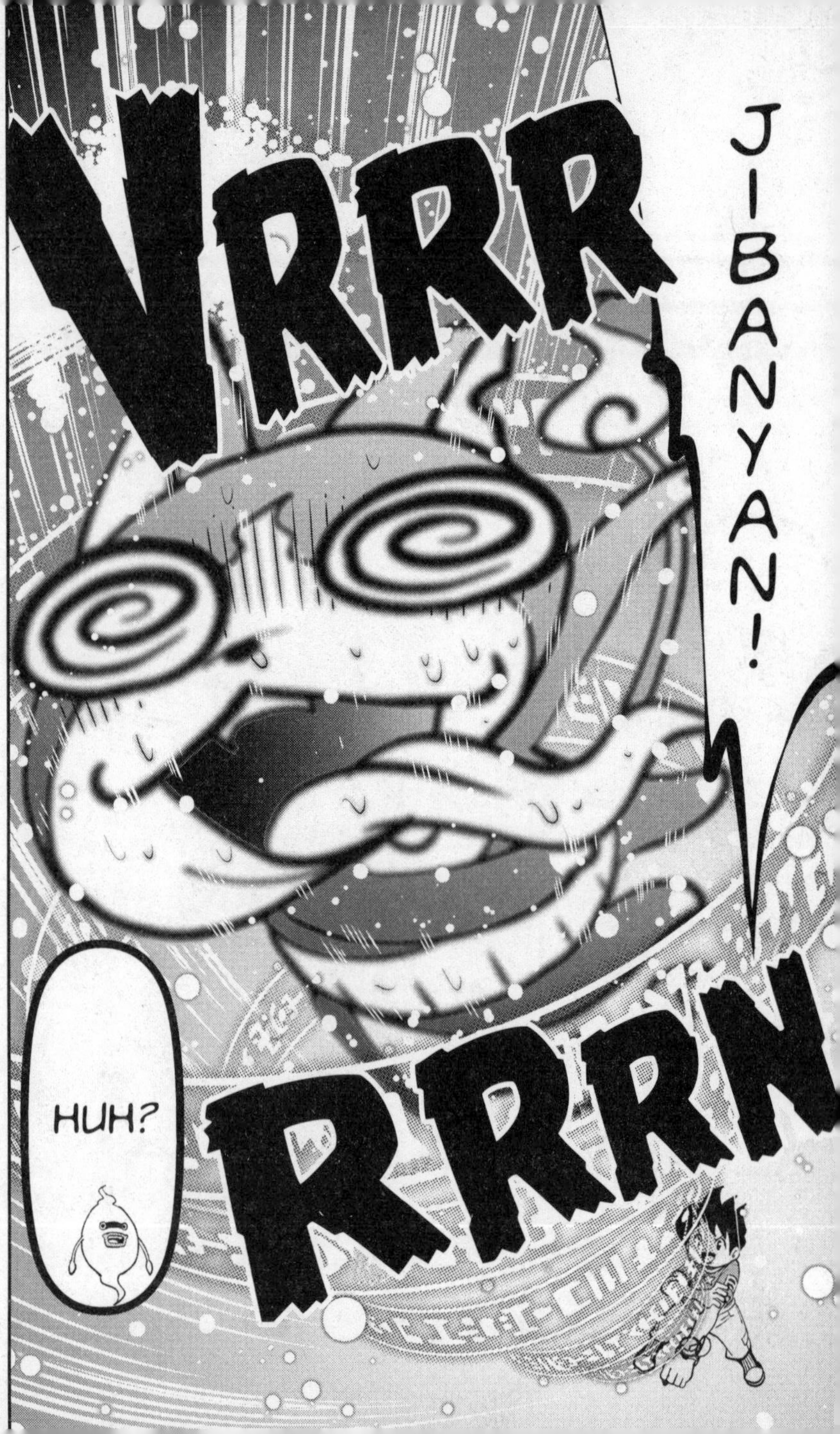
VRRR
JIBANYAN!
RRRN
HUH?

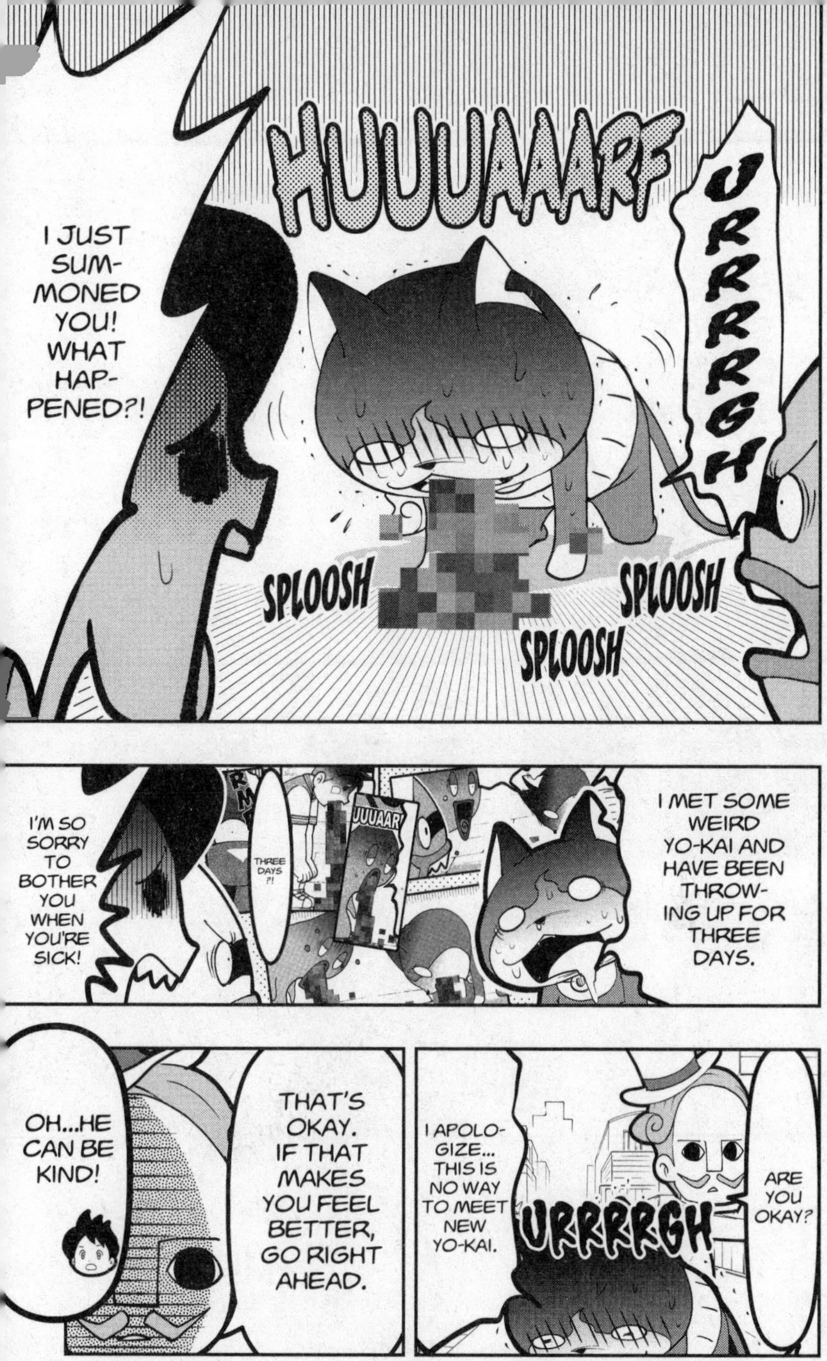
URRRRGH
HUUUAAARF
I JUST SUMMONED YOU! WHAT HAPPENED?!
SPLOOSH
SPLOOSH
SPLOOSH
I MET SOME WEIRD YO-KAI AND HAVE BEEN THROWING UP FOR THREE DAYS.
JUUUAAR!
THREE DAYS?!
I'M SO SORRY TO BOTHER YOU WHEN YOU'RE SICK!
ARE YOU OKAY?
URRRRGH
I APOLOGIZE... THIS IS NO WAY TO MEET NEW YO-KAI.
THAT'S OKAY. IF THAT MAKES YOU FEEL BETTER, GO RIGHT AHEAD.
OH...HE CAN BE KIND!

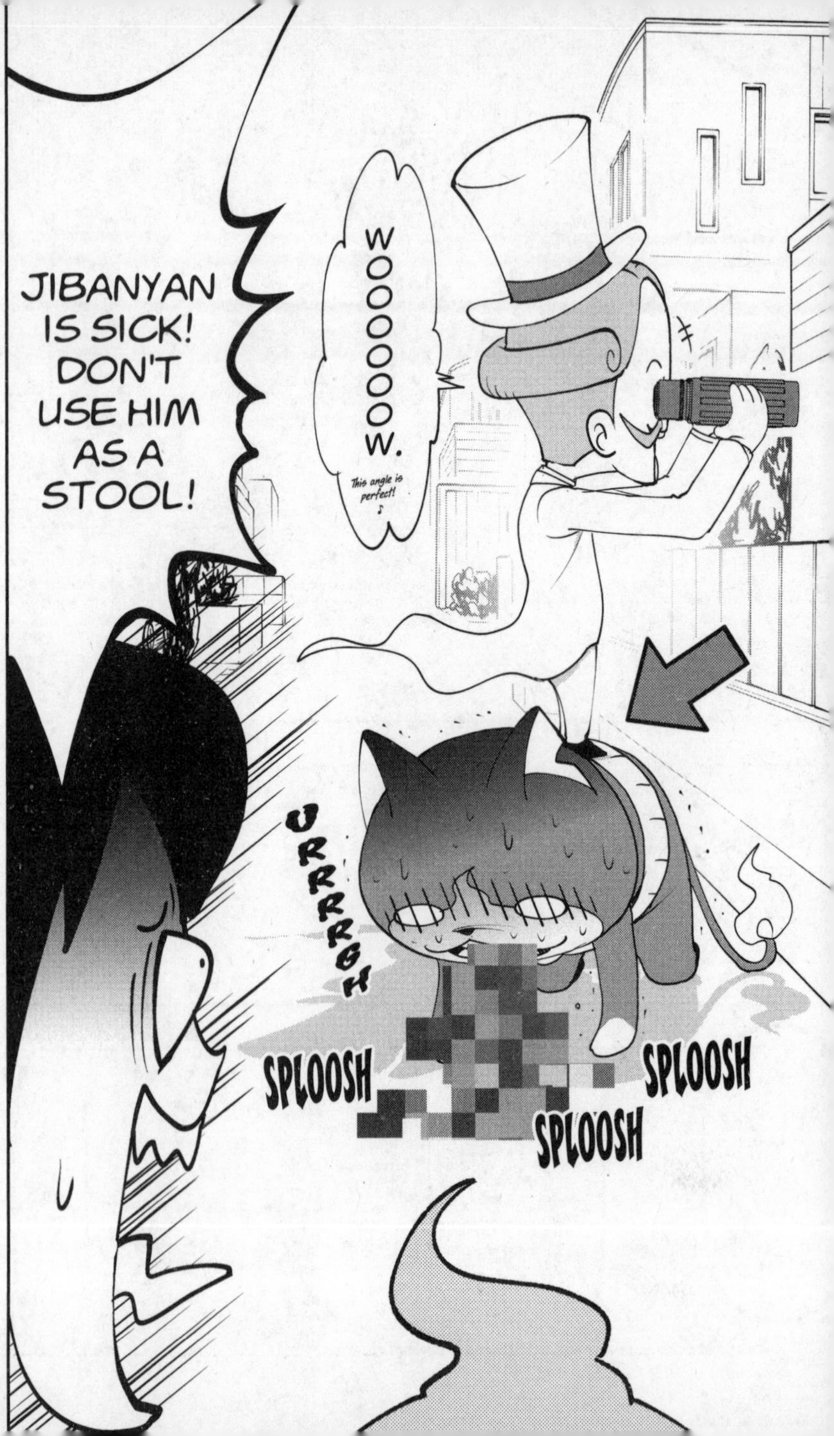
WOOOOOOW.
This angle is perfect! ♪
JIBANYAN IS SICK! DON'T USE HIM AS A STOOL!
URRRGH
SPLOOSH
SPLOOSH
SPLOOSH

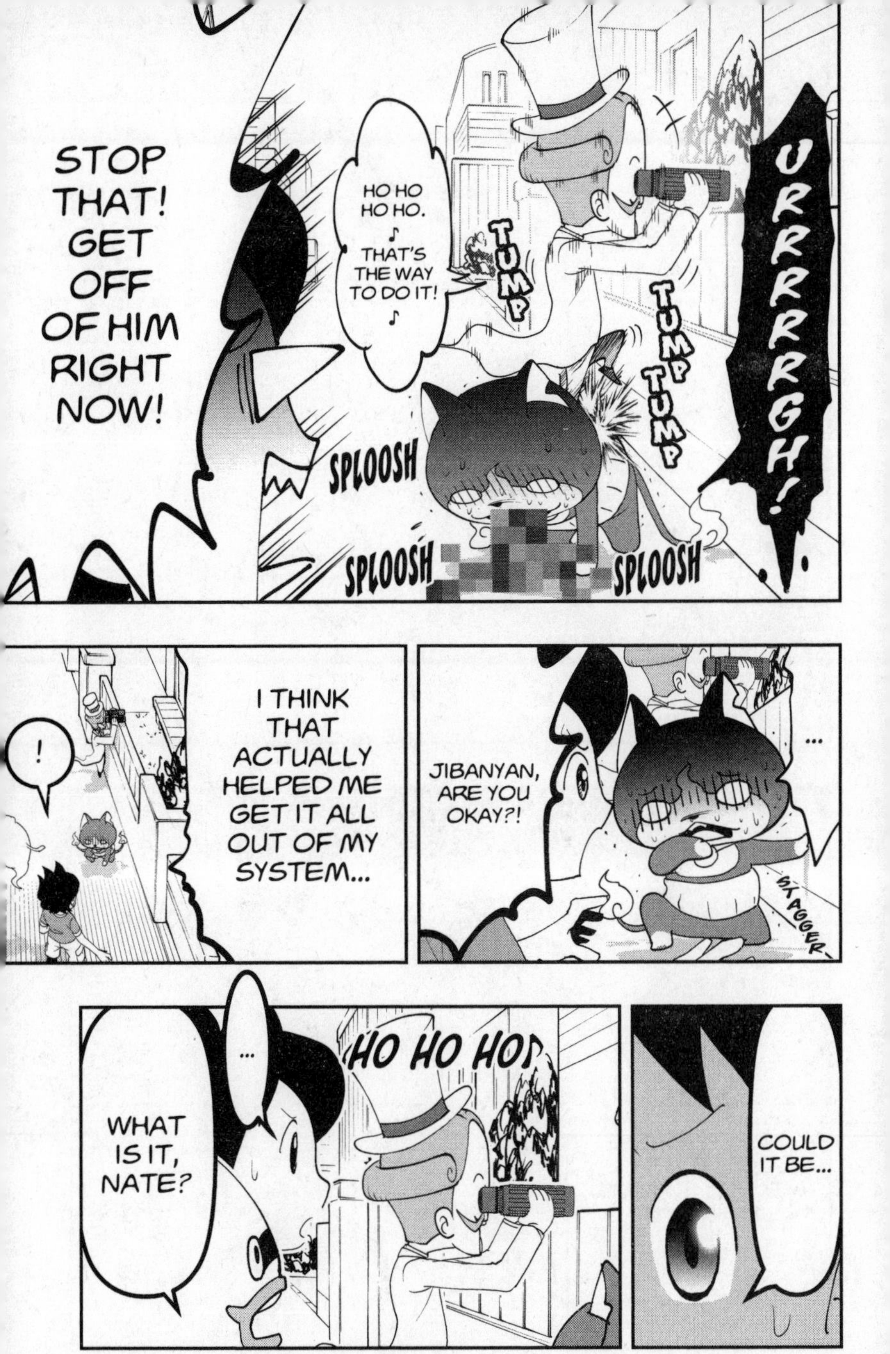
URRRRRGH!
TUMP TUMP TUMP
HO HO HO HO. ♪ THAT'S THE WAY TO DO IT! ♪
TUMP
SPLOOSH
SPLOOSH
SPLOOSH
STOP THAT! GET OFF OF HIM RIGHT NOW!
...
JIBANYAN, ARE YOU OKAY?!
STAGGER
I THINK THAT ACTUALLY HELPED ME GET IT ALL OUT OF MY SYSTEM...
!
COULD IT BE...
HO HO HO
...
WHAT IS IT, NATE?

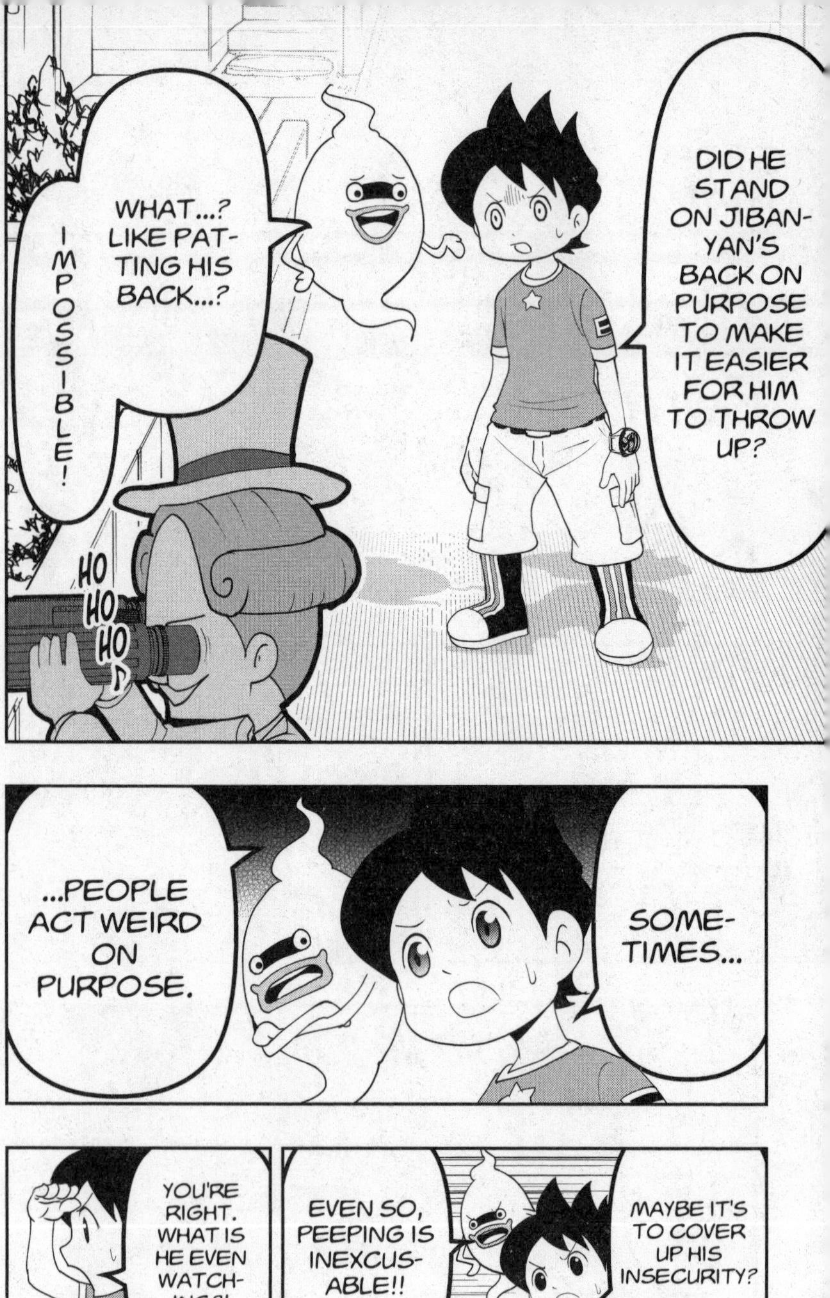
DID HE STAND ON JIBANYAN'S BACK ON PURPOSE TO MAKE IT EASIER FOR HIM TO THROW UP?
WHAT...? LIKE PATTING HIS BACK...?
IMPOSSIBLE!
HO HO HO ♪
SOMETIMES...
...PEOPLE ACT WEIRD ON PURPOSE.
MAYBE IT'S TO COVER UP HIS INSECURITY?
EVEN SO, PEEPING IS INEXCUSABLE!!
YOU'RE RIGHT. WHAT IS HE EVEN WATCHING?!

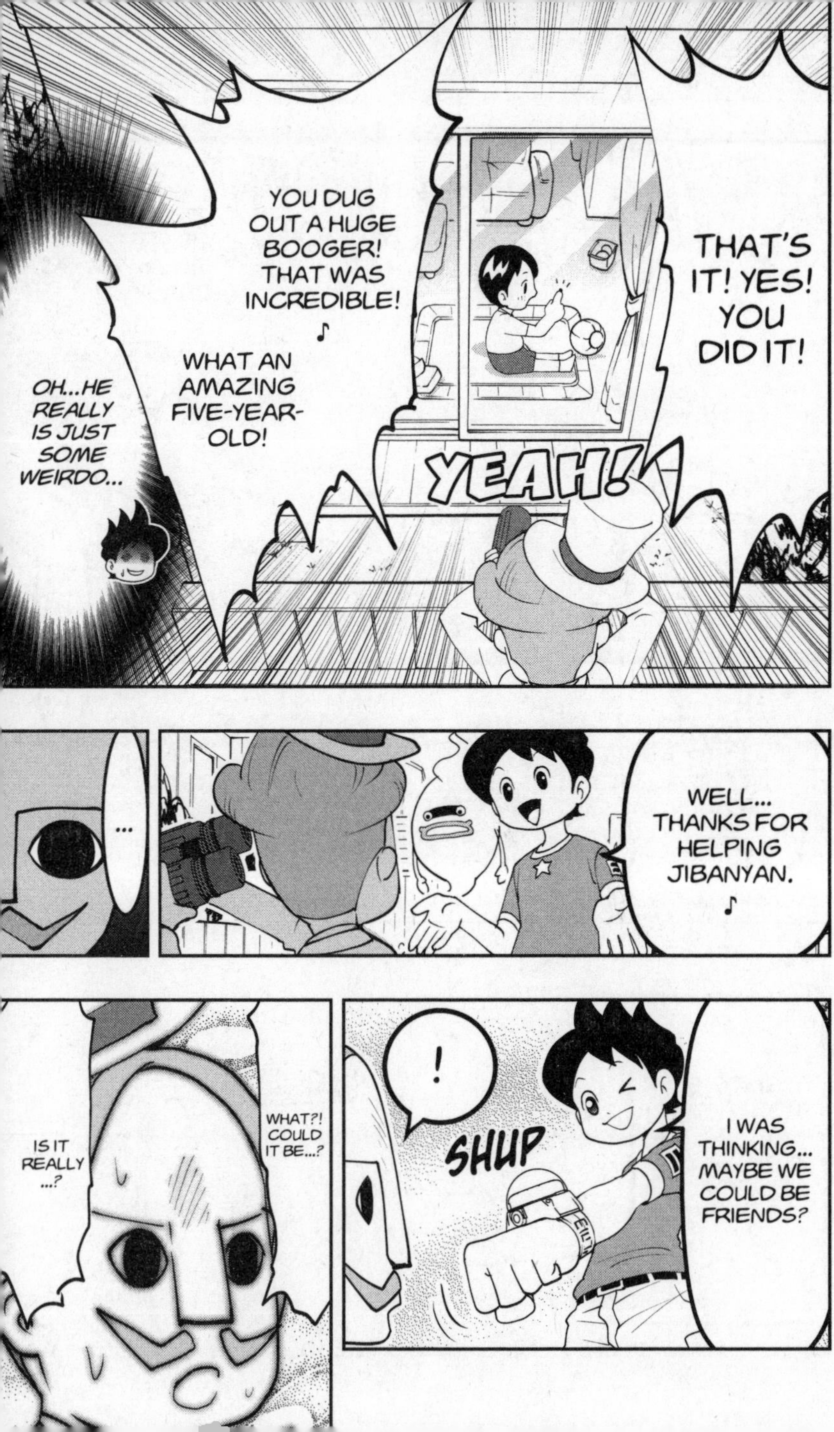
THAT'S IT! YES! YOU DID IT!
YOU DUG OUT A HUGE BOOGER! THAT WAS INCREDIBLE! ♪
WHAT AN AMAZING FIVE-YEAR-OLD!
YEAH!
OH...HE REALLY IS JUST SOME WEIRDO...
WELL... THANKS FOR HELPING JIBANYAN. ♪
...
I WAS THINKING... MAYBE WE COULD BE FRIENDS?
!
SHUP
WHAT?! COULD IT BE...?
IS IT REALLY ...?

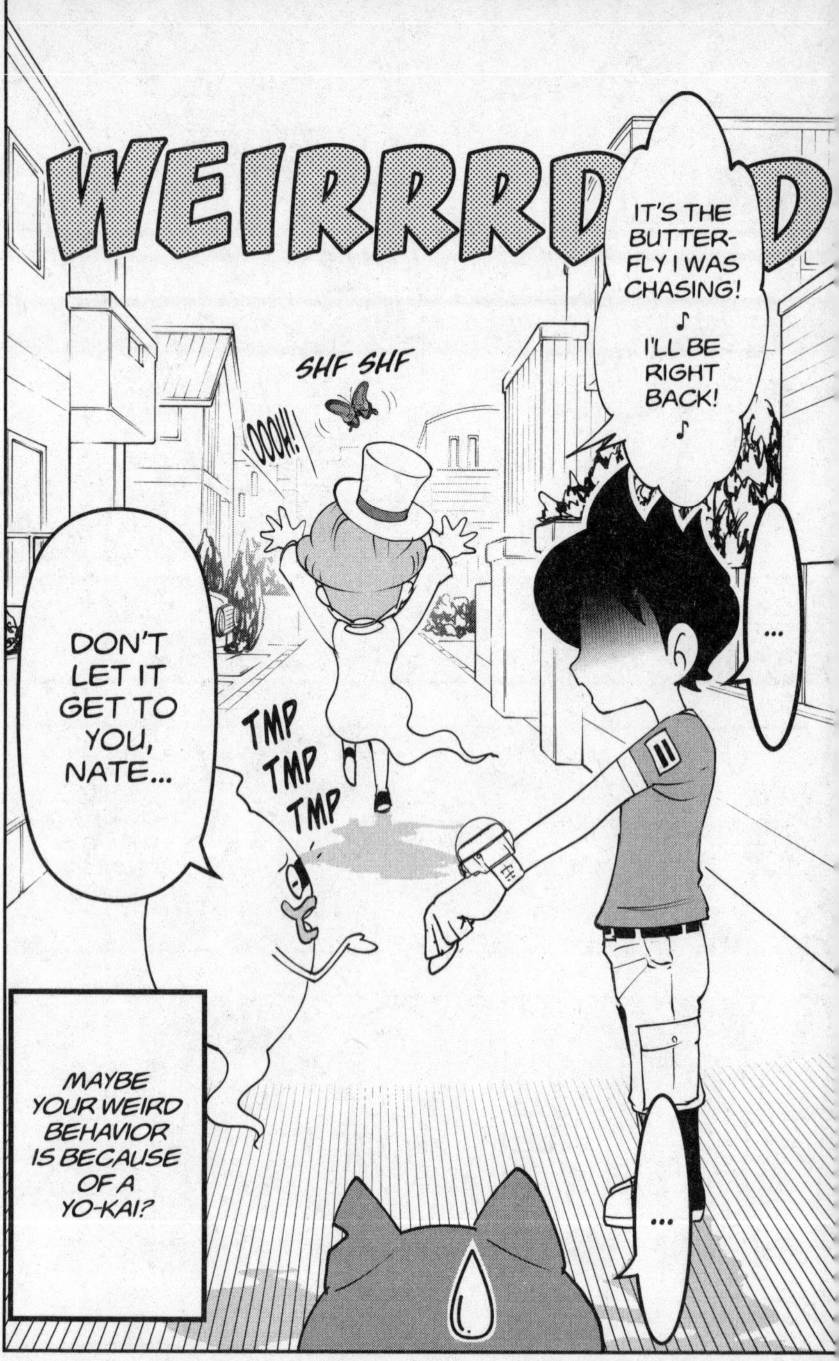
WEIRRRD
IT'S THE BUTTER-FLY I WAS CHASING! ♪ I'LL BE RIGHT BACK! ♪
SHF SHF
OOOH!
...
DON'T LET IT GET TO YOU, NATE...
TMP TMP TMP
...
MAYBE YOUR WEIRD BEHAVIOR IS BECAUSE OF A YO-KAI?

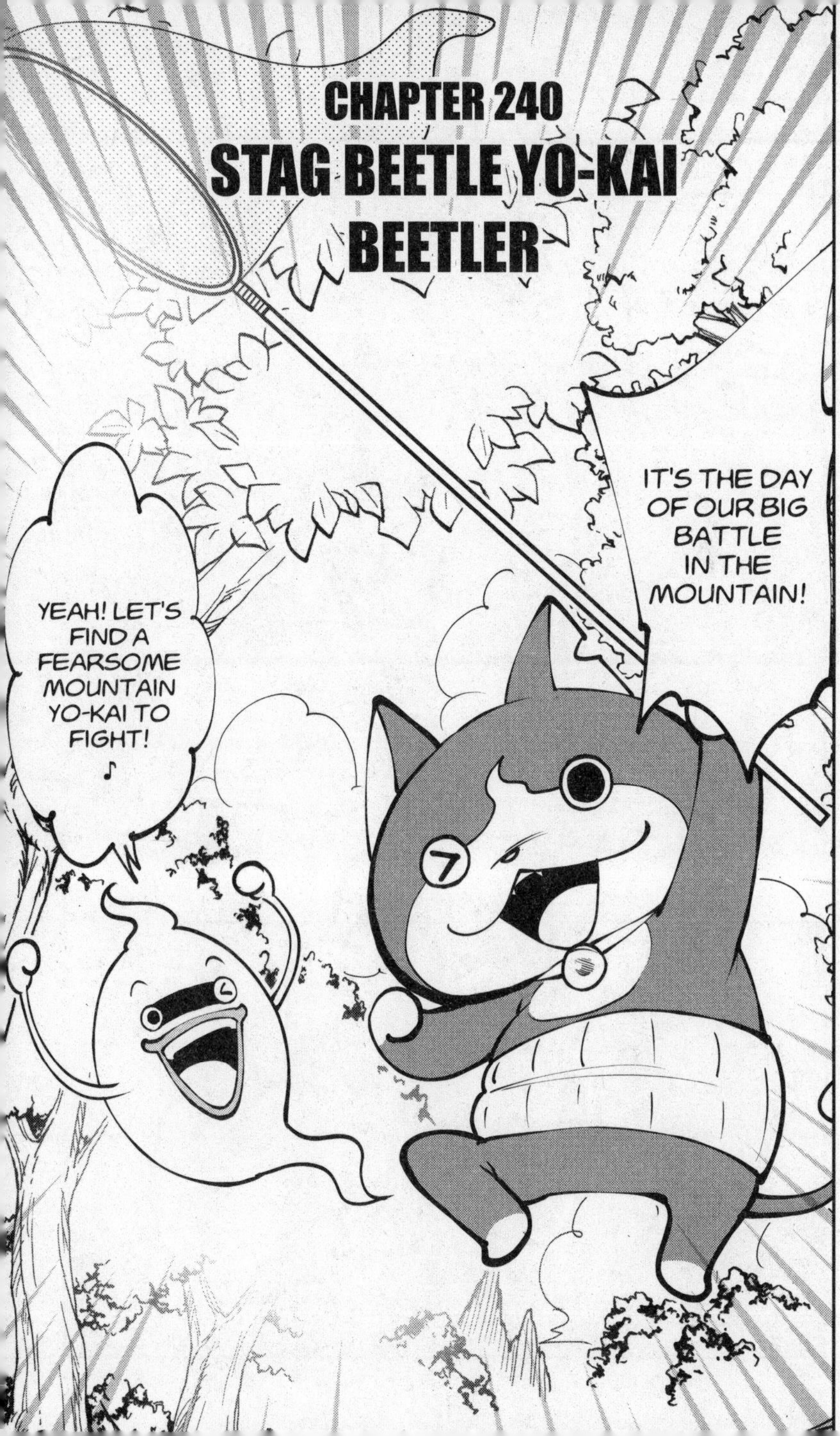
CHAPTER 240
STAG BEETLE YO-KAI BEETLER
IT'S THE DAY OF OUR BIG BATTLE IN THE MOUNTAIN!
YEAH! LET'S FIND A FEARSOME MOUNTAIN YO-KAI TO FIGHT! ♪

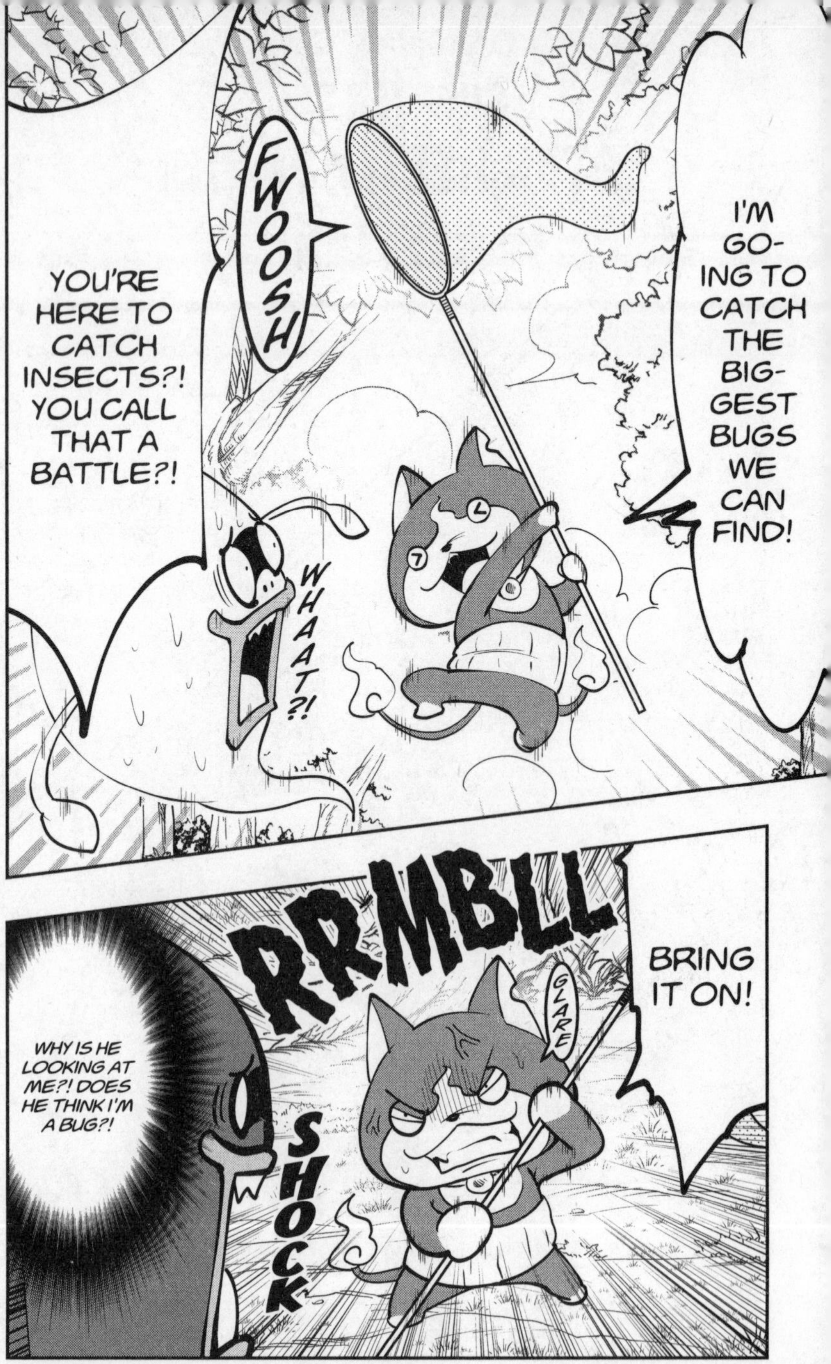
I'M GOING TO CATCH THE BIGGEST BUGS WE CAN FIND!
FWOOSH
YOU'RE HERE TO CATCH INSECTS?! YOU CALL THAT A BATTLE?!
WHAAAT?!
RRMBLL
BRING IT ON!
GLARE
WHY IS HE LOOKING AT ME?! DOES HE THINK I'M A BUG?!
SHOCK

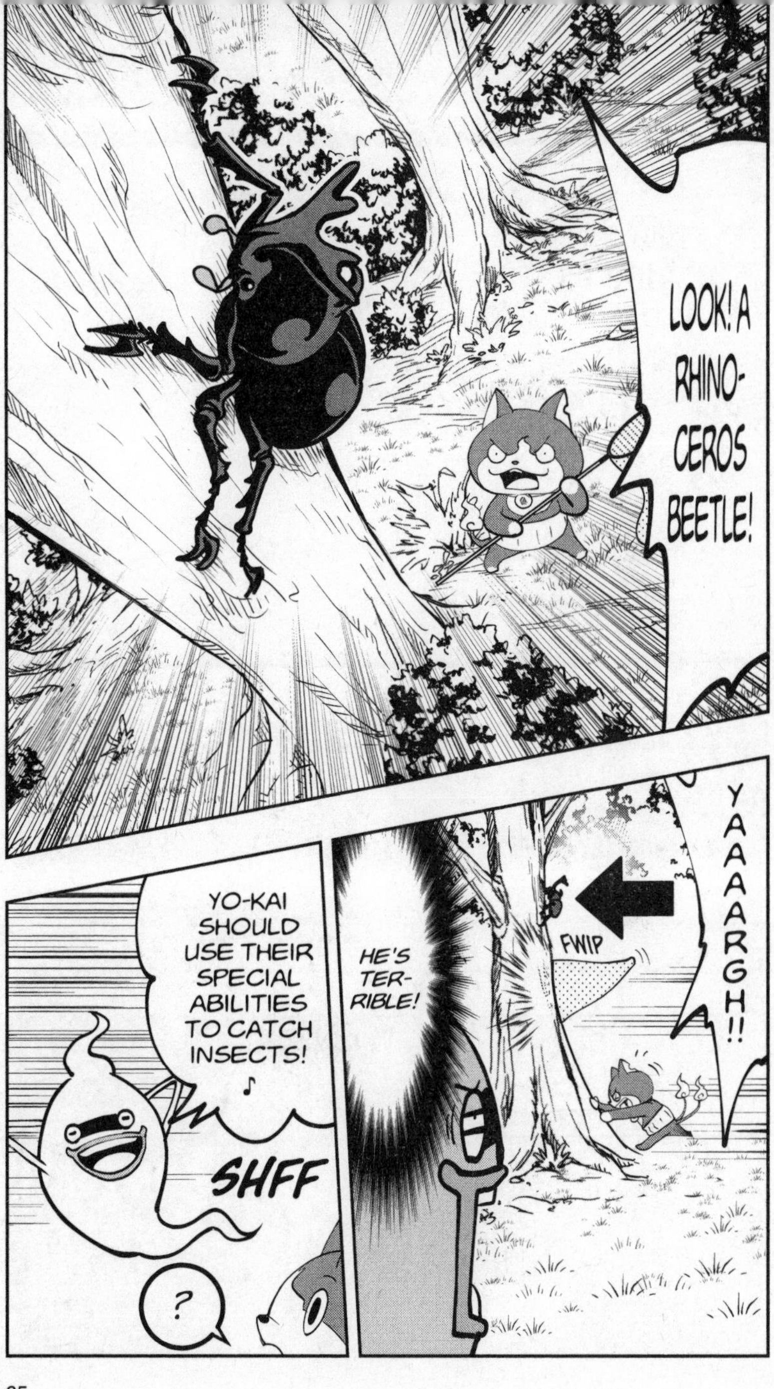
LOOK! A RHINO-CEROS BEETLE!
YAAAARGH!!
FWIP
HE'S TER-RIBLE!
YO-KAI SHOULD USE THEIR SPECIAL ABILITIES TO CATCH INSECTS! ♪
SHFF
?

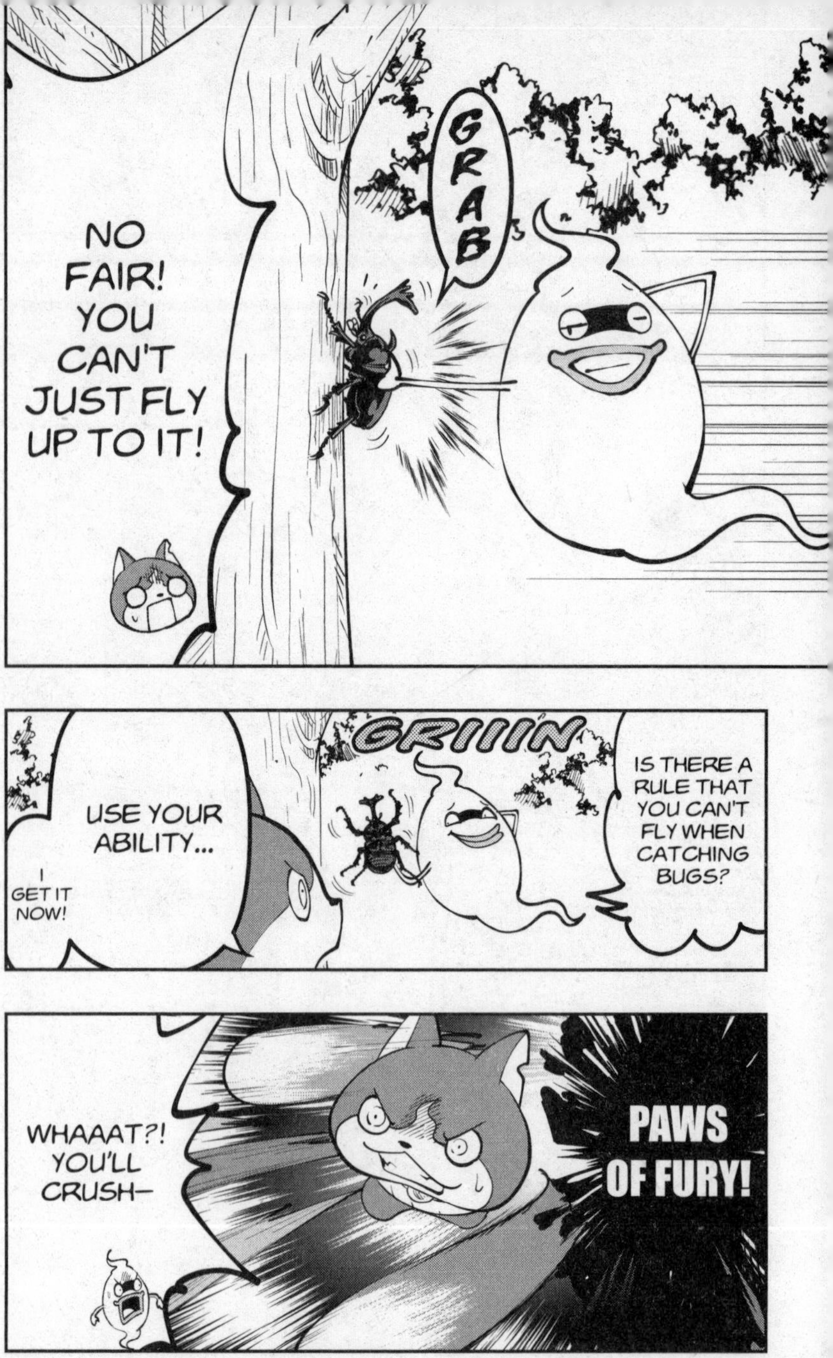
GRAB
NO FAIR! YOU CAN'T JUST FLY UP TO IT!
IS THERE A RULE THAT YOU CAN'T FLY WHEN CATCHING BUGS?
GRIIIN
USE YOUR ABILITY...
I GET IT NOW!
PAWS OF FURY!
WHAAAT?! YOU'LL CRUSH—

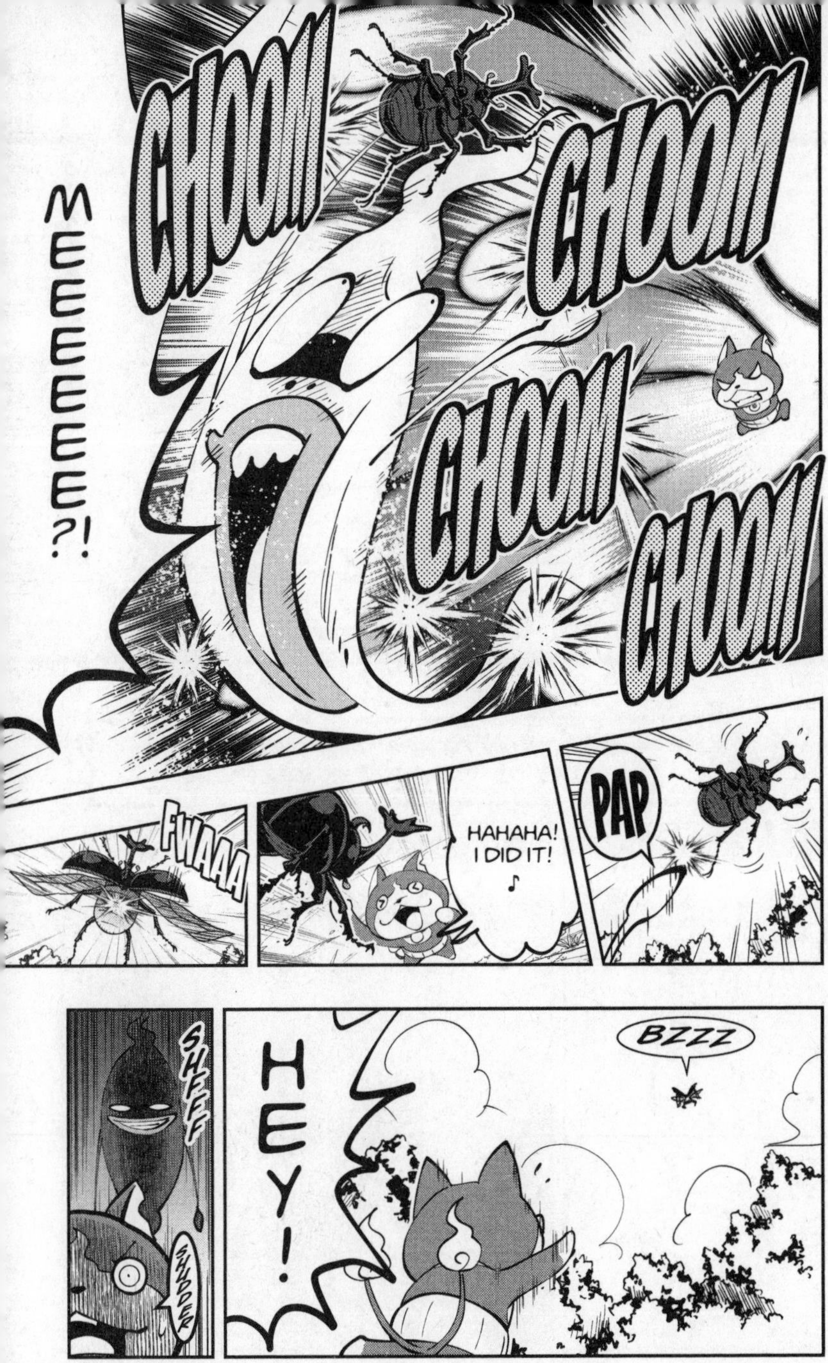
CHOOM
CHOOM
CHOOM
CHOOM
MEEEEEEE?!
PAP
HAHAHA! I DID IT! ♪
FWAAA
BZZZ
HEY!
SHFFF
SHUDDER

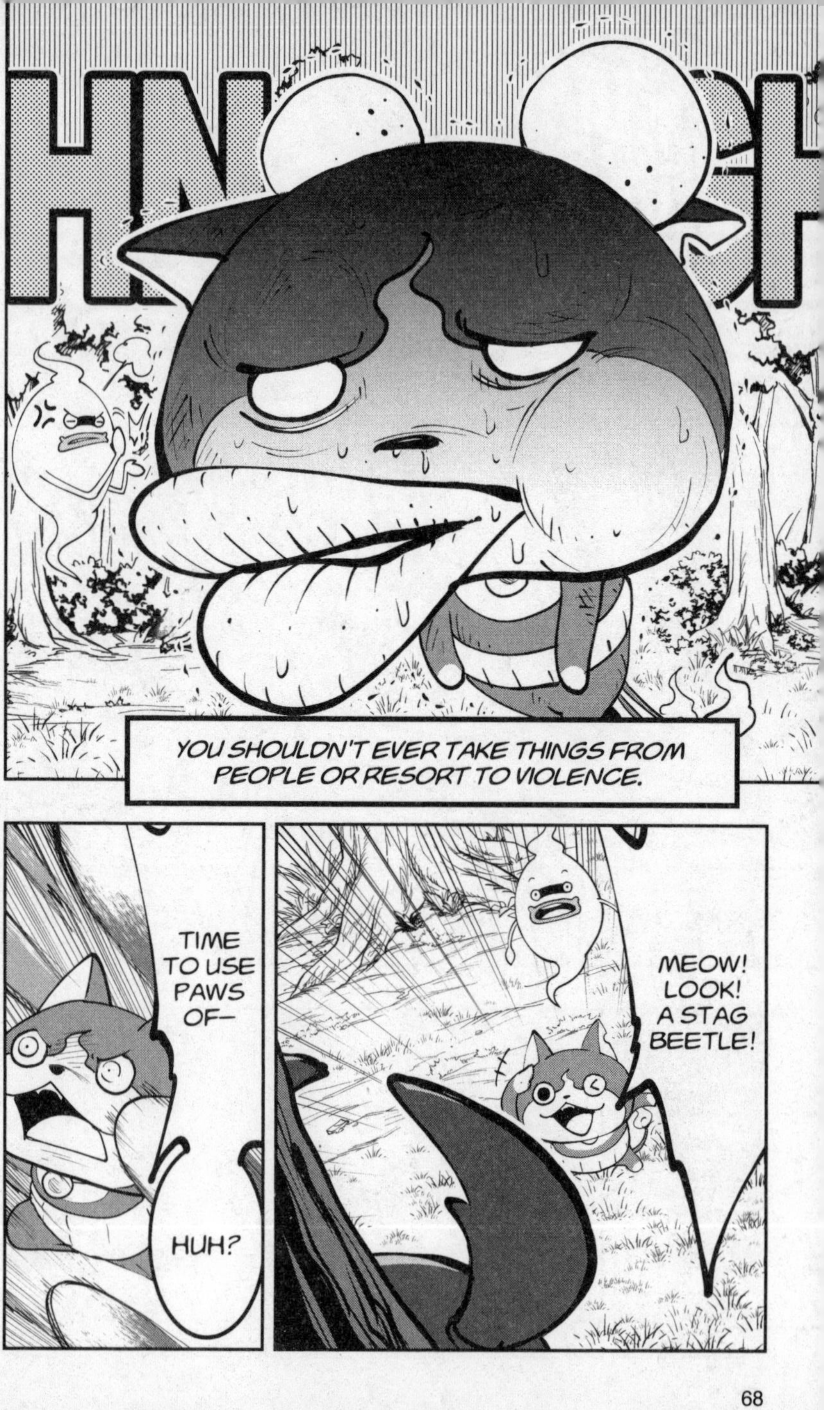
YOU SHOULDN'T EVER TAKE THINGS FROM PEOPLE OR RESORT TO VIOLENCE.
MEOW! LOOK! A STAG BEETLE!
TIME TO USE PAWS OF—
HUH?

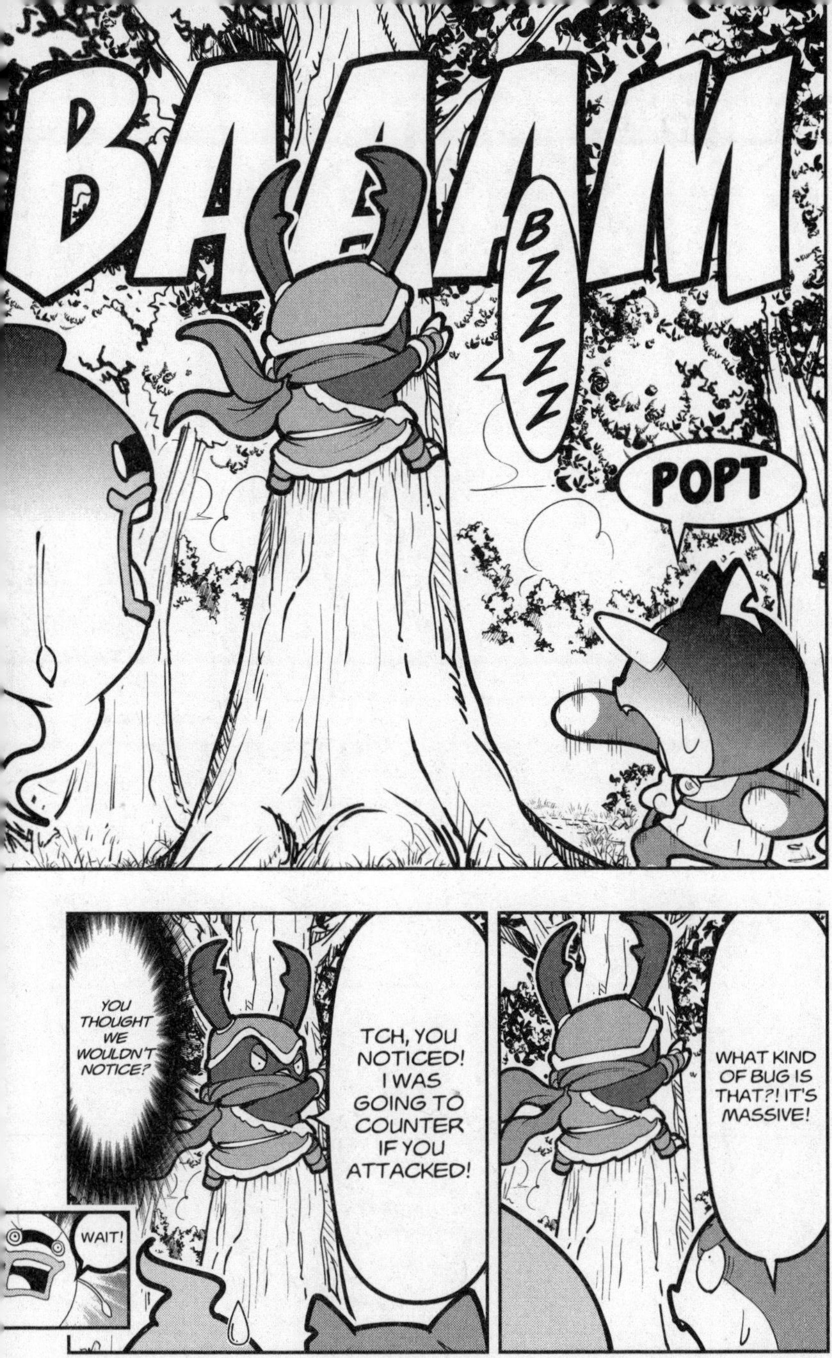
BAAM
BZZZZ
POPT
WHAT KIND OF BUG IS THAT?! IT'S MASSIVE!
TCH, YOU NOTICED! I WAS GOING TO COUNTER IF YOU ATTACKED!
YOU THOUGHT WE WOULDN'T NOTICE?
WAIT!

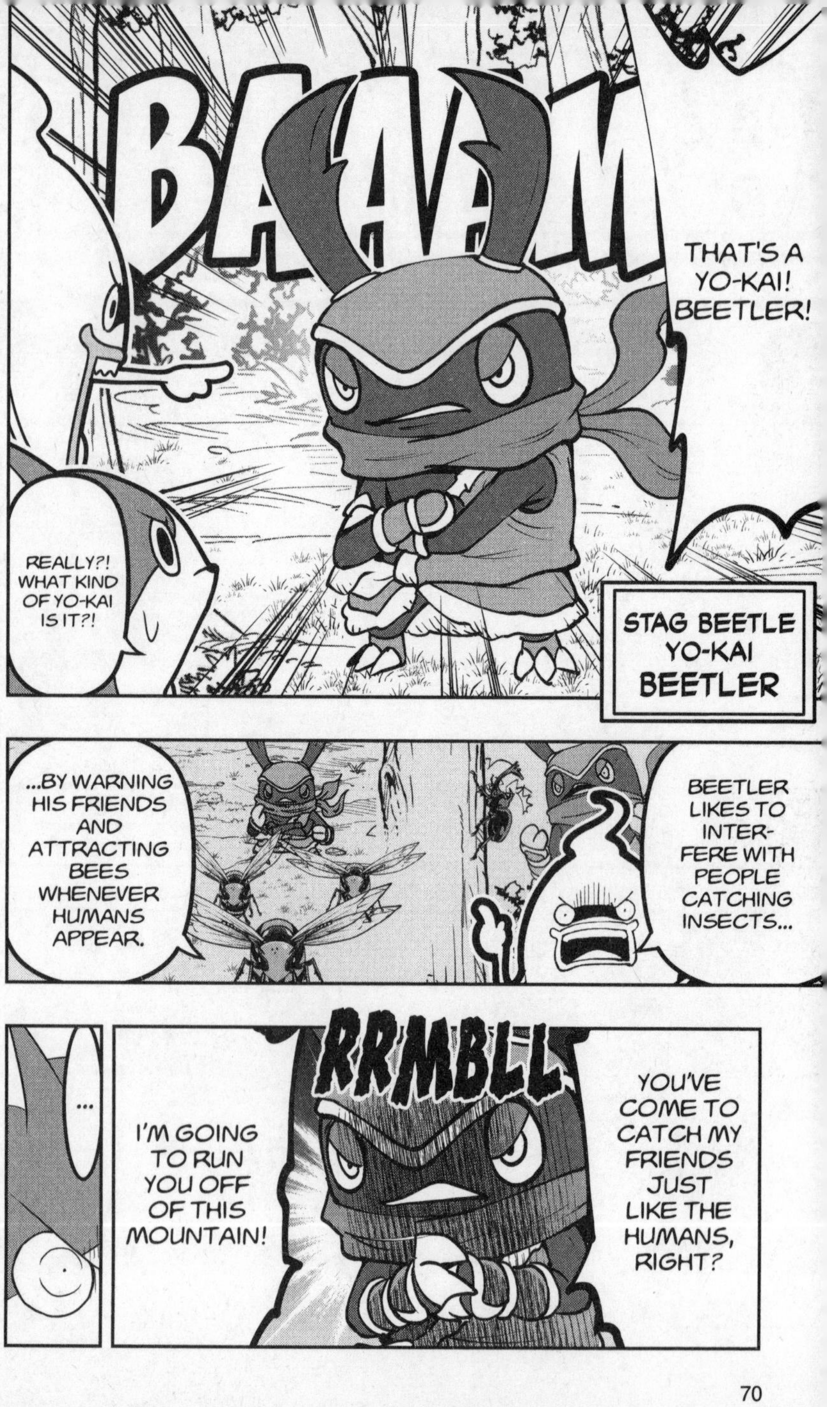
BAAM
THAT'S A YO-KAI! BEETLER!
STAG BEETLE YO-KAI BEETLER
REALLY?! WHAT KIND OF YO-KAI IS IT?!
BEETLER LIKES TO INTERFERE WITH PEOPLE CATCHING INSECTS...
...BY WARNING HIS FRIENDS AND ATTRACTING BEES WHENEVER HUMANS APPEAR.
RRMBLL
YOU'VE COME TO CATCH MY FRIENDS JUST LIKE THE HUMANS, RIGHT?
I'M GOING TO RUN YOU OFF OF THIS MOUNTAIN!
...

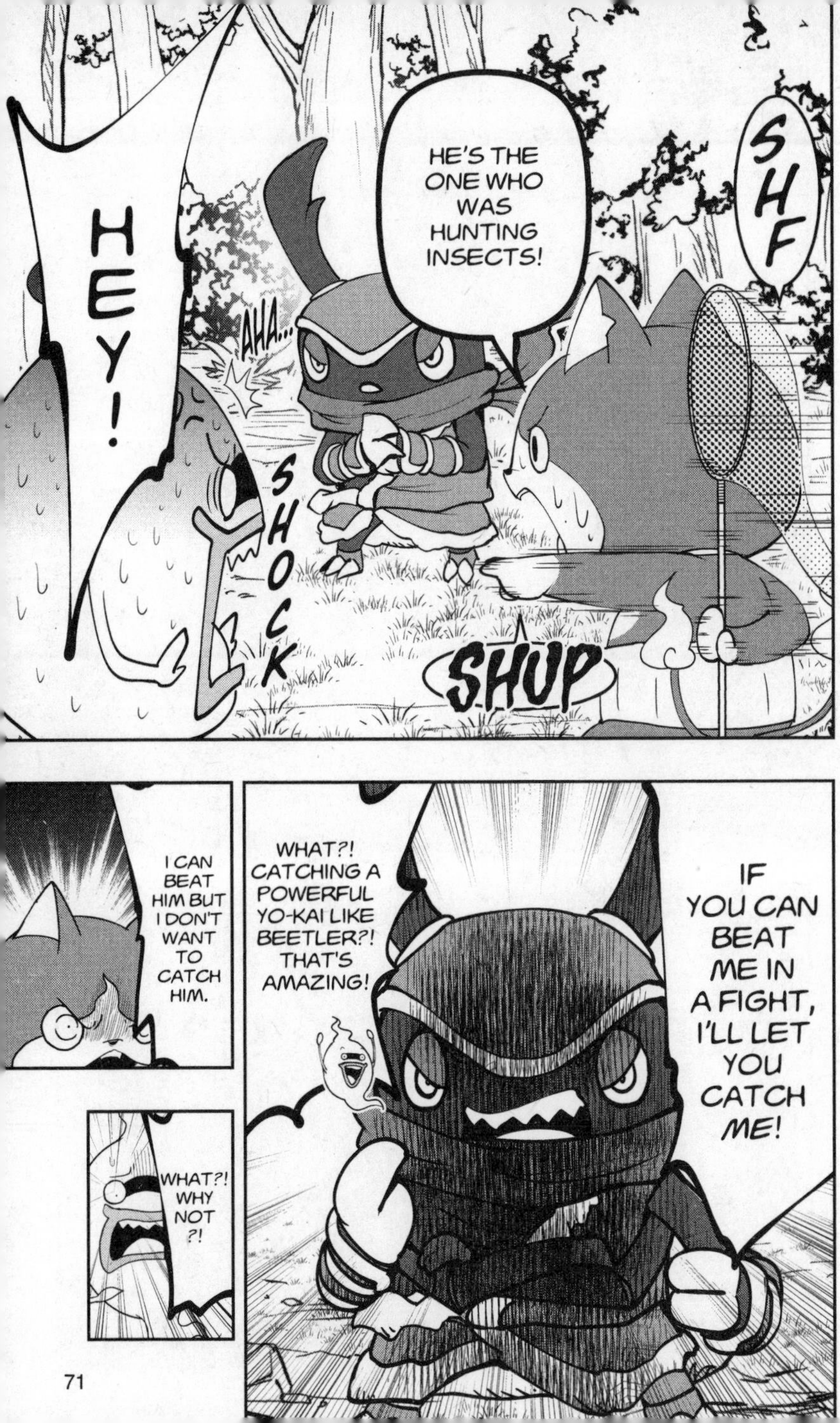
SHF
HE'S THE ONE WHO WAS HUNTING INSECTS!
HEY!
AHA...
SHOCK
SHUP
IF YOU CAN BEAT ME IN A FIGHT, I'LL LET YOU CATCH ME!
WHAT?! CATCHING A POWERFUL YO-KAI LIKE BEETLER?! THAT'S AMAZING!
I CAN BEAT HIM BUT I DON'T WANT TO CATCH HIM.
WHAT?! WHY NOT?!

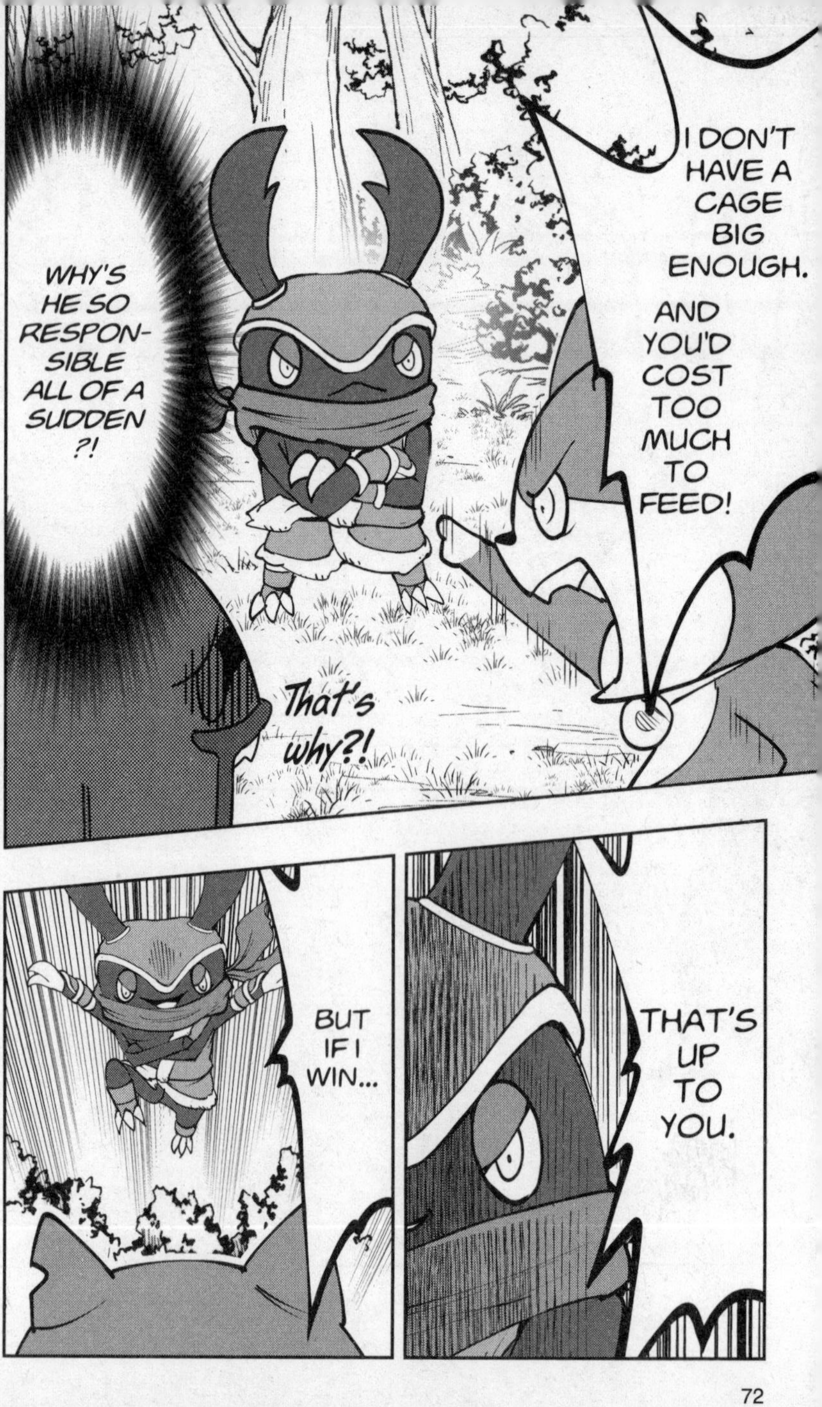
I DON'T HAVE A CAGE BIG ENOUGH.
AND YOU'D COST TOO MUCH TO FEED!
WHY'S HE SO RESPON-SIBLE ALL OF A SUDDEN ?!
That's why?!
THAT'S UP TO YOU.
BUT IF I WIN...

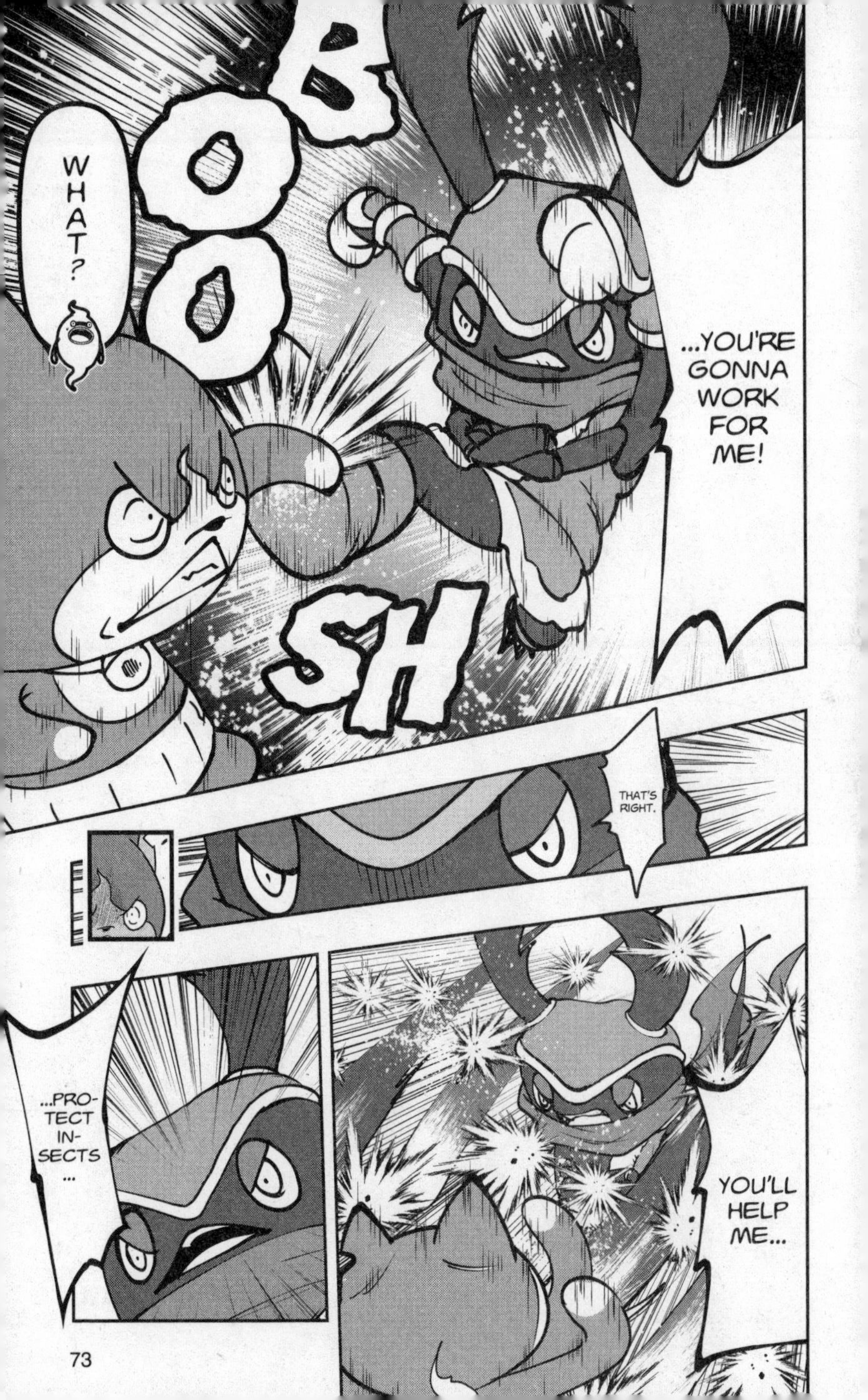
BOO
WHAT?
...YOU'RE GONNA WORK FOR ME!
SH
THAT'S RIGHT.
YOU'LL HELP ME...
...PRO-TECT IN-SECTS...

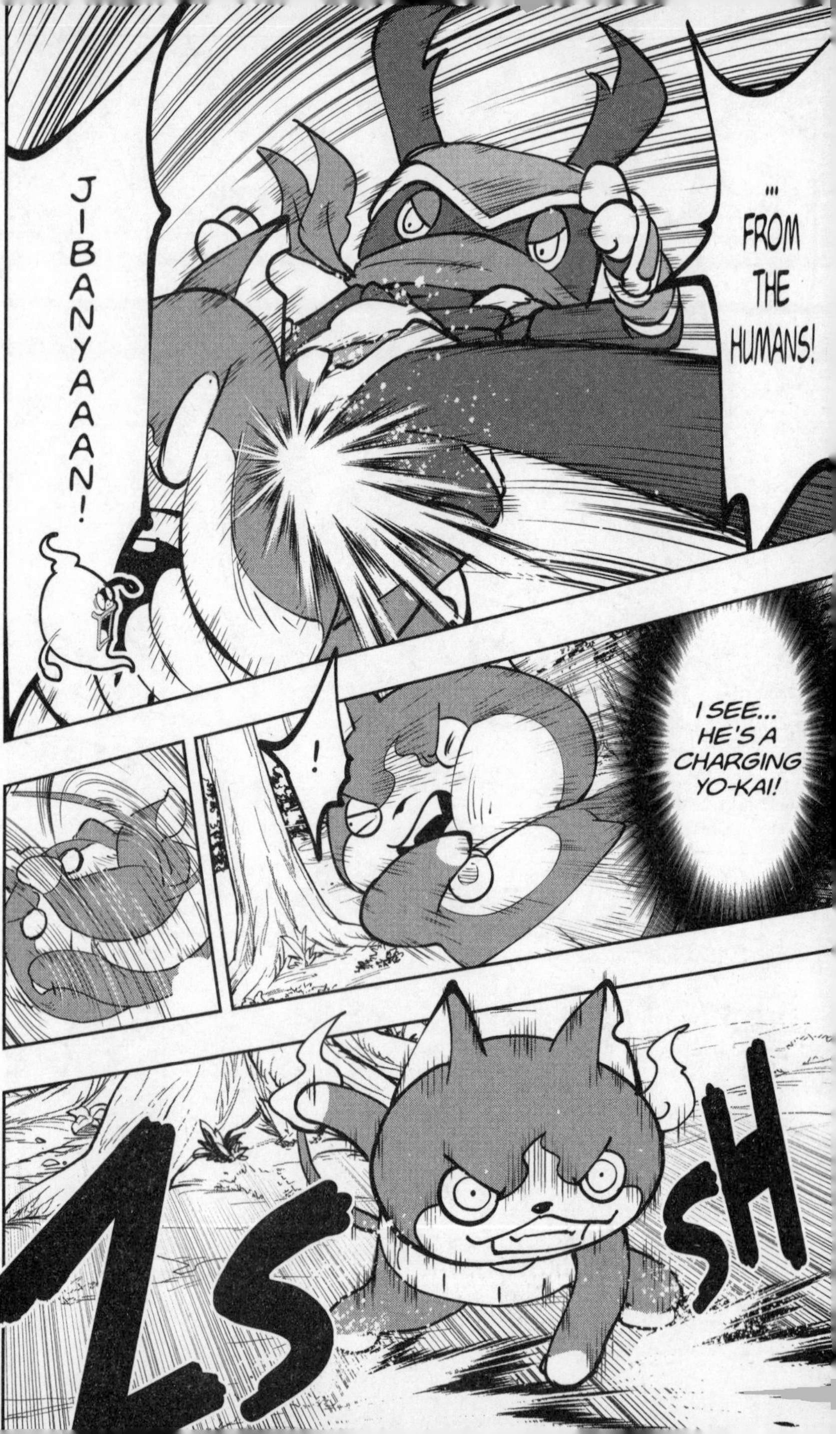
...FROM THE HUMANS!
JIBANYAAAAAN!
I SEE... HE'S A CHARGING YO-KAI!
!

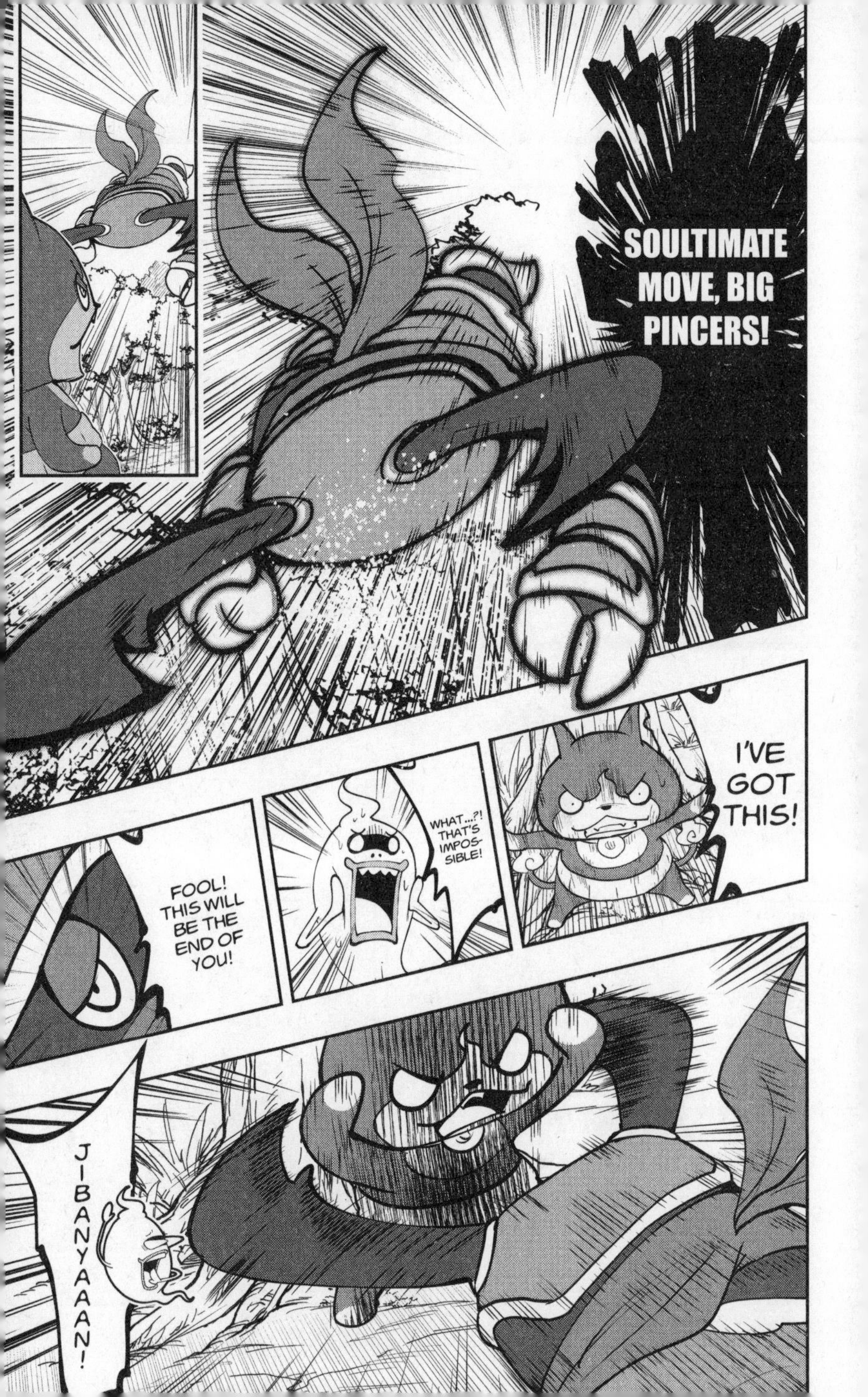
SOULTIMATE MOVE, BIG PINCERS!
I'VE GOT THIS!
WHAT...?! THAT'S IMPOSSIBLE!
FOOL! THIS WILL BE THE END OF YOU!
JIBANYAAAAN!

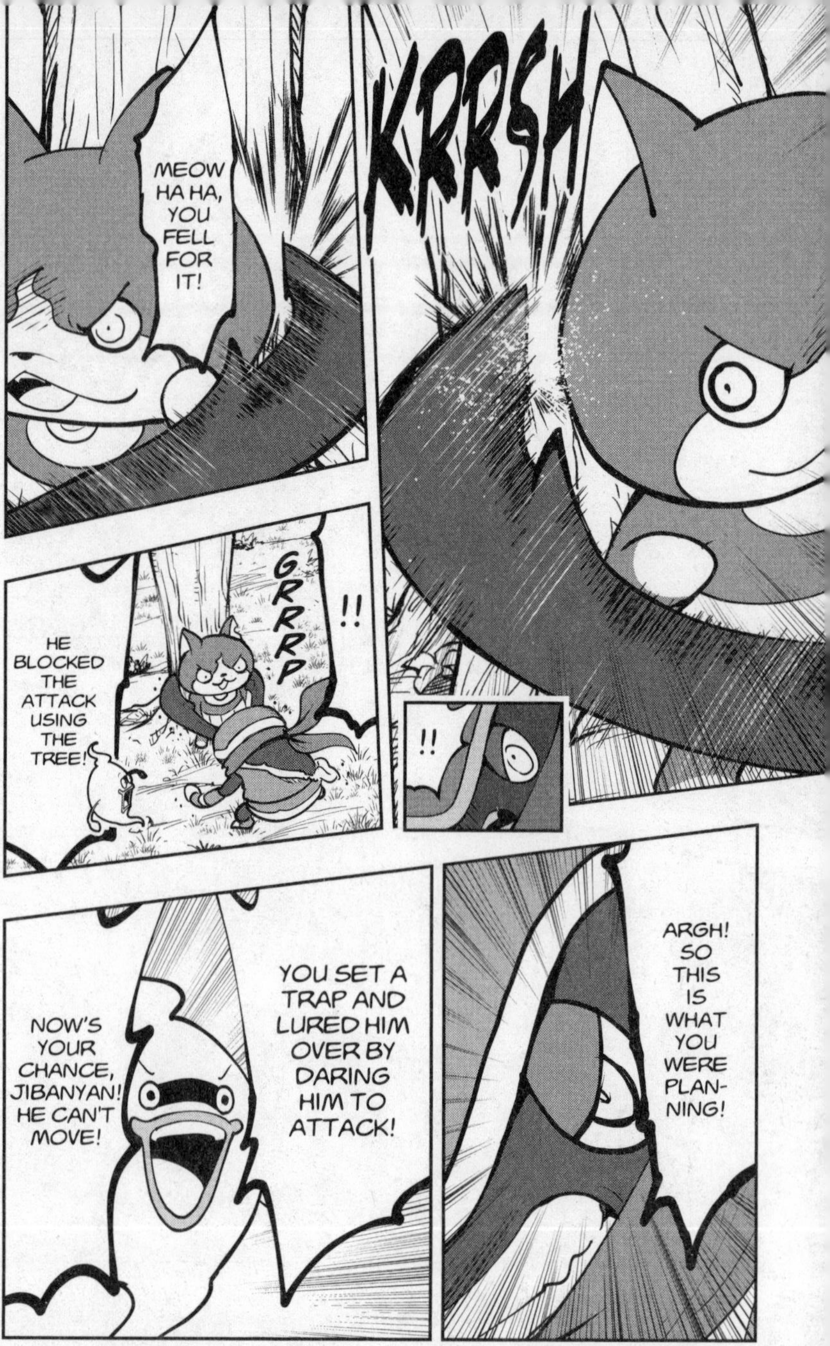
KRRSH
MEOW HA HA, YOU FELL FOR IT!
GRRRP
!!
HE BLOCKED THE ATTACK USING THE TREE!
!!
ARGH! SO THIS IS WHAT YOU WERE PLAN-NING!
YOU SET A TRAP AND LURED HIM OVER BY DARING HIM TO ATTACK!
NOW'S YOUR CHANCE, JIBANYAN! HE CAN'T MOVE!

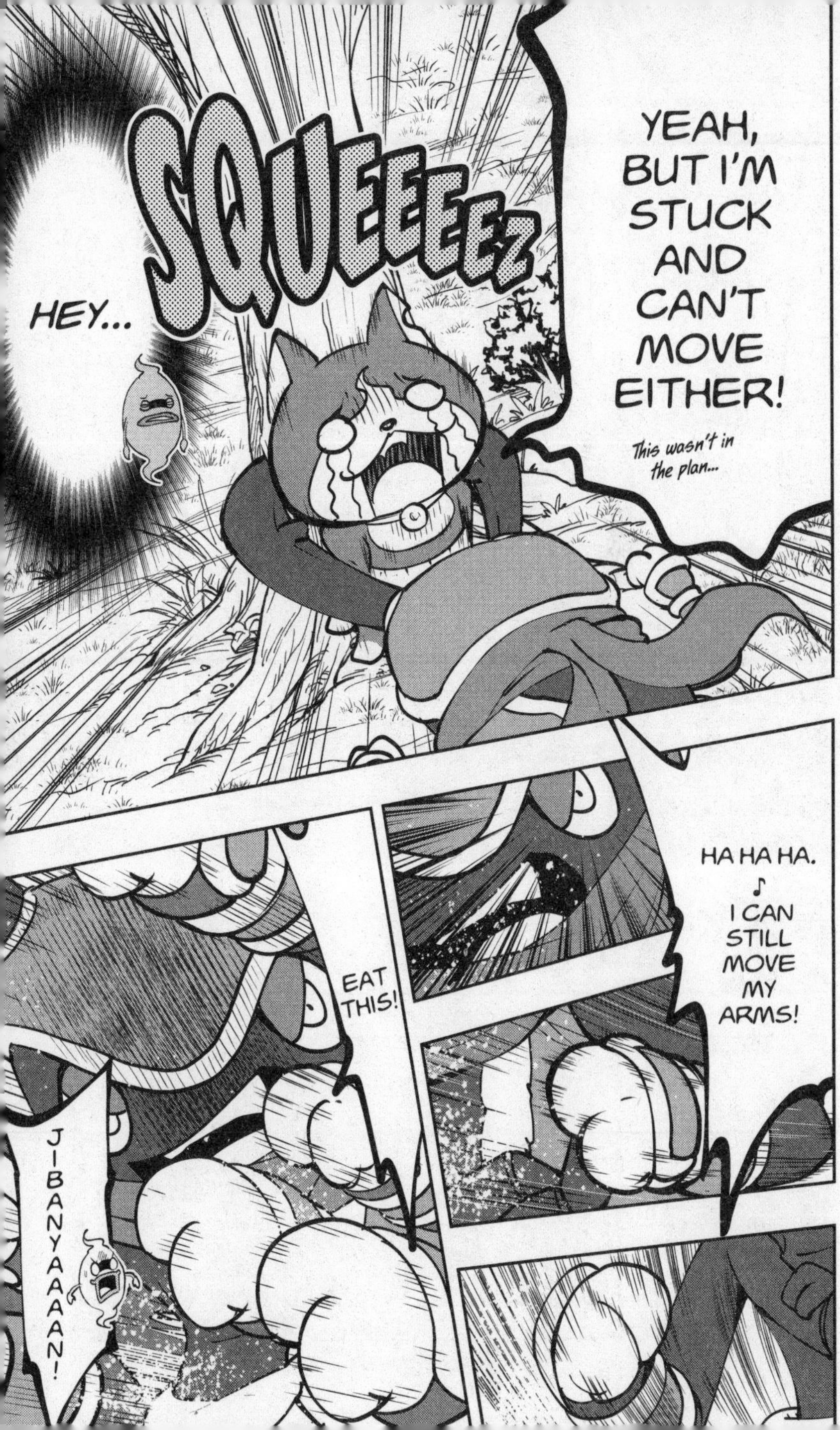
YEAH, BUT I'M STUCK AND CAN'T MOVE EITHER!
SQUEEEZ
This wasn't in the plan...
HEY...
HA HA HA. ♪ I CAN STILL MOVE MY ARMS!
EAT THIS!
JIBANYAAAAAN!

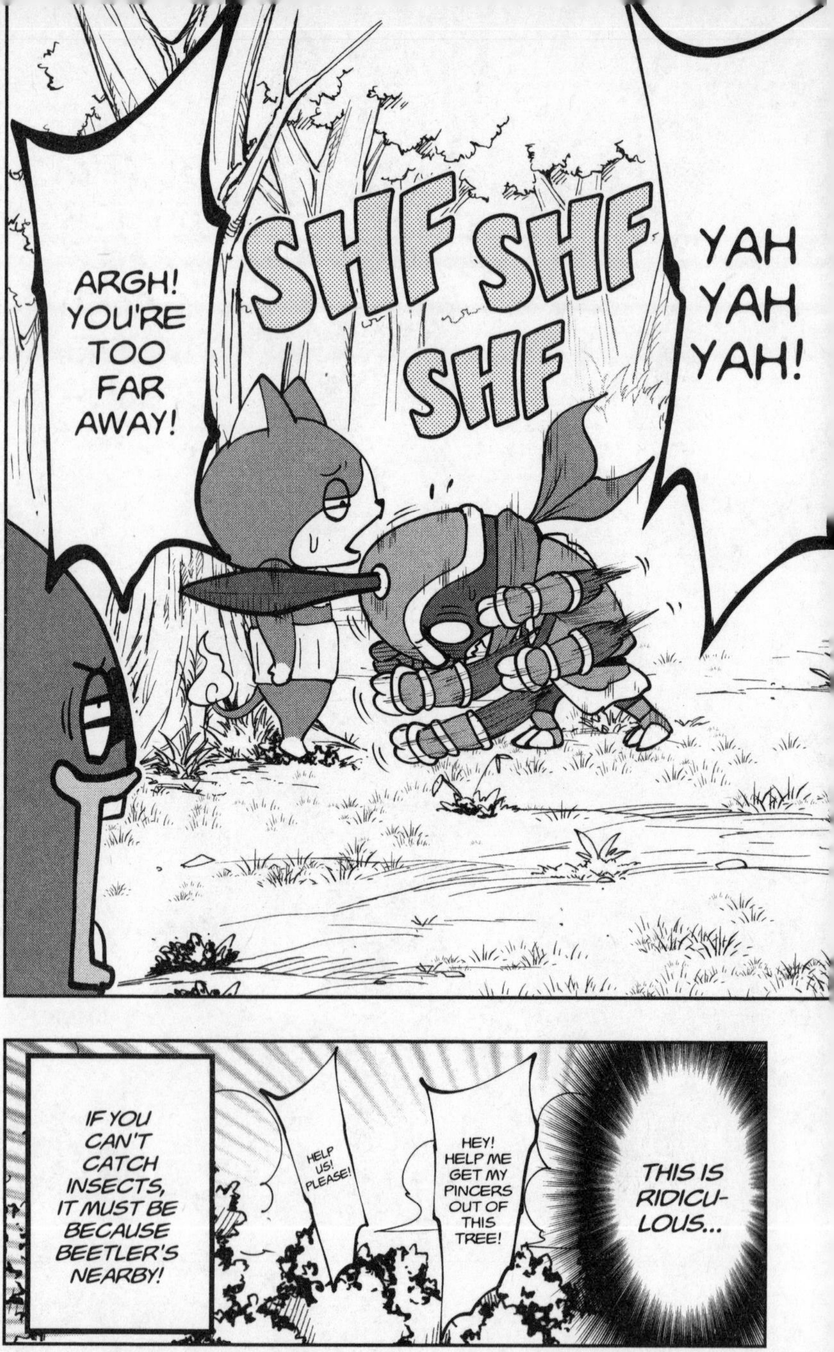
YAH YAH YAH!
SHF SHF SHF
ARGH! YOU'RE TOO FAR AWAY!
THIS IS RIDICU-LOUS...
HEY! HELP ME GET MY PINCERS OUT OF THIS TREE!
HELP US! PLEASE!
IF YOU CAN'T CATCH INSECTS, IT MUST BE BECAUSE BEETLER'S NEARBY!

CHAPTER 241
RHINOCEROS BEETLE YO-KAI RHINOGGIN

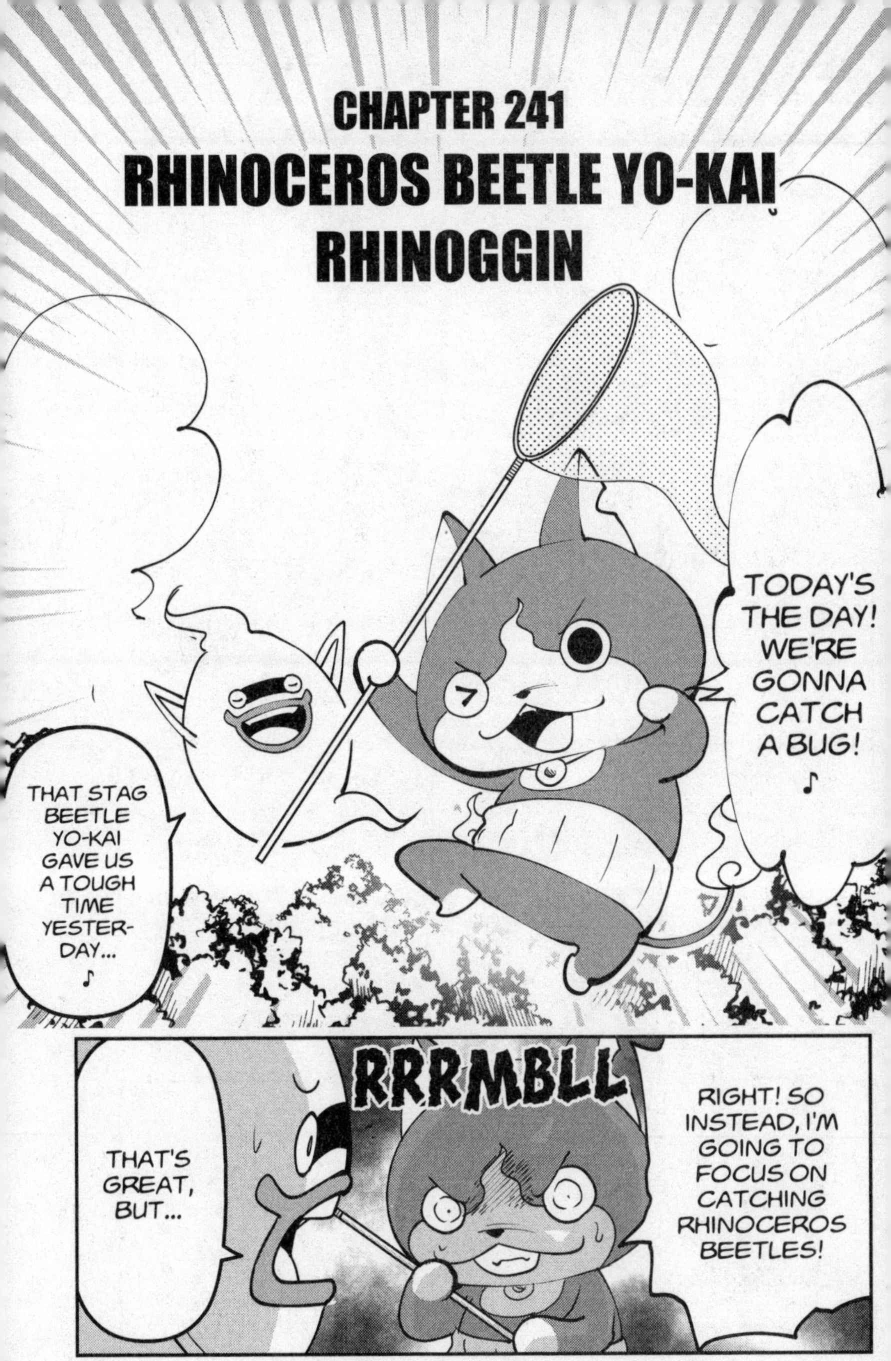
TODAY'S THE DAY! WE'RE GONNA CATCH A BUG! ♪
THAT STAG BEETLE YO-KAI GAVE US A TOUGH TIME YESTER-DAY... ♪
RIGHT! SO INSTEAD, I'M GOING TO FOCUS ON CATCHING RHINOCEROS BEETLES!
RRRMBLL
THAT'S GREAT, BUT...

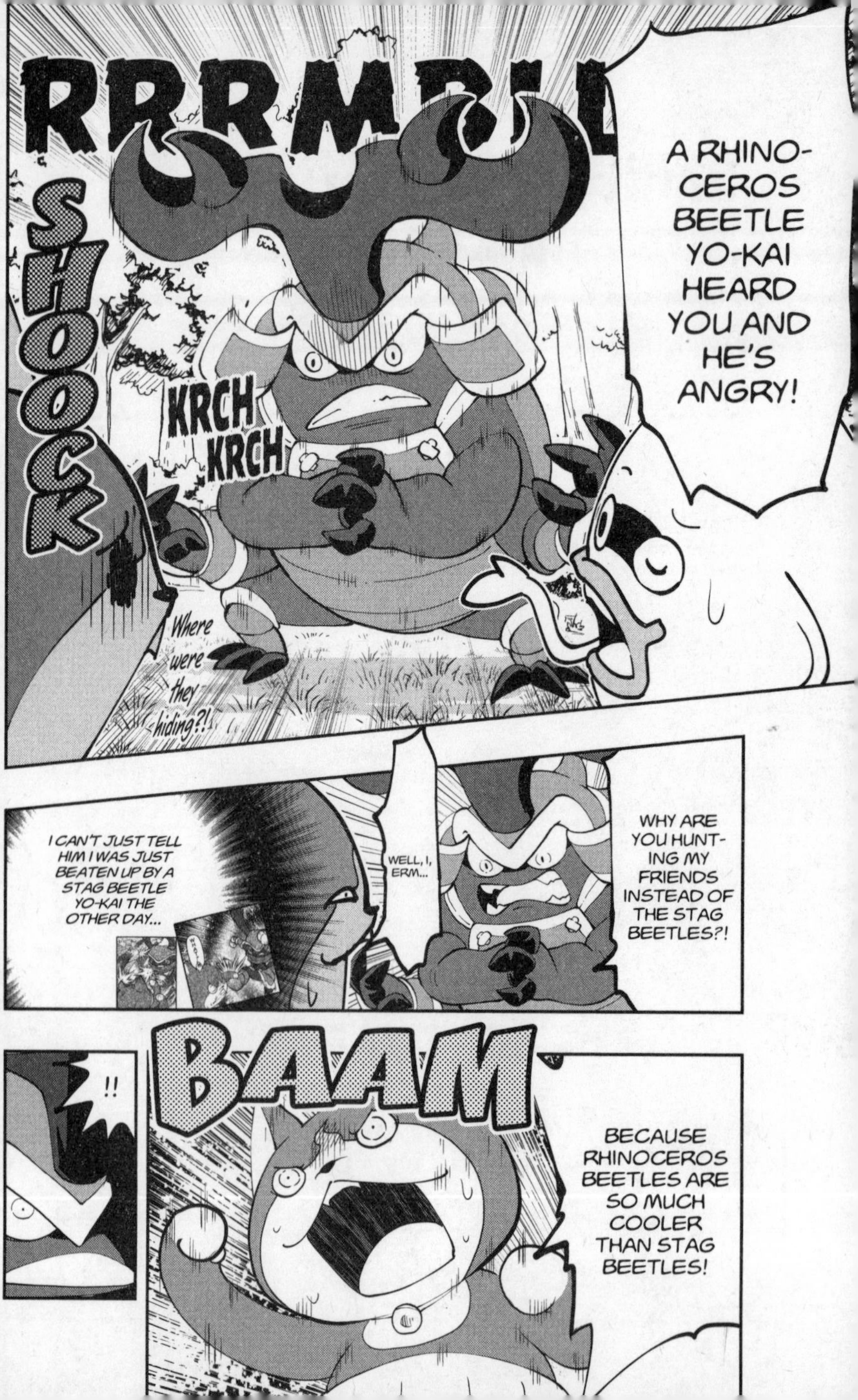
RRRMBLL
A RHINO-
CEROS
BEETLE
YO-KAI
HEARD
YOU AND
HE'S
ANGRY!
SHOOCK
KRCH
KRCH
Where were they hiding?!
WHY ARE YOU HUNTING MY FRIENDS INSTEAD OF THE STAG BEETLES?!
WELL, I, ERM...
I CAN'T JUST TELL HIM I WAS JUST BEATEN UP BY A STAG BEETLE YO-KAI THE OTHER DAY...
BAAM
BECAUSE RHINOCEROS BEETLES ARE SO MUCH COOLER THAN STAG BEETLES!
!!

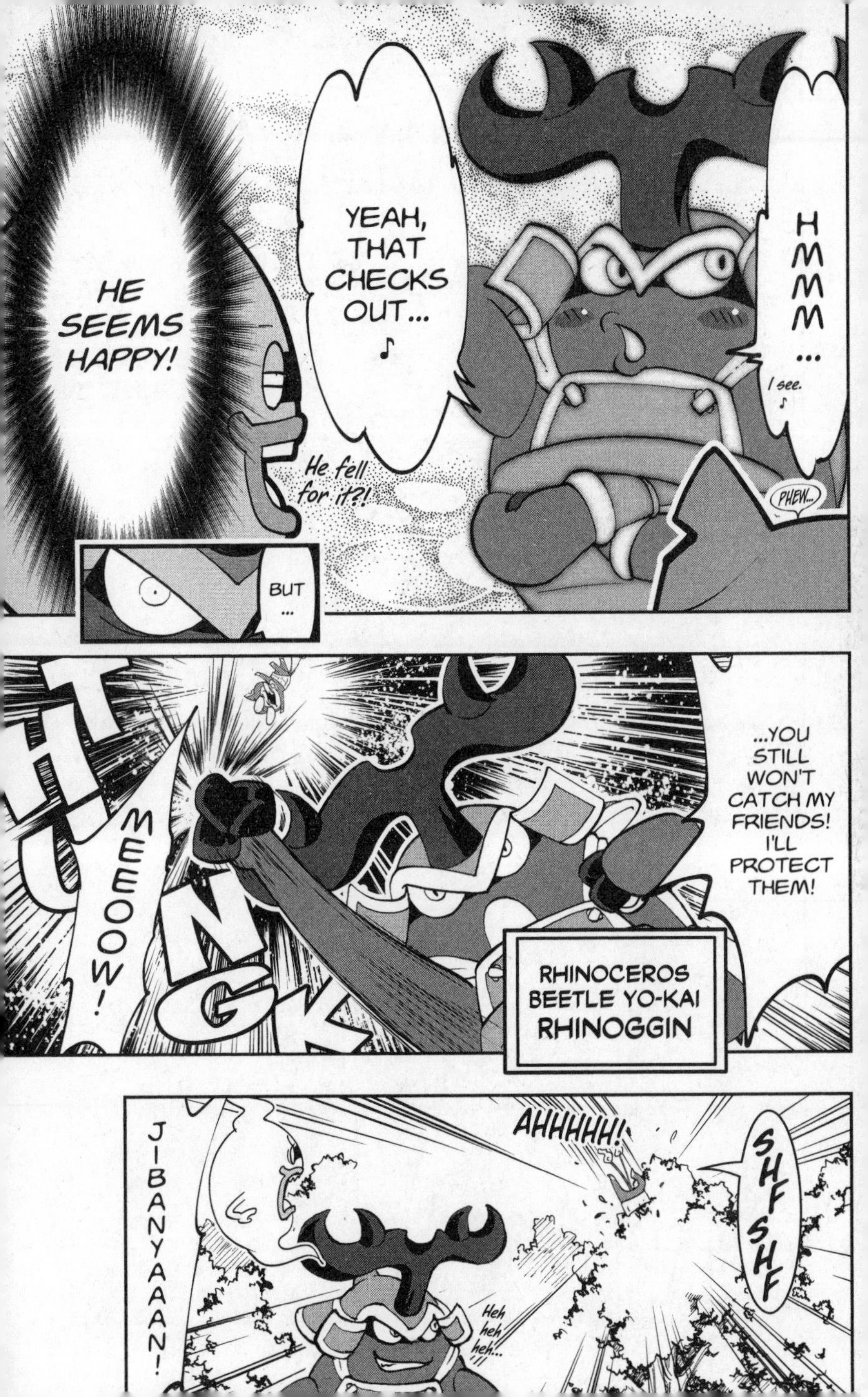
HMMM...
I see. ♪
PHEW...
YEAH, THAT CHECKS OUT... ♪
He fell for it?!
HE SEEMS HAPPY!
BUT...
...YOU STILL WON'T CATCH MY FRIENDS! I'LL PROTECT THEM!
RHINOCEROS BEETLE YO-KAI RHINOGGIN
THUNGK
MEEEOOW!
SHF SHF
AHHHHH!
Heh heh heh...
JIBANYAAAAN!

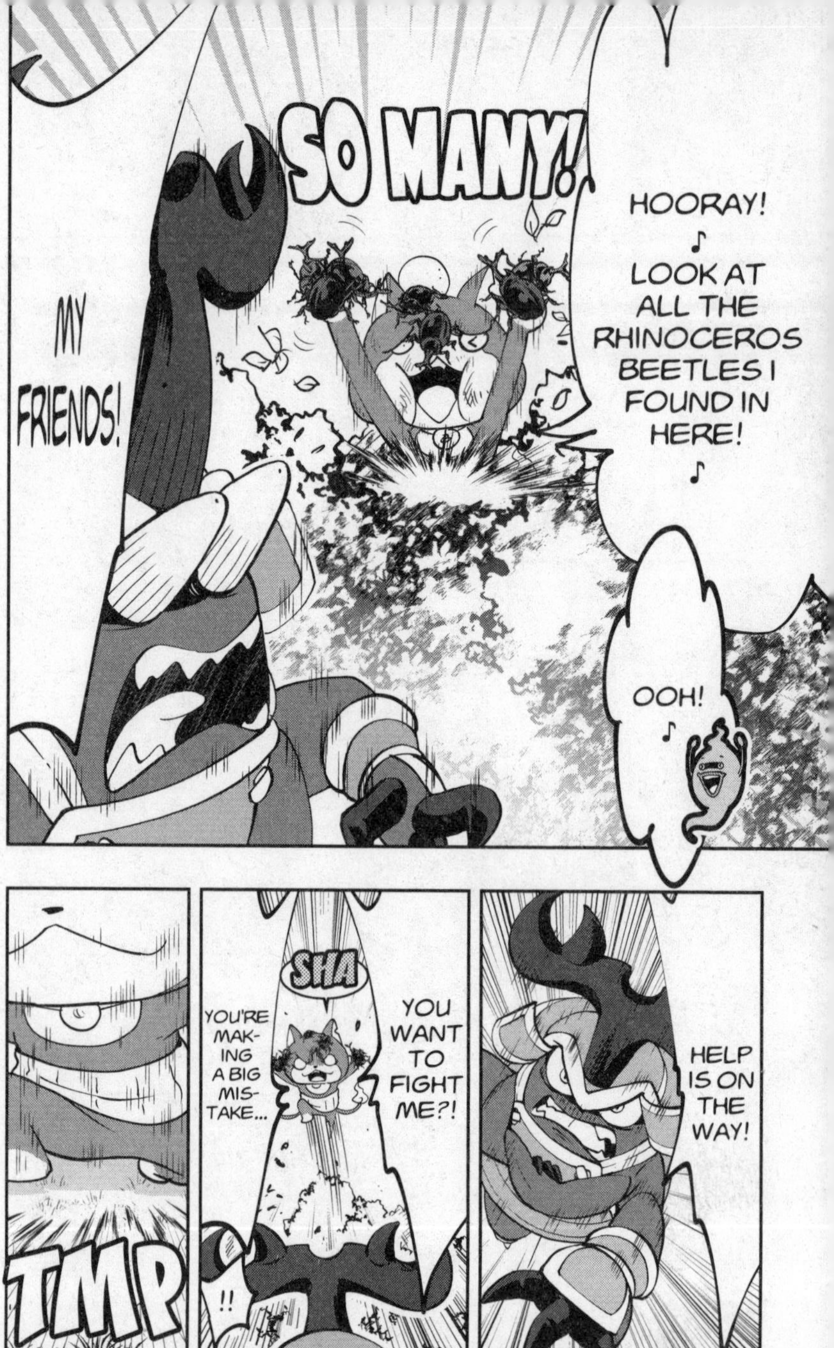
HOORAY! ♪ LOOK AT ALL THE RHINOCEROS BEETLES I FOUND IN HERE! ♪
SO MANY!
MY FRIENDS!
OOH! ♪
HELP IS ON THE WAY!
SHA
YOU WANT TO FIGHT ME?!
YOU'RE MAK-ING A BIG MIS-TAKE...
!!
TMP

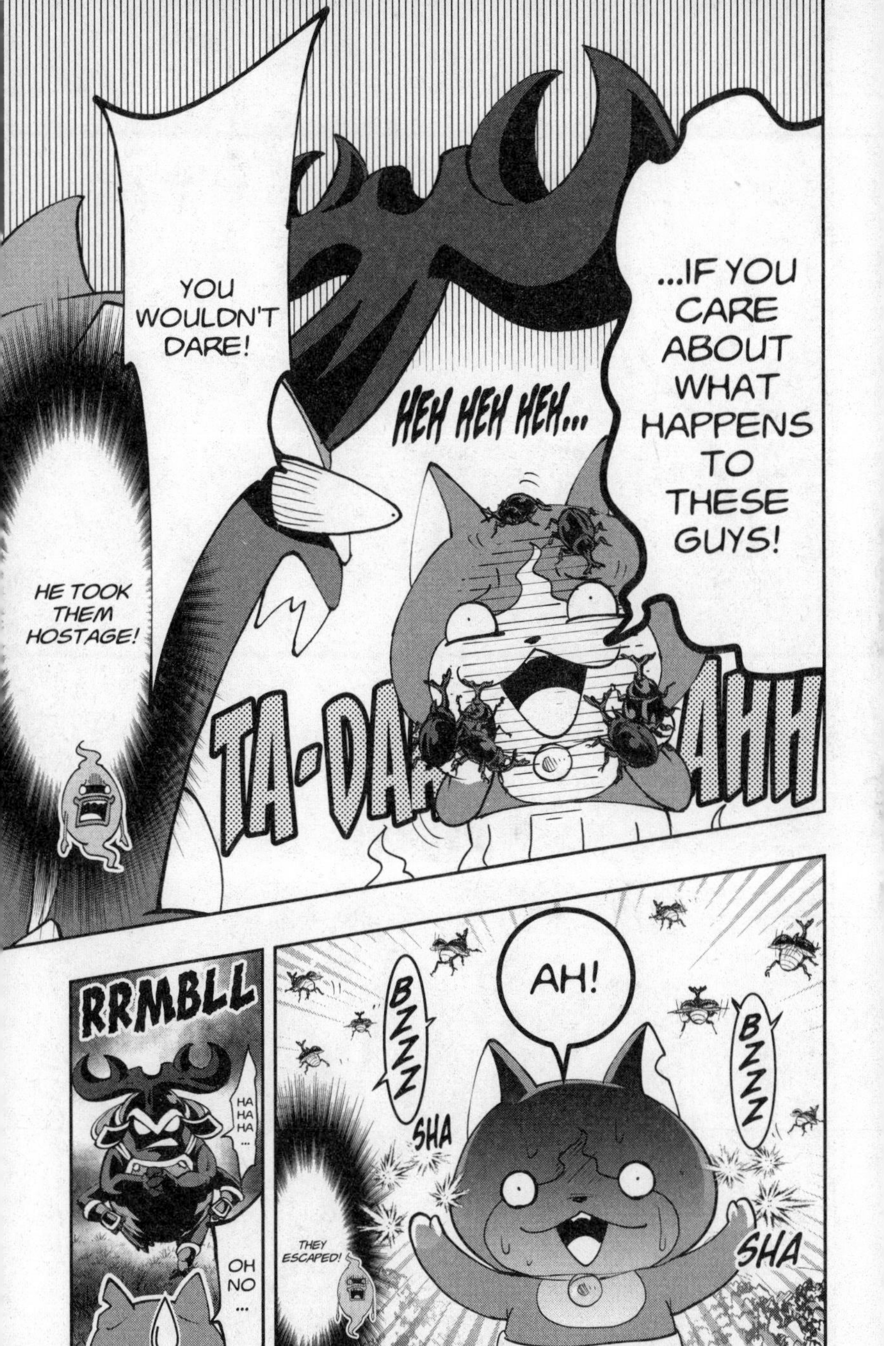
...IF YOU CARE ABOUT WHAT HAPPENS TO THESE GUYS!
HEH HEH HEH...
YOU WOULDN'T DARE!
TA-DA AHH
HE TOOK THEM HOSTAGE!
AH!
BZZZ
BZZZ
SHA
SHA
THEY ESCAPED!
RRMBLL
HA HA HA ...
OH NO ...

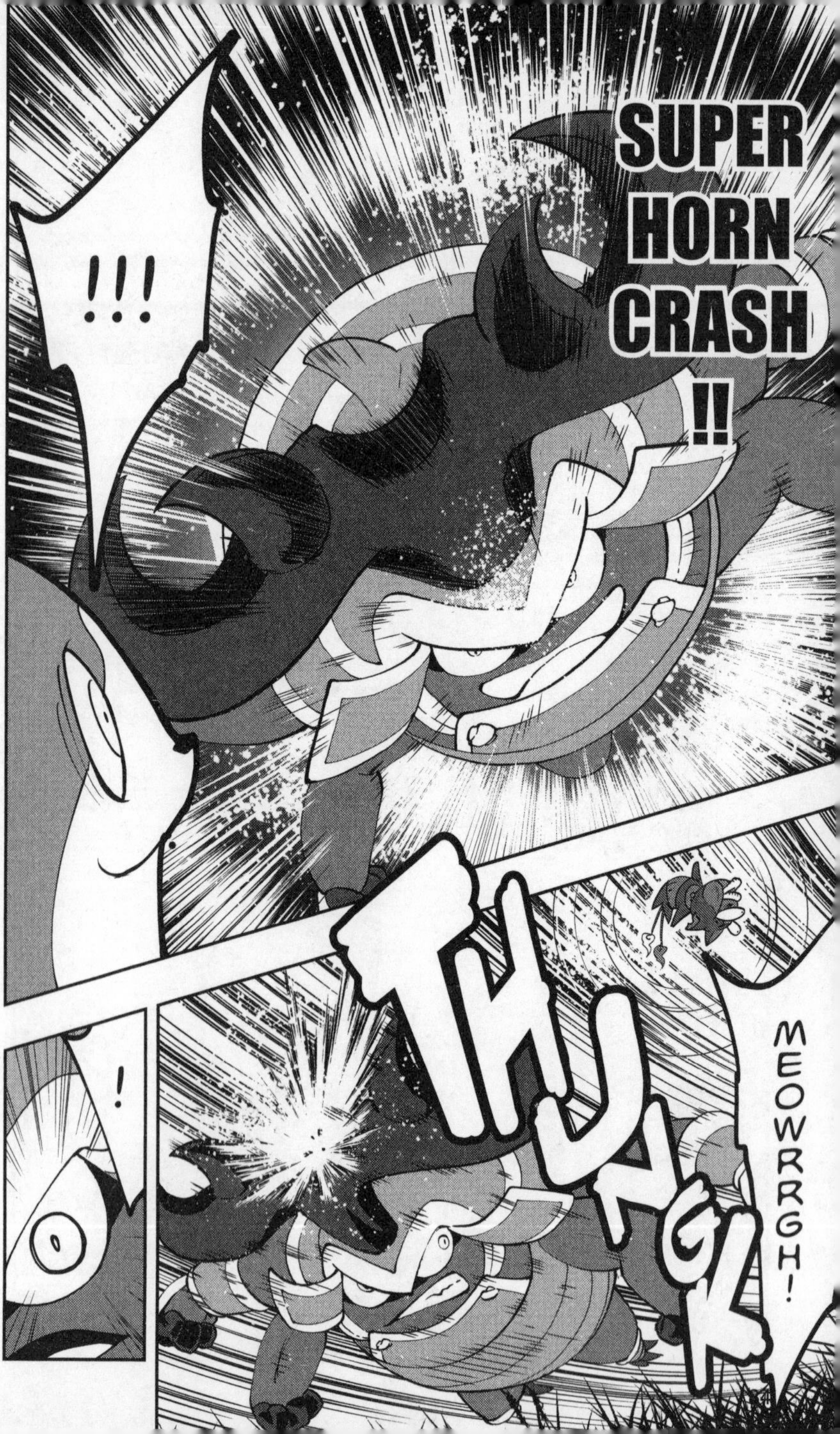
SUPER HORN CRASH!!
!!!
THUNGK
MEOWRRGH!
!

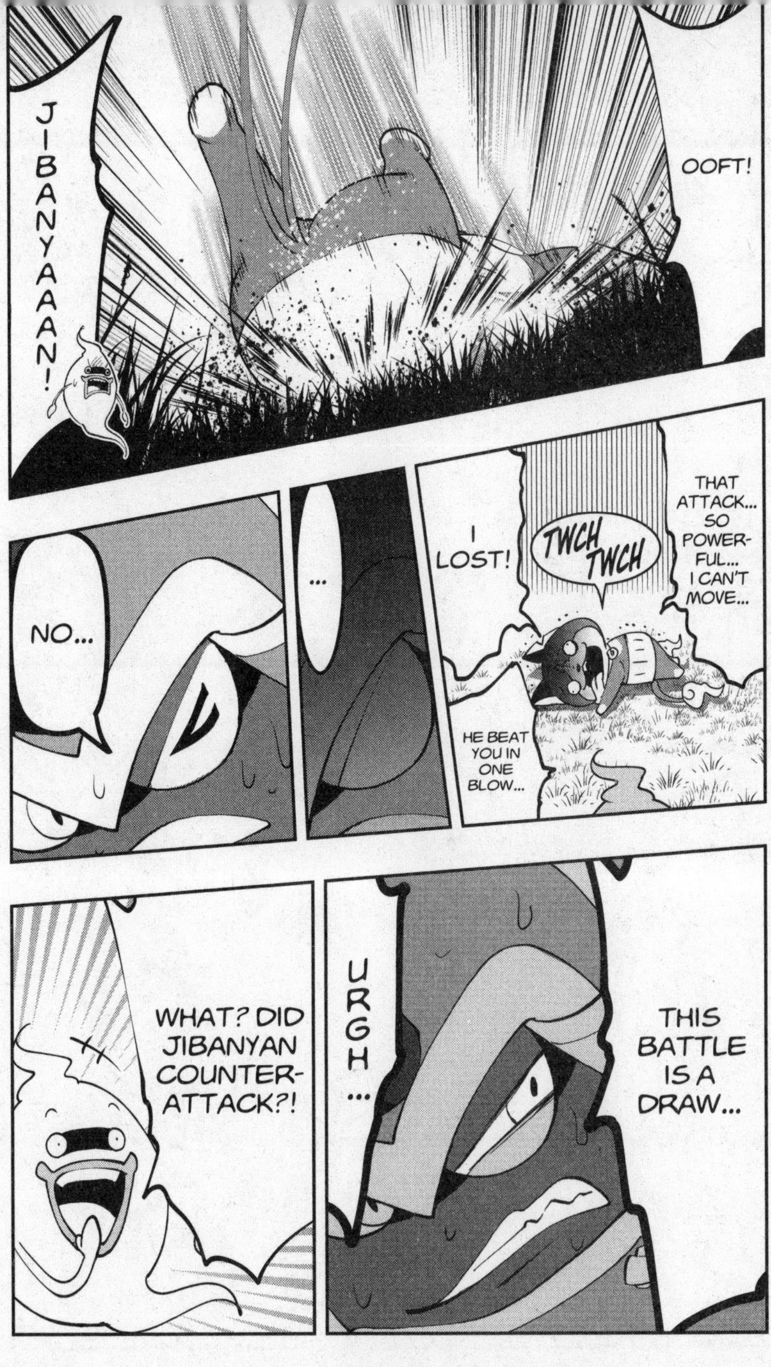
OOFT!
JIBANYAAAAN!
THAT ATTACK... SO POWER-FUL... I CAN'T MOVE...
TWCH TWCH
I LOST!
HE BEAT YOU IN ONE BLOW...
...
NO...
THIS BATTLE IS A DRAW...
URGH...
WHAT? DID JIBANYAN COUNTER-ATTACK?!

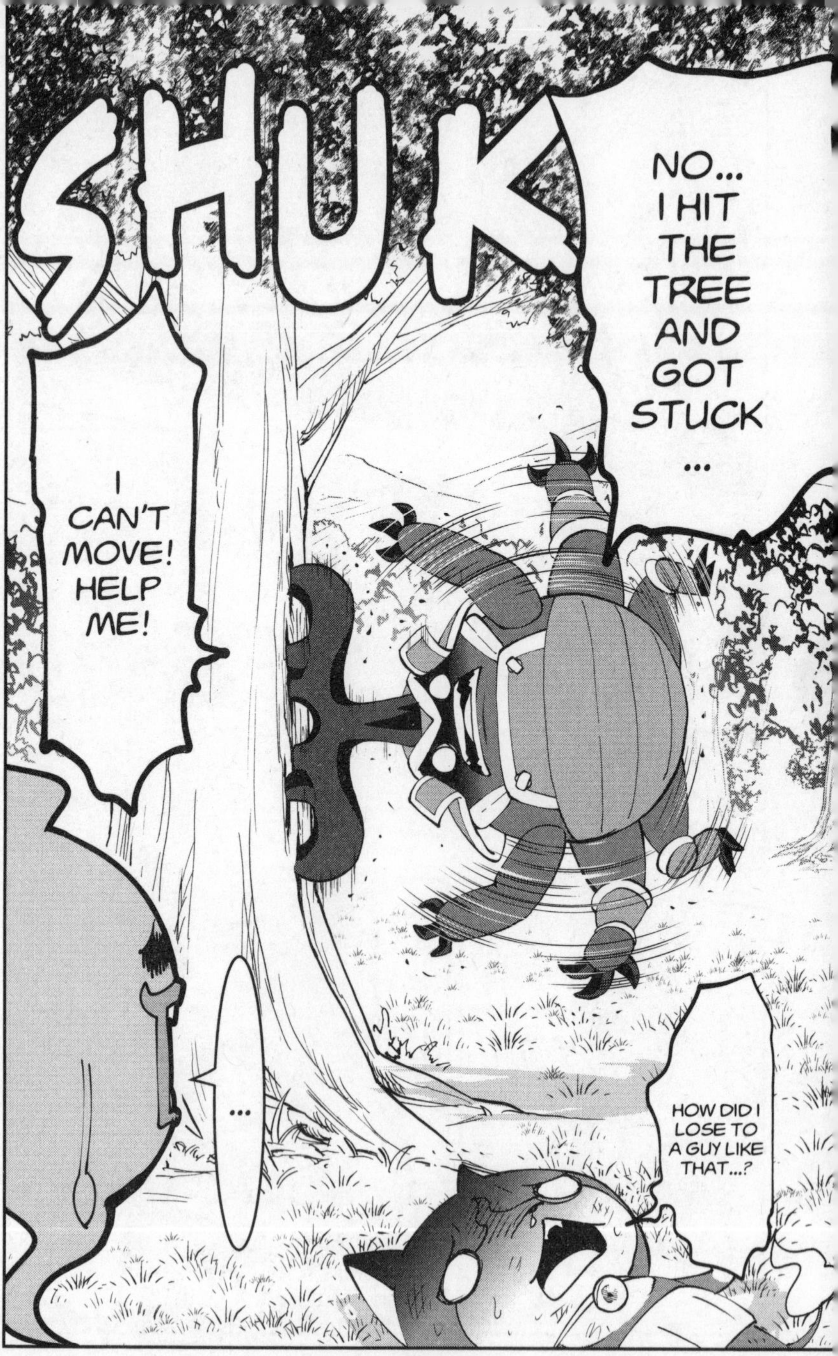
SHUK
NO... I HIT THE TREE AND GOT STUCK ...
I CAN'T MOVE! HELP ME!
HOW DID I LOSE TO A GUY LIKE THAT...?
...

CHAPTER 242
NEWBORN YO-KAI ORIGINYAN

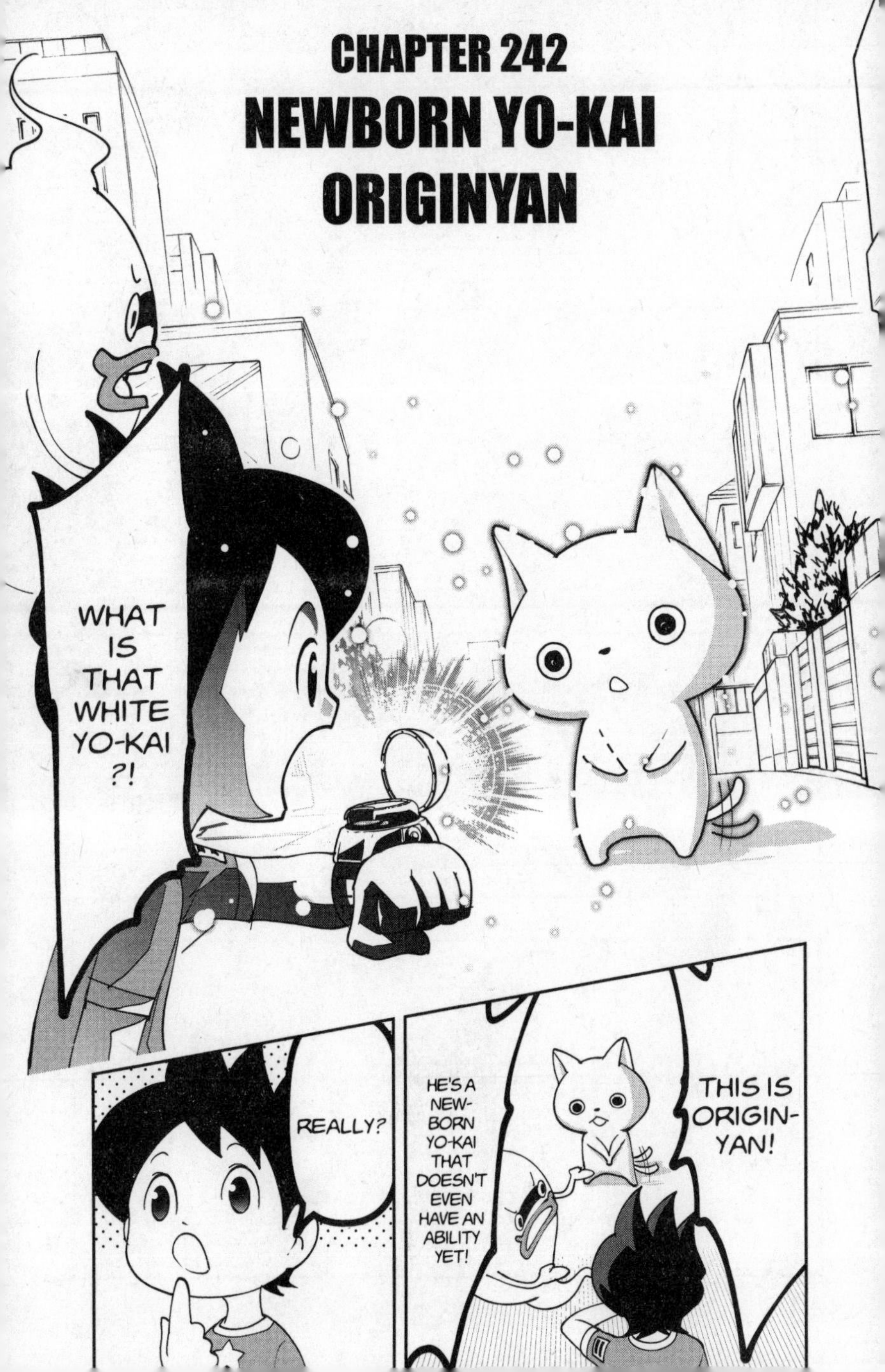
WHAT IS THAT WHITE YO-KAI?!
THIS IS ORIGIN-YAN!
HE'S A NEW-BORN YO-KAI THAT DOESN'T EVEN HAVE AN ABILITY YET!
REALLY?

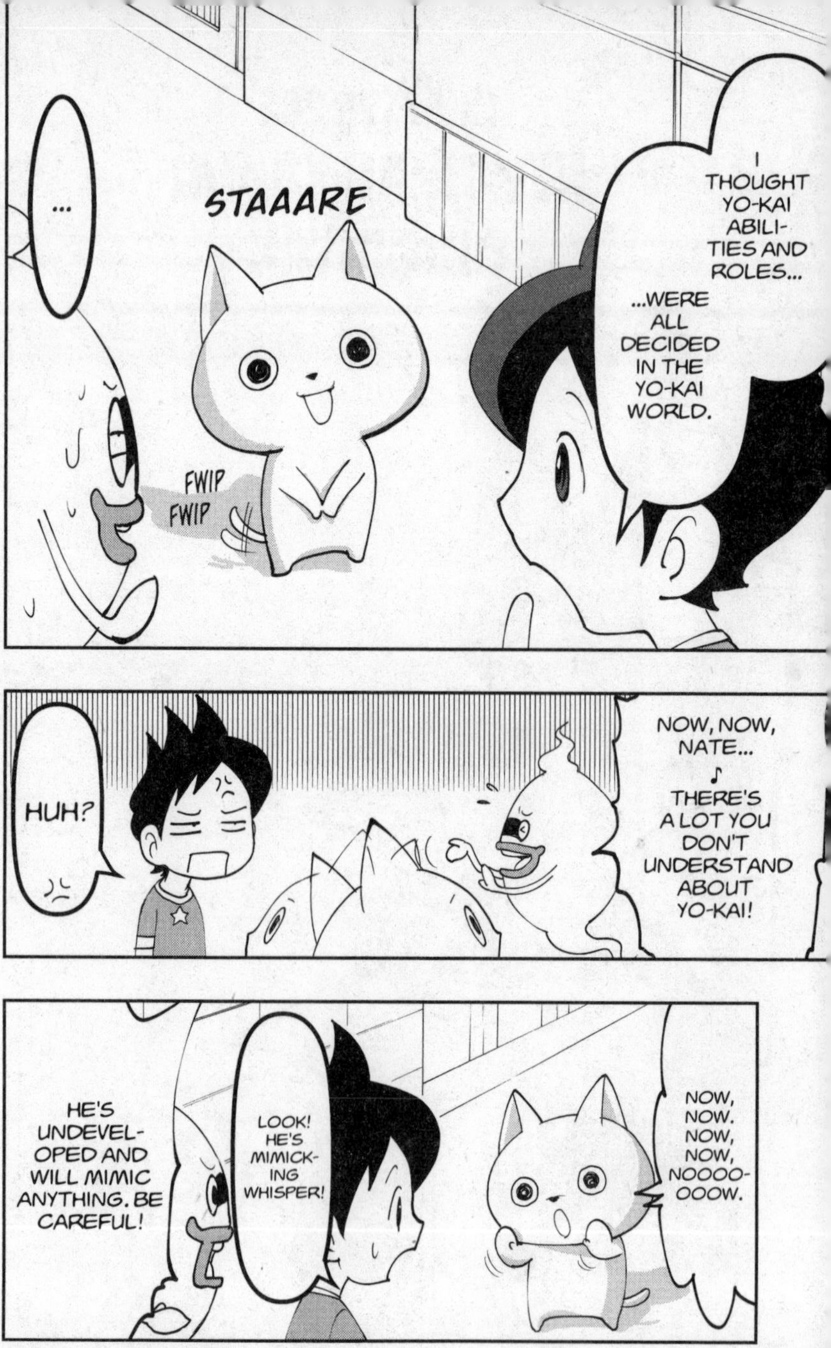
I THOUGHT YO-KAI ABILI-TIES AND ROLES...
...WERE ALL DECIDED IN THE YO-KAI WORLD.
STAAARE
FWIP FWIP
...
NOW, NOW, NATE... ♪ THERE'S A LOT YOU DON'T UNDERSTAND ABOUT YO-KAI!
HUH?
NOW, NOW. NOW, NOW, NOOOO-OOOW.
LOOK! HE'S MIMICK-ING WHISPER!
HE'S UNDEVEL-OPED AND WILL MIMIC ANYTHING. BE CAREFUL!

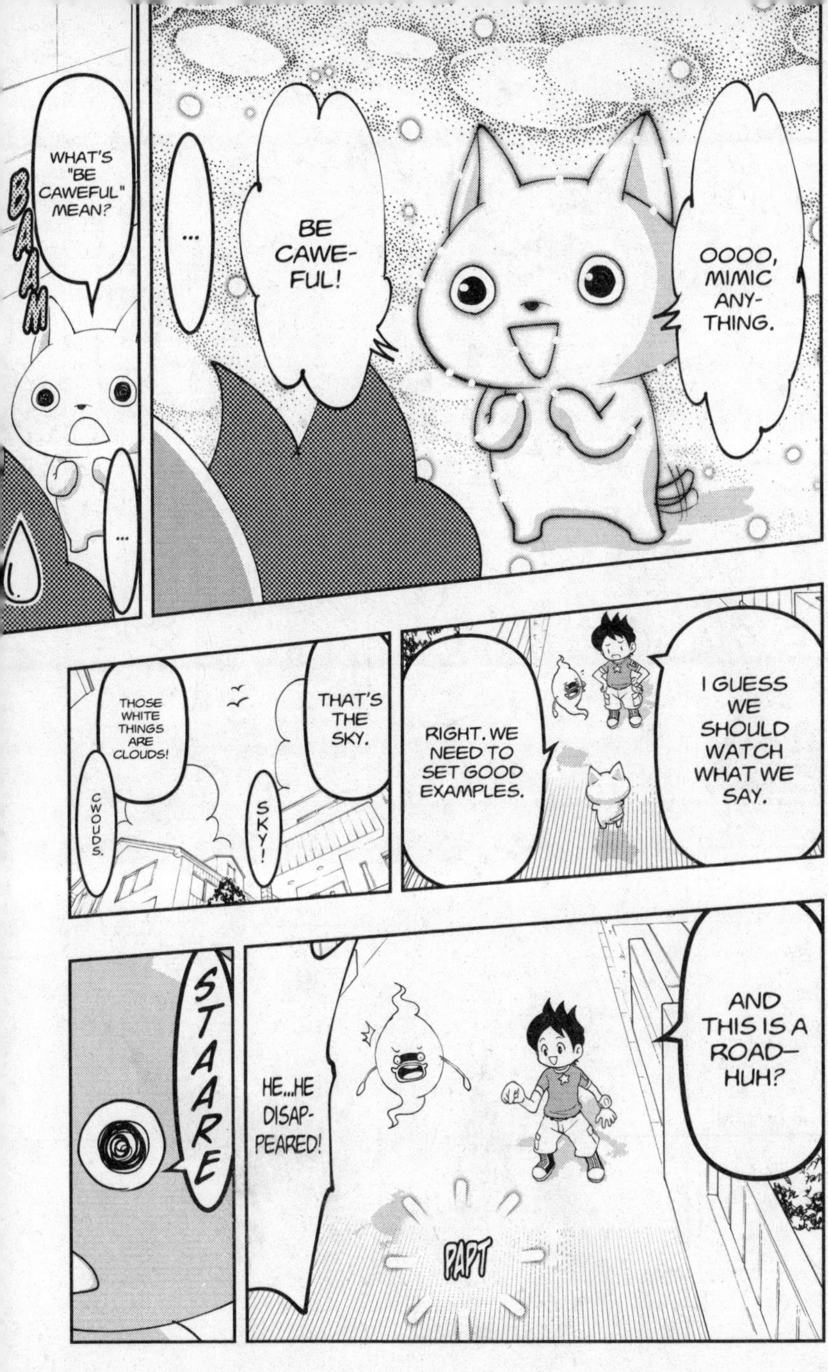
OOOO, MIMIC ANY-THING.
BE CAWE-FUL!
...
BAAM
WHAT'S "BE CAWEFUL" MEAN?
...
I GUESS WE SHOULD WATCH WHAT WE SAY.
RIGHT. WE NEED TO SET GOOD EXAMPLES.
THAT'S THE SKY.
SKY!
THOSE WHITE THINGS ARE CLOUDS!
CWOUDS.
AND THIS IS A ROAD—HUH?
HE...HE DISAP-PEARED!
PAPT
STAARE

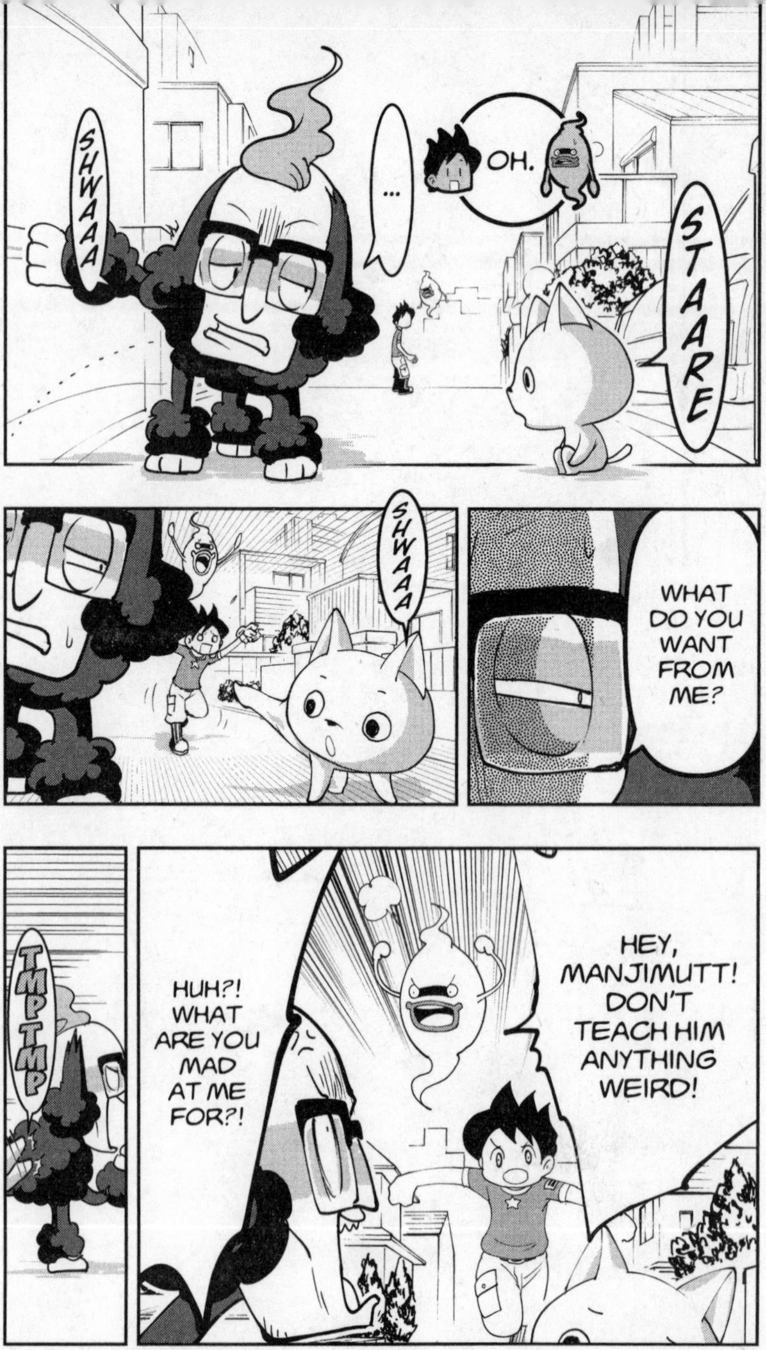
STAARE
OH.
...
SHWAAAA
WHAT DO YOU WANT FROM ME?
SHWAAA
HEY, MANJIMUTT! DON'T TEACH HIM ANYTHING WEIRD!
HUH?! WHAT ARE YOU MAD AT ME FOR?!
TMP TMP

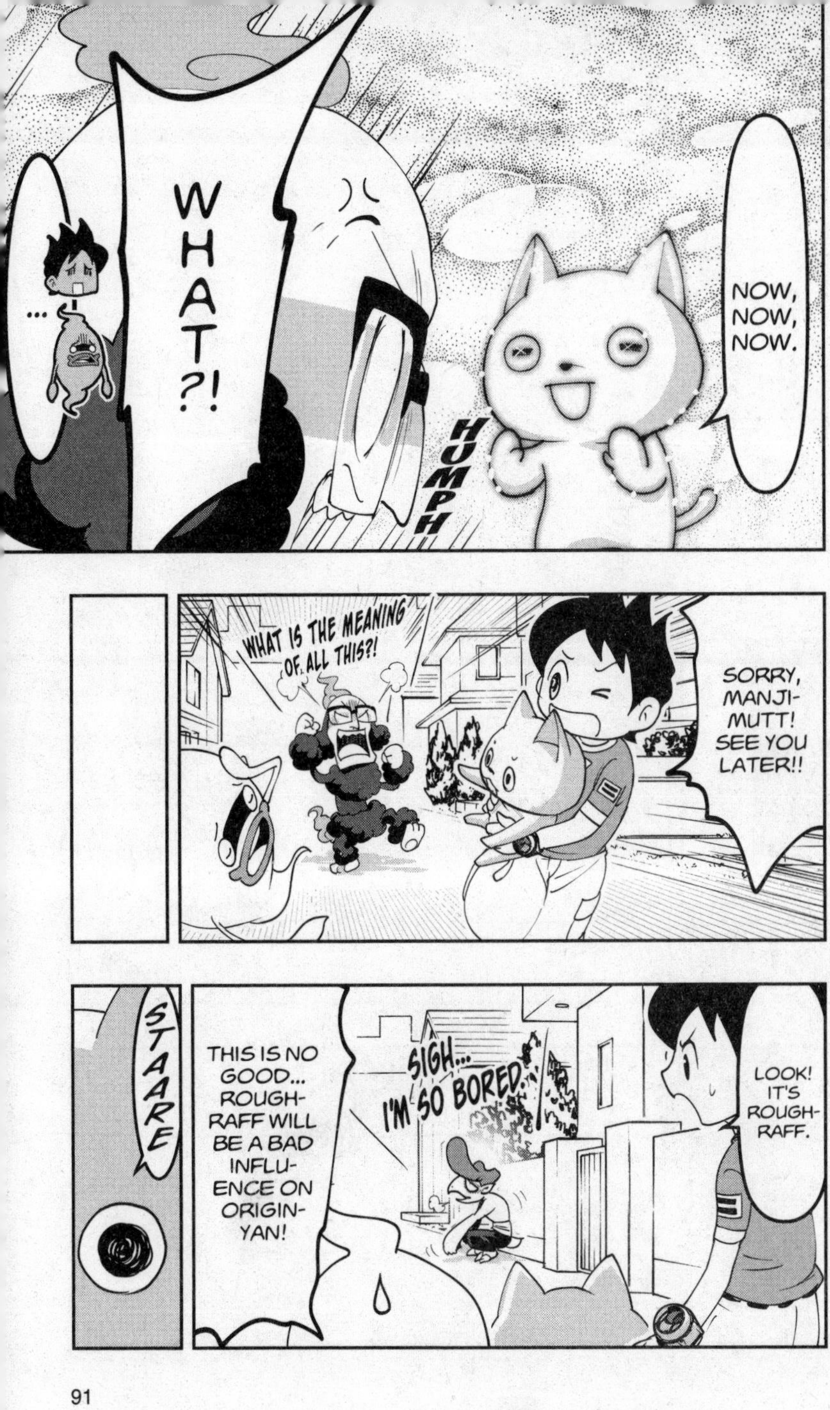
NOW, NOW, NOW.
HUMPH!
WHAT?!
...
SORRY, MANJI-MUTT! SEE YOU LATER!!
WHAT IS THE MEANING OF ALL THIS?!
LOOK! IT'S ROUGH-RAFF.
SIGH... I'M SO BORED.
THIS IS NO GOOD... ROUGH-RAFF WILL BE A BAD INFLU-ENCE ON ORIGIN-YAN!
STAARE

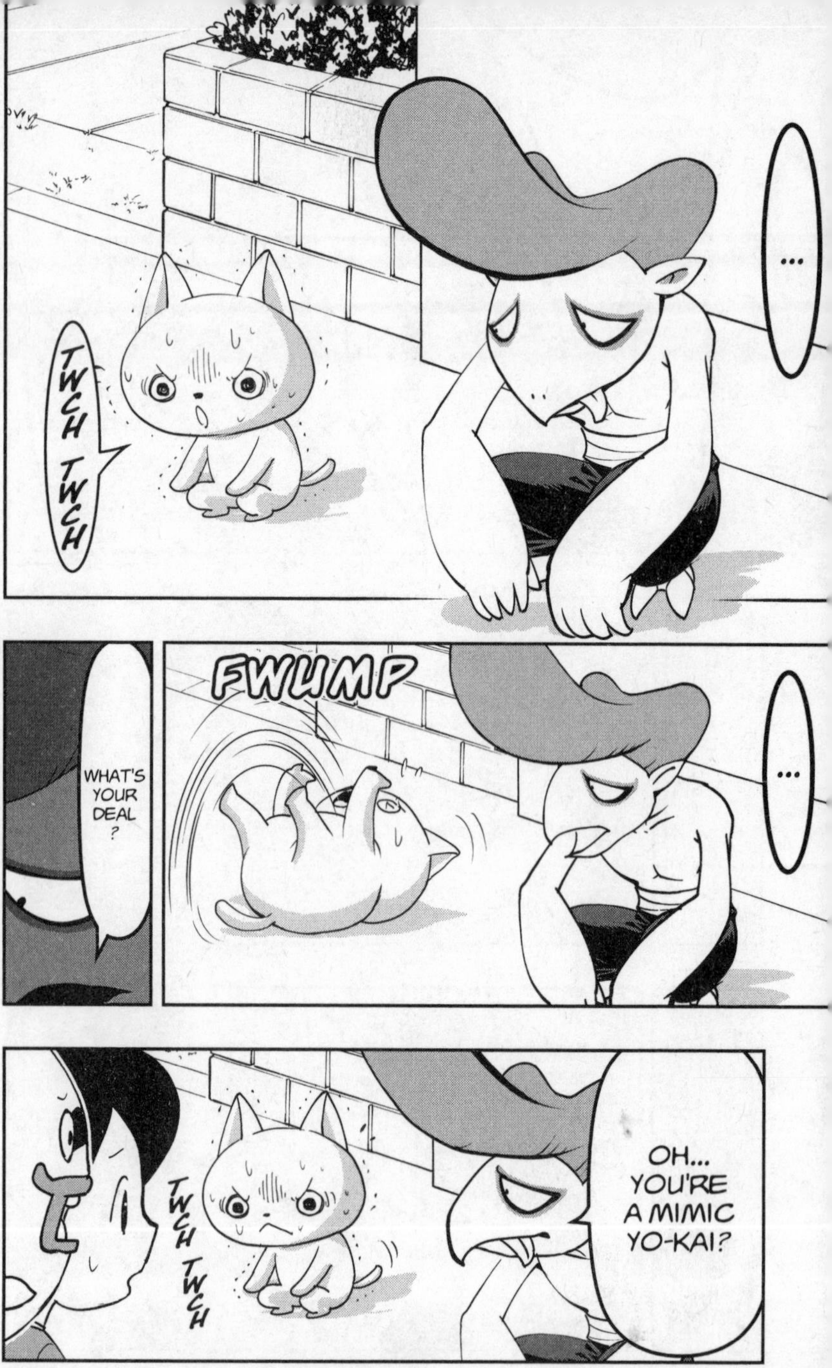
...
TWCH TWCH
...
FWUMP
WHAT'S YOUR DEAL?
OH... YOU'RE A MIMIC YO-KAI?
TWCH TWCH

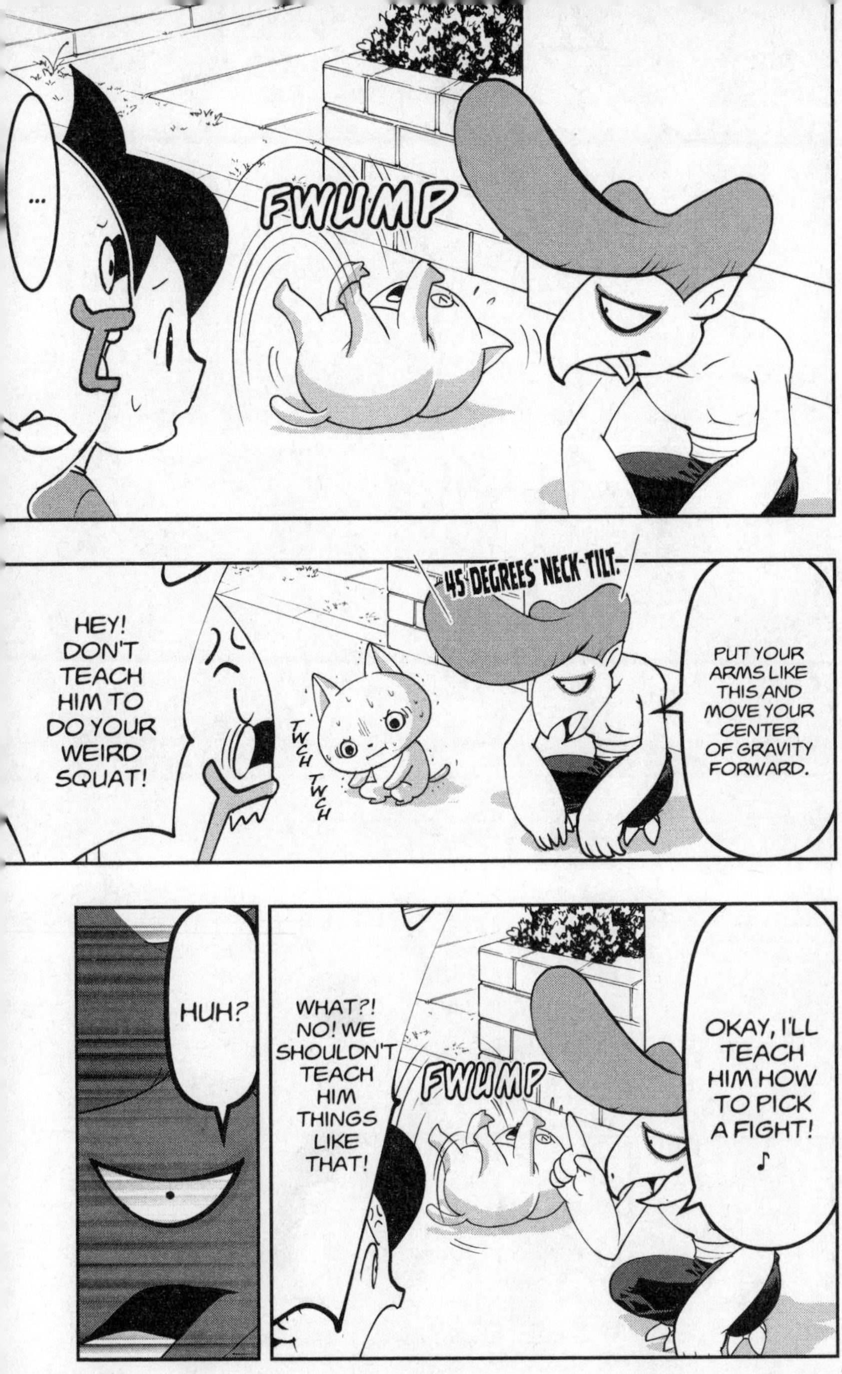
FWUMP
...
45 DEGREES NECK-TILT.
PUT YOUR ARMS LIKE THIS AND MOVE YOUR CENTER OF GRAVITY FORWARD.
TWCH TWCH
HEY! DON'T TEACH HIM TO DO YOUR WEIRD SQUAT!
OKAY, I'LL TEACH HIM HOW TO PICK A FIGHT! ♪
FWUMP
WHAT?! NO! WE SHOULDN'T TEACH HIM THINGS LIKE THAT!
HUH?

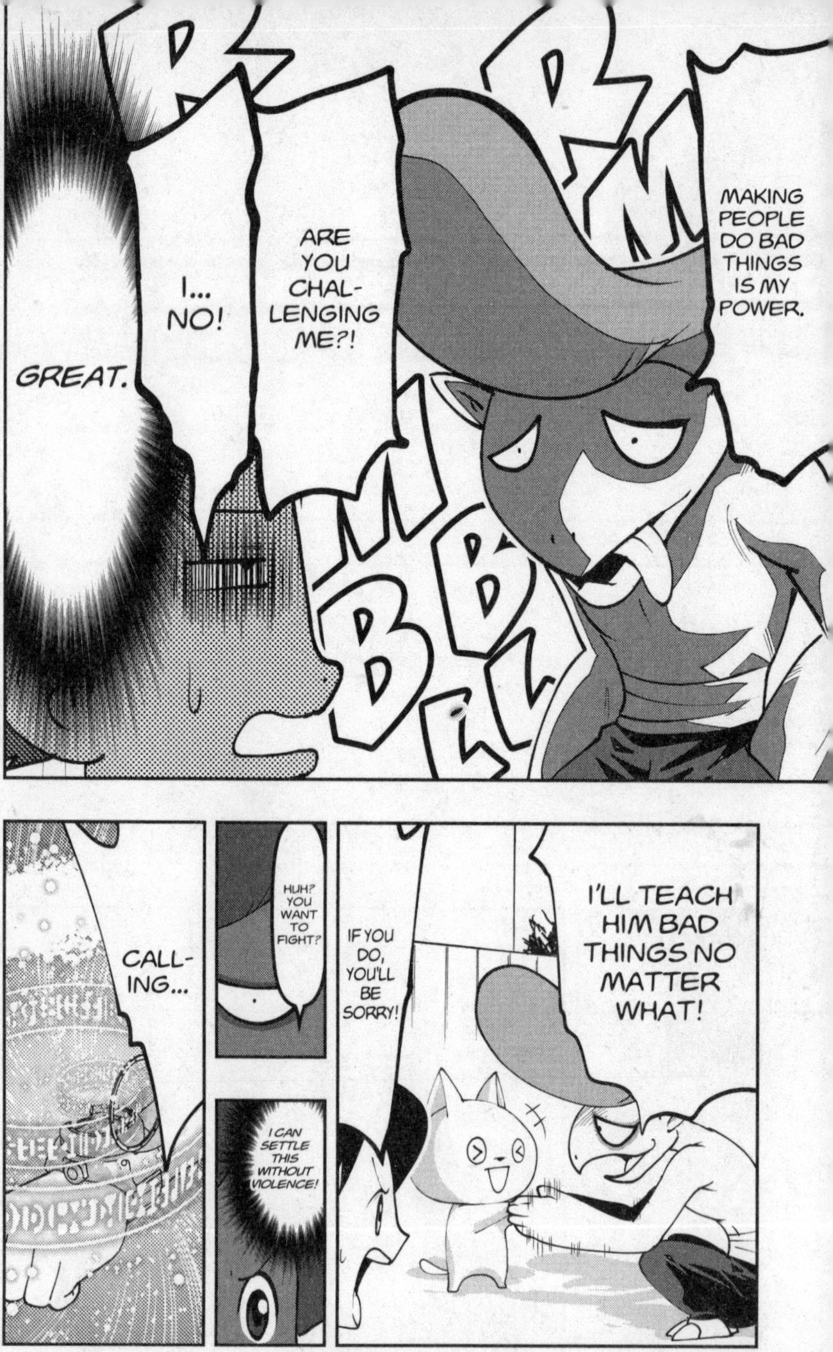
MAKING PEOPLE DO BAD THINGS IS MY POWER.
ARE YOU CHAL-LENGING ME?!
I... NO!
GREAT.
I'LL TEACH HIM BAD THINGS NO MATTER WHAT!
IF YOU DO, YOU'LL BE SORRY!
HUH? YOU WANT TO FIGHT?
I CAN SETTLE THIS WITHOUT VIOLENCE!
CALL-ING...

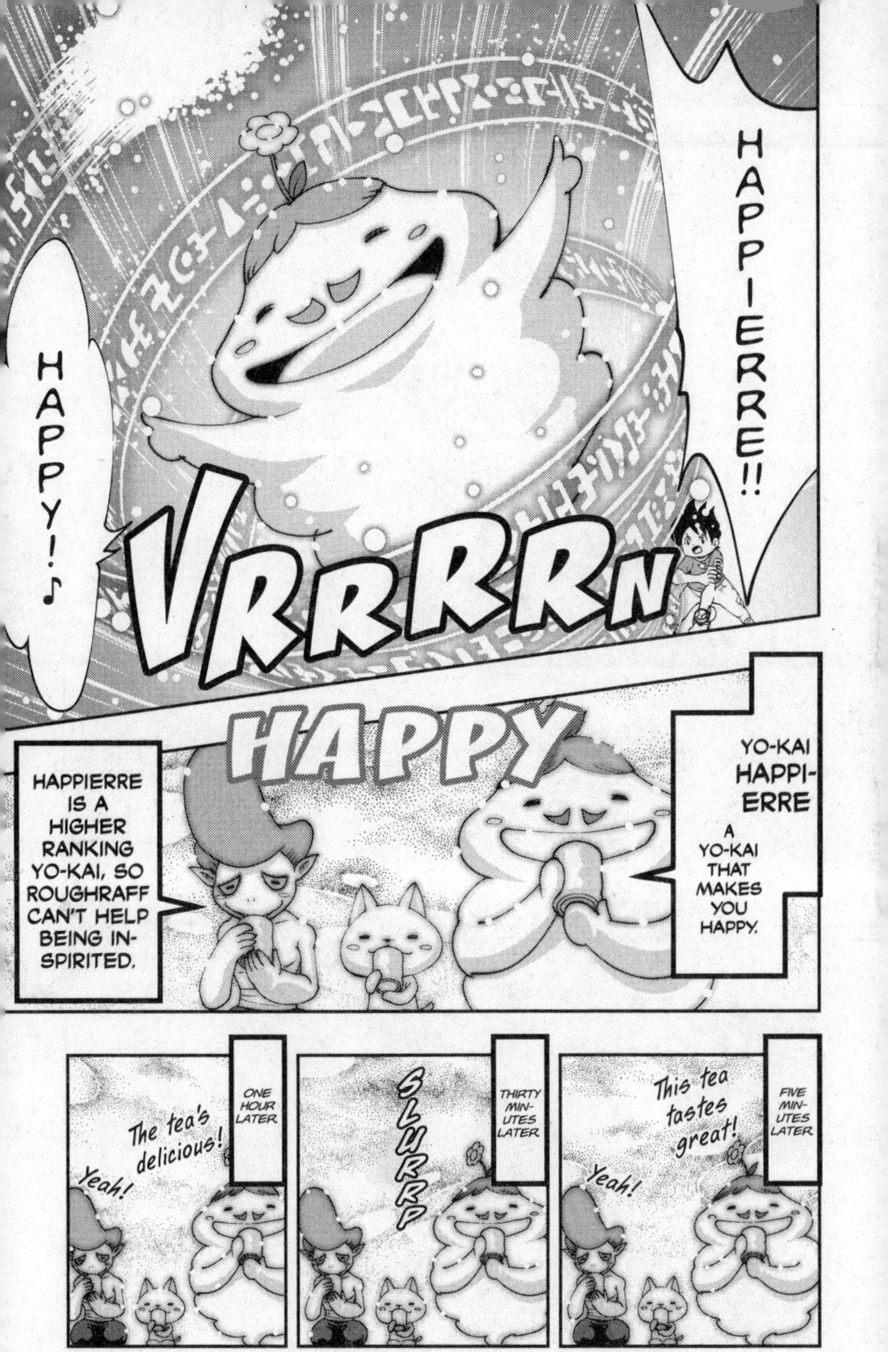
HAPPIERRE!!
HAPPY! ♪
VRRRRN
HAPPY
YO-KAI HAPPIERRE
A YO-KAI THAT MAKES YOU HAPPY.
HAPPIERRE IS A HIGHER RANKING YO-KAI, SO ROUGHRAFF CAN'T HELP BEING IN-SPIRITED.
FIVE MIN-UTES LATER
This tea tastes great!
Yeah!
THIRTY MIN-UTES LATER
SLURRP
ONE HOUR LATER
The tea's delicious!
Yeah!

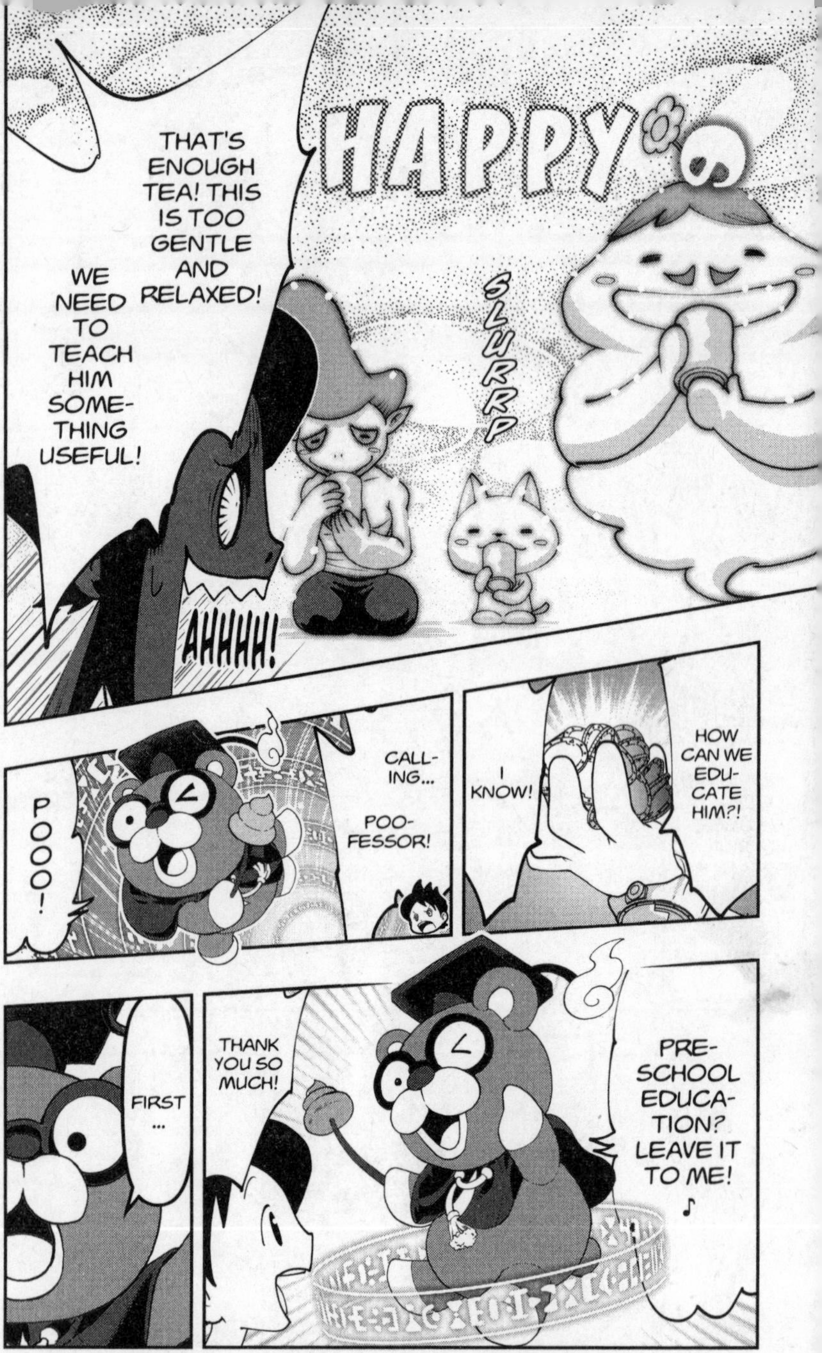
HAPPY
SLURRP
THAT'S ENOUGH TEA! THIS IS TOO GENTLE AND RELAXED!
WE NEED TO TEACH HIM SOME-THING USEFUL!
AHHHH!
HOW CAN WE EDU-CATE HIM?!
I KNOW!
CALL-ING...
POO-FESSOR!
POOOO!
PRE-SCHOOL EDUCA-TION? LEAVE IT TO ME! ♪
THANK YOU SO MUCH!
FIRST ...

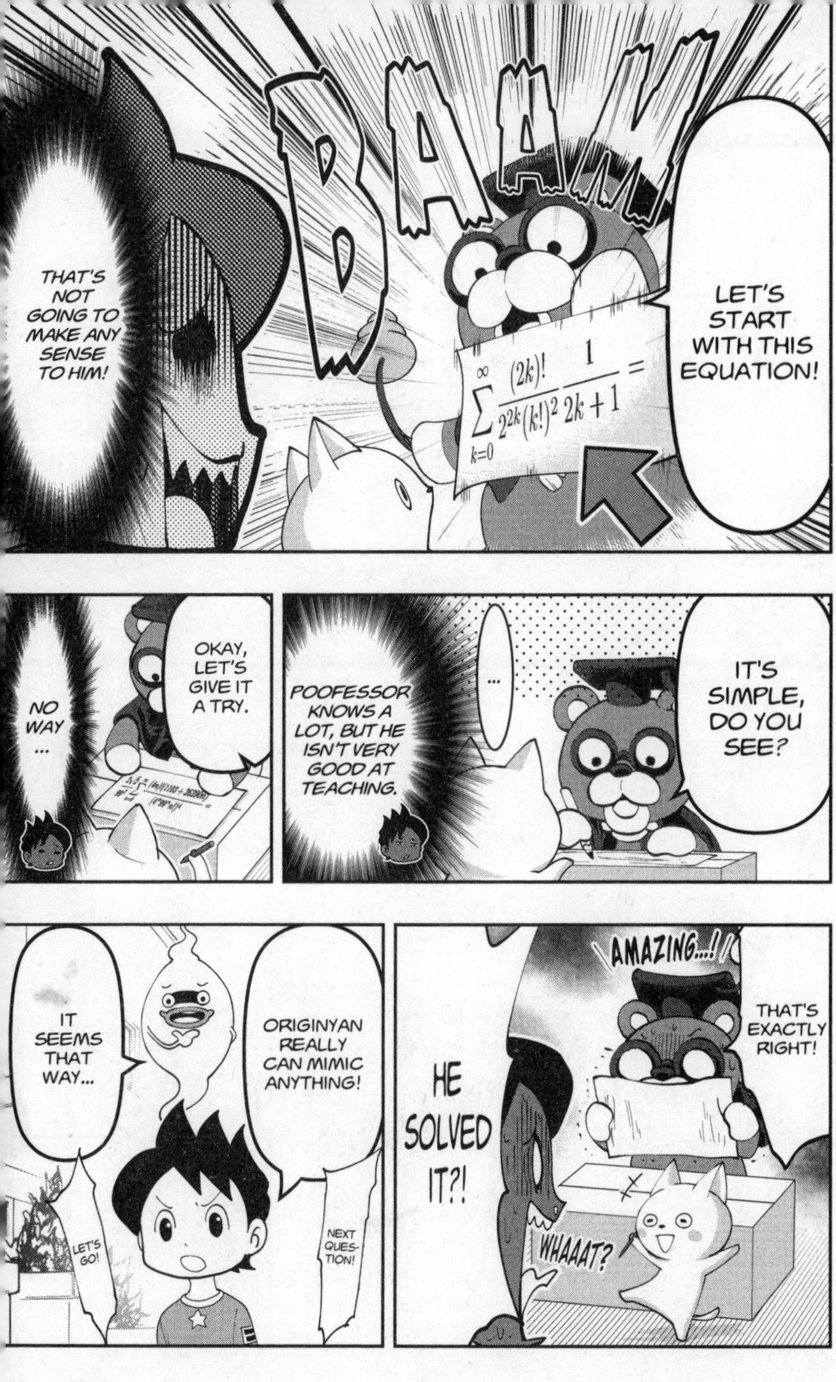
LET'S START WITH THIS EQUATION!
BAAM
$\sum_{k=0}^{\infty} \frac{(2k)!}{2^{2k}(k!)^2} \frac{1}{2k+1} =$
THAT'S NOT GOING TO MAKE ANY SENSE TO HIM!
IT'S SIMPLE, DO YOU SEE?
...
POOFESSOR KNOWS A LOT, BUT HE ISN'T VERY GOOD AT TEACHING.
OKAY, LET'S GIVE IT A TRY.
NO WAY ...
AMAZING...!
THAT'S EXACTLY RIGHT!
HE SOLVED IT?!
WHAAAT?
ORIGINYAN REALLY CAN MIMIC ANYTHING!
NEXT QUESTION!
IT SEEMS THAT WAY...
LET'S GO!

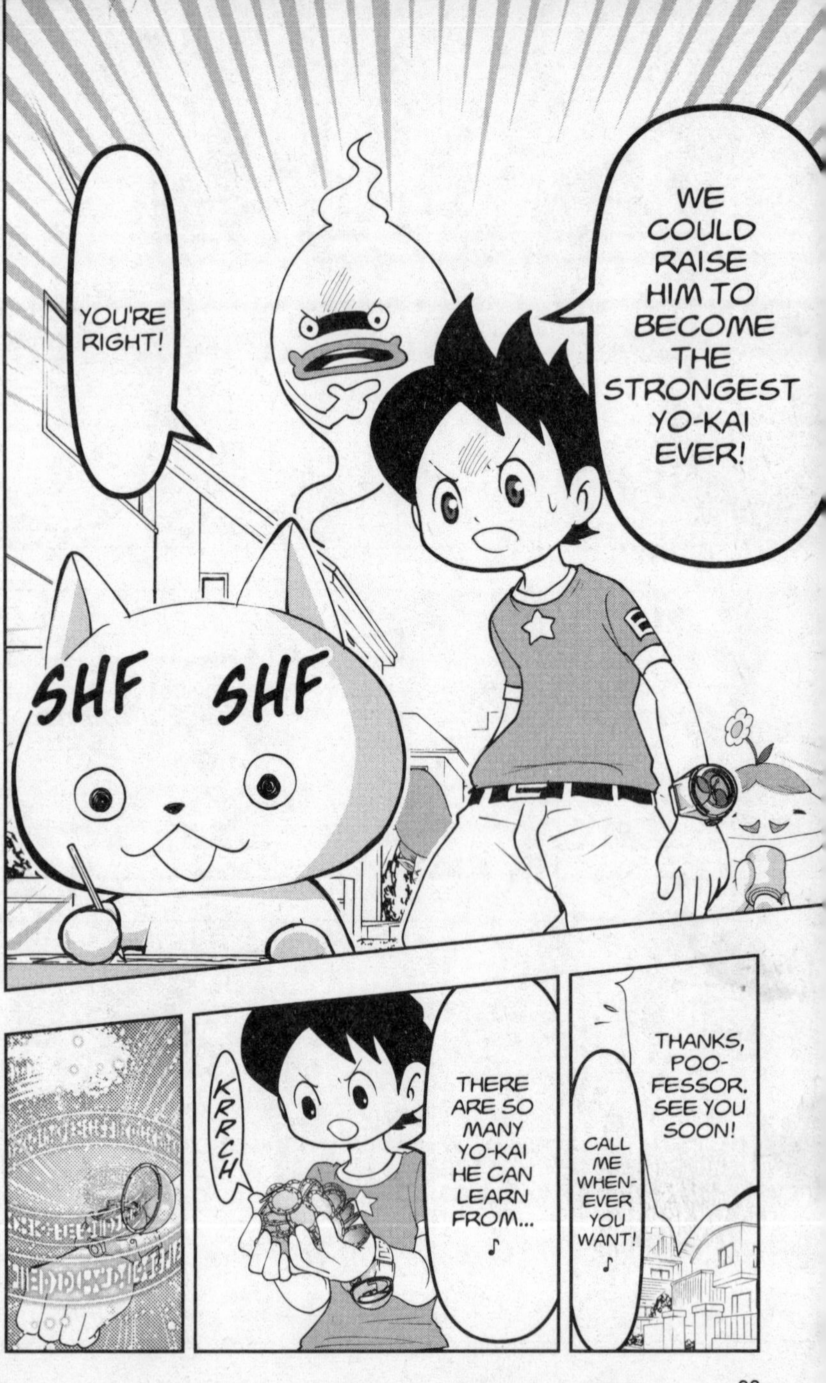
WE COULD RAISE HIM TO BECOME THE STRONGEST YO-KAI EVER!
YOU'RE RIGHT!
SHF SHF
THANKS, POO-FESSOR. SEE YOU SOON!
CALL ME WHEN-EVER YOU WANT! ♪
THERE ARE SO MANY YO-KAI HE CAN LEARN FROM... ♪
KRRCH

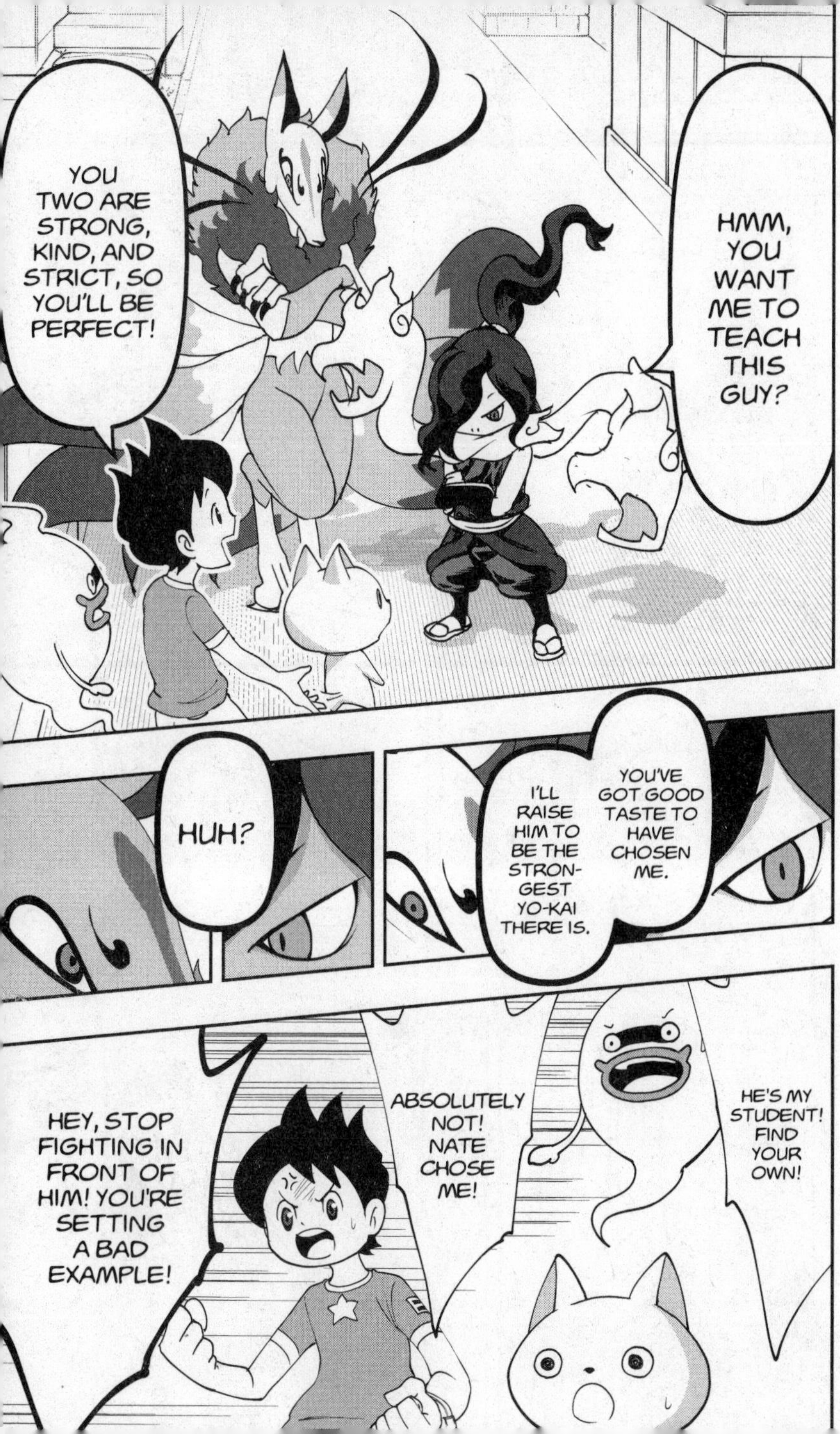
HMM, YOU WANT ME TO TEACH THIS GUY?
YOU TWO ARE STRONG, KIND, AND STRICT, SO YOU'LL BE PERFECT!
YOU'VE GOT GOOD TASTE TO HAVE CHOSEN ME.
I'LL RAISE HIM TO BE THE STRON-GEST YO-KAI THERE IS.
HUH?
HE'S MY STUDENT! FIND YOUR OWN!
ABSOLUTELY NOT! NATE CHOSE ME!
HEY, STOP FIGHTING IN FRONT OF HIM! YOU'RE SETTING A BAD EXAMPLE!

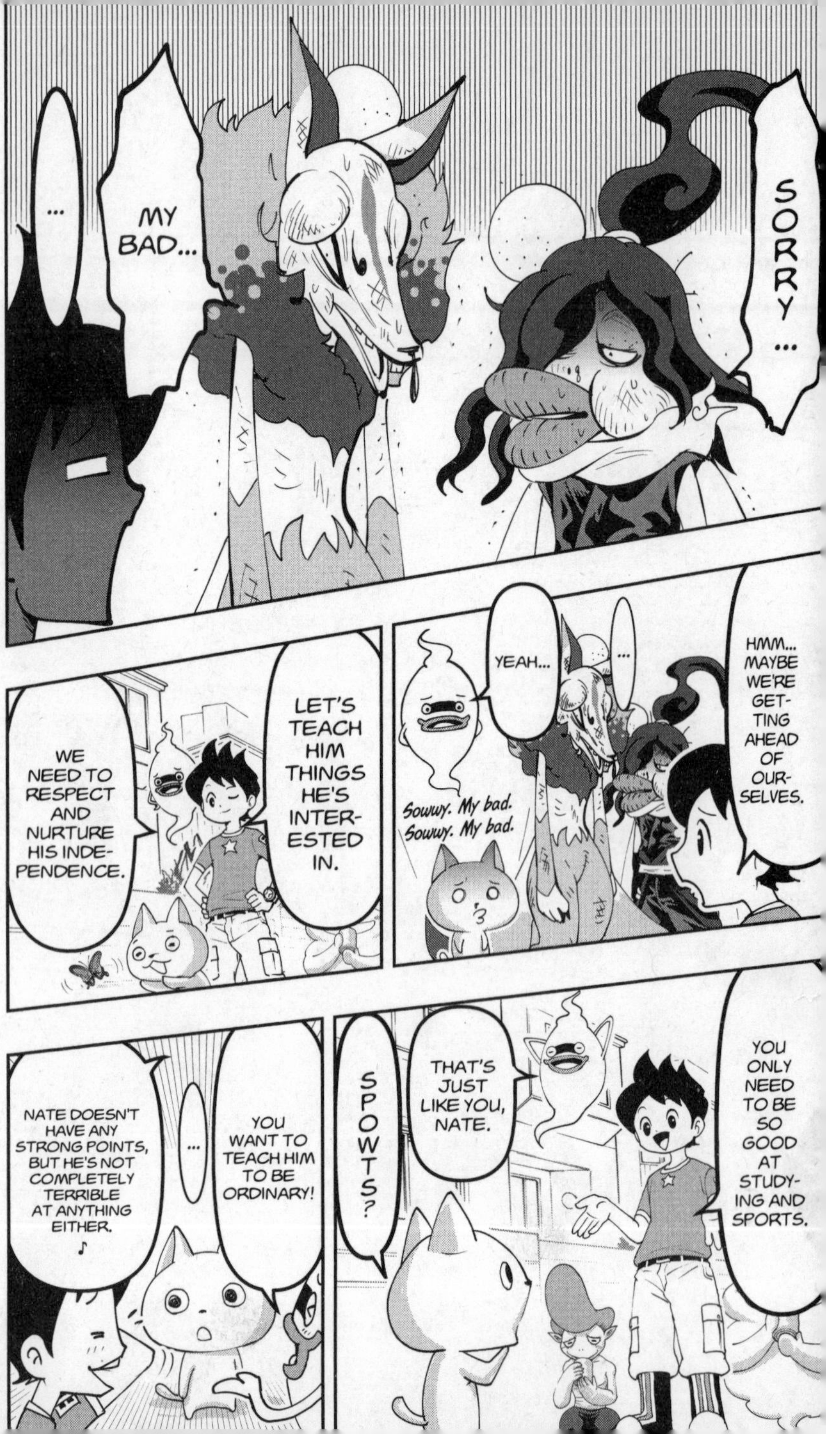
SORRY...
MY BAD...
...
HMM... MAYBE WE'RE GET-TING AHEAD OF OUR-SELVES.
...
YEAH...
Sowwy. My bad. Sowwy. My bad.
LET'S TEACH HIM THINGS HE'S INTER-ESTED IN.
WE NEED TO RESPECT AND NURTURE HIS INDE-PENDENCE.
YOU ONLY NEED TO BE SO GOOD AT STUDY-ING AND SPORTS.
THAT'S JUST LIKE YOU, NATE.
SPOWTS?
YOU WANT TO TEACH HIM TO BE ORDINARY!
...
NATE DOESN'T HAVE ANY STRONG POINTS, BUT HE'S NOT COMPLETELY TERRIBLE AT ANYTHING EITHER. ♪

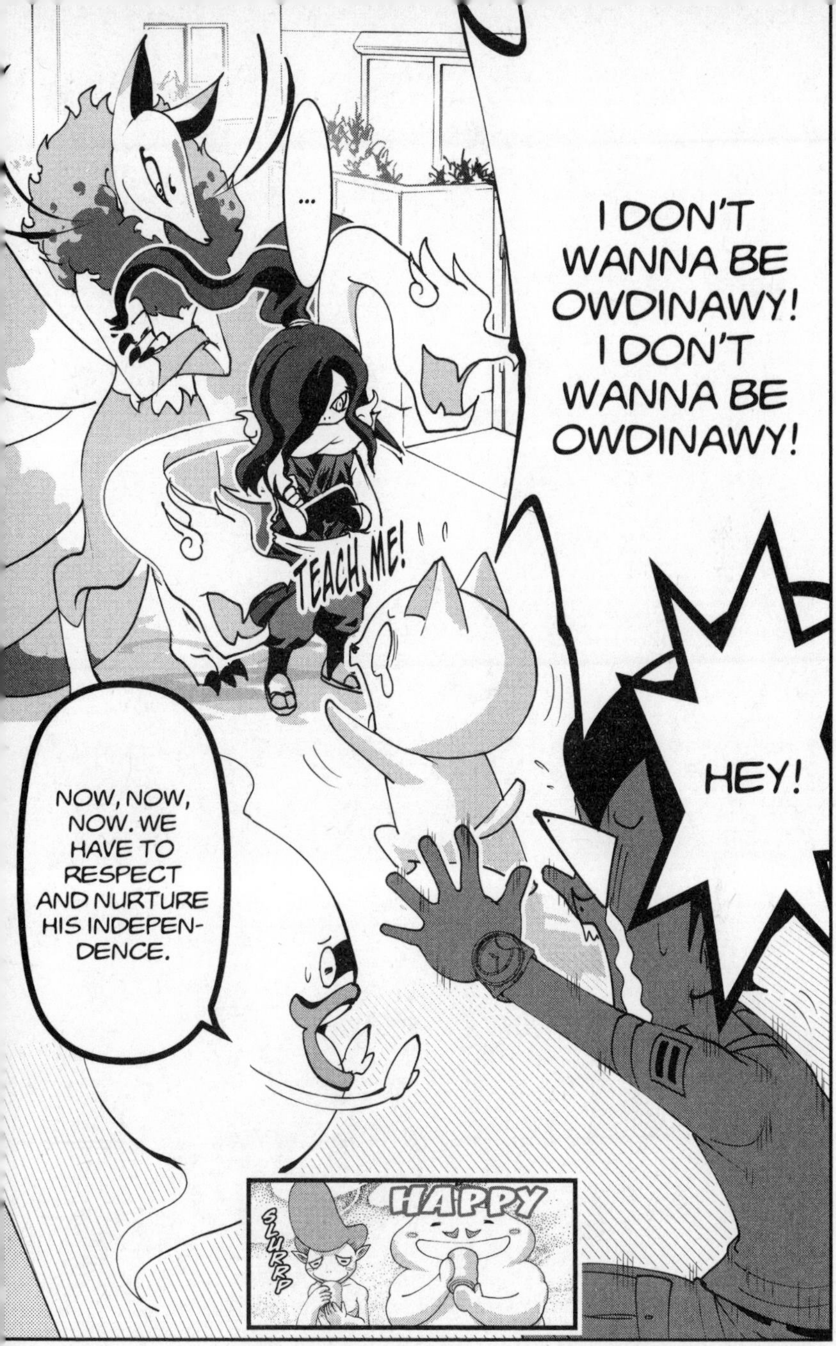
I DON'T WANNA BE OWDINAWY! I DON'T WANNA BE OWDINAWY!
...
TEACH ME!
HEY!
NOW, NOW, NOW. WE HAVE TO RESPECT AND NURTURE HIS INDEPEN-DENCE.
HAPPY
SLURRP

CHAPTER 243
SUMO CHALLENGER YO-KAI KINTARONYAN

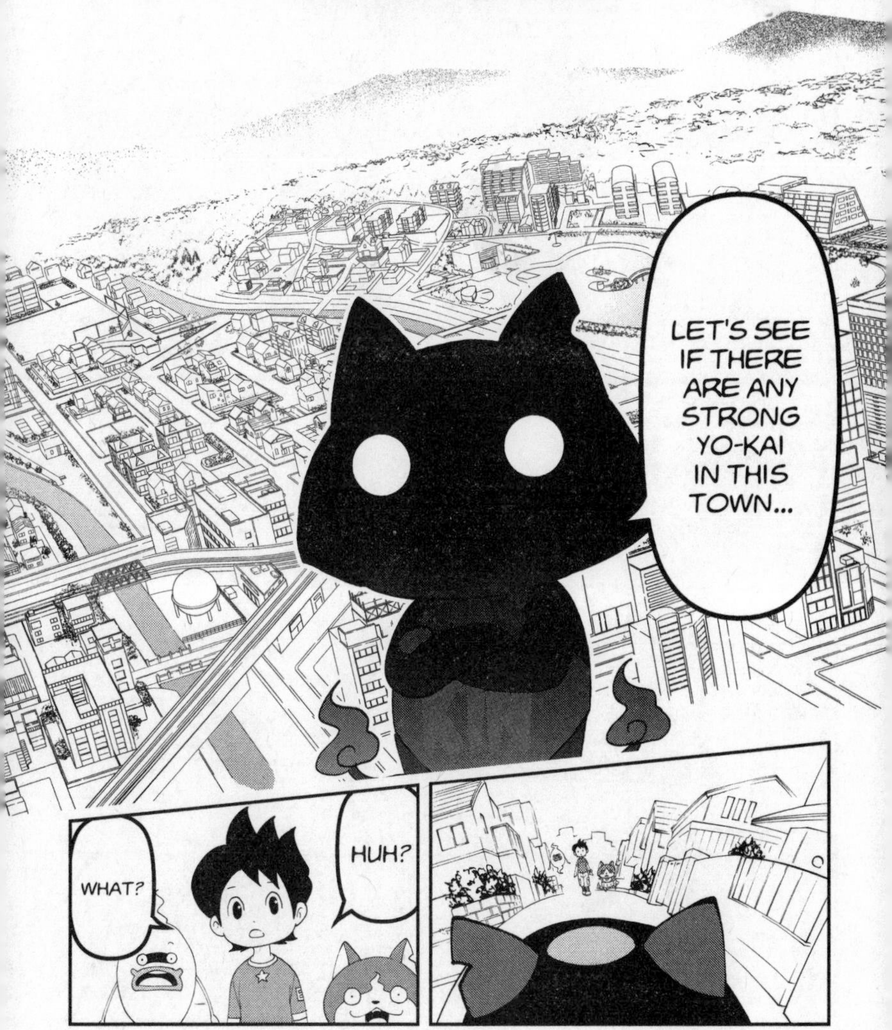

LET'S SEE IF THERE ARE ANY STRONG YO-KAI IN THIS TOWN...
HUH?
WHAT?

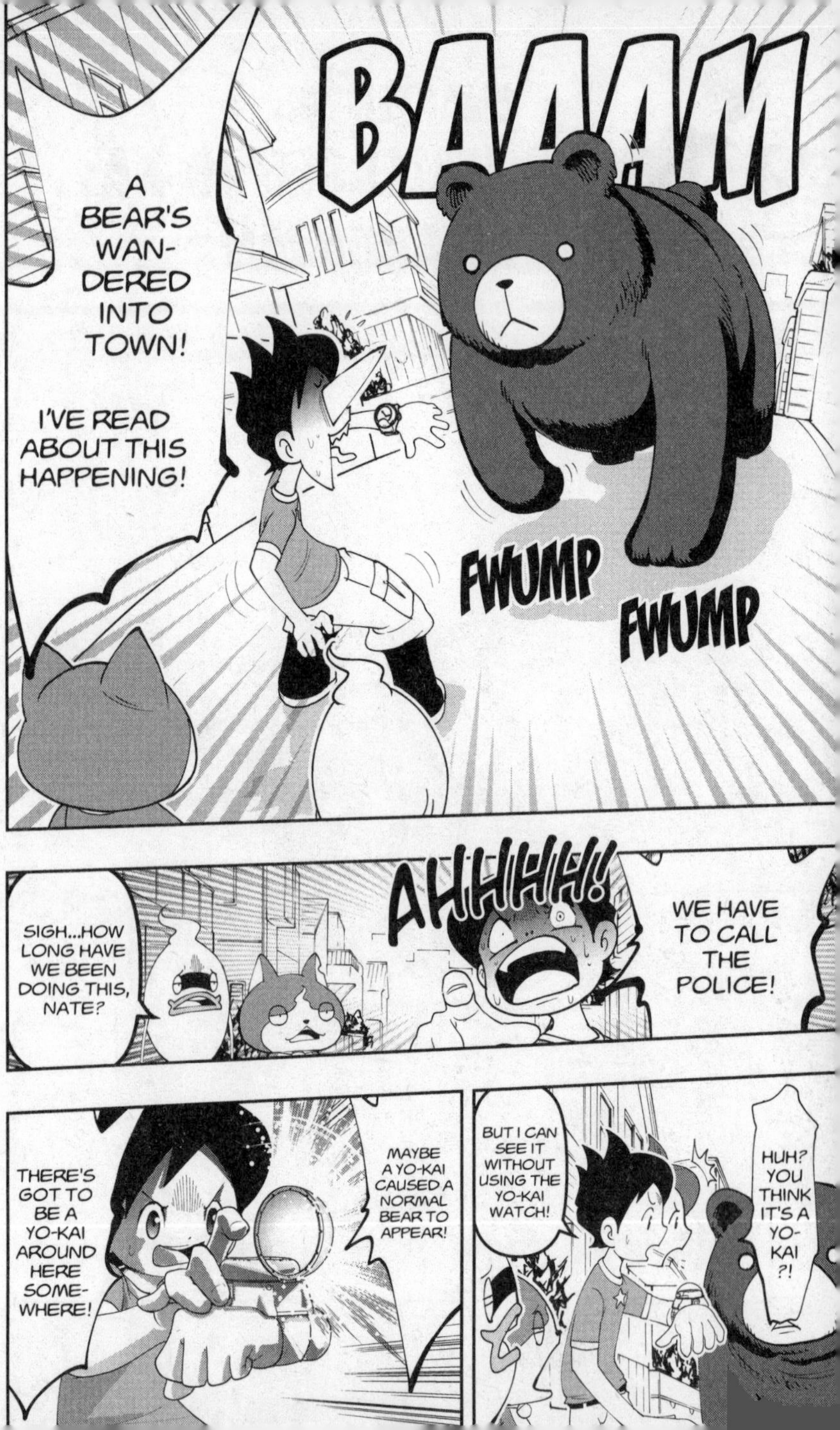
BAAAM
A BEAR'S WANDERED INTO TOWN!
I'VE READ ABOUT THIS HAPPENING!
FWUMP
FWUMP
AHHHH!
WE HAVE TO CALL THE POLICE!
SIGH...HOW LONG HAVE WE BEEN DOING THIS, NATE?
HUH? YOU THINK IT'S A YO-KAI?!
BUT I CAN SEE IT WITHOUT USING THE YO-KAI WATCH!
MAYBE A YO-KAI CAUSED A NORMAL BEAR TO APPEAR!
THERE'S GOT TO BE A YO-KAI AROUND HERE SOMEWHERE!

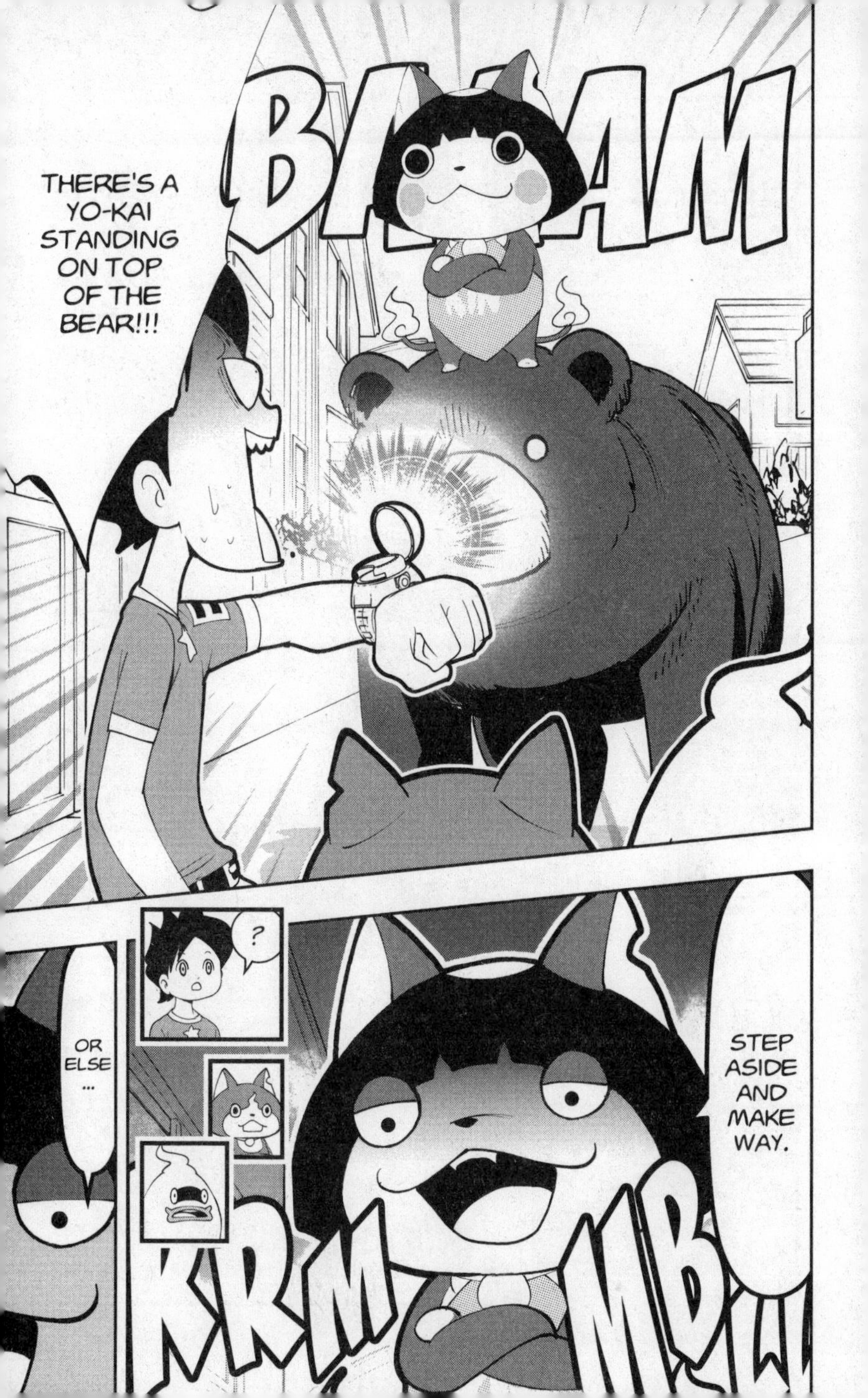
THERE'S A YO-KAI STANDING ON TOP OF THE BEAR!!!
STEP ASIDE AND MAKE WAY.
?
OR ELSE ...

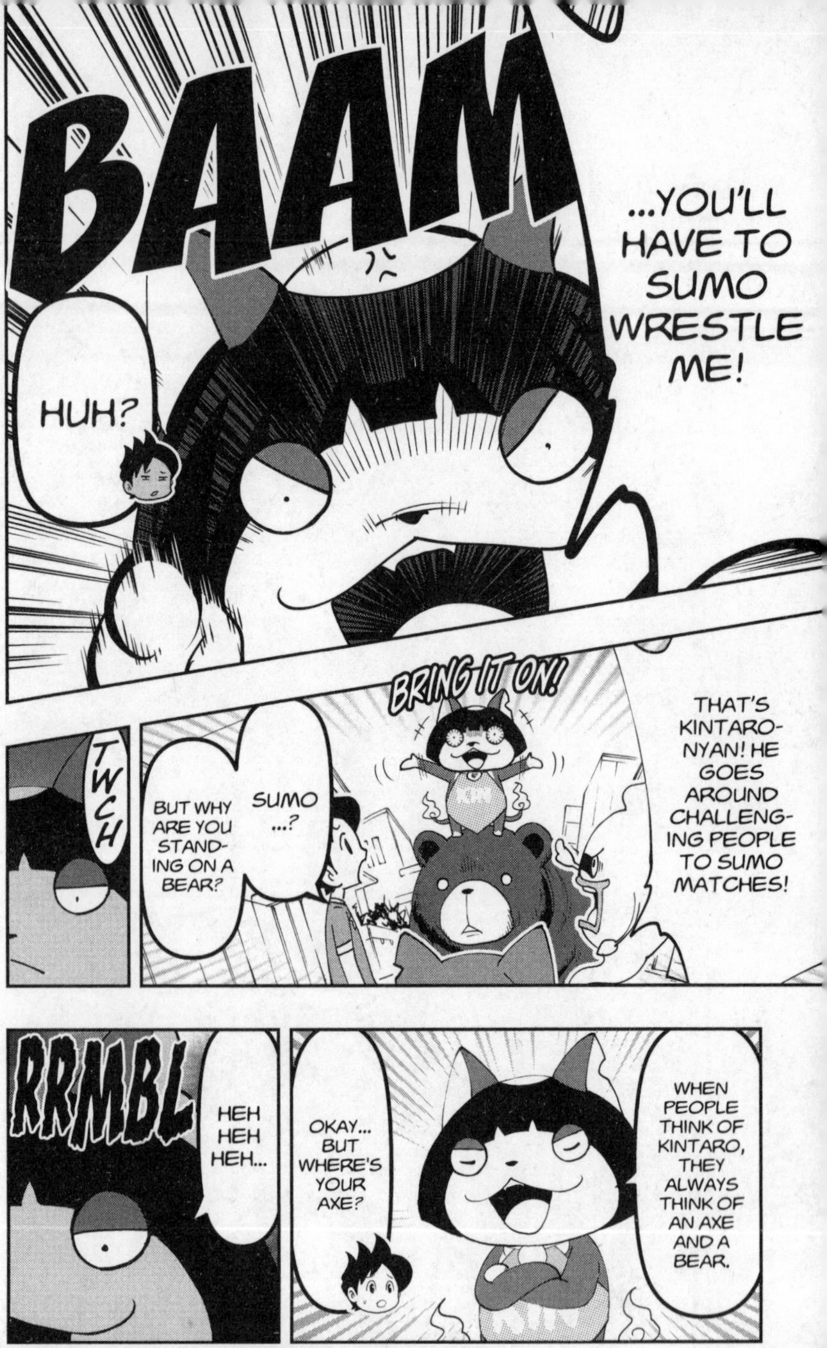
BAAM
...YOU'LL HAVE TO SUMO WRESTLE ME!
HUH?
THAT'S KINTARO-NYAN! HE GOES AROUND CHALLENG-ING PEOPLE TO SUMO MATCHES!
BRING IT ON!
SUMO ...?
BUT WHY ARE YOU STAND-ING ON A BEAR?
TWCH
WHEN PEOPLE THINK OF KINTARO, THEY ALWAYS THINK OF AN AXE AND A BEAR.
OKAY... BUT WHERE'S YOUR AXE?
HEH HEH HEH...
RRMBL

KINTARO REFERS TO THE HERO OF A JAPANESE FOLK STORY WHO HAD A TAME BEAR. -ED.

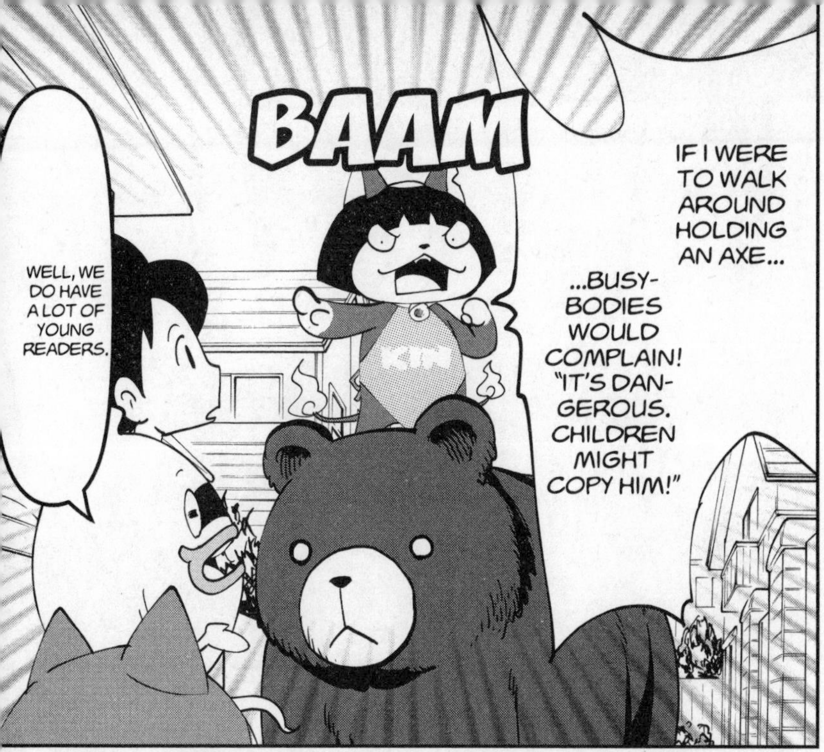
BAAM
IF I WERE TO WALK AROUND HOLDING AN AXE...
...BUSYBODIES WOULD COMPLAIN! "IT'S DANGEROUS. CHILDREN MIGHT COPY HIM!"
WELL, WE DO HAVE A LOT OF YOUNG READERS.

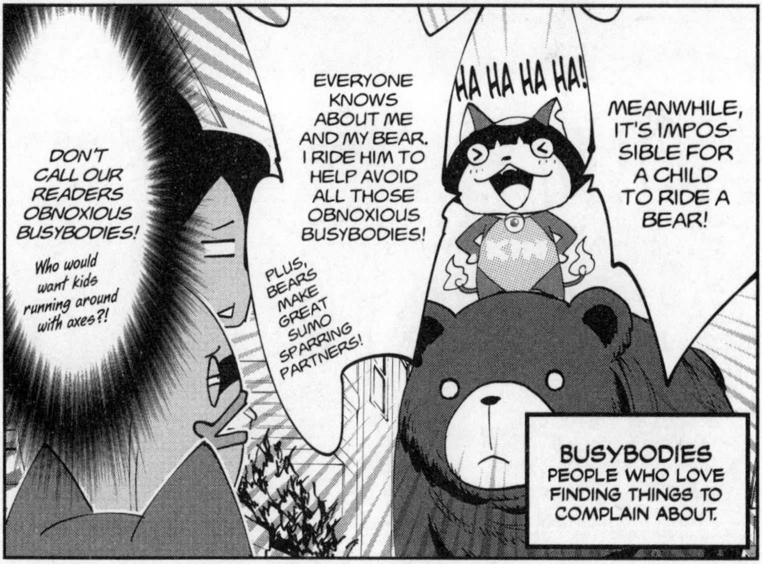
MEANWHILE, IT'S IMPOSSIBLE FOR A CHILD TO RIDE A BEAR!
HA HA HA HA!
EVERYONE KNOWS ABOUT ME AND MY BEAR. I RIDE HIM TO HELP AVOID ALL THOSE OBNOXIOUS BUSYBODIES!
PLUS, BEARS MAKE GREAT SUMO SPARRING PARTNERS!
DON'T CALL OUR READERS OBNOXIOUS BUSYBODIES!
Who would want kids running around with axes?!
BUSYBODIES
PEOPLE WHO LOVE FINDING THINGS TO COMPLAIN ABOUT.

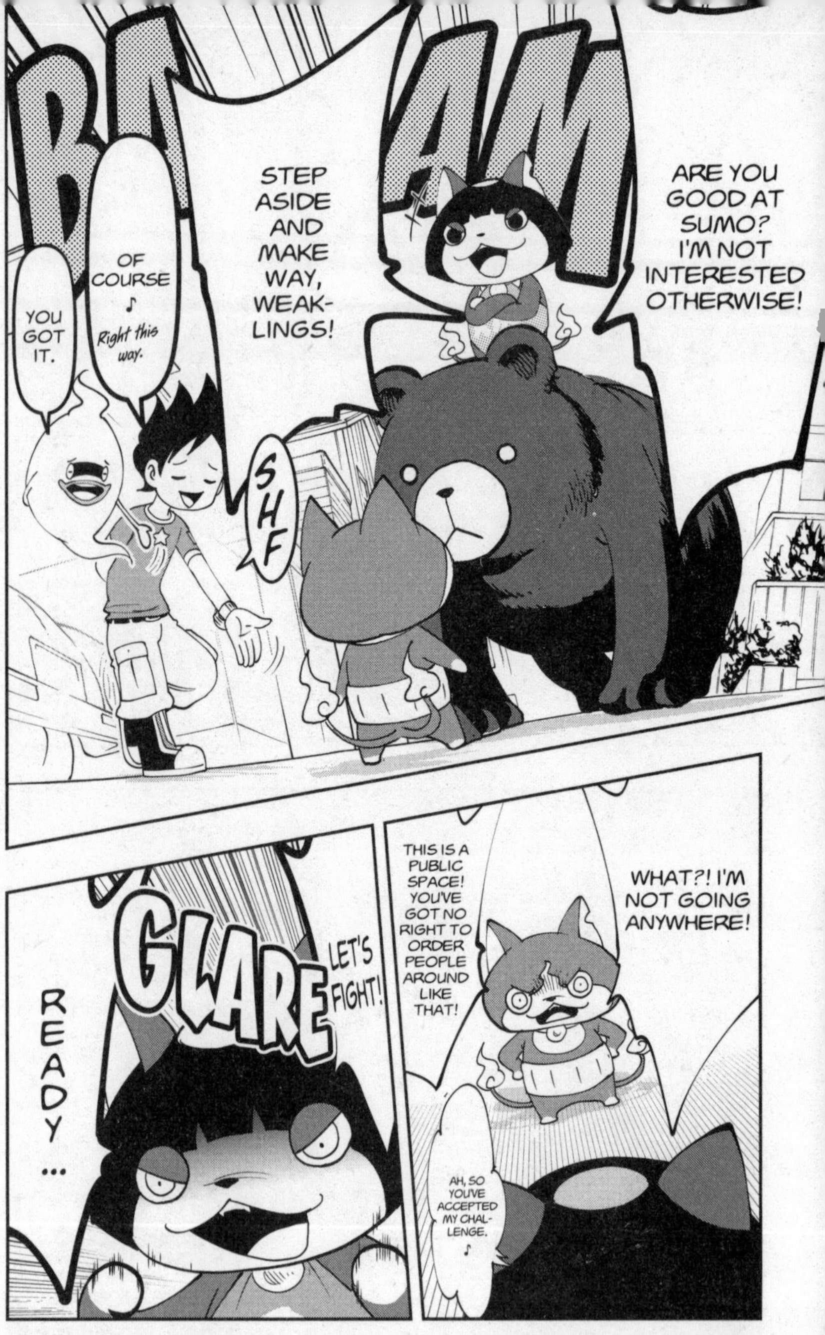
ARE YOU GOOD AT SUMO? I'M NOT INTERESTED OTHERWISE!
BAM
STEP ASIDE AND MAKE WAY, WEAK-LINGS!
OF COURSE ♪ Right this way.
YOU GOT IT.
SHF
WHAT?! I'M NOT GOING ANYWHERE!
THIS IS A PUBLIC SPACE! YOU'VE GOT NO RIGHT TO ORDER PEOPLE AROUND LIKE THAT!
AH, SO YOU'VE ACCEPTED MY CHAL-LENGE. ♪
LET'S FIGHT!
GLARE
READY...

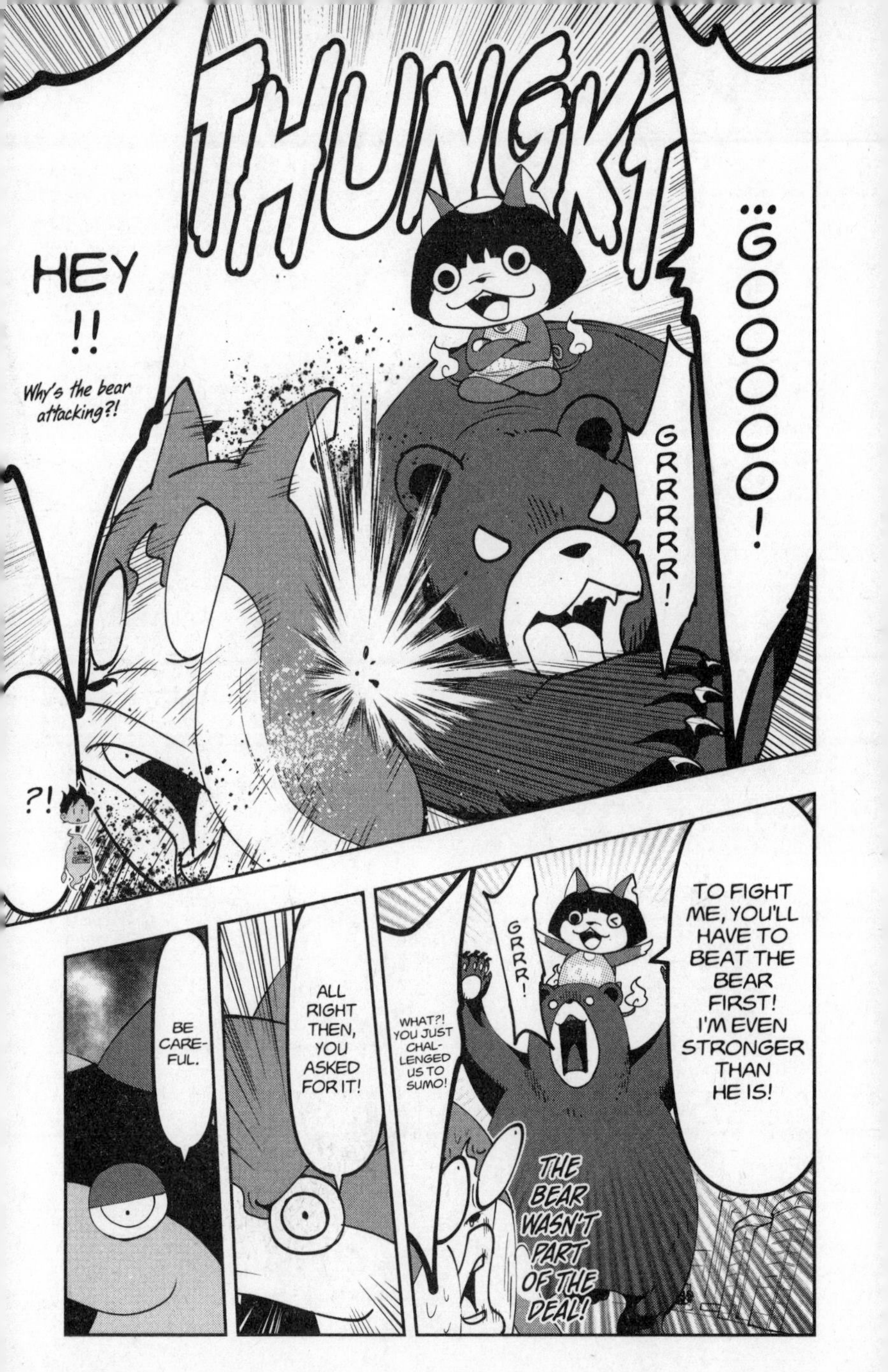
THUNK!
...GOOOOOO!
GRRRRR!
HEY!!
Why's the bear attacking?!
?!
TO FIGHT ME, YOU'LL HAVE TO BEAT THE BEAR FIRST! I'M EVEN STRONGER THAN HE IS!
GRRR!
WHAT?! YOU JUST CHALLENGED US TO SUMO!
THE BEAR WASN'T PART OF THE DEAL!
ALL RIGHT THEN, YOU ASKED FOR IT!
BE CAREFUL.

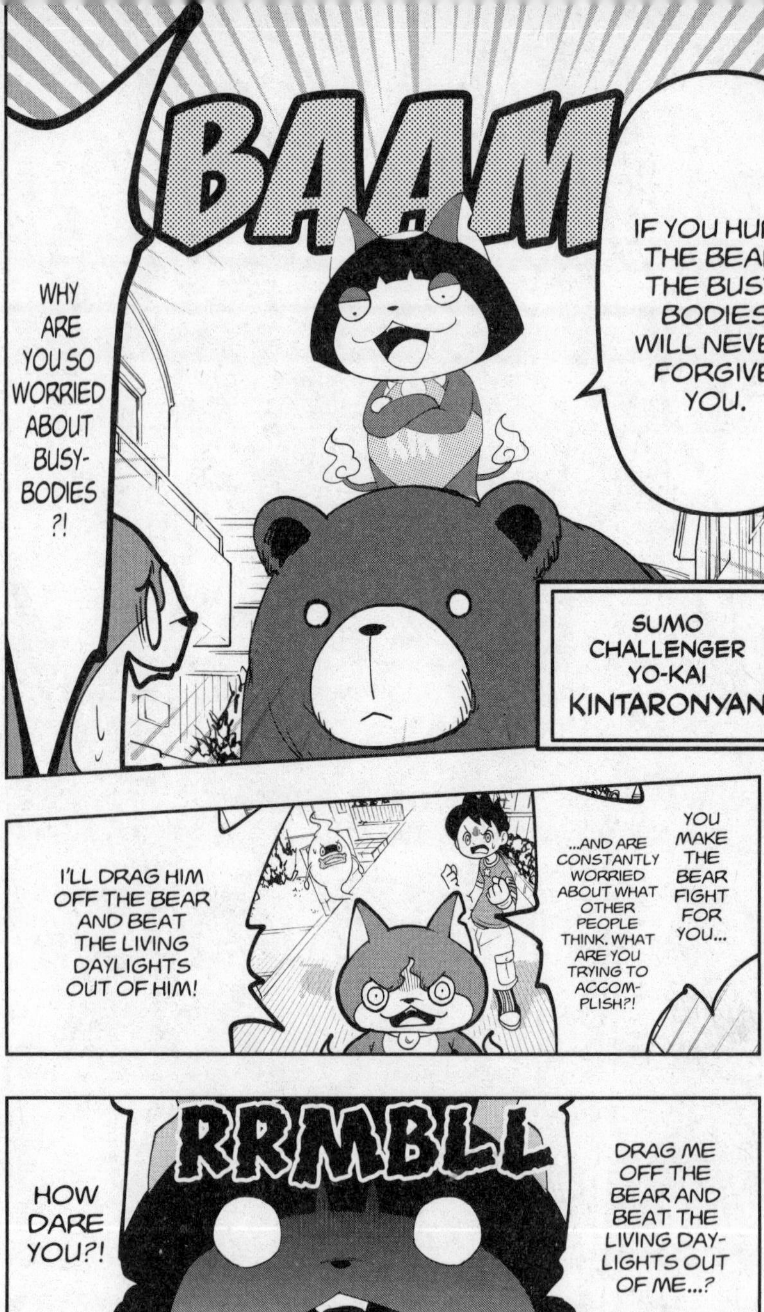

IF YOU HURT THE BEAR, THE BUSY-BODIES WILL NEVER FORGIVE YOU.
BAAM
WHY ARE YOU SO WORRIED ABOUT BUSY-BODIES?!
SUMO CHALLENGER YO-KAI KINTARONYAN
YOU MAKE THE BEAR FIGHT FOR YOU...
...AND ARE CONSTANTLY WORRIED ABOUT WHAT OTHER PEOPLE THINK. WHAT ARE YOU TRYING TO ACCOM-PLISH?!
I'LL DRAG HIM OFF THE BEAR AND BEAT THE LIVING DAYLIGHTS OUT OF HIM!
DRAG ME OFF THE BEAR AND BEAT THE LIVING DAY-LIGHTS OUT OF ME...?
RRMBLL
HOW DARE YOU?!

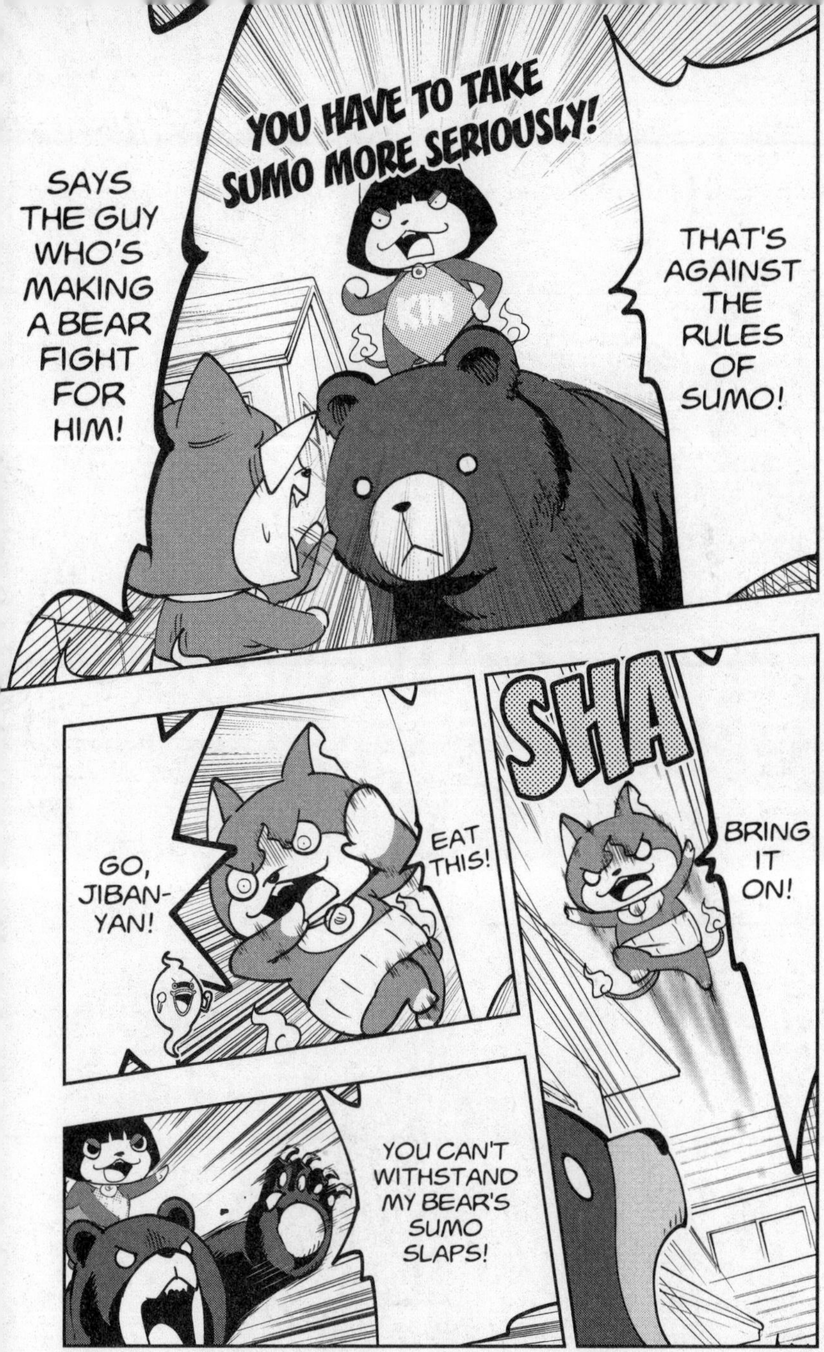
YOU HAVE TO TAKE SUMO MORE SERIOUSLY!
THAT'S AGAINST THE RULES OF SUMO!
SAYS THE GUY WHO'S MAKING A BEAR FIGHT FOR HIM!
SHA
BRING IT ON!
EAT THIS!
GO, JIBAN-YAN!
YOU CAN'T WITHSTAND MY BEAR'S SUMO SLAPS!

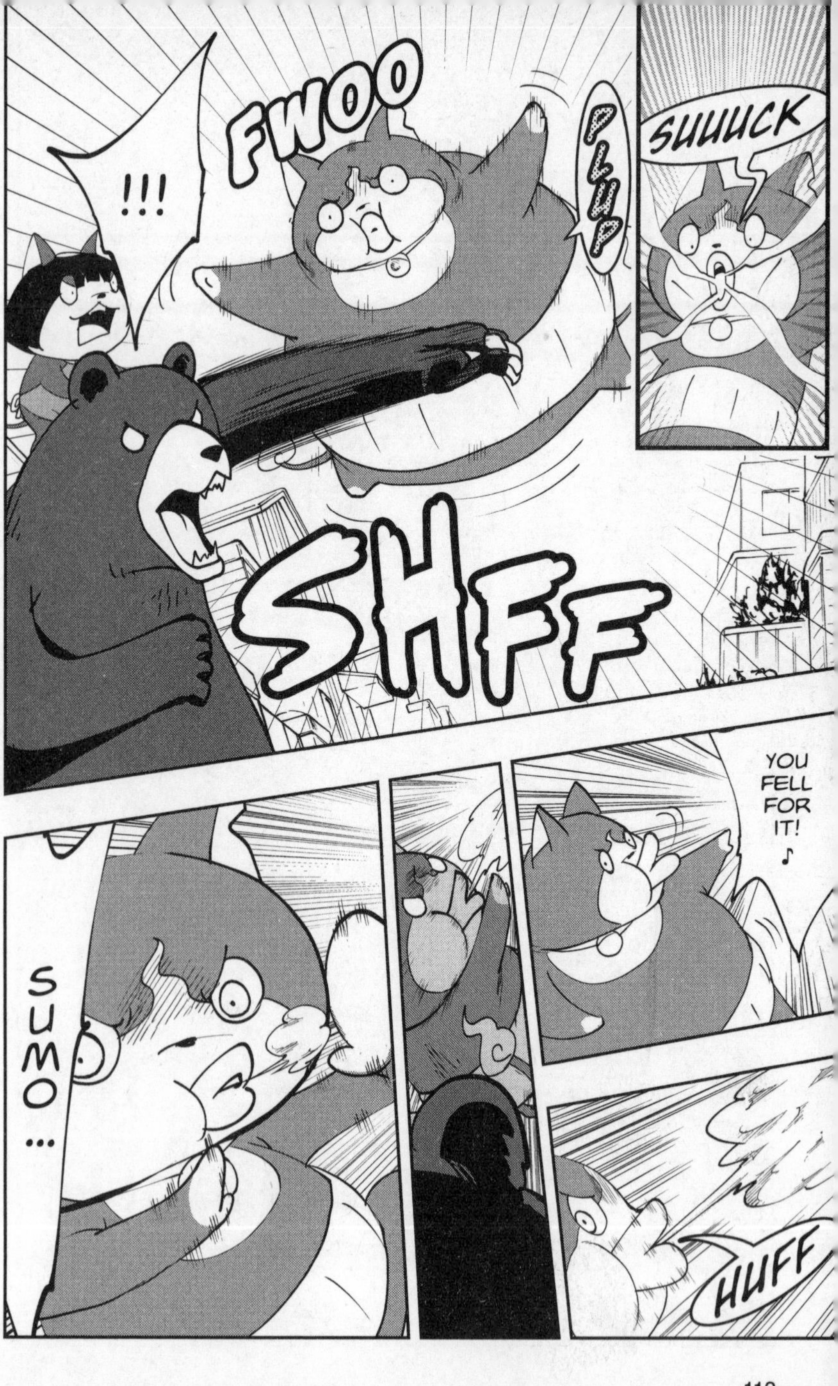
SUUUCK
PLUP
FWOO
!!!
SHFF
YOU FELL FOR IT! ♪
HUFF
SUMO...

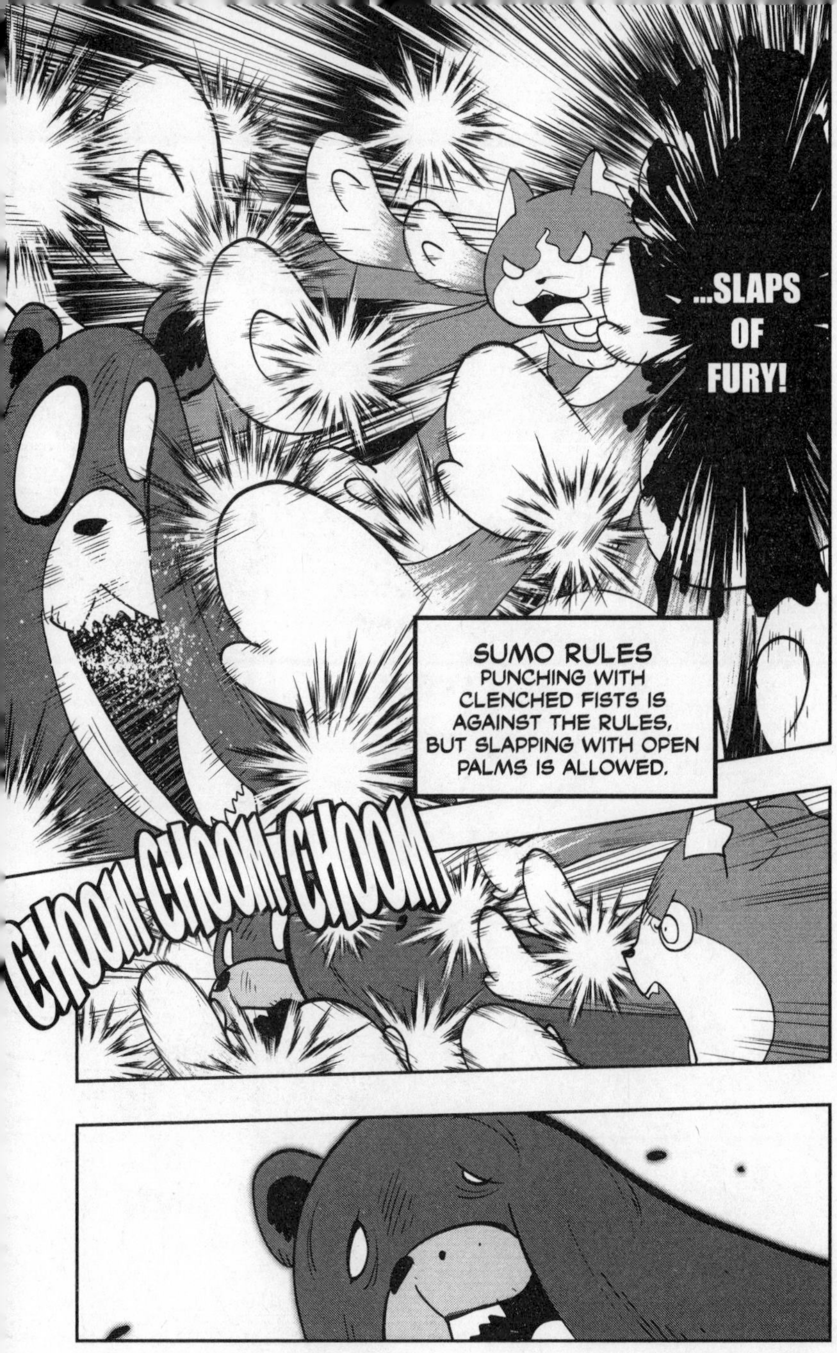
...SLAPS OF FURY!
SUMO RULES
PUNCHING WITH CLENCHED FISTS IS AGAINST THE RULES, BUT SLAPPING WITH OPEN PALMS IS ALLOWED.
CHOOM CHOOM CHOOM

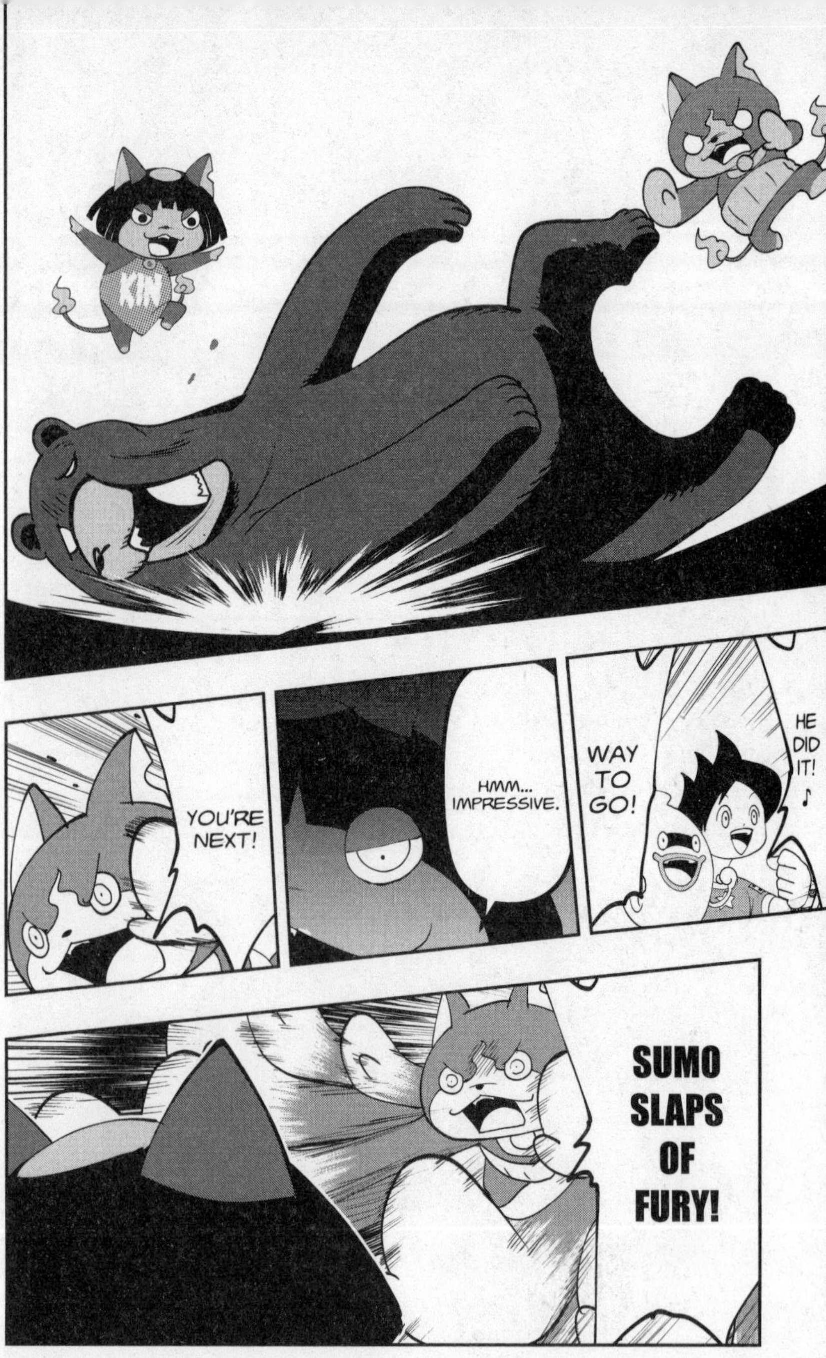
KIN
HE DID IT! ♪
WAY TO GO!
HMM... IMPRESSIVE.
YOU'RE NEXT!
SUMO SLAPS OF FURY!

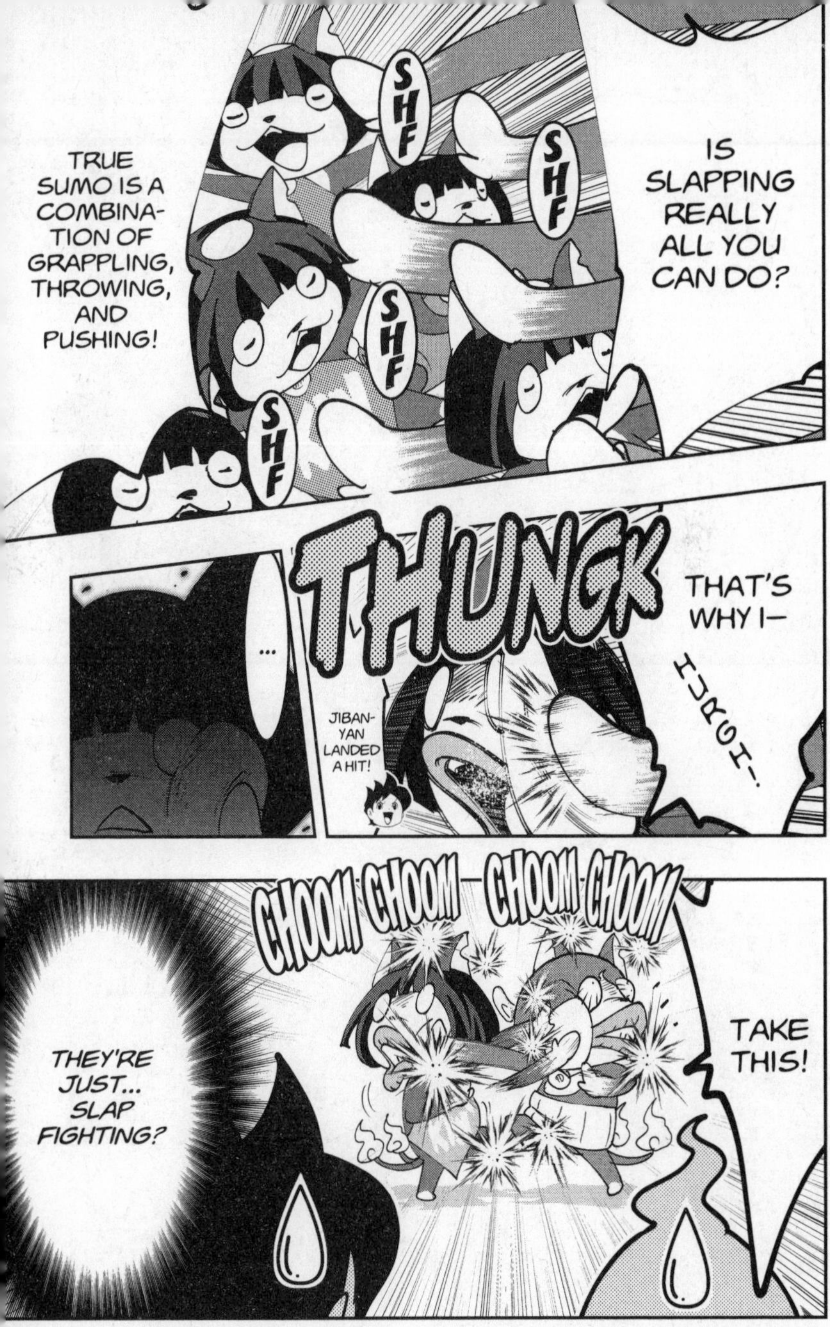
IS SLAPPING REALLY ALL YOU CAN DO?
SHF
SHF
SHF
SHF
TRUE SUMO IS A COMBINATION OF GRAPPLING, THROWING, AND PUSHING!
THUNCK
THAT'S WHY I—
JIBAN-YAN LANDED A HIT!
...
CHOOM CHOOM CHOOM CHOOM
TAKE THIS!
THEY'RE JUST... SLAP FIGHTING?

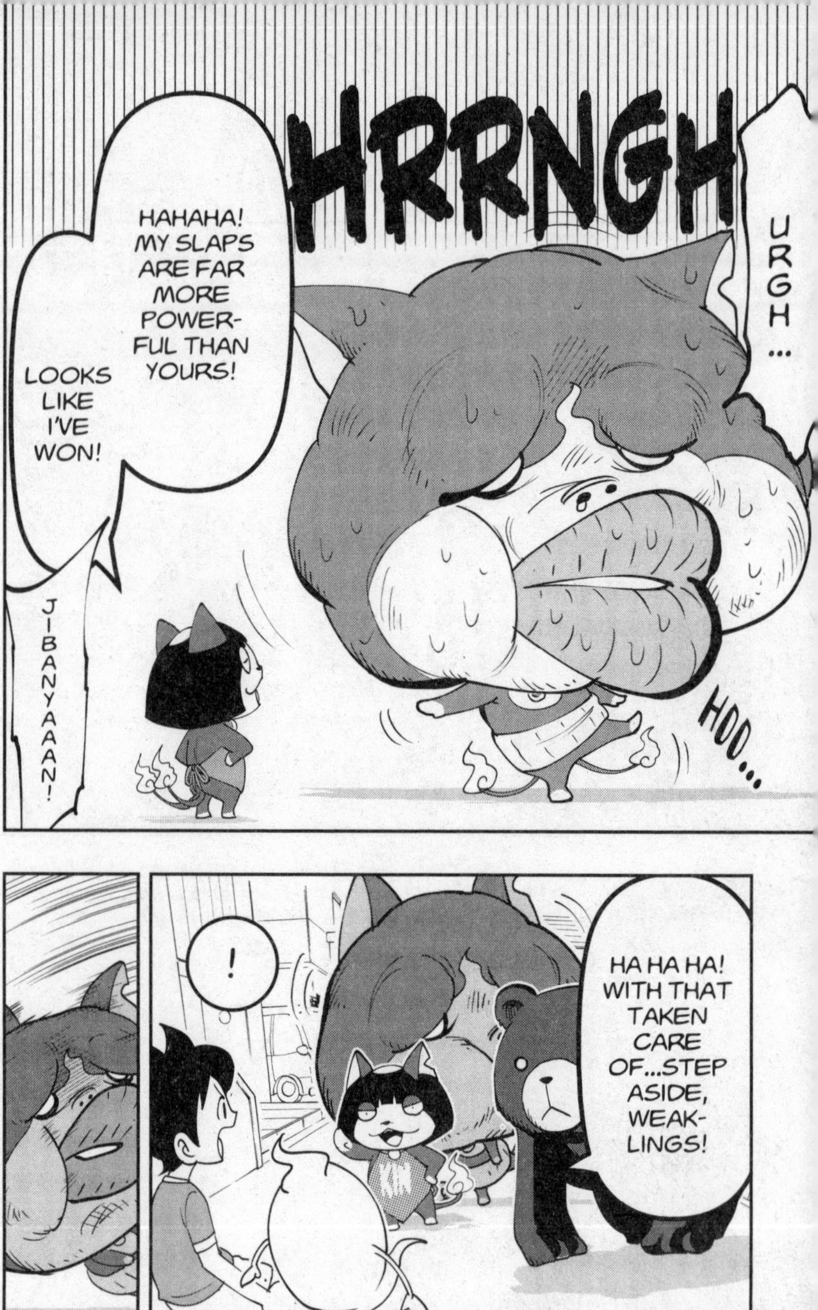
HRRNGH
URGH...
HAHAHA! MY SLAPS ARE FAR MORE POWER-FUL THAN YOURS! LOOKS LIKE I'VE WON!
HOO...
JIBANYAAAAN!
HA HA HA! WITH THAT TAKEN CARE OF...STEP ASIDE, WEAK-LINGS!
!

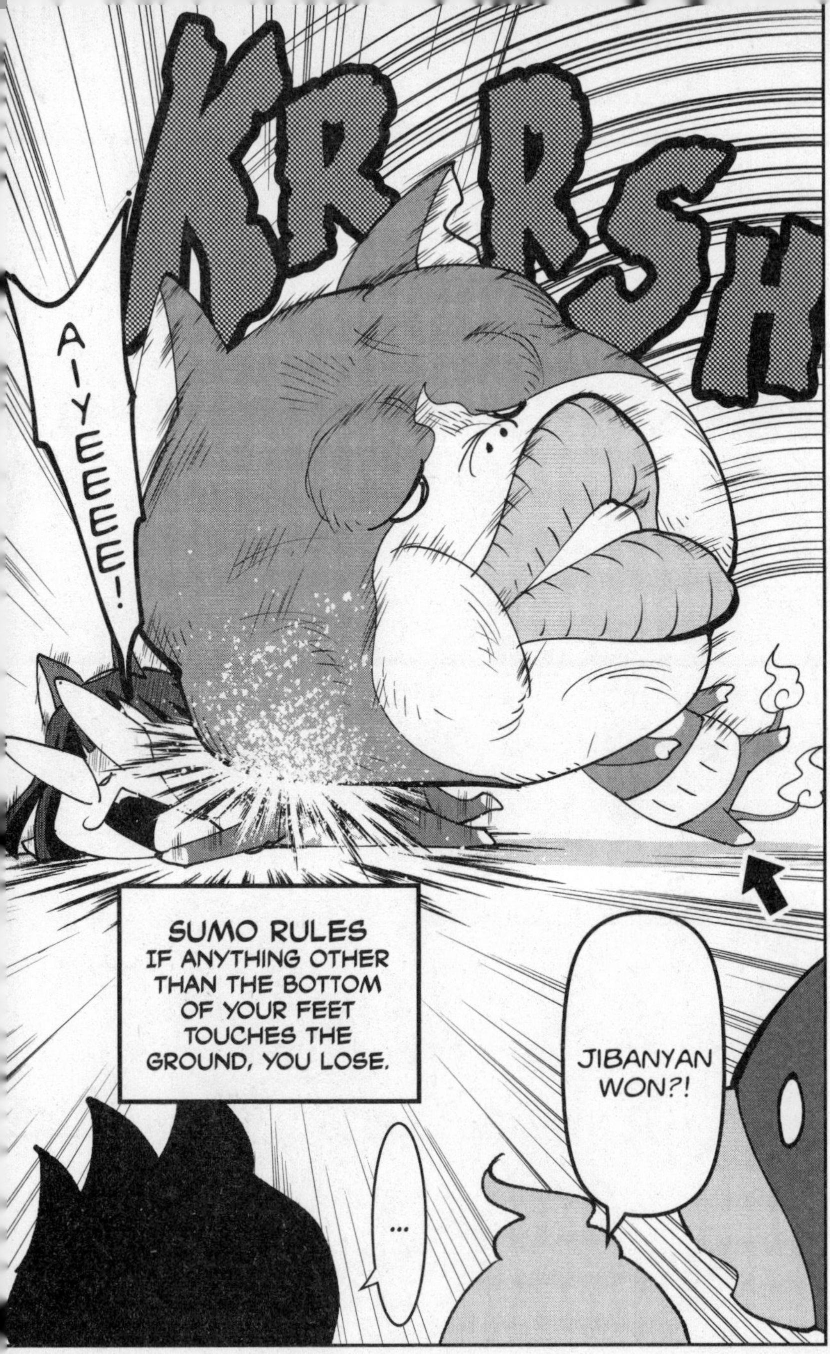
KRRSH
AIYEEEEE!
SUMO RULES IF ANYTHING OTHER THAN THE BOTTOM OF YOUR FEET TOUCHES THE GROUND, YOU LOSE.
JIBANYAN WON?!
...

CHAPTER 244
UNDERSEA PALACE RETURNEE YO-KAI ODYSSEYNYAN

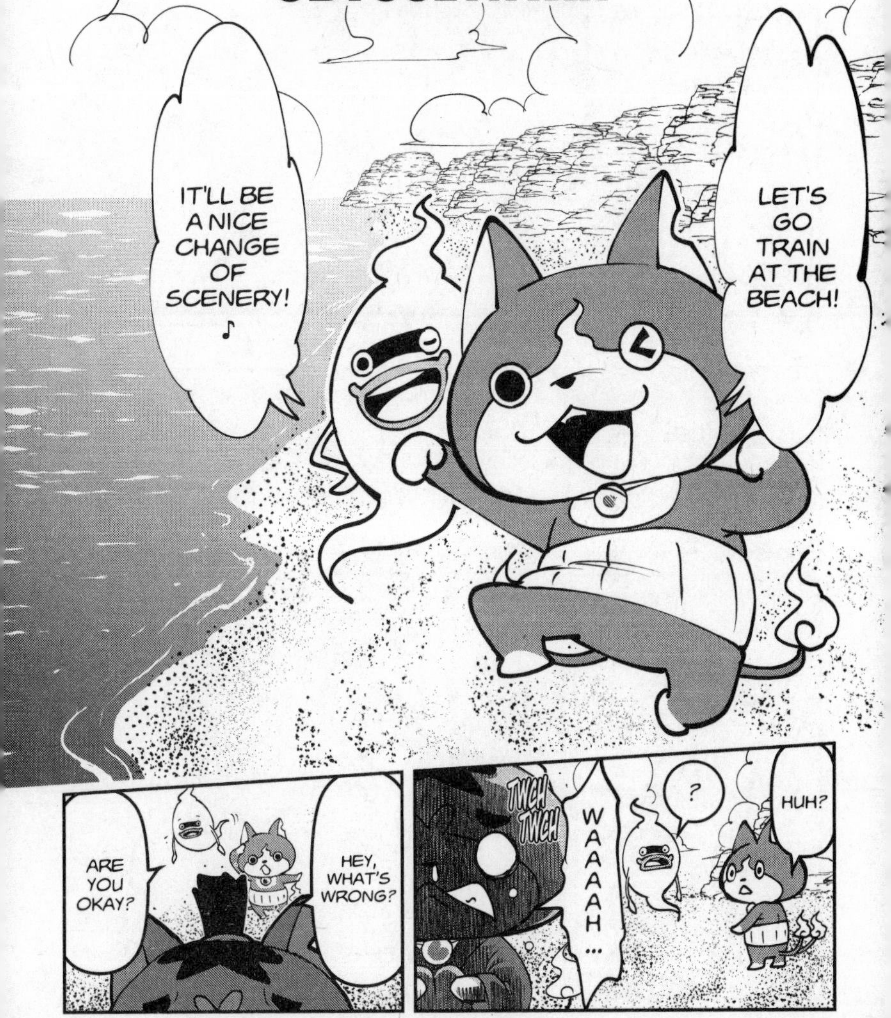
LET'S GO TRAIN AT THE BEACH!
IT'LL BE A NICE CHANGE OF SCENERY! ♪
HUH?
?
WAAAAAH...
TWCH TWCH
HEY, WHAT'S WRONG?
ARE YOU OKAY?

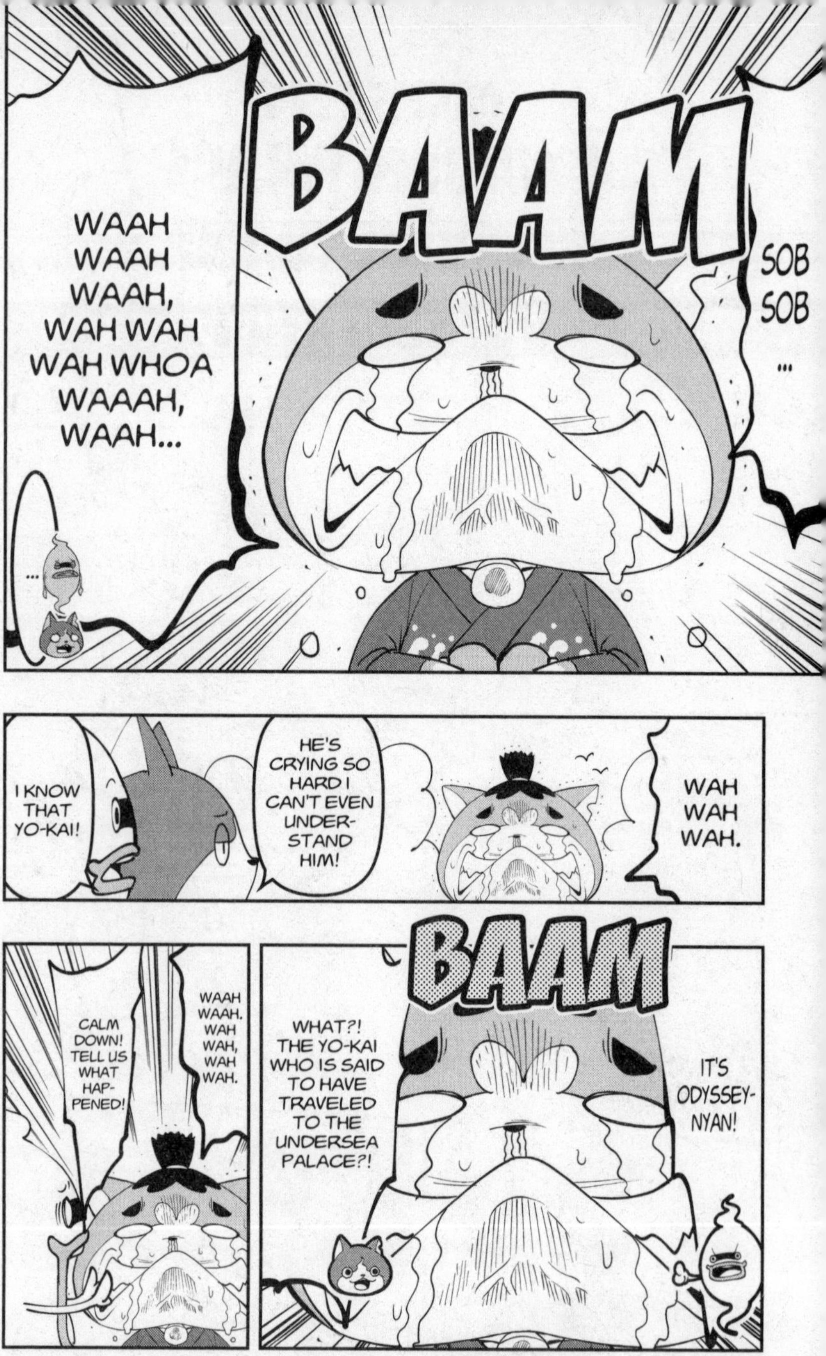
BAAM
SOB SOB ...
WAAH WAAH WAAH, WAH WAH WAH WHOA WAAAH, WAAH...
...
WAH WAH WAH.
HE'S CRYING SO HARD I CAN'T EVEN UNDER-STAND HIM!
I KNOW THAT YO-KAI!
BAAM
IT'S ODYSSEY-NYAN!
WHAT?! THE YO-KAI WHO IS SAID TO HAVE TRAVELED TO THE UNDERSEA PALACE?!
WAAH WAAH. WAH WAH, WAH WAH.
CALM DOWN! TELL US WHAT HAP-PENED!

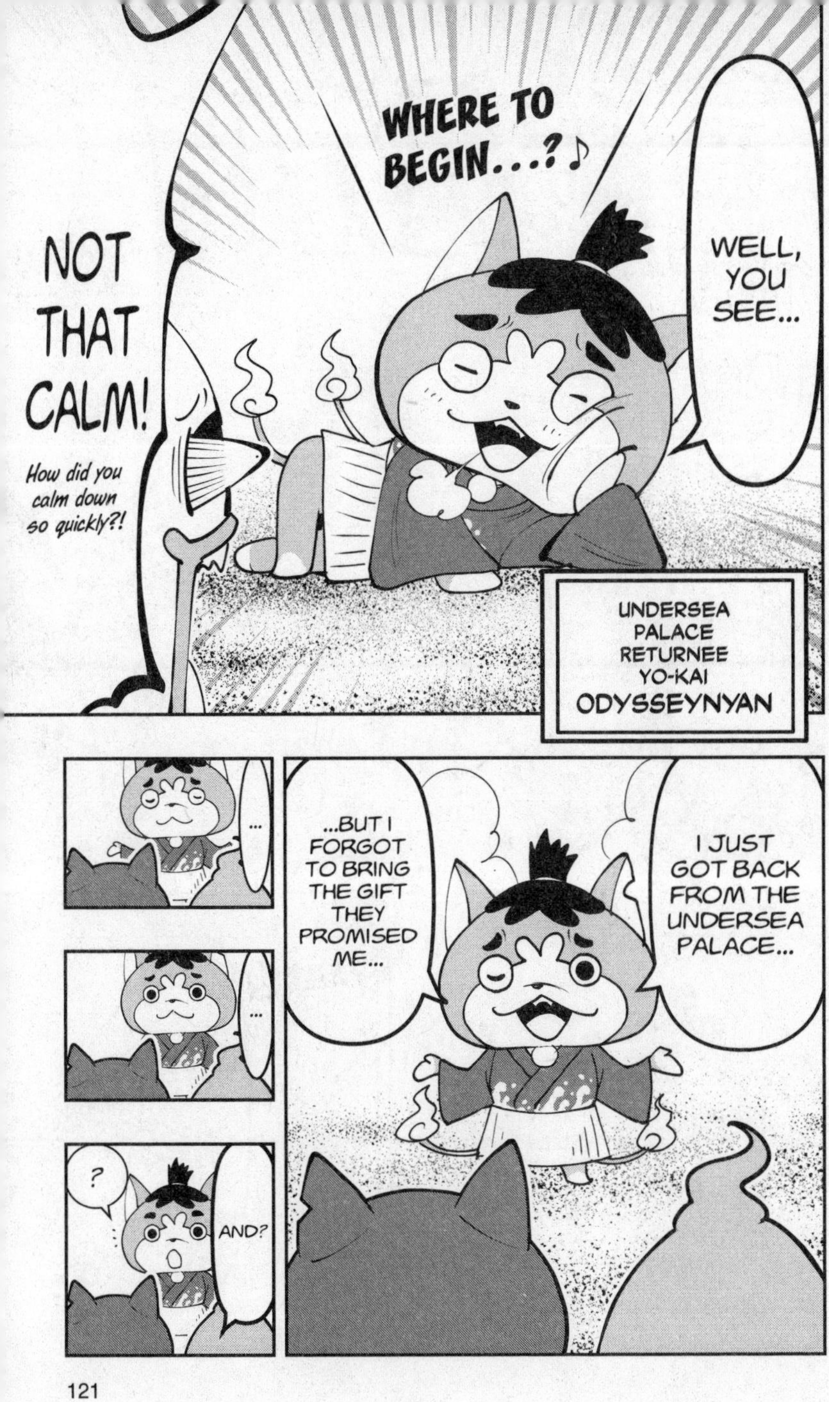
WELL, YOU SEE...
WHERE TO BEGIN...?♪
NOT THAT CALM!
How did you calm down so quickly?!
UNDERSEA PALACE RETURNEE YO-KAI
ODYSSEYNYAN
I JUST GOT BACK FROM THE UNDERSEA PALACE...
...BUT I FORGOT TO BRING THE GIFT THEY PROMISED ME...
...
...
AND?
?

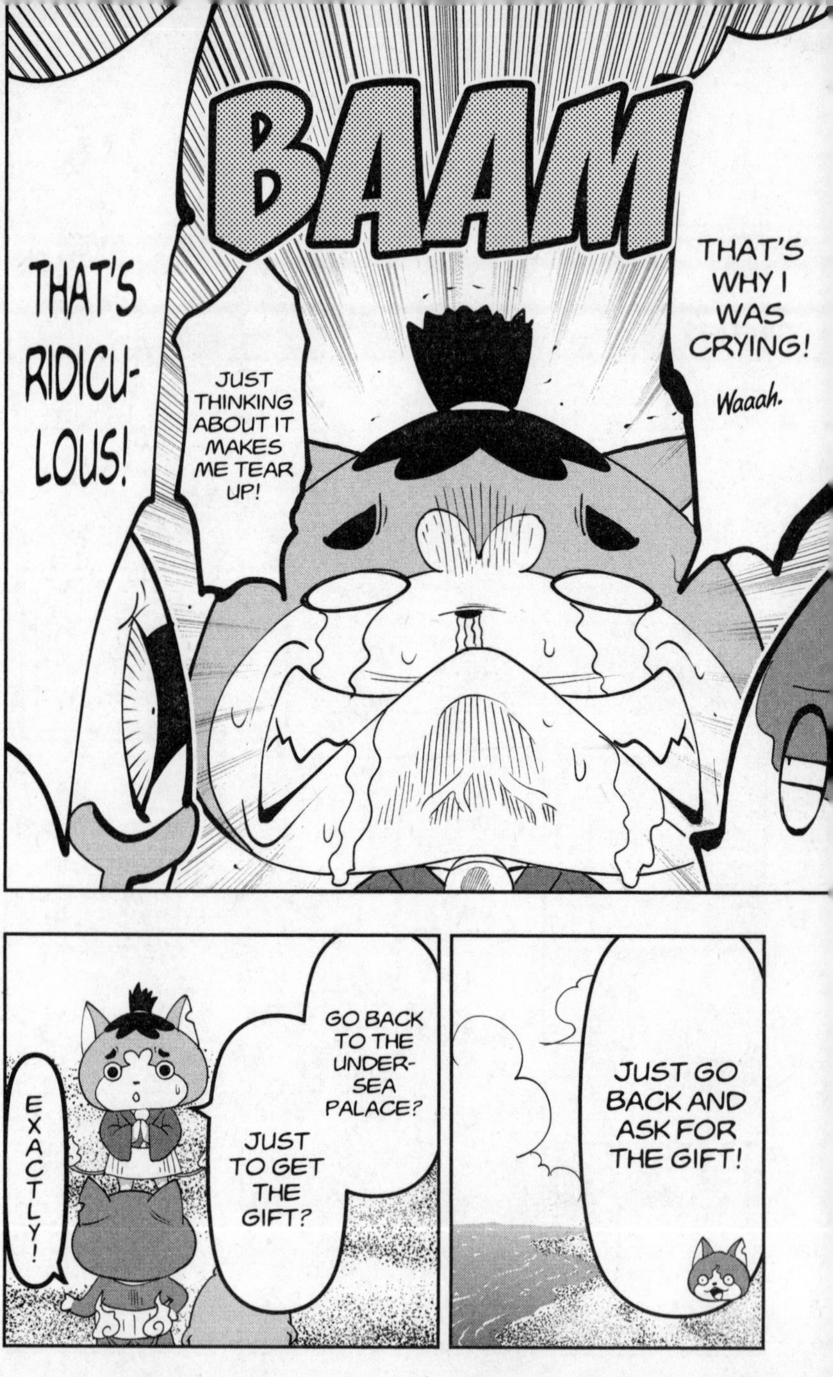
BAAM
THAT'S WHY I WAS CRYING!
Waaah.
JUST THINKING ABOUT IT MAKES ME TEAR UP!
THAT'S RIDICU-LOUS!
JUST GO BACK AND ASK FOR THE GIFT!
GO BACK TO THE UNDER-SEA PALACE?
JUST TO GET THE GIFT?
EXACTLY!

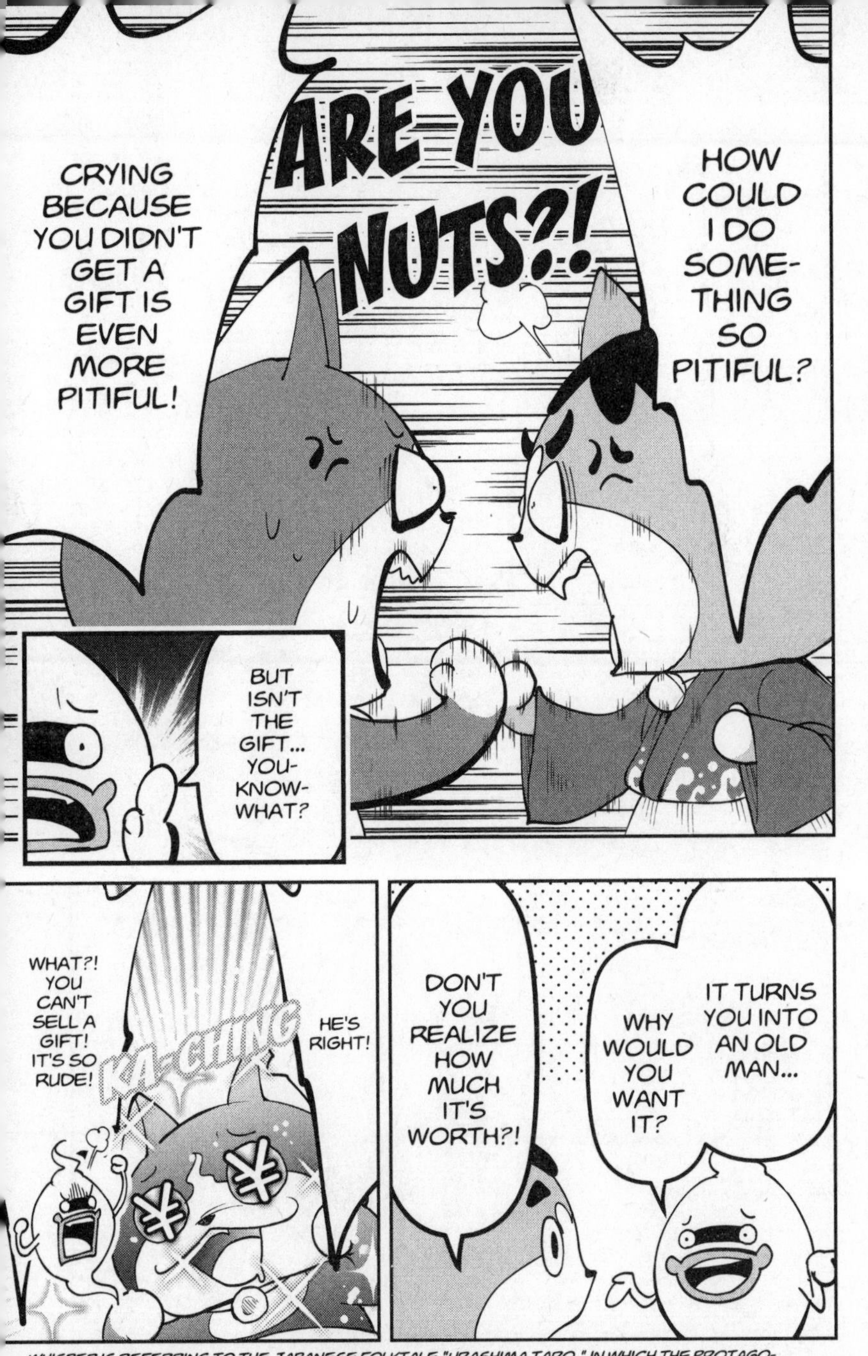
HOW COULD I DO SOMETHING SO PITIFUL?
ARE YOU NUTS?!
CRYING BECAUSE YOU DIDN'T GET A GIFT IS EVEN MORE PITIFUL!
BUT ISN'T THE GIFT... YOU-KNOW-WHAT?
IT TURNS YOU INTO AN OLD MAN...
WHY WOULD YOU WANT IT?
DON'T YOU REALIZE HOW MUCH IT'S WORTH?!
HE'S RIGHT!
KA-CHING
WHAT?! YOU CAN'T SELL A GIFT! IT'S SO RUDE!

WHISPER IS REFERRING TO THE JAPANESE FOLKTALE "URASHIMA TARO," IN WHICH THE PROTAGONIST RIDES A TURTLE TO AN UNDERSEA PALACE AND HIS OLD AGE IS KEPT IN A BOX GIVEN TO HIM BY THE PRINCESS OTOHIME. —ED.

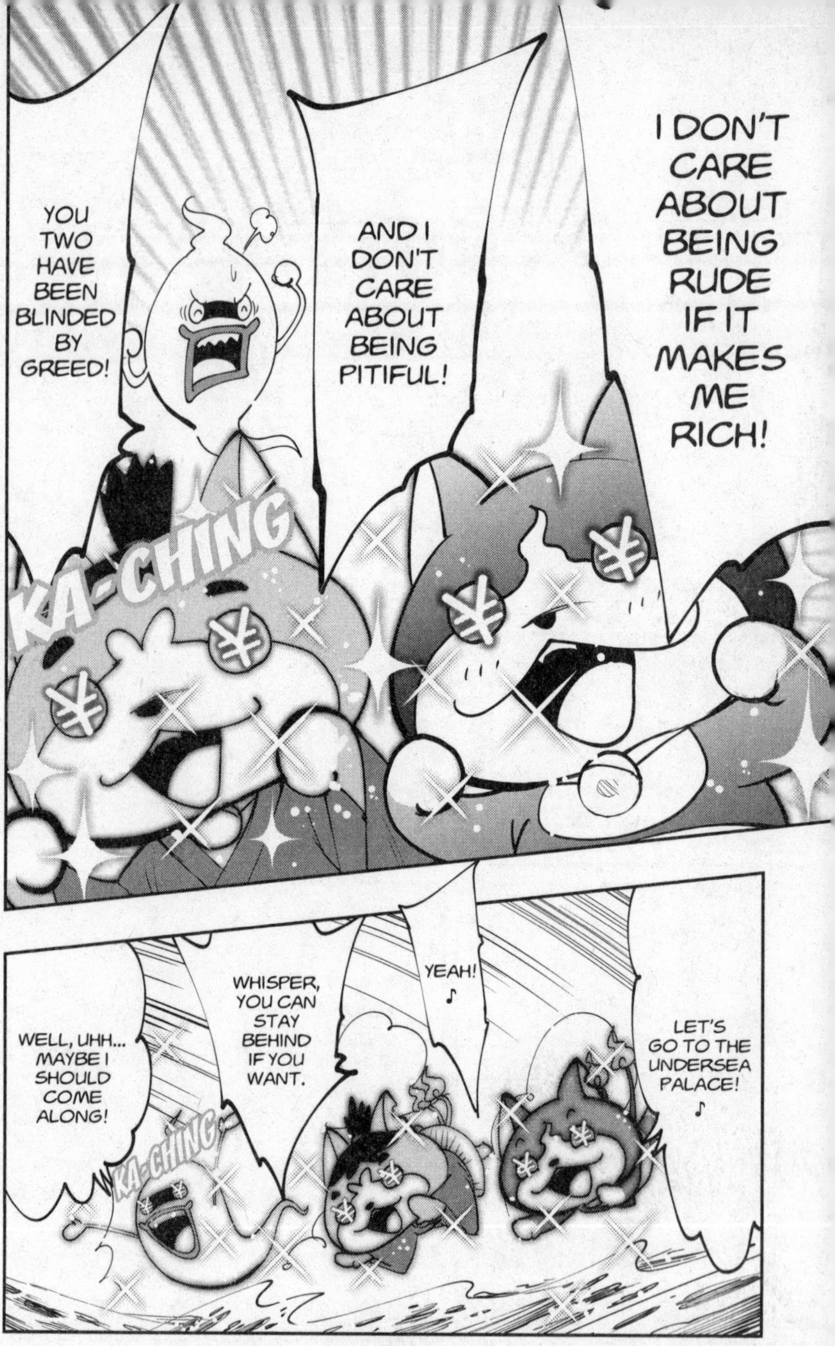
I DON'T CARE ABOUT BEING RUDE IF IT MAKES ME RICH!
AND I DON'T CARE ABOUT BEING PITIFUL!
YOU TWO HAVE BEEN BLINDED BY GREED!
KA-CHING
LET'S GO TO THE UNDERSEA PALACE! ♪
YEAH! ♪
WHISPER, YOU CAN STAY BEHIND IF YOU WANT.
WELL, UHH... MAYBE I SHOULD COME ALONG!
KA-CHING

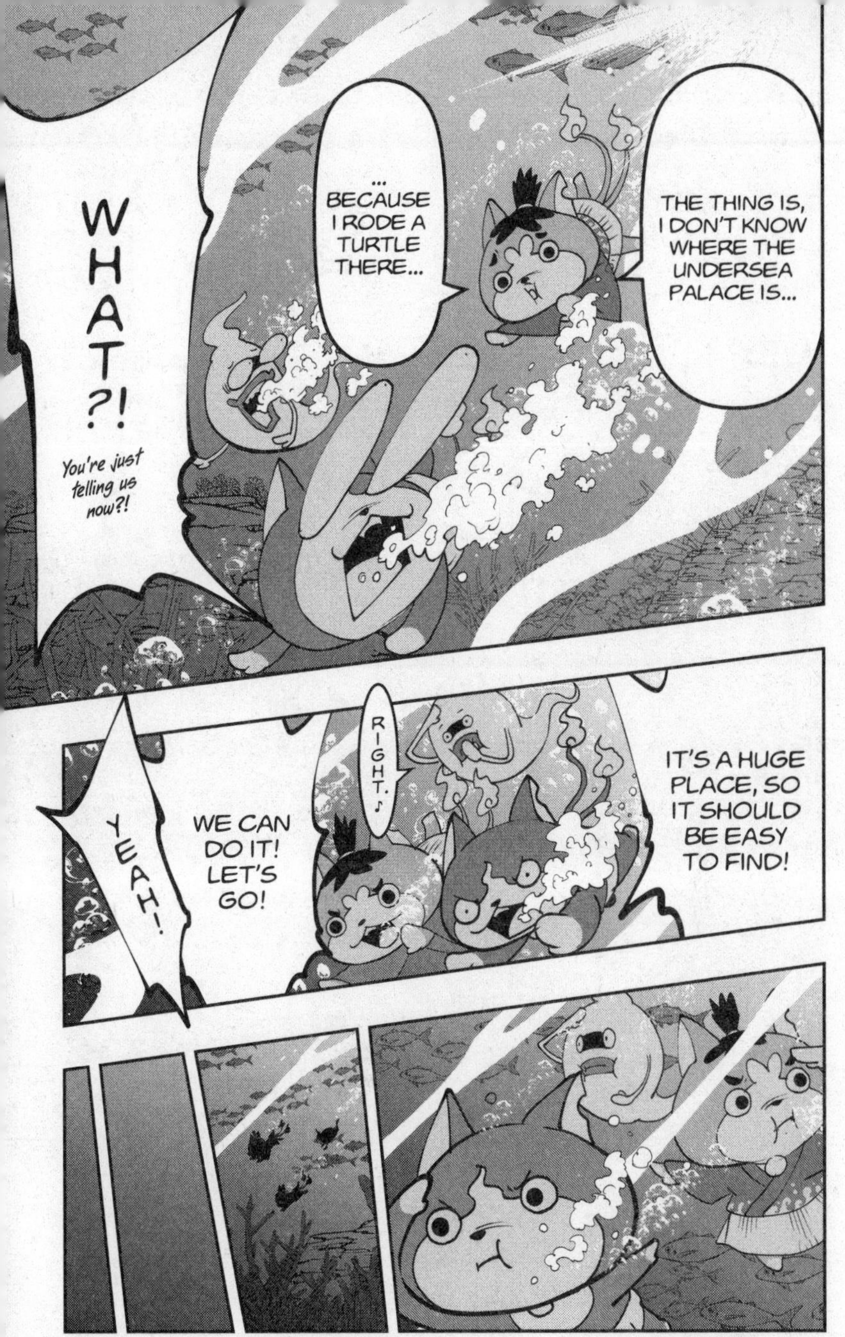
THE THING IS, I DON'T KNOW WHERE THE UNDERSEA PALACE IS...
...BECAUSE I RODE A TURTLE THERE...
WHAT?!
You're just telling us now?!
IT'S A HUGE PLACE, SO IT SHOULD BE EASY TO FIND!
RIGHT.♪
WE CAN DO IT! LET'S GO!
YEAH!

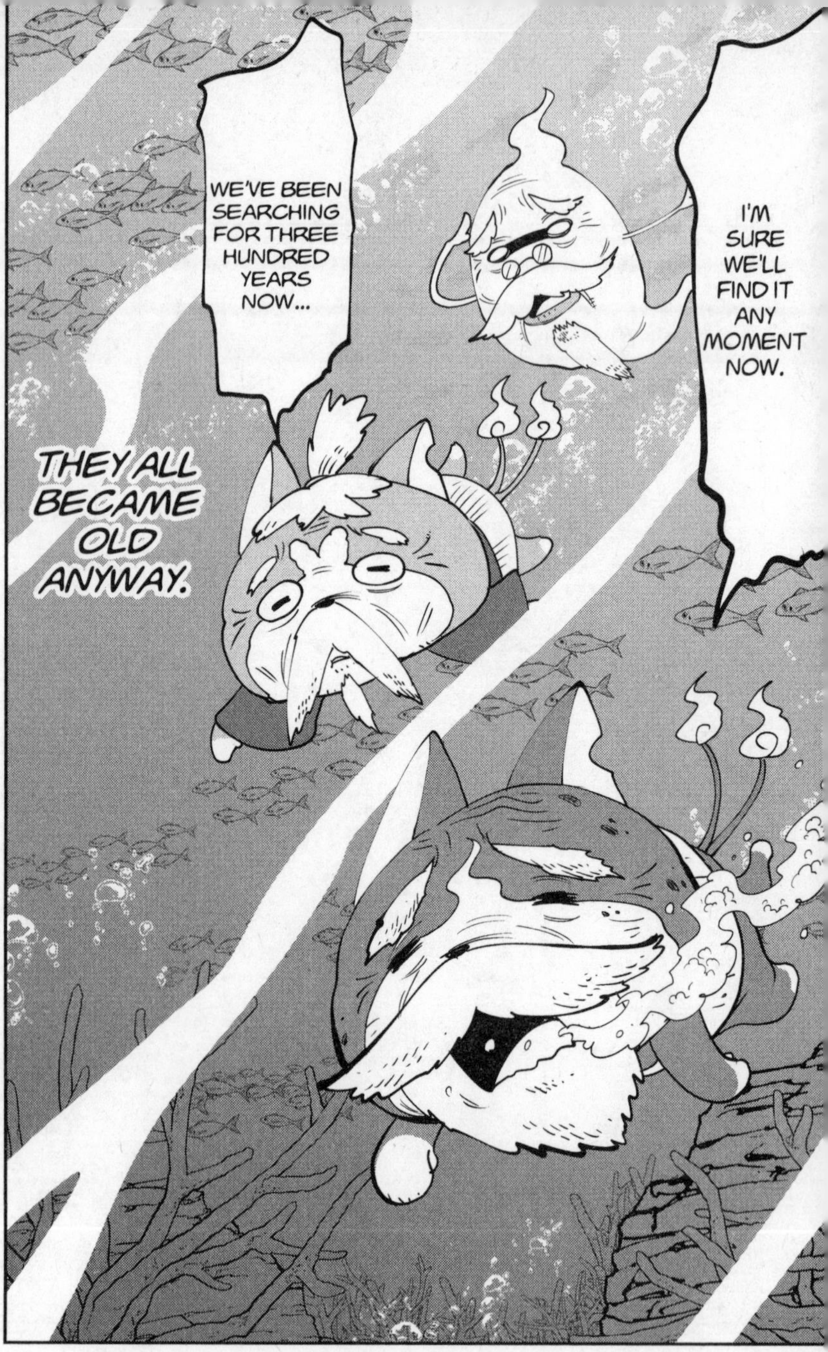
I'M SURE WE'LL FIND IT ANY MOMENT NOW.
WE'VE BEEN SEARCHING FOR THREE HUNDRED YEARS NOW...
THEY ALL BECAME OLD ANYWAY.

CHAPTER 245
DESTRUCTION YO-KAI D-STROY

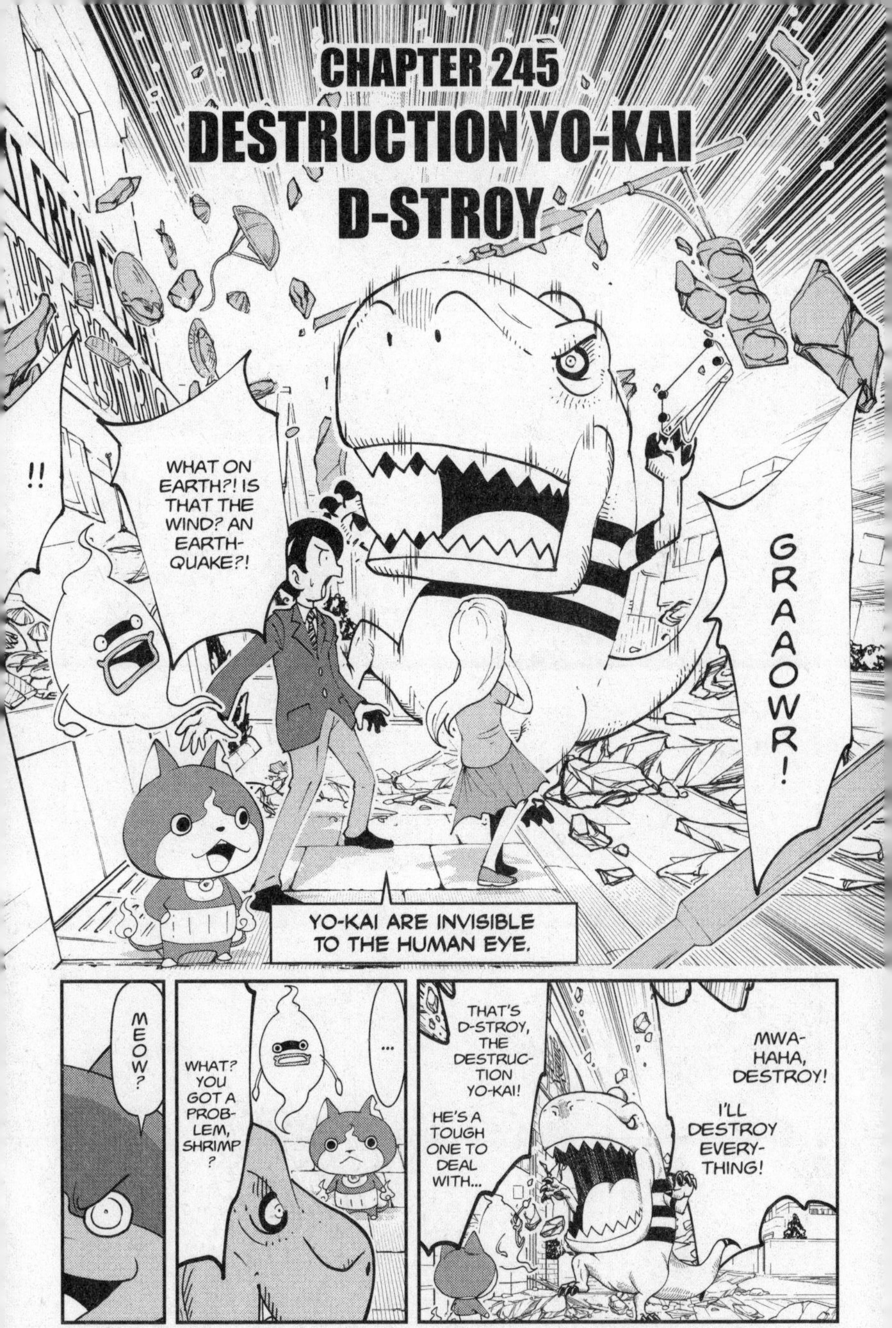
GRAAAOWR!
WHAT ON EARTH?! IS THAT THE WIND? AN EARTHQUAKE?!
!!
YO-KAI ARE INVISIBLE TO THE HUMAN EYE.
MWA-HAHA, DESTROY!
I'LL DESTROY EVERYTHING!
THAT'S D-STROY, THE DESTRUCTION YO-KAI!
HE'S A TOUGH ONE TO DEAL WITH...
...
WHAT? YOU GOT A PROBLEM, SHRIMP?
MEOW?

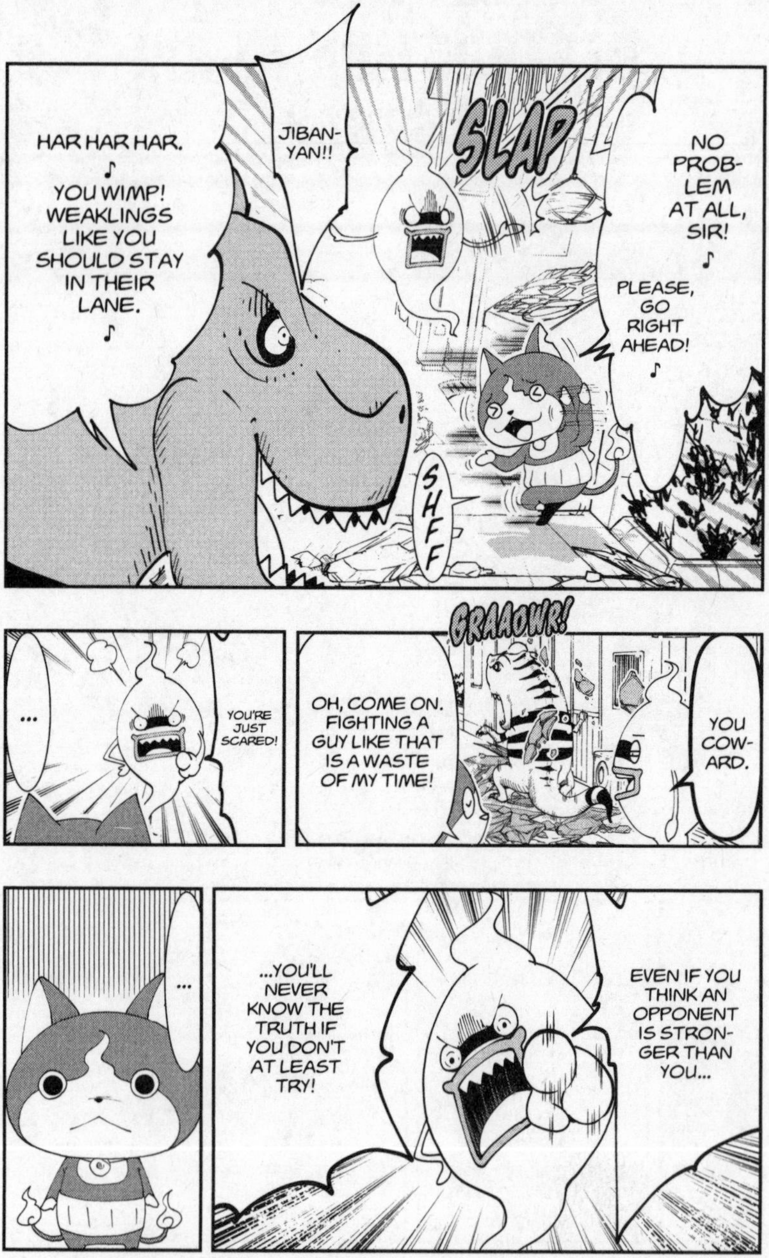
NO PROBLEM AT ALL, SIR! ♪
PLEASE, GO RIGHT AHEAD! ♪
SLAP
JIBAN-YAN!!
HAR HAR HAR. ♪ YOU WIMP! WEAKLINGS LIKE YOU SHOULD STAY IN THEIR LANE. ♪
SHFF
GRAAOWR!
YOU COWARD.
OH, COME ON. FIGHTING A GUY LIKE THAT IS A WASTE OF MY TIME!
YOU'RE JUST SCARED!
...
EVEN IF YOU THINK AN OPPONENT IS STRONGER THAN YOU...
...YOU'LL NEVER KNOW THE TRUTH IF YOU DON'T AT LEAST TRY!
...

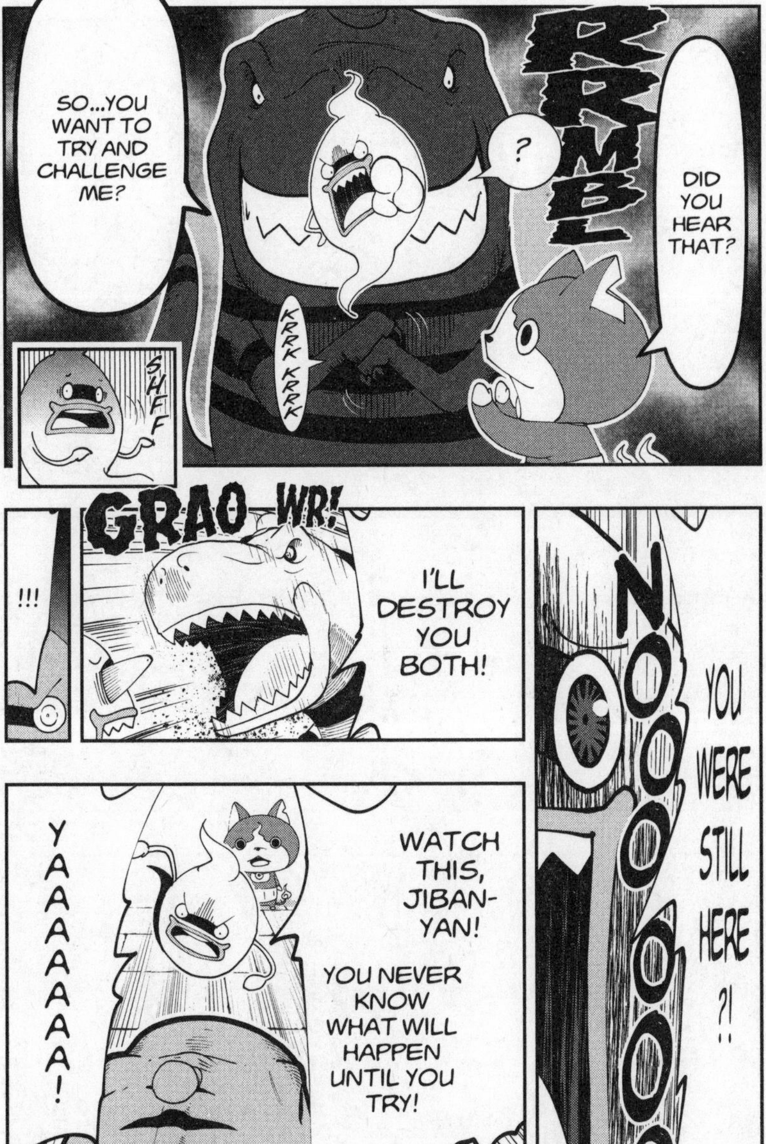
DID YOU HEAR THAT?
RRMBL
?
SO...YOU WANT TO TRY AND CHALLENGE ME?
KRRK KRRK
SHFF
NOOOOOOOOOO
YOU WERE STILL HERE ?!
GRAO WR!
I'LL DESTROY YOU BOTH!
!!!
WATCH THIS, JIBAN-YAN!
YOU NEVER KNOW WHAT WILL HAPPEN UNTIL YOU TRY!
YAAAAAAAAA!

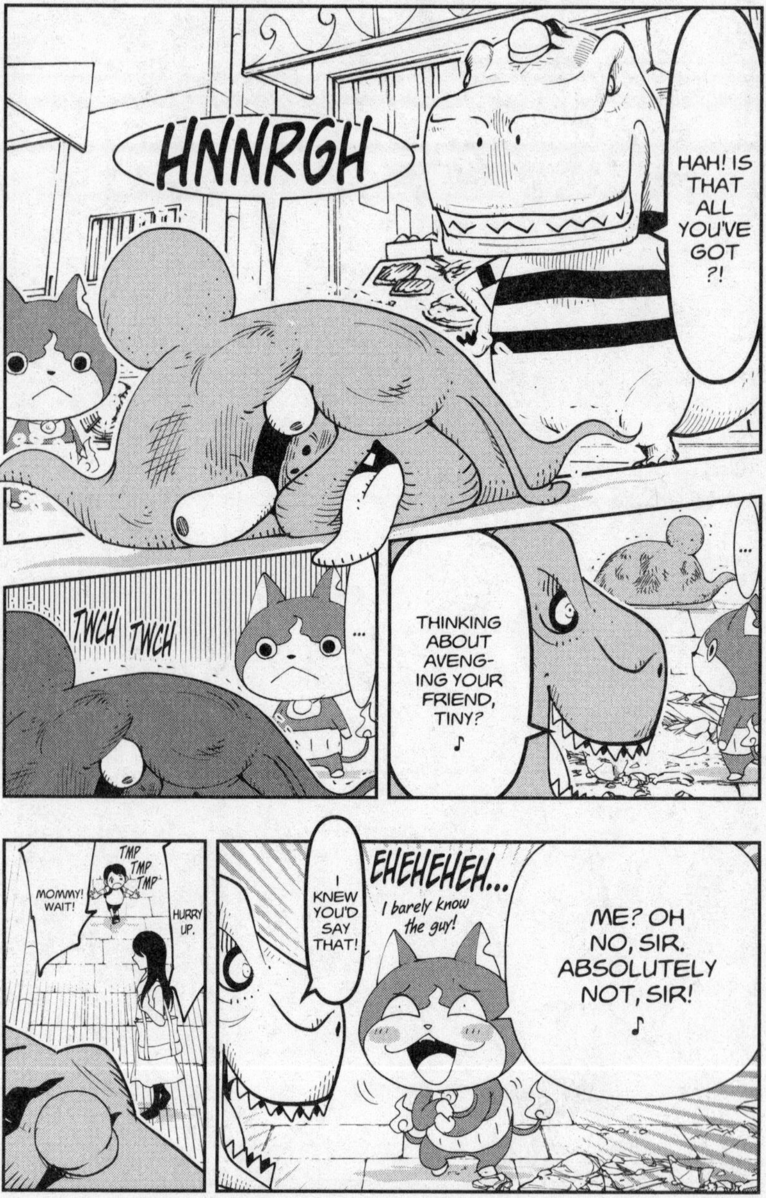
HAH! IS THAT ALL YOU'VE GOT ?!
HNNRGH
...
THINKING ABOUT AVENG-ING YOUR FRIEND, TINY? ♪
...
TWCH TWCH
ME? OH NO, SIR. ABSOLUTELY NOT, SIR! ♪
EHEHEHEH...
I barely know the guy!
I KNEW YOU'D SAY THAT!
HURRY UP.
TMP TMP TMP
MOMMY! WAIT!

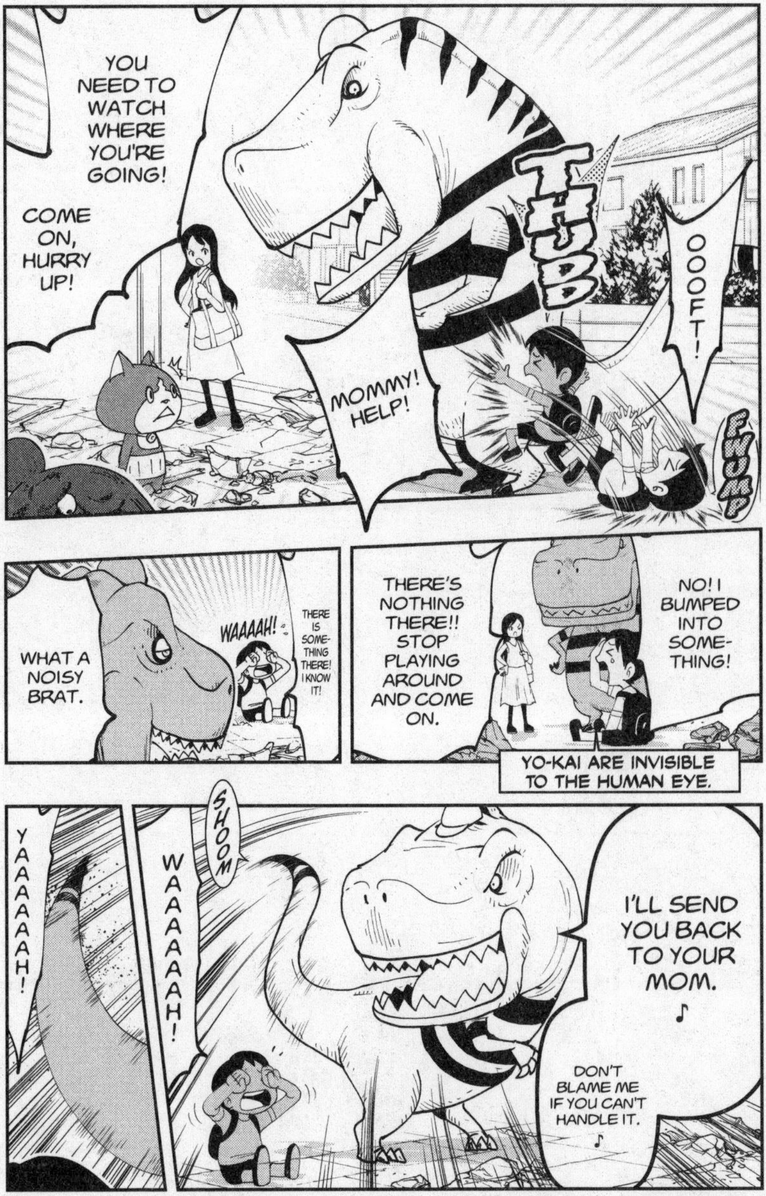
OOOFT!
THUD
YOU NEED TO WATCH WHERE YOU'RE GOING!
COME ON, HURRY UP!
MOMMY! HELP!
FWUMP
NO! I BUMPED INTO SOME-THING!
THERE'S NOTHING THERE!! STOP PLAYING AROUND AND COME ON.
YO-KAI ARE INVISIBLE TO THE HUMAN EYE.
THERE IS SOME-THING THERE! I KNOW IT!
WAAAAH!
WHAT A NOISY BRAT.
I'LL SEND YOU BACK TO YOUR MOM. ♪
DON'T BLAME ME IF YOU CAN'T HANDLE IT. ♪
SHOOM
WAAAAAAAH!
YAAAAAAAH!

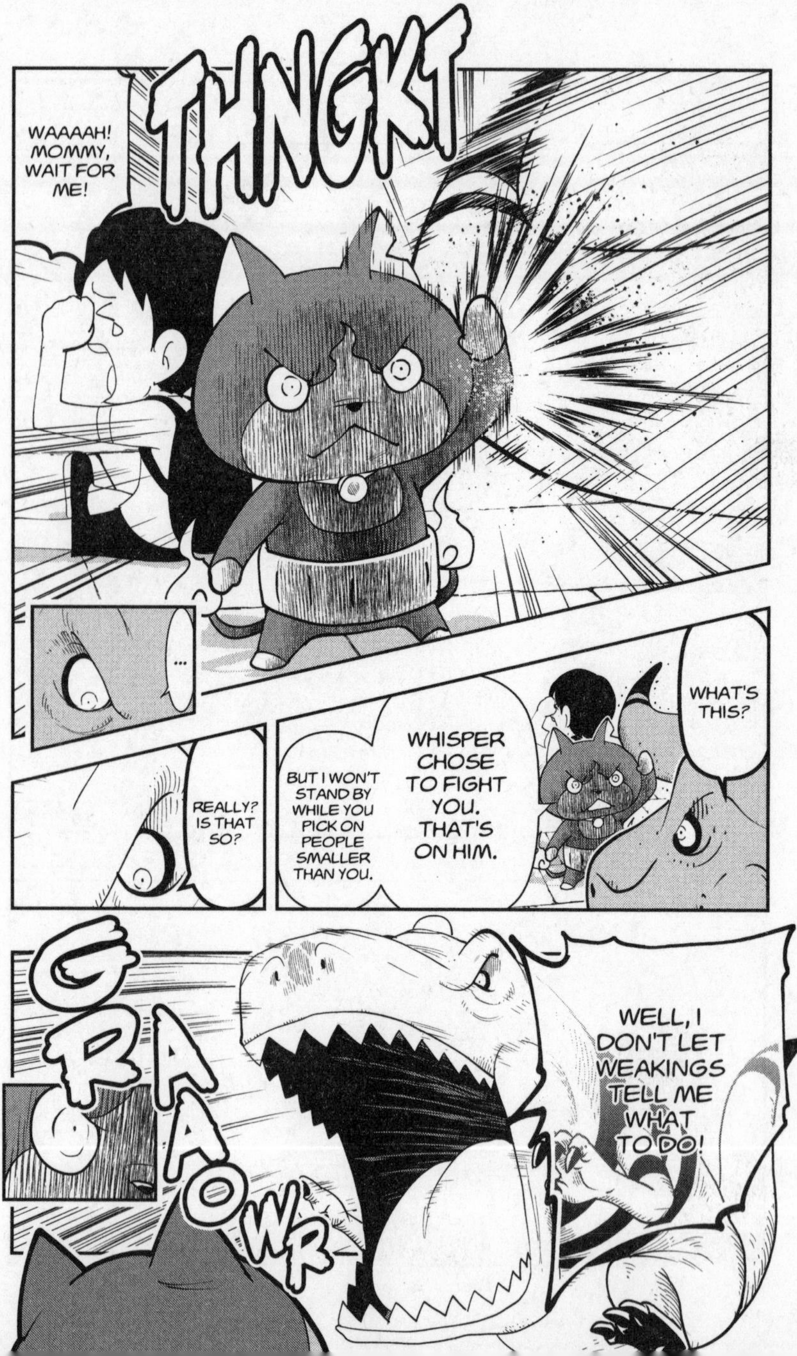
THNGKT
WAAAAH! MOMMY, WAIT FOR ME!
WHAT'S THIS?
...
WHISPER CHOSE TO FIGHT YOU. THAT'S ON HIM.
BUT I WON'T STAND BY WHILE YOU PICK ON PEOPLE SMALLER THAN YOU.
REALLY? IS THAT SO?
WELL, I DON'T LET WEAKINGS TELL ME WHAT TO DO!
GRAAOWR

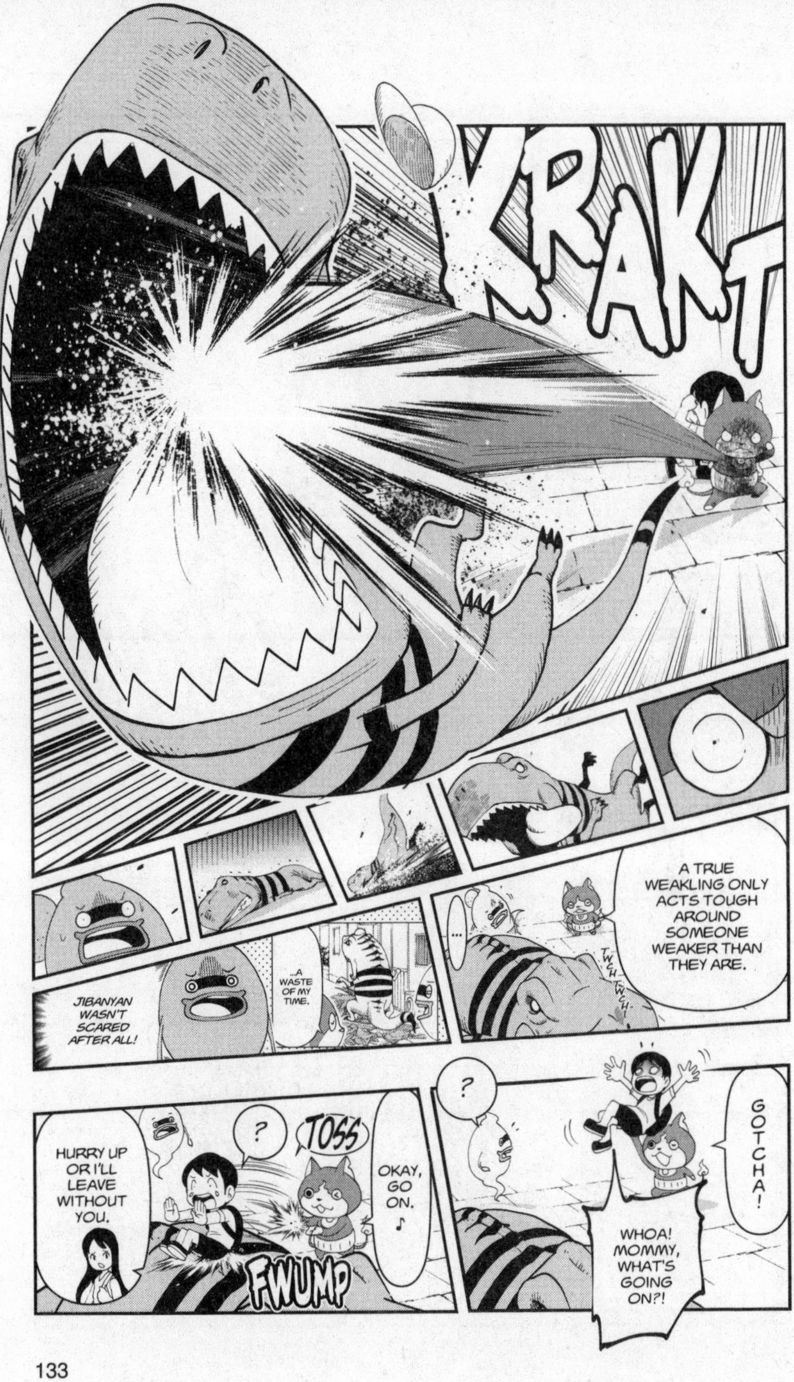
KRAKT
A TRUE WEAKLING ONLY ACTS TOUGH AROUND SOMEONE WEAKER THAN THEY ARE.
TWCH TWCH
...
...A WASTE OF MY TIME.
JIBANYAN WASN'T SCARED AFTER ALL!
GOTCHA!
?
WHOA! MOMMY, WHAT'S GOING ON?!
OKAY, GO ON. ♪
TOSS
?
HURRY UP OR I'LL LEAVE WITHOUT YOU.
FWUMP

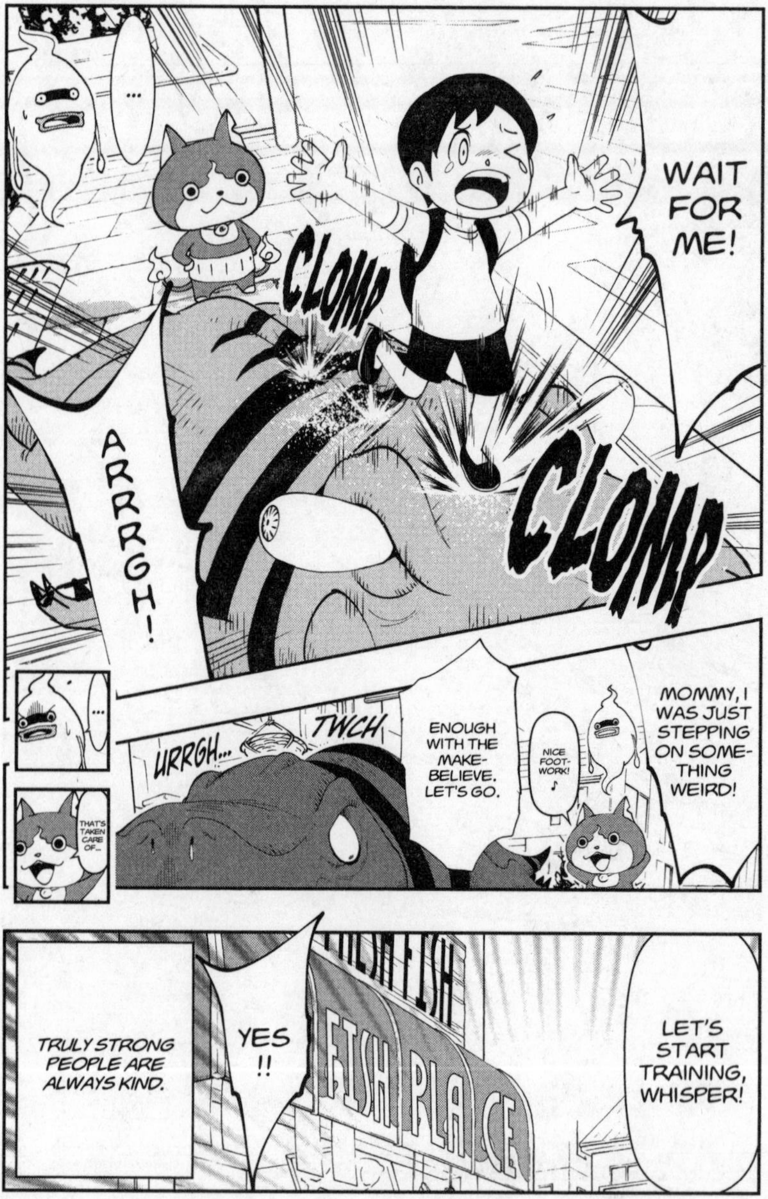
WAIT FOR ME!
CLOMP
CLOMP
...
ARRRGH!
MOMMY, I WAS JUST STEPPING ON SOMETHING WEIRD!
NICE FOOTWORK! ♪
ENOUGH WITH THE MAKE-BELIEVE. LET'S GO.
TWCH
URRGH...
...
THAT'S TAKEN CARE OF...
LET'S START TRAINING, WHISPER!
FISH PLACE
YES !!
TRULY STRONG PEOPLE ARE ALWAYS KIND.

CHAPTER 246
RECKLESS DRIVING YO-KAI SPEEDEMOUNTAIN

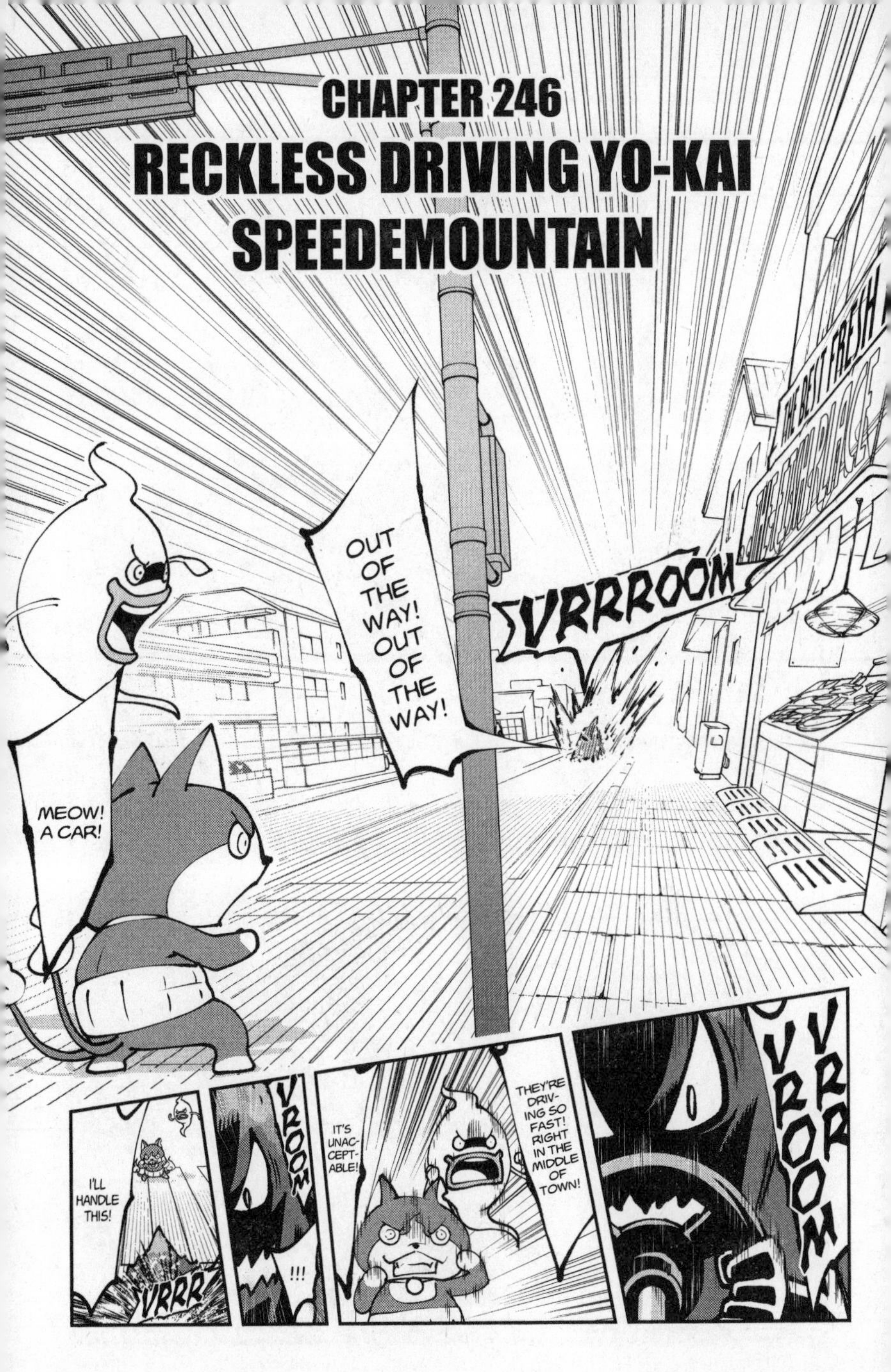
VRRROOM
OUT OF THE WAY! OUT OF THE WAY!
MEOW! A CAR!
VRRROOM
VROOM
THEY'RE DRIVING SO FAST! RIGHT IN THE MIDDLE OF TOWN!
IT'S UNACCEPTABLE!
VROOM
!!!
I'LL HANDLE THIS!
VRRR

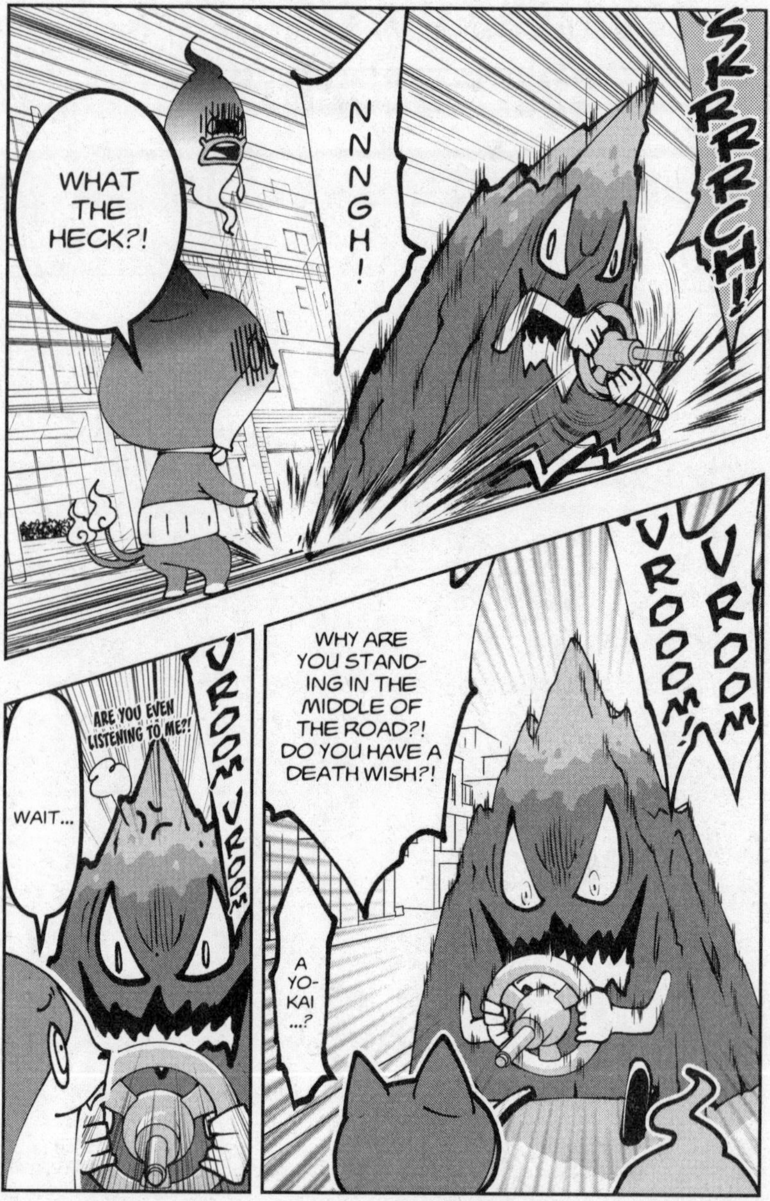
SKRRRCH!!
NNNGH!
WHAT THE HECK?!
VROOM
VROOOOM!
WHY ARE YOU STANDING IN THE MIDDLE OF THE ROAD?! DO YOU HAVE A DEATH WISH?!
A YO-KAI...?
VROOM VROOM
ARE YOU EVEN LISTENING TO ME?!
WAIT...

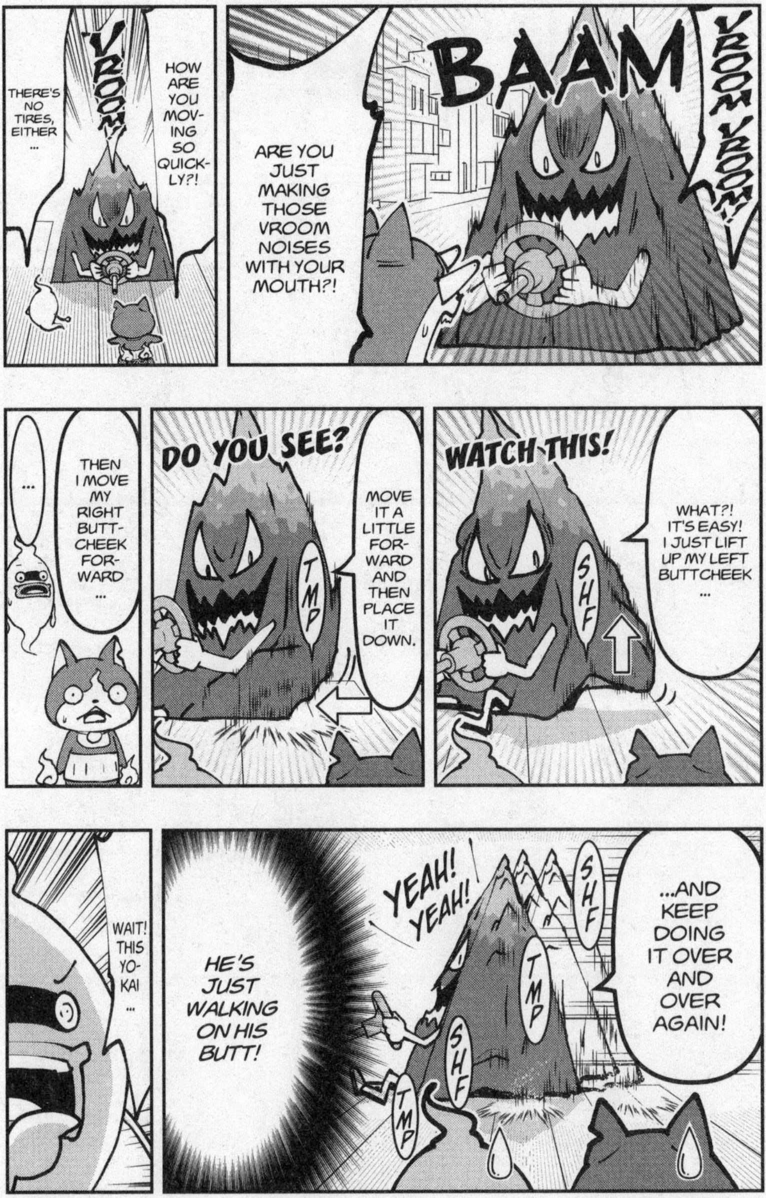
VROOM VROOM!!
BAAM
ARE YOU JUST MAKING THOSE VROOM NOISES WITH YOUR MOUTH?!
VROOM!
HOW ARE YOU MOVING SO QUICKLY?!
THERE'S NO TIRES, EITHER ...
WATCH THIS!
WHAT?! IT'S EASY! I JUST LIFT UP MY LEFT BUTTCHEEK ...
SHF
DO YOU SEE?
MOVE IT A LITTLE FORWARD AND THEN PLACE IT DOWN.
TMP
THEN I MOVE MY RIGHT BUTTCHEEK FORWARD ...
...
...AND KEEP DOING IT OVER AND OVER AGAIN!
SHF
YEAH! YEAH!
TMP
SHF
TMP
HE'S JUST WALKING ON HIS BUTT!
WAIT! THIS YOKAI ...

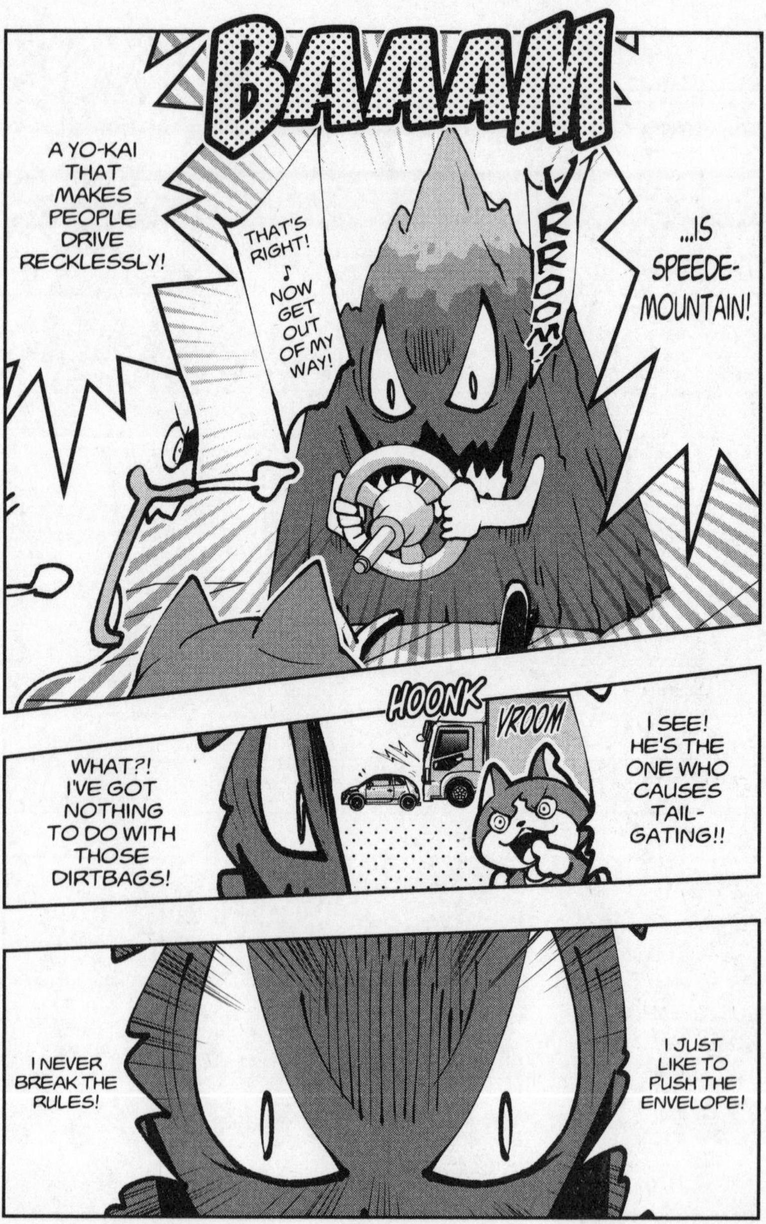
BAAAM
VRROOM!
A YO-KAI THAT MAKES PEOPLE DRIVE RECKLESSLY!
...IS SPEEDE-MOUNTAIN!
THAT'S RIGHT! ♪ NOW GET OUT OF MY WAY!
I SEE! HE'S THE ONE WHO CAUSES TAIL-GATING!!
VROOM
HOONK
WHAT?! I'VE GOT NOTHING TO DO WITH THOSE DIRTBAGS!
I JUST LIKE TO PUSH THE ENVELOPE!
I NEVER BREAK THE RULES!

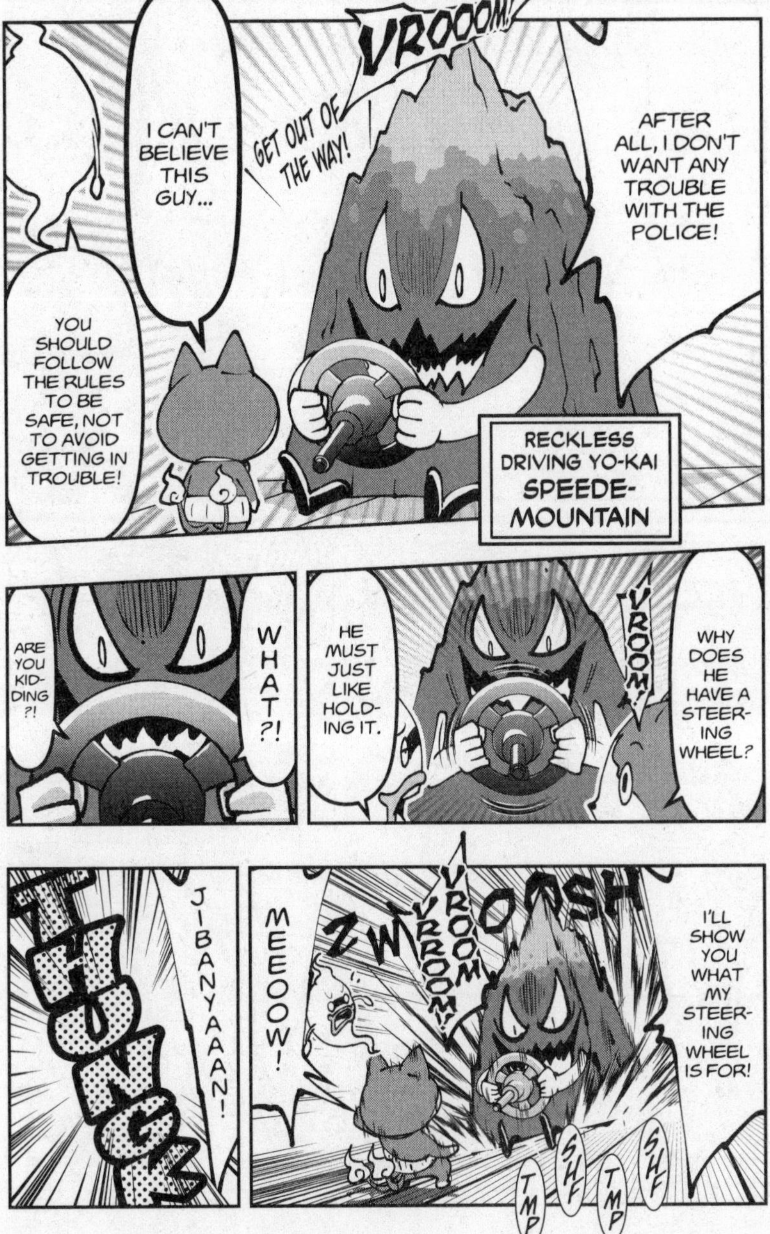
AFTER ALL, I DON'T WANT ANY TROUBLE WITH THE POLICE!
VROOOM!
GET OUT OF THE WAY!
I CAN'T BELIEVE THIS GUY...
YOU SHOULD FOLLOW THE RULES TO BE SAFE, NOT TO AVOID GETTING IN TROUBLE!
RECKLESS DRIVING YO-KAI SPEEDE-MOUNTAIN
WHY DOES HE HAVE A STEERING WHEEL?
VROOOM!
HE MUST JUST LIKE HOLDING IT.
WHAT?!
ARE YOU KIDDING?!
I'LL SHOW YOU WHAT MY STEERING WHEEL IS FOR!
ZWOOSH
VROOM VROOM VROOM!
MEEEOOW!
SHF TMP SHF TMP
JIBANYAAAN!
THUNG!

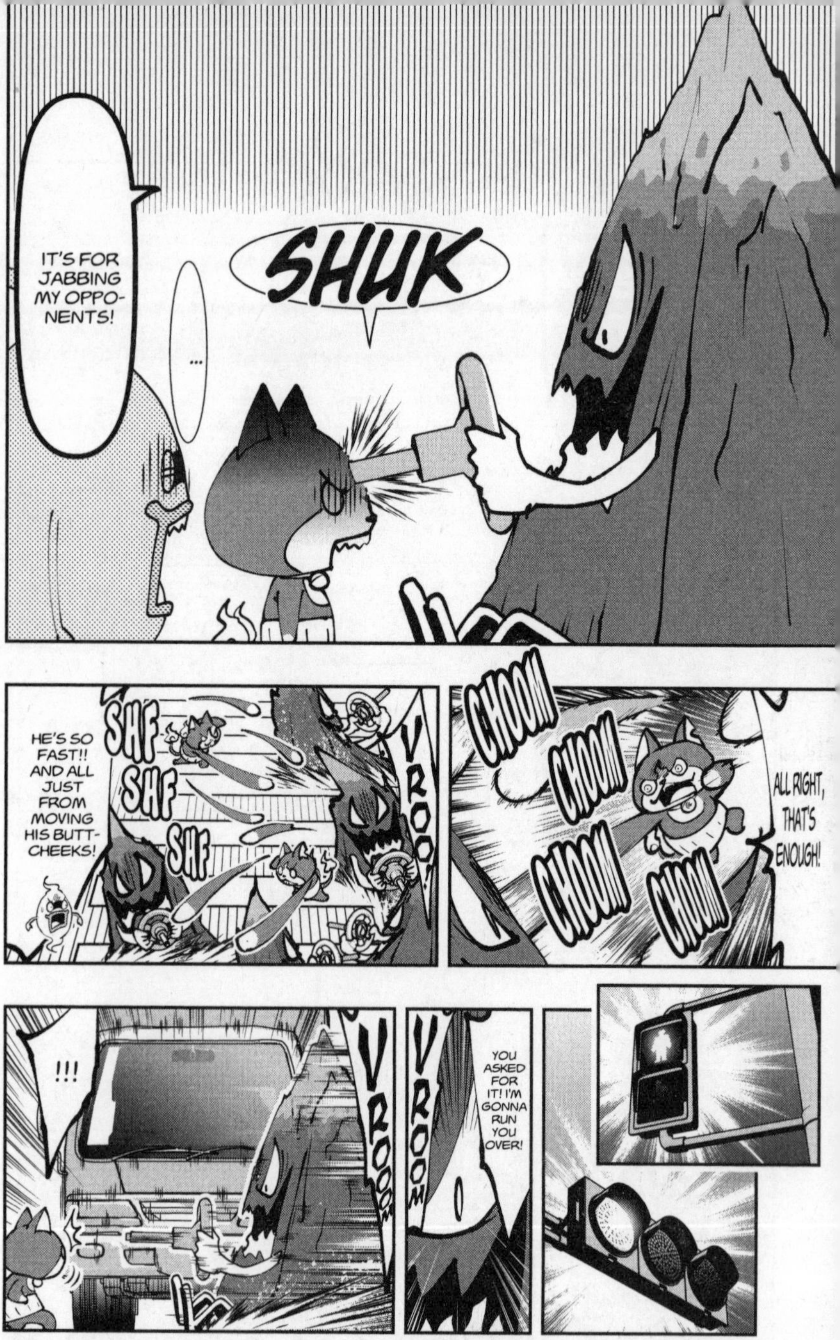
SHUK
...
IT'S FOR JABBING MY OPPONENTS!
CHOOM
CHOOM
CHOOM
CHOOM
ALL RIGHT, THAT'S ENOUGH!
VROOOM!
SHF
SHF
SHF
HE'S SO FAST!! AND ALL JUST FROM MOVING HIS BUTT-CHEEKS!
YOU ASKED FOR IT! I'M GONNA RUN YOU OVER!
VROOOM
VROOOOM
!!!

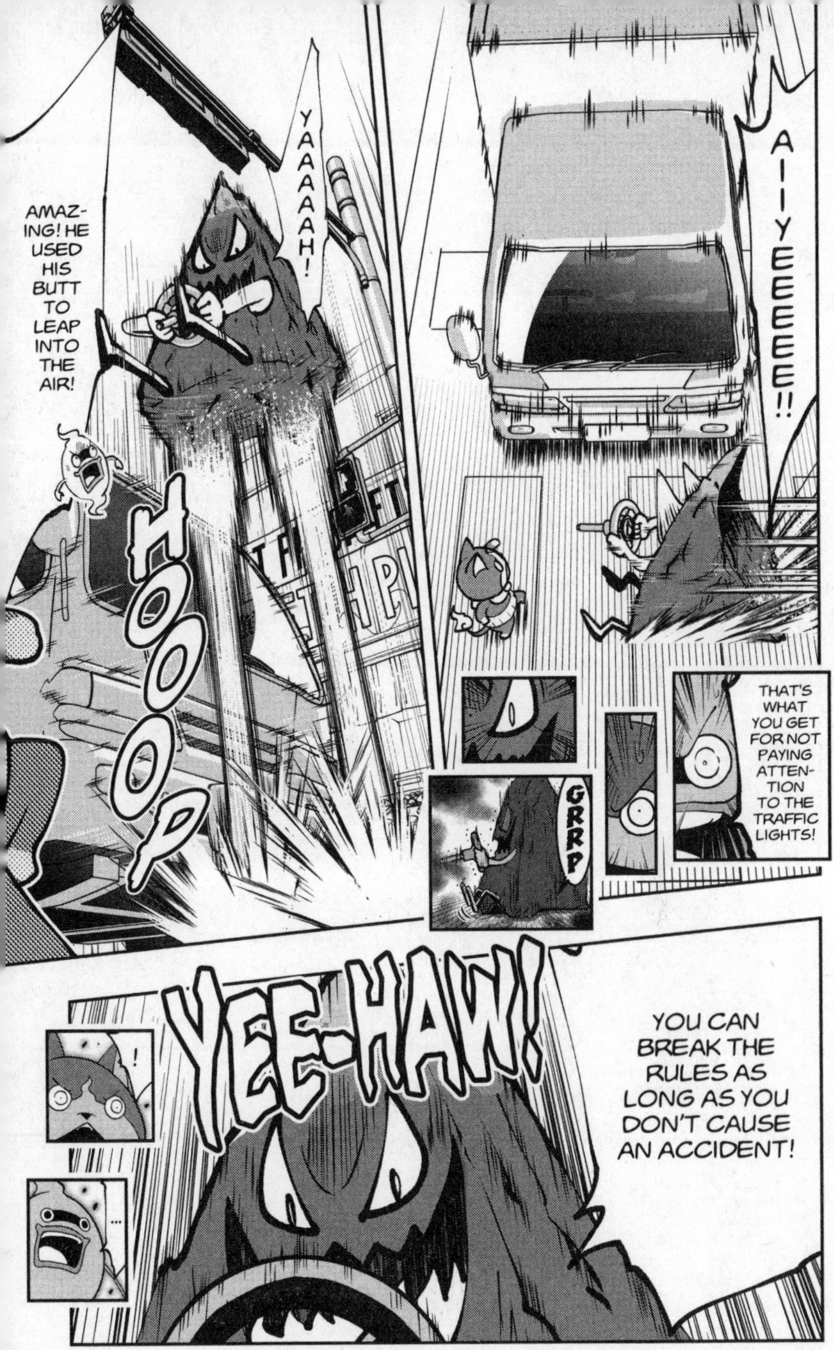
AIIYEEEEEE!!
THAT'S WHAT YOU GET FOR NOT PAYING ATTEN-TION TO THE TRAFFIC LIGHTS!
GRRP
YAAAAAAH!
AMAZ-ING! HE USED HIS BUTT TO LEAP INTO THE AIR!
HOOOOP
YOU CAN BREAK THE RULES AS LONG AS YOU DON'T CAUSE AN ACCIDENT!
YEE-HAW!
!
...

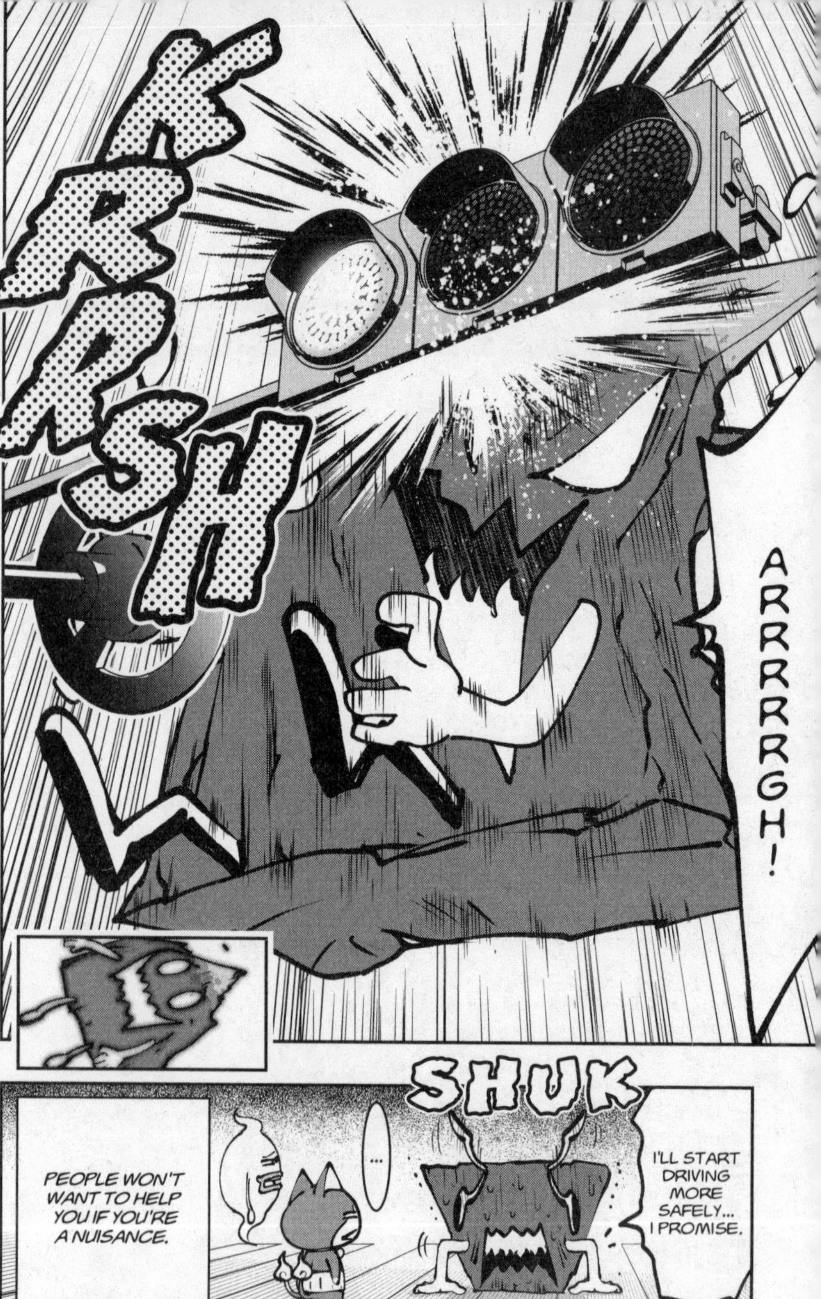
KRRSH
ARRRRRGH!
SHUK
I'LL START DRIVING MORE SAFELY... I PROMISE.
...
PEOPLE WON'T WANT TO HELP YOU IF YOU'RE A NUISANCE.

CHAPTER 247
MASTER DANCER YO-KAI SEAWEED SENSEI

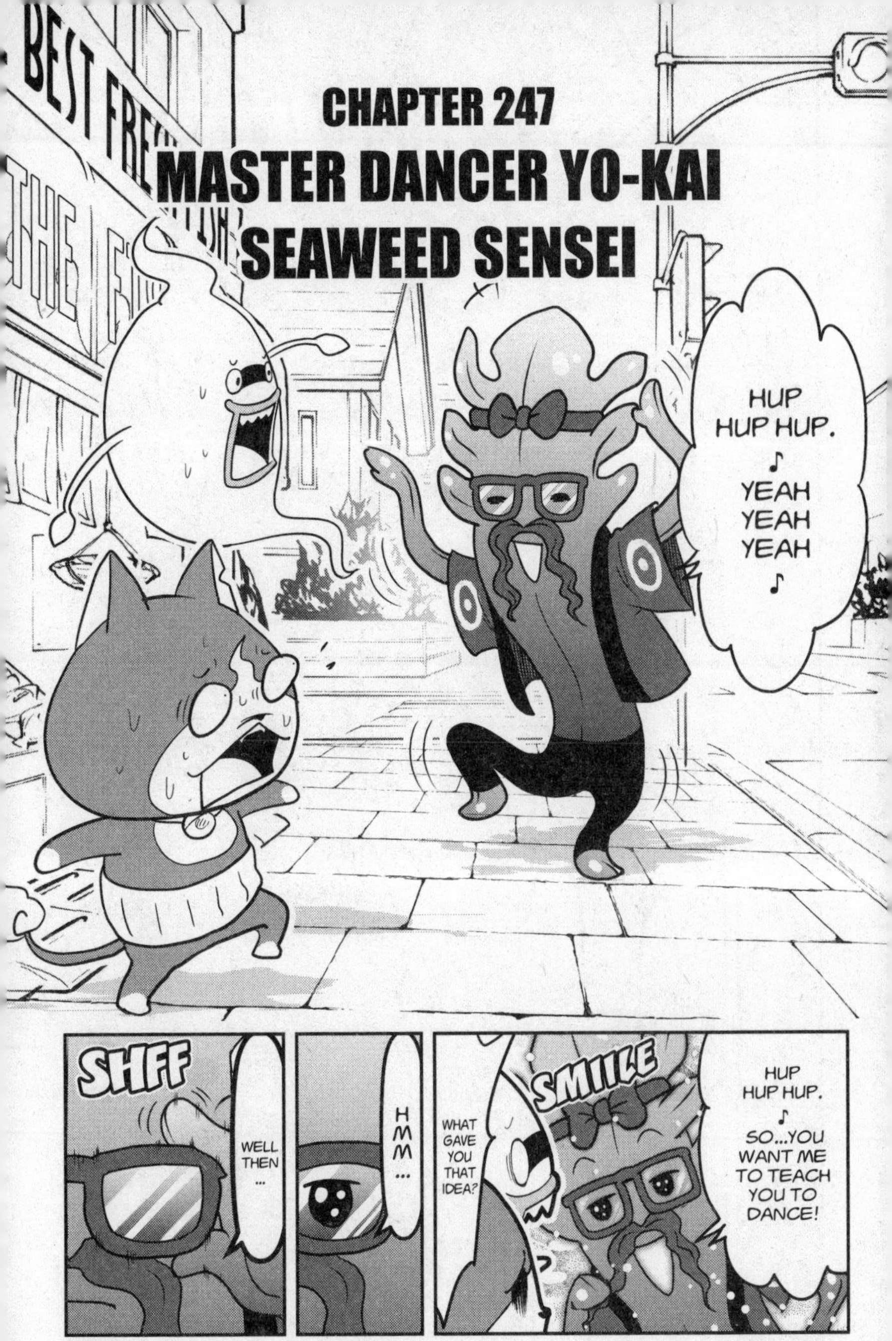
HUP HUP HUP. ♪ YEAH YEAH YEAH ♪
SMIILE
HUP HUP HUP. ♪ SO...YOU WANT ME TO TEACH YOU TO DANCE!
WHAT GAVE YOU THAT IDEA?
HMM...
SHFF
WELL THEN...

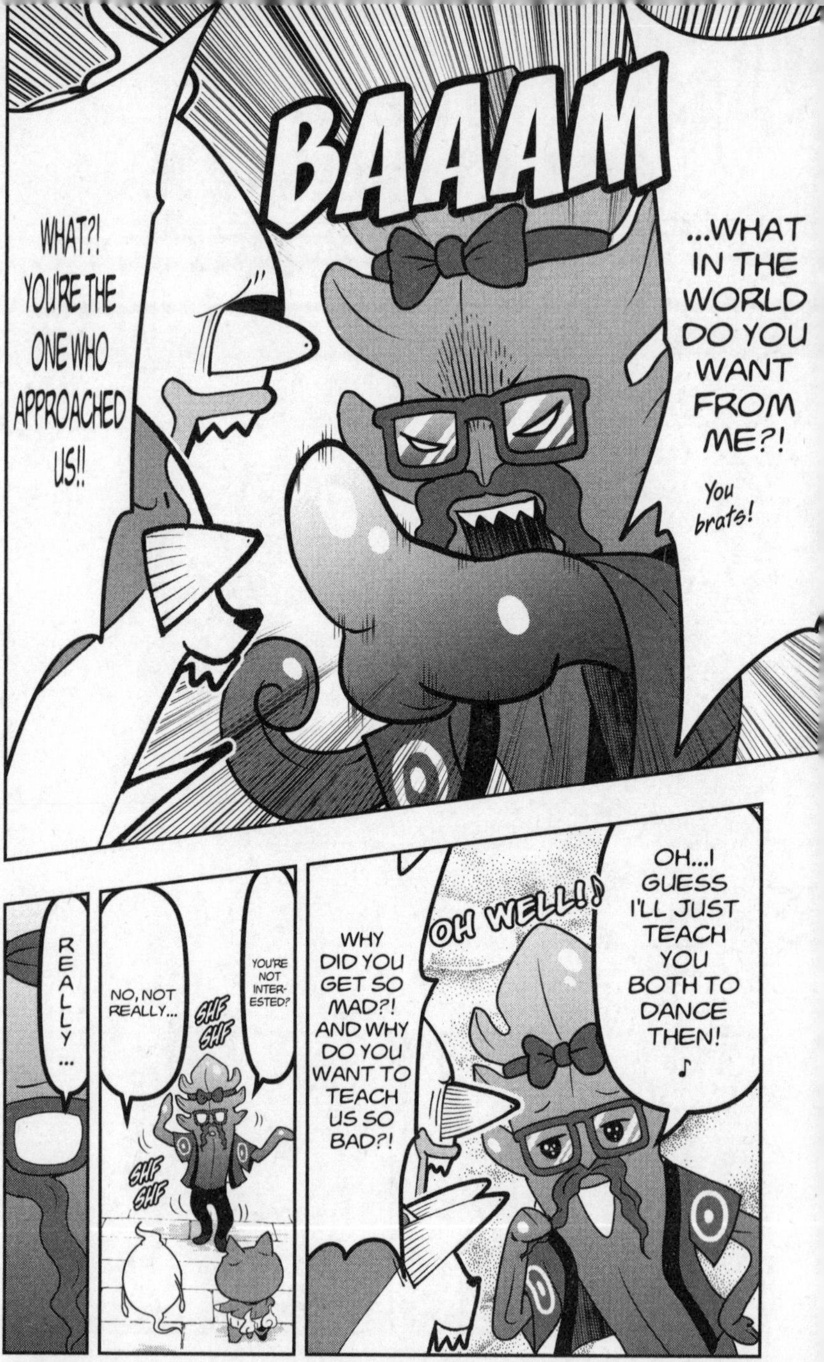
BAAAM
...WHAT IN THE WORLD DO YOU WANT FROM ME?!
You brats!
WHAT?! YOU'RE THE ONE WHO APPROACHED US!!
OH...I GUESS I'LL JUST TEACH YOU BOTH TO DANCE THEN! ♪
OH WELL!♪
WHY DID YOU GET SO MAD?! AND WHY DO YOU WANT TO TEACH US SO BAD?!
YOU'RE NOT INTERESTED?
SHF SHF
NO, NOT REALLY...
SHF SHF
REALLY...

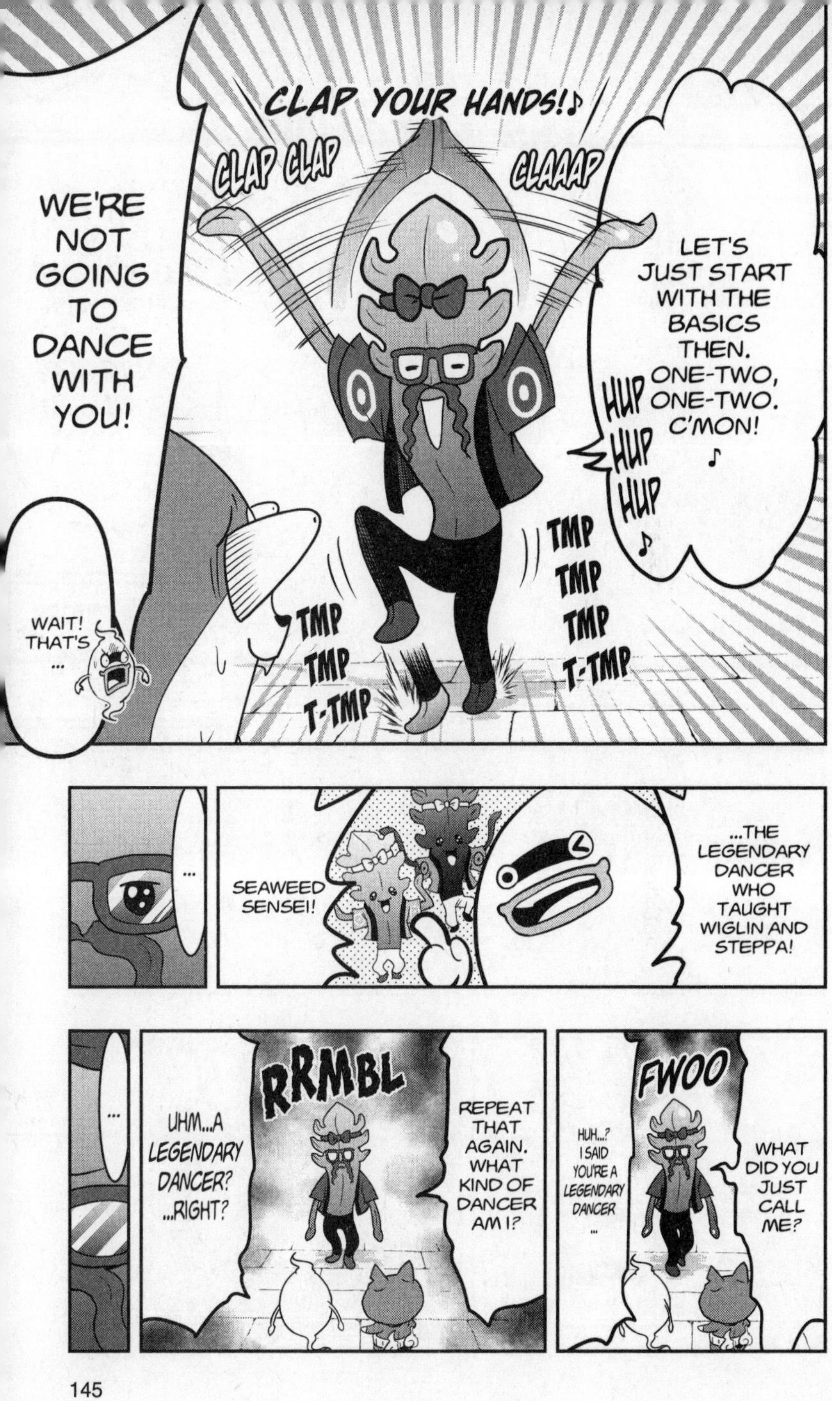
CLAP YOUR HANDS!♪
CLAAAP
CLAP CLAP
LET'S JUST START WITH THE BASICS THEN. ONE-TWO, ONE-TWO. C'MON! ♪
HUP HUP HUP ♪
WE'RE NOT GOING TO DANCE WITH YOU!
TMP TMP TMP T-TMP
TMP TMP T-TMP
WAIT! THAT'S ...
...THE LEGENDARY DANCER WHO TAUGHT WIGLIN AND STEPPA!
SEAWEED SENSEI!
...
FWOO
WHAT DID YOU JUST CALL ME?
HUH...? I SAID YOU'RE A LEGENDARY DANCER ...
RRMBL
REPEAT THAT AGAIN. WHAT KIND OF DANCER AM I?
UHM...A LEGENDARY DANCER? ...RIGHT?
...

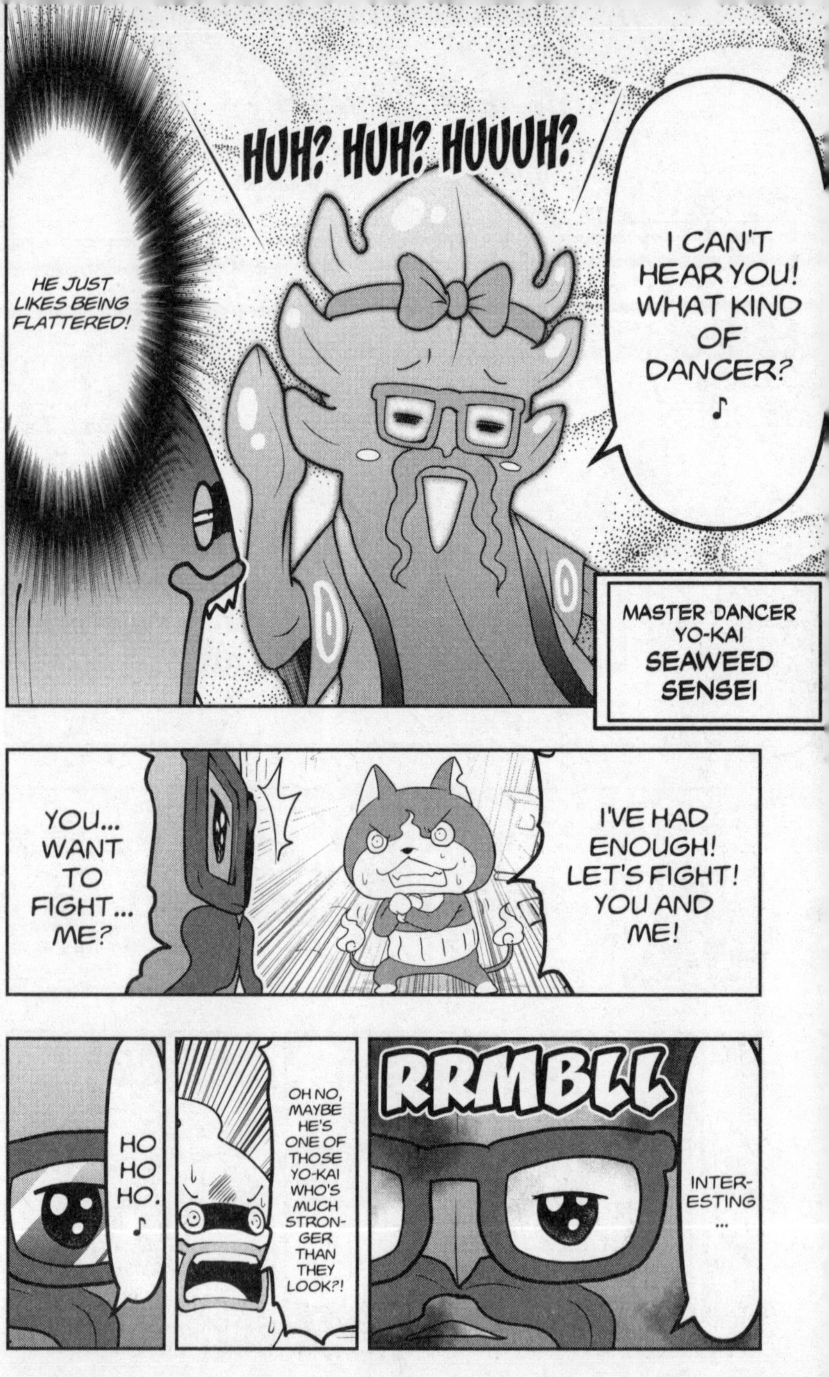
I CAN'T HEAR YOU! WHAT KIND OF DANCER? ♪
HUH? HUH? HUUUH?
HE JUST LIKES BEING FLATTERED!
MASTER DANCER YO-KAI SEAWEED SENSEI
I'VE HAD ENOUGH! LET'S FIGHT! YOU AND ME!
YOU... WANT TO FIGHT... ME?
RRMBLL
INTER-ESTING...
OH NO, MAYBE HE'S ONE OF THOSE YO-KAI WHO'S MUCH STRONGER THAN THEY LOOK?!
HO HO HO. ♪

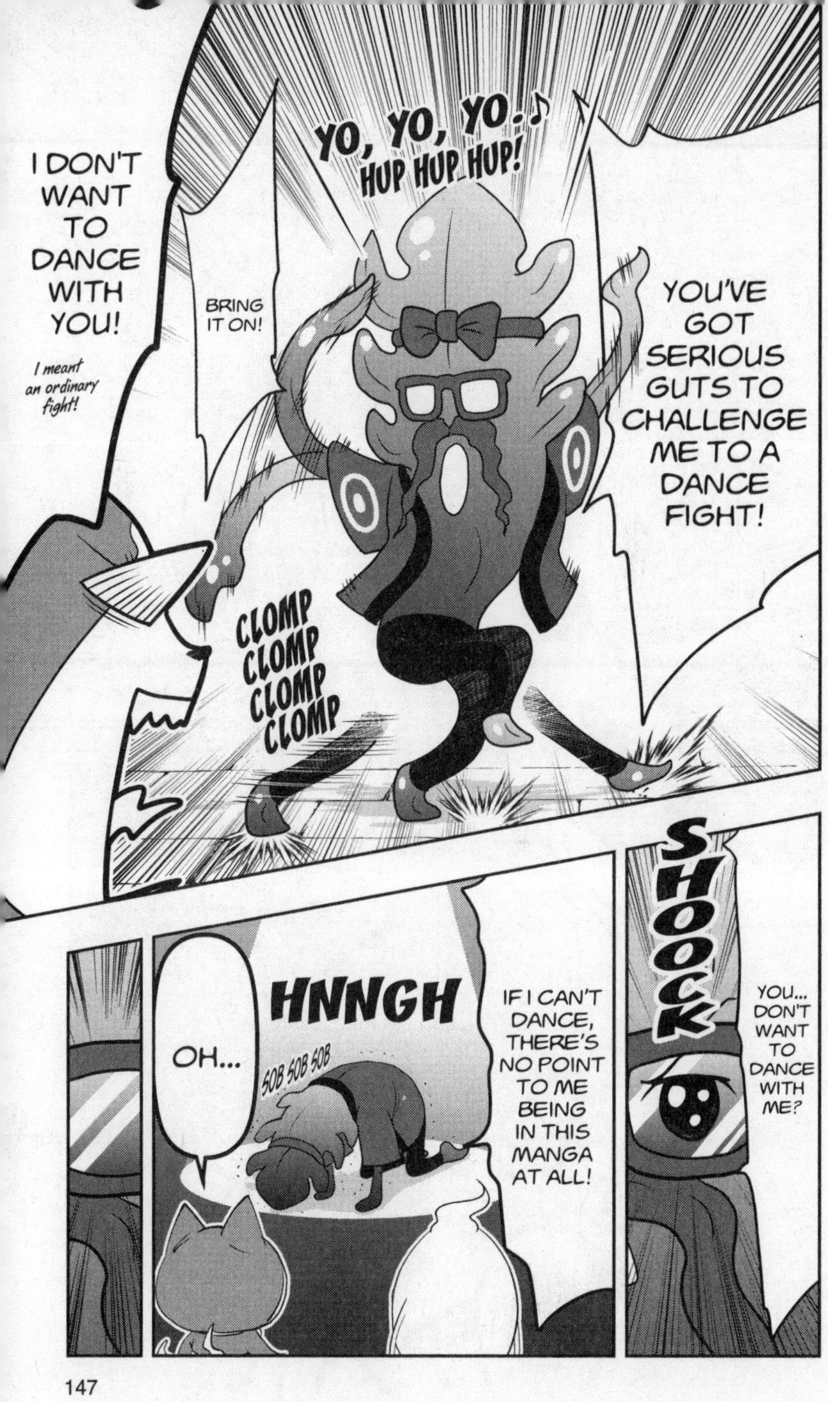
YO, YO, YO♪
HUP HUP HUP!
YOU'VE GOT SERIOUS GUTS TO CHALLENGE ME TO A DANCE FIGHT!
BRING IT ON!
I DON'T WANT TO DANCE WITH YOU!
I meant an ordinary fight!
CLOMP CLOMP CLOMP CLOMP
SHOOCK
YOU... DON'T WANT TO DANCE WITH ME?
IF I CAN'T DANCE, THERE'S NO POINT TO ME BEING IN THIS MANGA AT ALL!
HNNGH
OH...
SOB SOB SOB

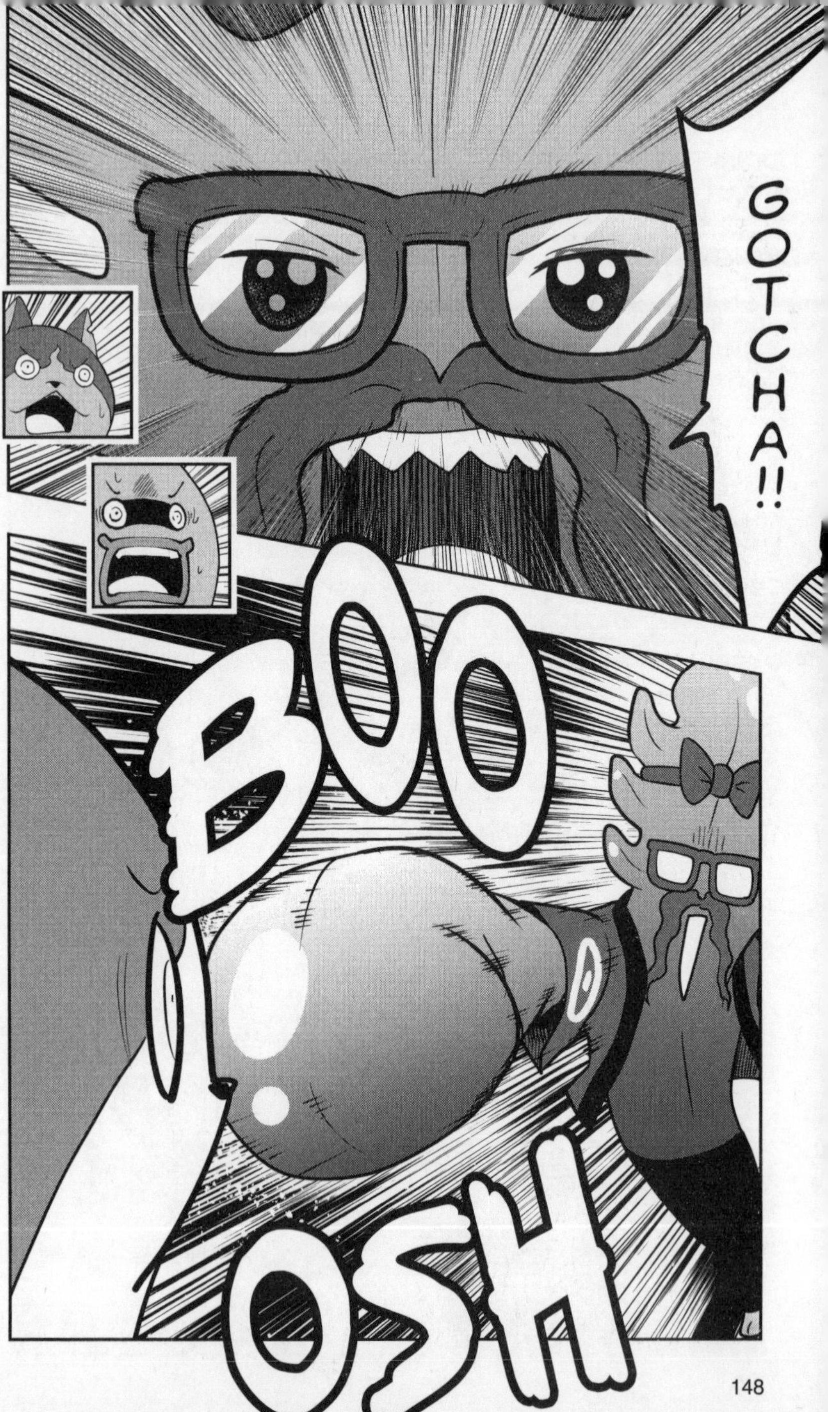
GOTCHA!!
BOOOSH

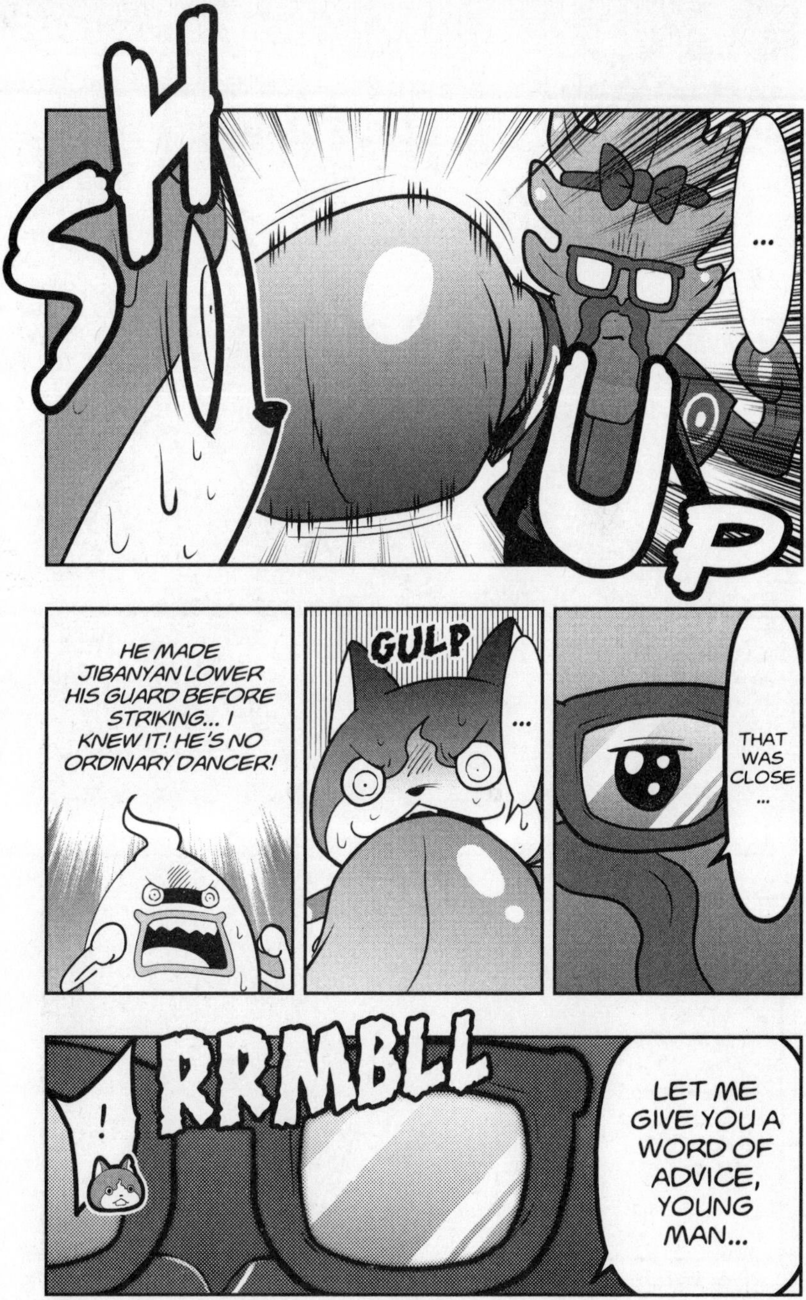
...
SHUP
THAT WAS CLOSE ...
GULP
...
HE MADE JIBANYAN LOWER HIS GUARD BEFORE STRIKING... I KNEW IT! HE'S NO ORDINARY DANCER!
LET ME GIVE YOU A WORD OF ADVICE, YOUNG MAN...
RRMBLL
!

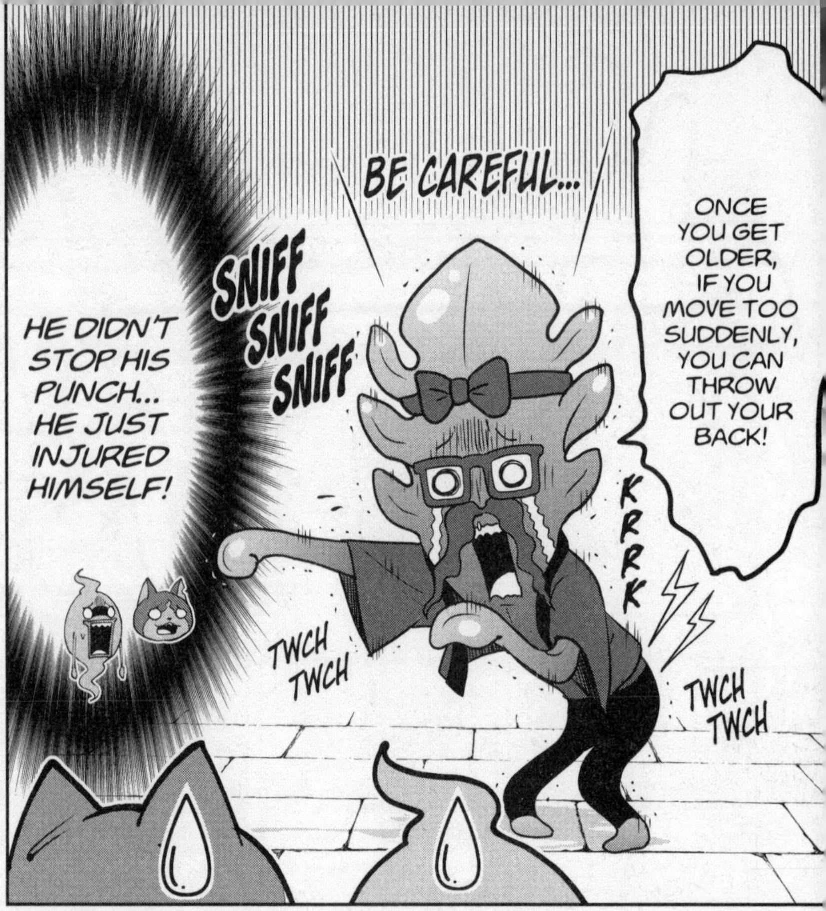
ONCE YOU GET OLDER, IF YOU MOVE TOO SUDDENLY, YOU CAN THROW OUT YOUR BACK!
BE CAREFUL...
KRRK
SNIFF SNIFF SNIFF
TWCH TWCH
HE DIDN'T STOP HIS PUNCH... HE JUST INJURED HIMSELF!
TWCH TWCH

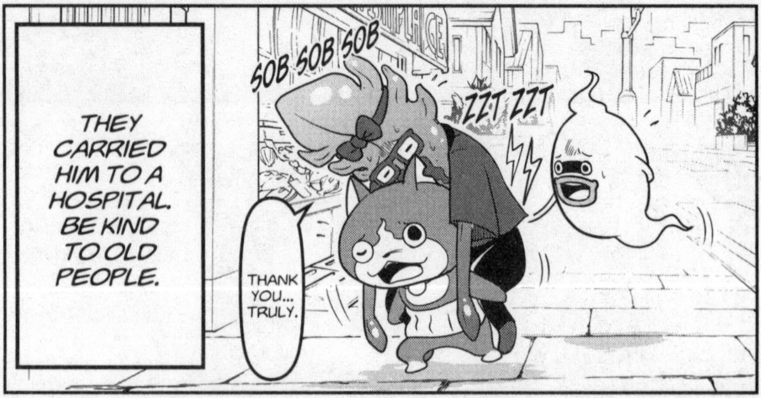
ZZT ZZT
SOB SOB SOB
THANK YOU... TRULY.
THEY CARRIED HIM TO A HOSPITAL. BE KIND TO OLD PEOPLE.

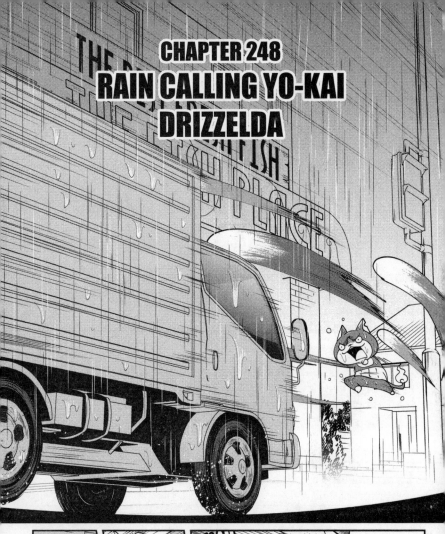

CHAPTER 248
RAIN CALLING YO-KAI DRIZZELDA

SLIP

SLIP

CHOOM

CHOOM

CHOOM

I'M COMING FOR YOU, TRUCK! MEOW MEOW!

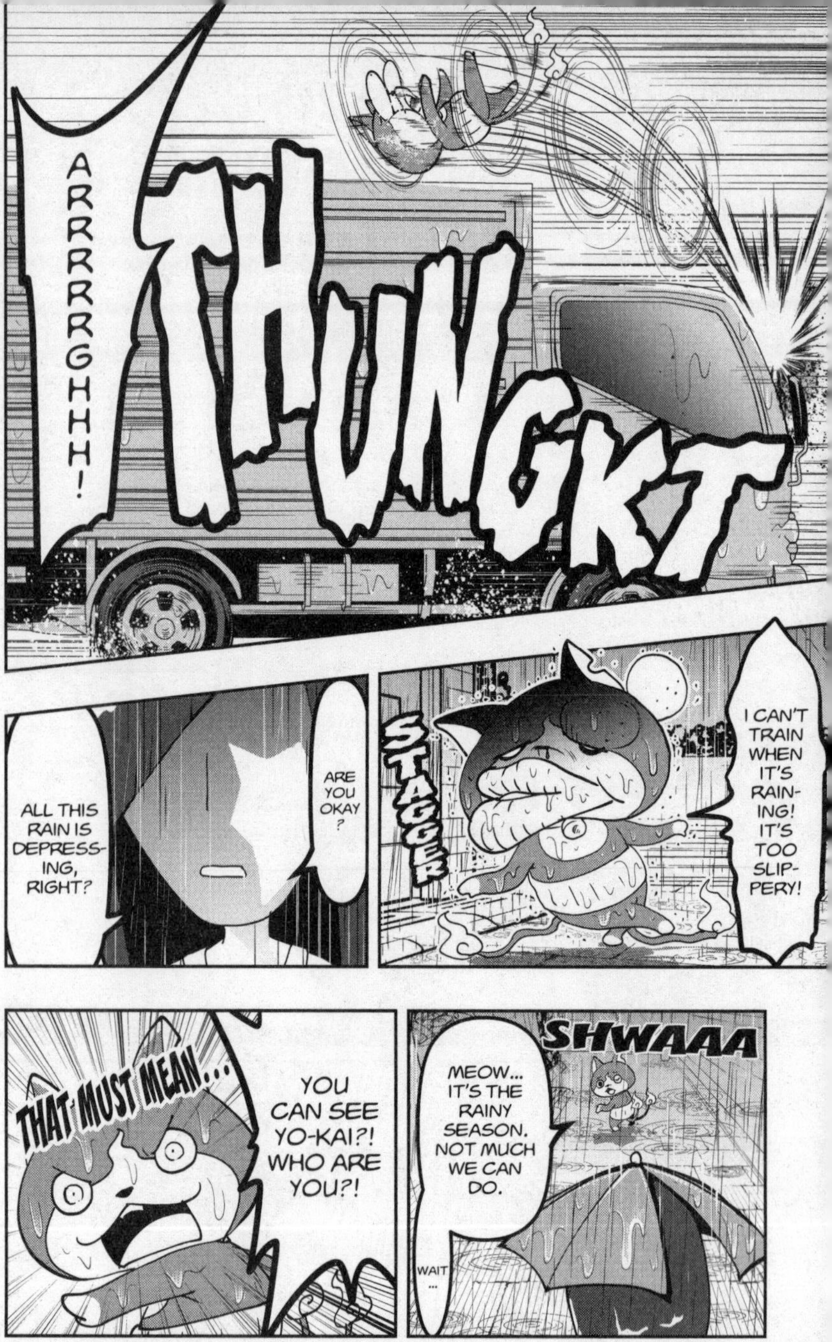
THUNGKT
ARRRRRGHHH!
I CAN'T TRAIN WHEN IT'S RAIN-ING! IT'S TOO SLIP-PERY!
STAGGER
ARE YOU OKAY?
ALL THIS RAIN IS DEPRESS-ING, RIGHT?
SHWAAA
MEOW... IT'S THE RAINY SEASON. NOT MUCH WE CAN DO.
WAIT...
YOU CAN SEE YO-KAI?! WHO ARE YOU?!
THAT MUST MEAN...

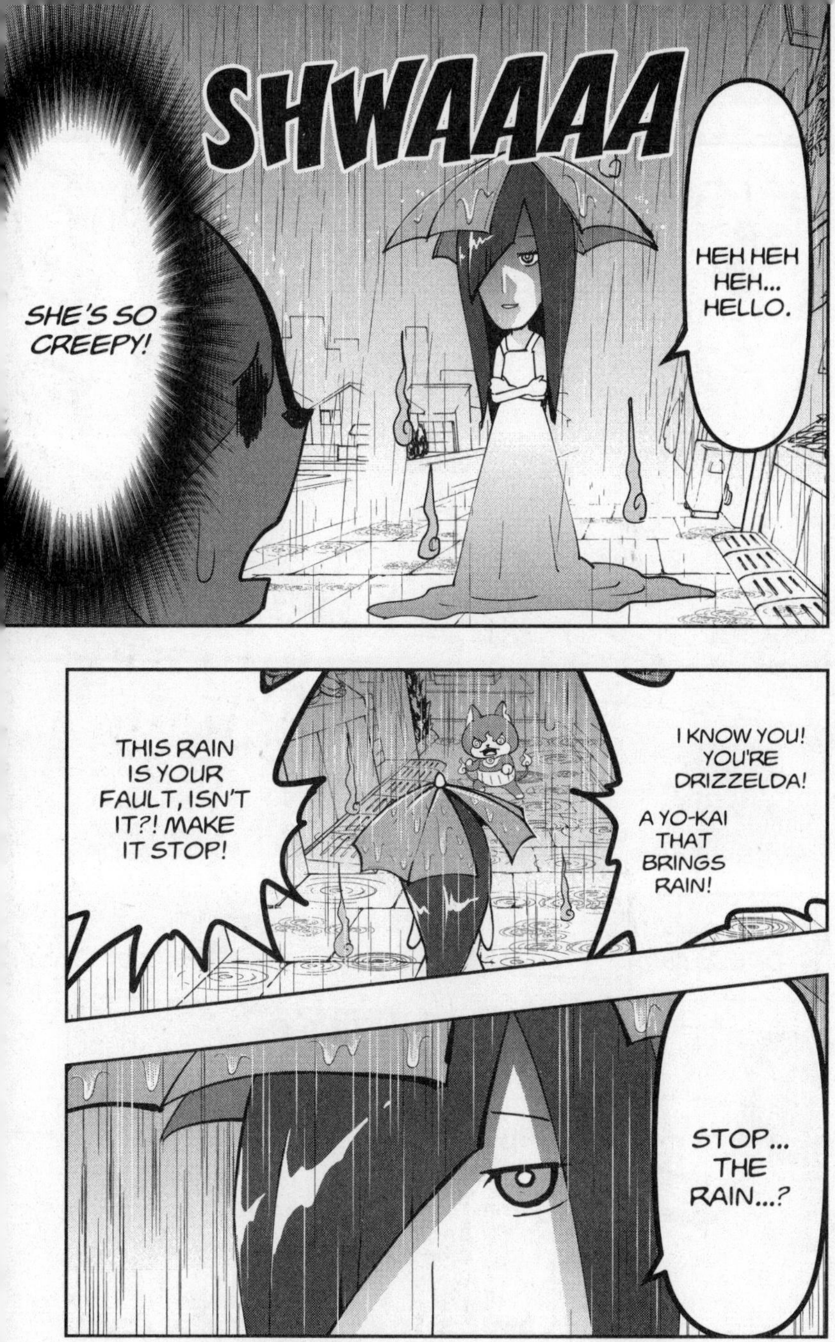
SHWAAAA
HEH HEH HEH... HELLO.
SHE'S SO CREEPY!
I KNOW YOU! YOU'RE DRIZZELDA!
A YO-KAI THAT BRINGS RAIN!
THIS RAIN IS YOUR FAULT, ISN'T IT?! MAKE IT STOP!
STOP... THE RAIN...?

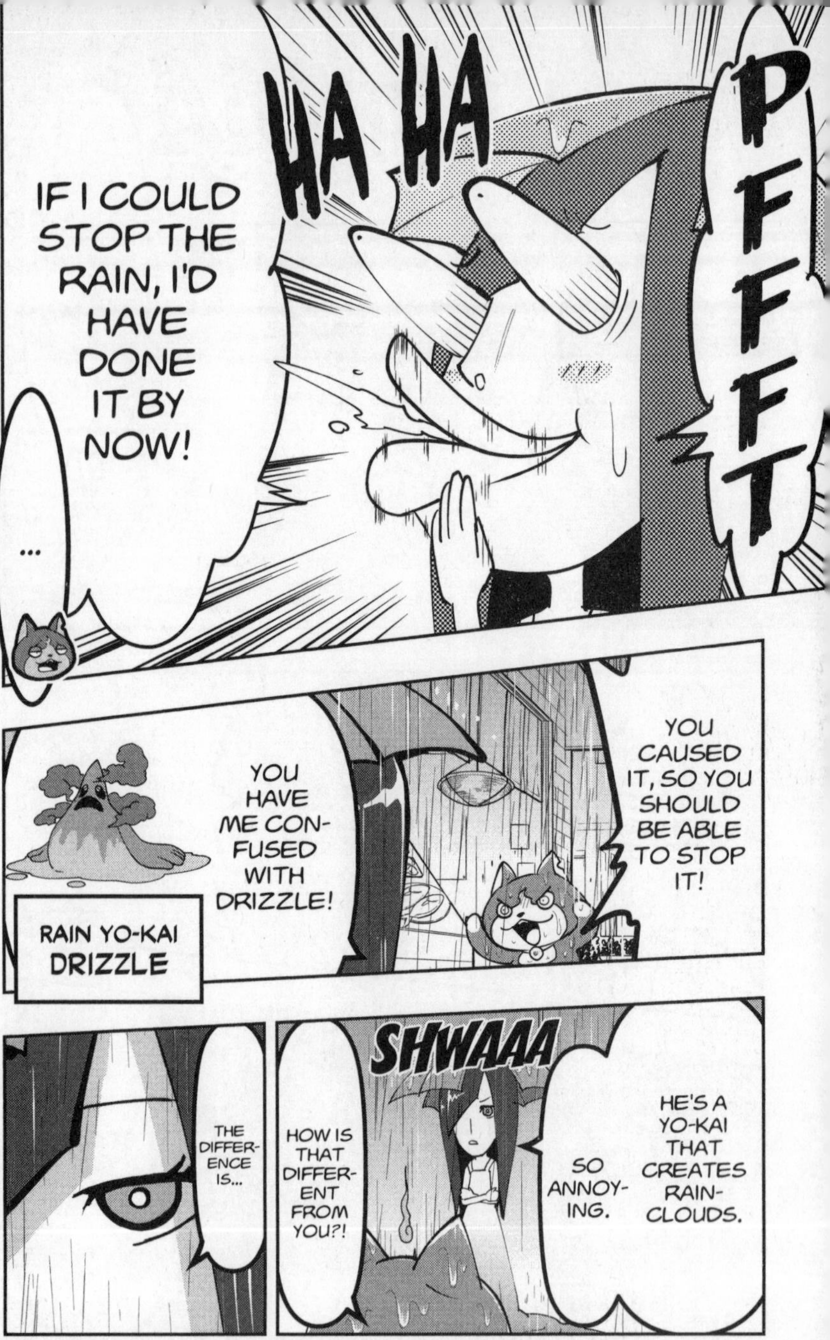

PFFFT
HA HA
IF I COULD STOP THE RAIN, I'D HAVE DONE IT BY NOW!
...
YOU CAUSED IT, SO YOU SHOULD BE ABLE TO STOP IT!
YOU HAVE ME CONFUSED WITH DRIZZLE!
RAIN YO-KAI DRIZZLE
SHWAAA
HE'S A YO-KAI THAT CREATES RAINCLOUDS.
SO ANNOYING.
HOW IS THAT DIFFERENT FROM YOU?!
THE DIFFERENCE IS...

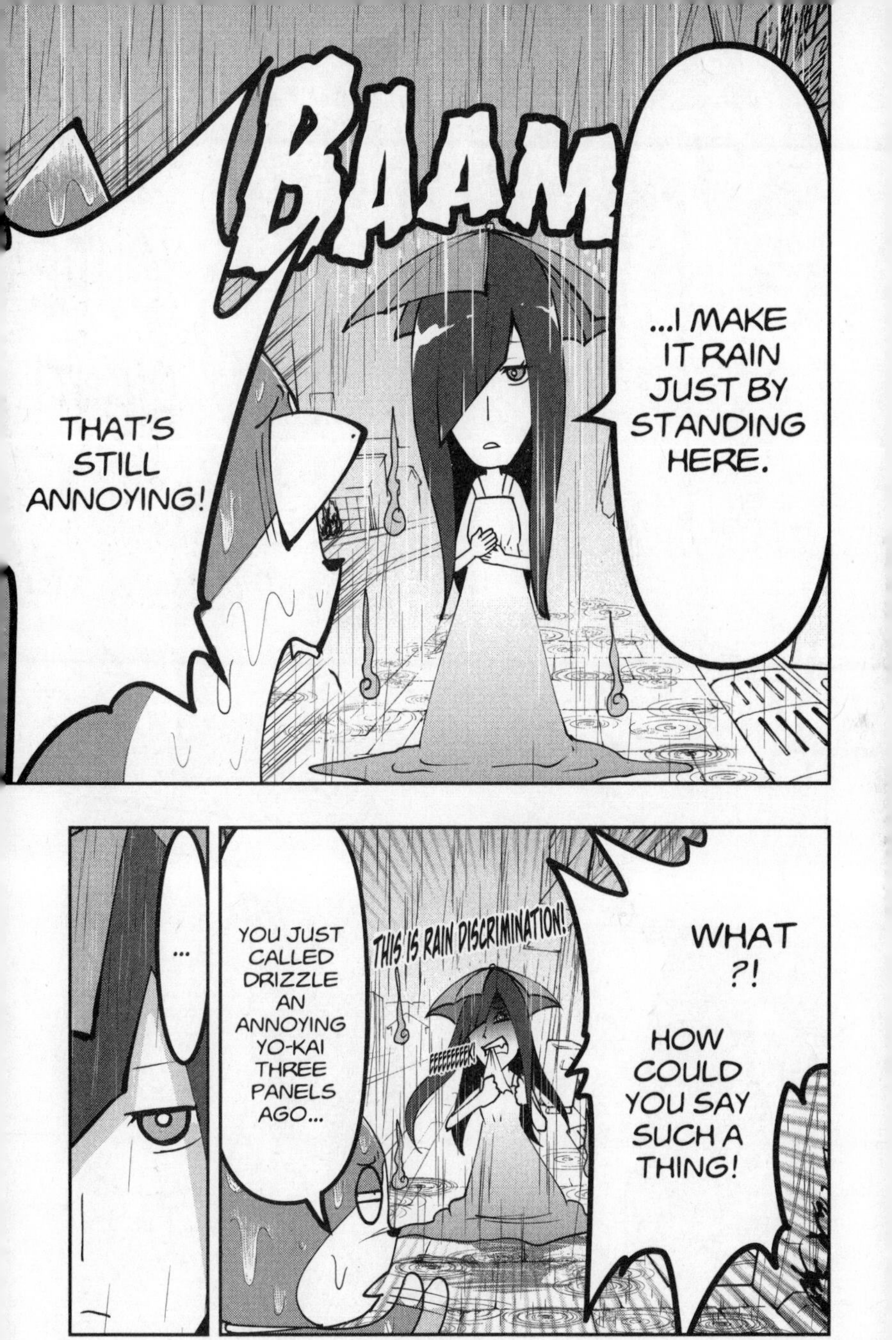
BAAM
...I MAKE IT RAIN JUST BY STANDING HERE.
THAT'S STILL ANNOYING!
WHAT?!
HOW COULD YOU SAY SUCH A THING!
THIS IS RAIN DISCRIMINATION!
YOU JUST CALLED DRIZZLE AN ANNOYING YO-KAI THREE PANELS AGO...
...

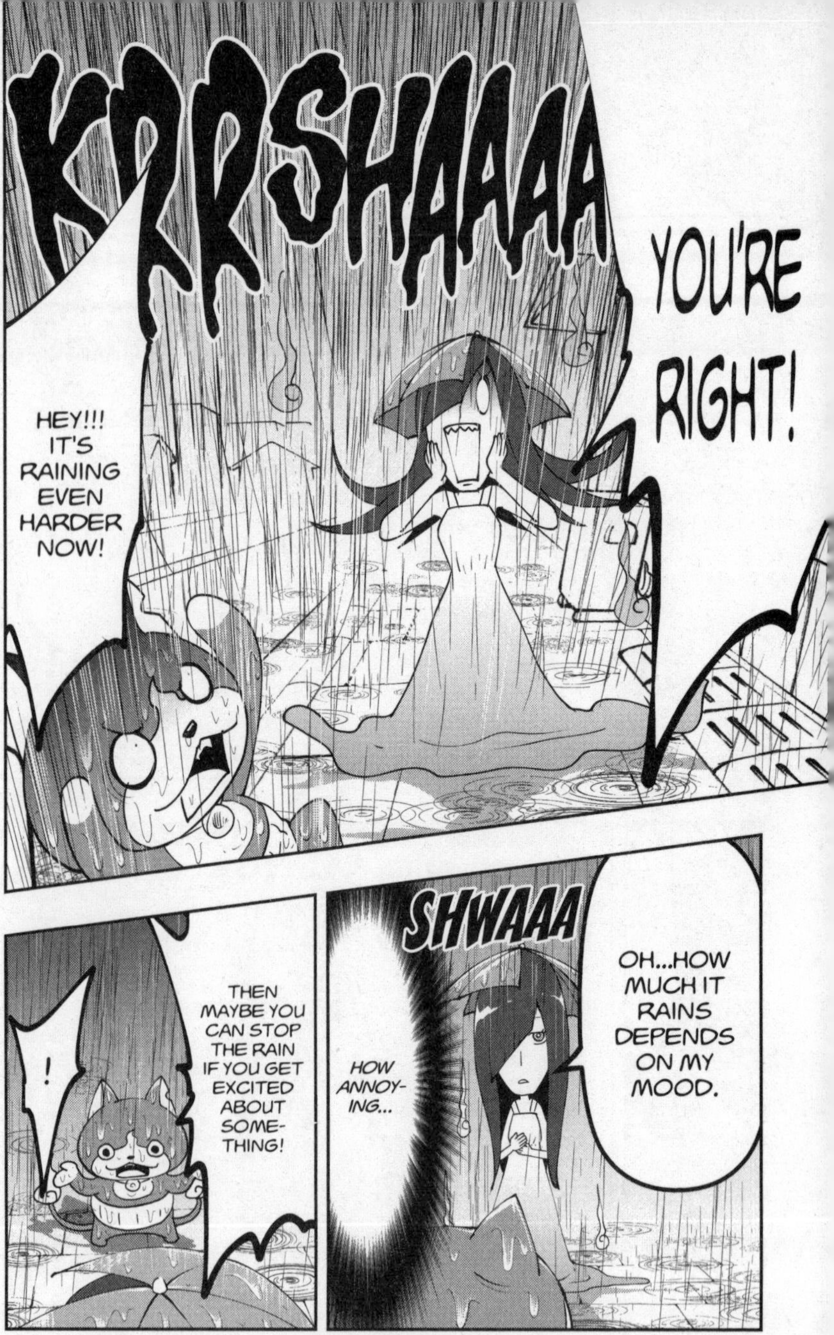
KRRSHAAAA
YOU'RE RIGHT!
HEY!!! IT'S RAINING EVEN HARDER NOW!
SHWAAA
OH...HOW MUCH IT RAINS DEPENDS ON MY MOOD.
HOW ANNOY-ING...
THEN MAYBE YOU CAN STOP THE RAIN IF YOU GET EXCITED ABOUT SOME-THING!
!

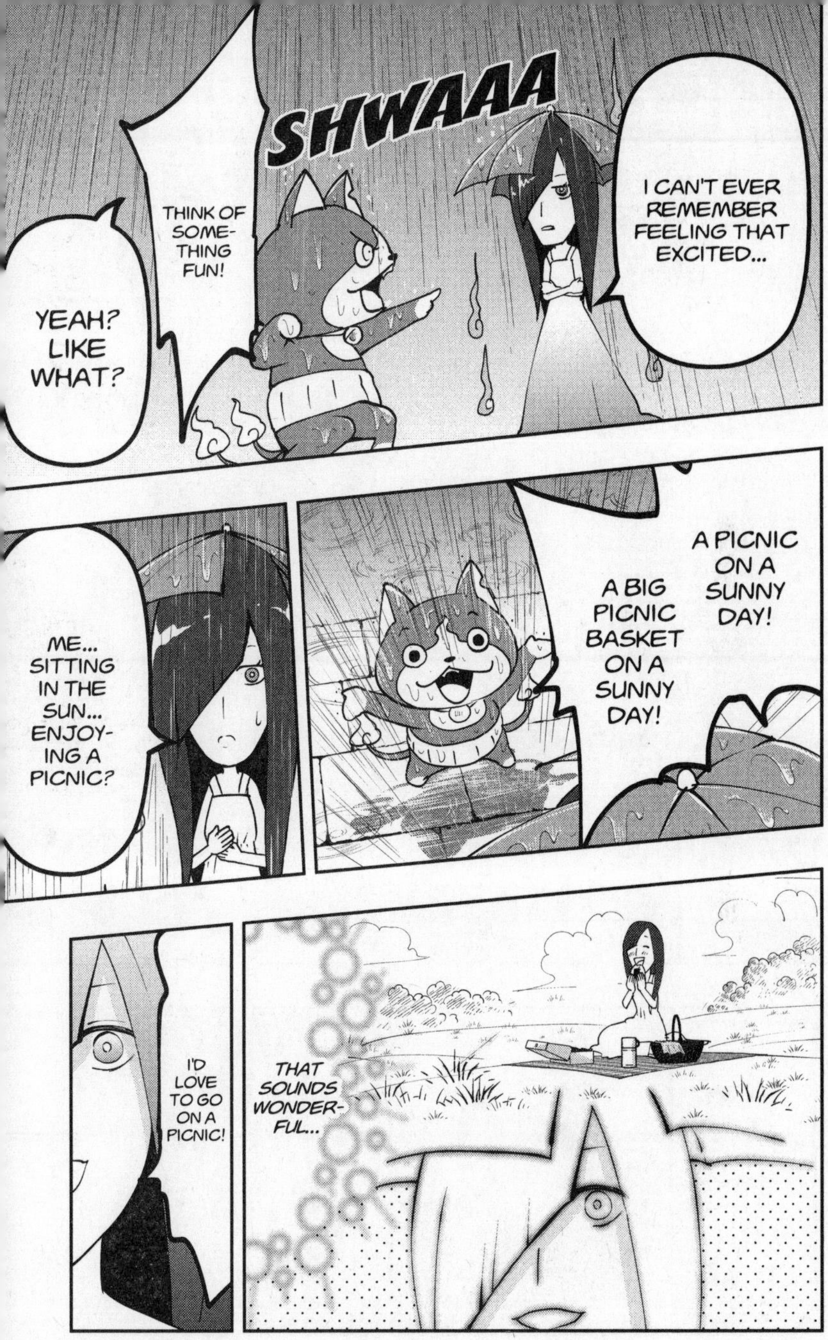
I CAN'T EVER REMEMBER FEELING THAT EXCITED...
SHWAAA
THINK OF SOME-THING FUN!
YEAH? LIKE WHAT?
A PICNIC ON A SUNNY DAY!
A BIG PICNIC BASKET ON A SUNNY DAY!
ME... SITTING IN THE SUN... ENJOY-ING A PICNIC?
THAT SOUNDS WONDER-FUL...
I'D LOVE TO GO ON A PICNIC!

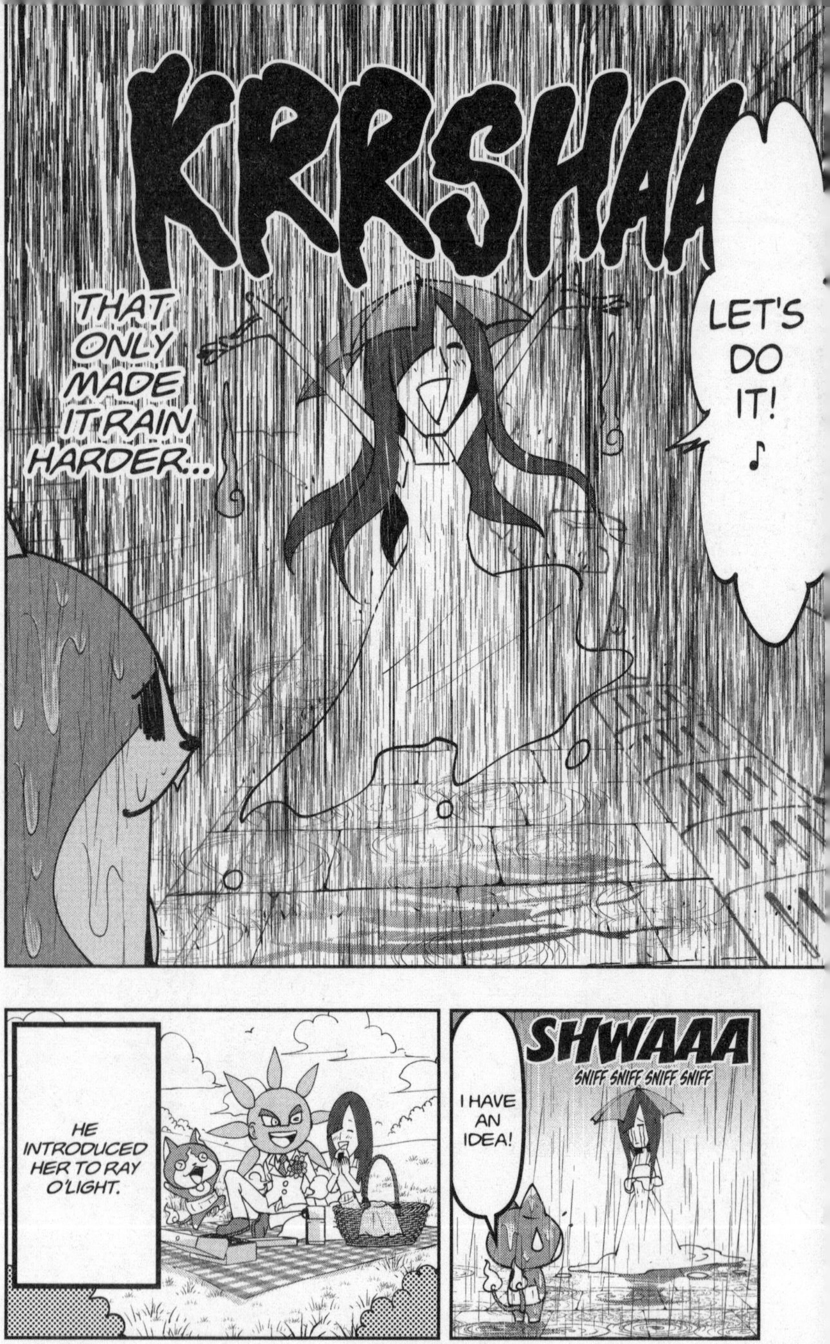
KRRSHAA
LET'S DO IT! ♪
THAT ONLY MADE IT RAIN HARDER...
SHWAAA
SNIFF SNIFF SNIFF SNIFF
I HAVE AN IDEA!
HE INTRODUCED HER TO RAY O'LIGHT.

CHAPTER 249
SPACE LOVING YO-KAI USAPYON

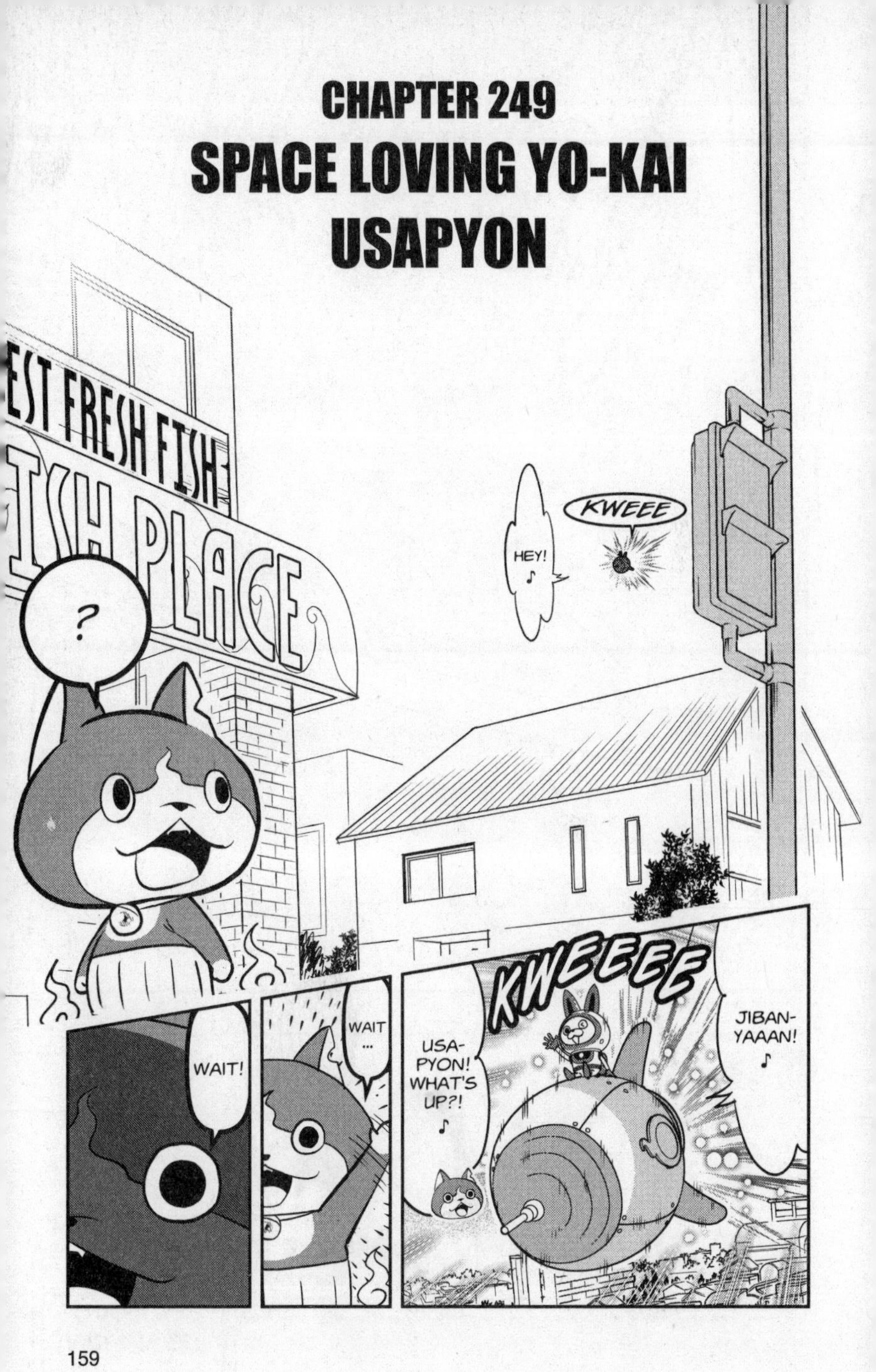
KWEEE
HEY! ♪
?
EST FRESH FISH
ISH PLACE
JIBAN-YAAAN! ♪
KWEEEEE
USA-PYON! WHAT'S UP?! ♪
WAIT ...
WAIT!

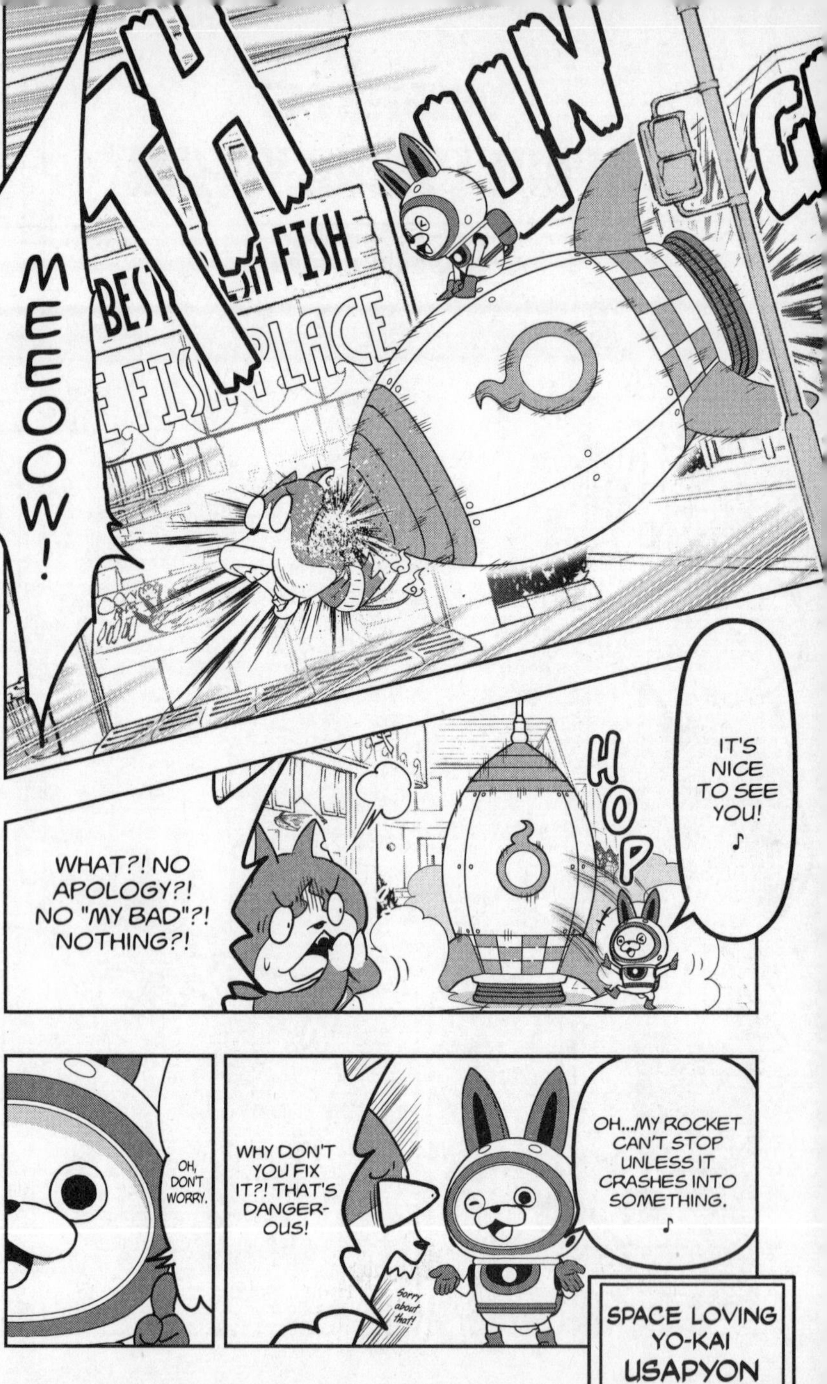
MEEOOW!
HOP
IT'S NICE TO SEE YOU! ♪
WHAT?! NO APOLOGY?! NO "MY BAD"?! NOTHING?!
OH...MY ROCKET CAN'T STOP UNLESS IT CRASHES INTO SOMETHING. ♪
WHY DON'T YOU FIX IT?! THAT'S DANGER-OUS!
Sorry about that!
SPACE LOVING YO-KAI USAPYON
OH, DON'T WORRY.

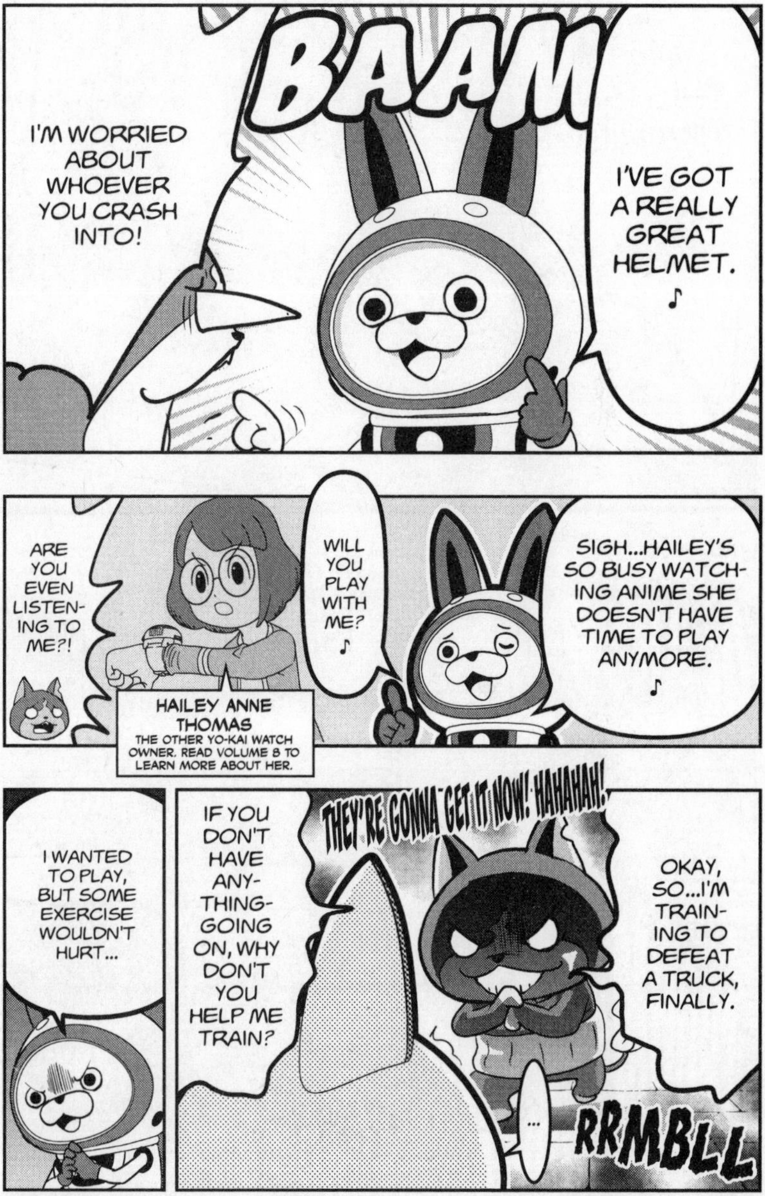
BAAM
I'VE GOT A REALLY GREAT HELMET. ♪
I'M WORRIED ABOUT WHOEVER YOU CRASH INTO!
SIGH...HAILEY'S SO BUSY WATCH-ING ANIME SHE DOESN'T HAVE TIME TO PLAY ANYMORE. ♪
WILL YOU PLAY WITH ME? ♪
ARE YOU EVEN LISTEN-ING TO ME?!
HAILEY ANNE THOMAS
THE OTHER YO-KAI WATCH OWNER. READ VOLUME 8 TO LEARN MORE ABOUT HER.
THEY'RE GONNA GET IT NOW! HAHAHAH!
OKAY, SO...I'M TRAIN-ING TO DEFEAT A TRUCK, FINALLY.
IF YOU DON'T HAVE ANY-THING-GOING ON, WHY DON'T YOU HELP ME TRAIN?
...
RRMBLL
I WANTED TO PLAY, BUT SOME EXERCISE WOULDN'T HURT...

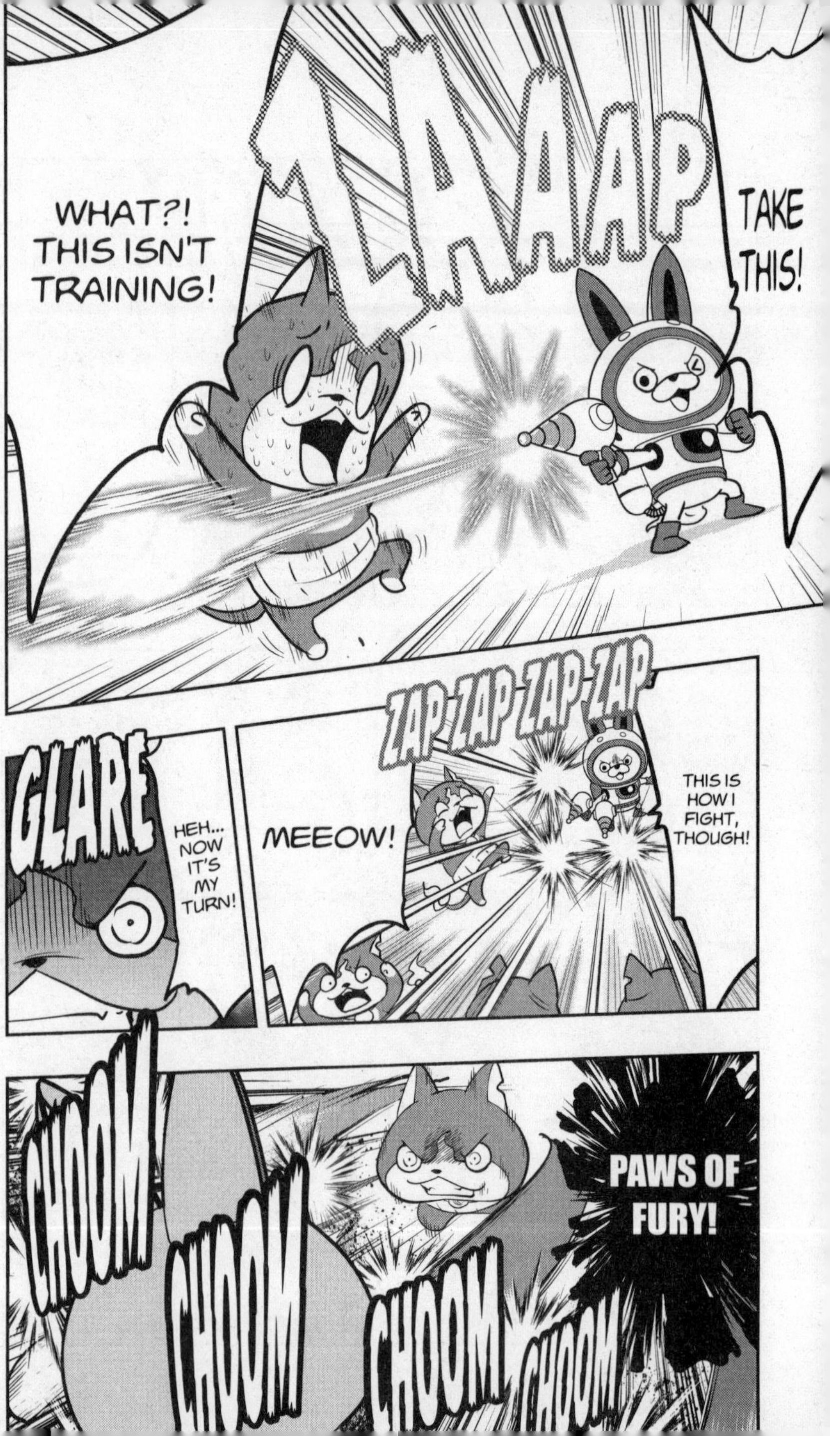
TAKE THIS!
ZZAAAP
WHAT?! THIS ISN'T TRAINING!
ZAP ZAP ZAP ZAP
THIS IS HOW I FIGHT, THOUGH!
MEEOW!
HEH... NOW IT'S MY TURN!
GLARE
PAWS OF FURY!
CHOOM
CHOOM
CHOOM
CHOOM

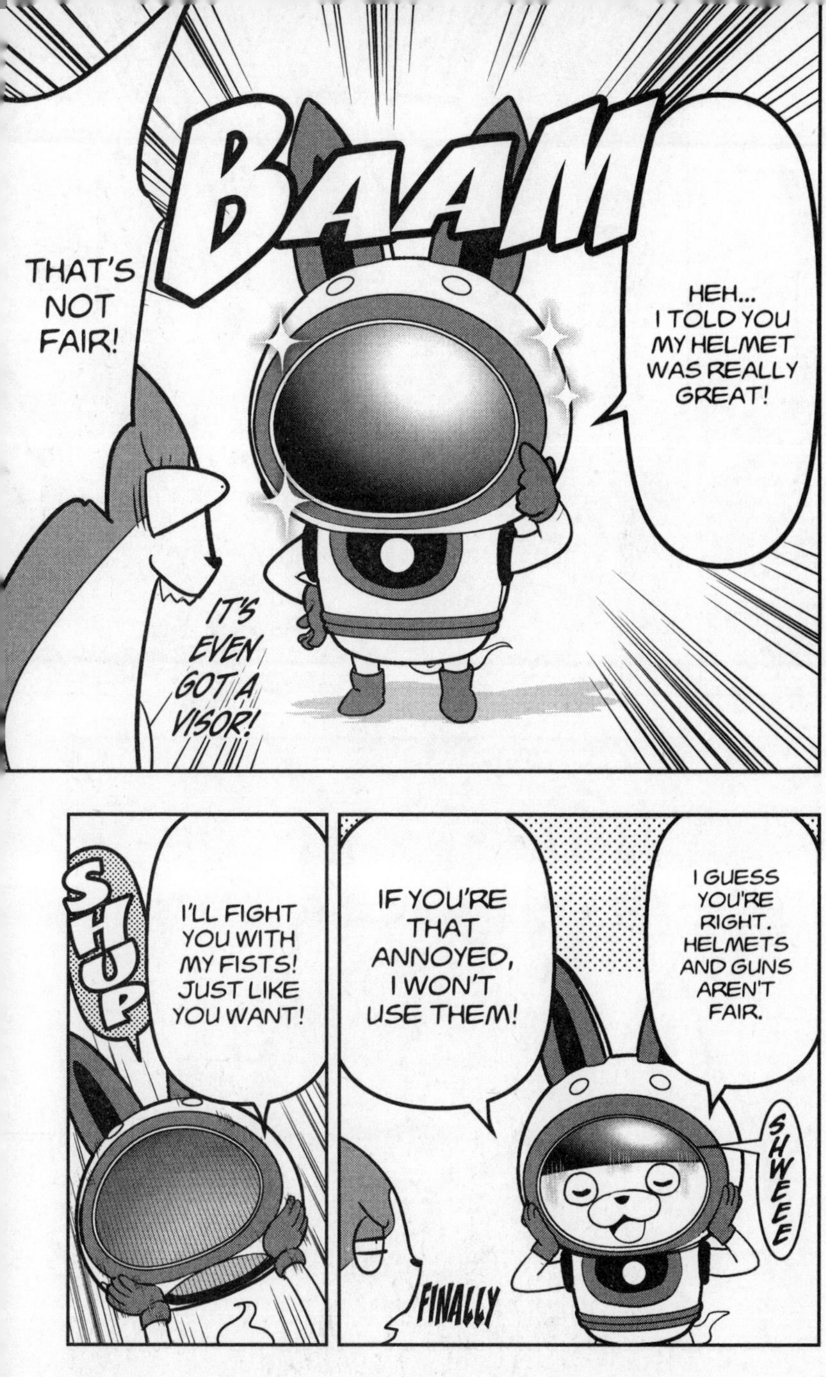
BAAM
HEH... I TOLD YOU MY HELMET WAS REALLY GREAT!
THAT'S NOT FAIR!
IT'S EVEN GOT A VISOR!
I GUESS YOU'RE RIGHT. HELMETS AND GUNS AREN'T FAIR.
IF YOU'RE THAT ANNOYED, I WON'T USE THEM!
SHWEEE
FINALLY
I'LL FIGHT YOU WITH MY FISTS! JUST LIKE YOU WANT!
SHUP

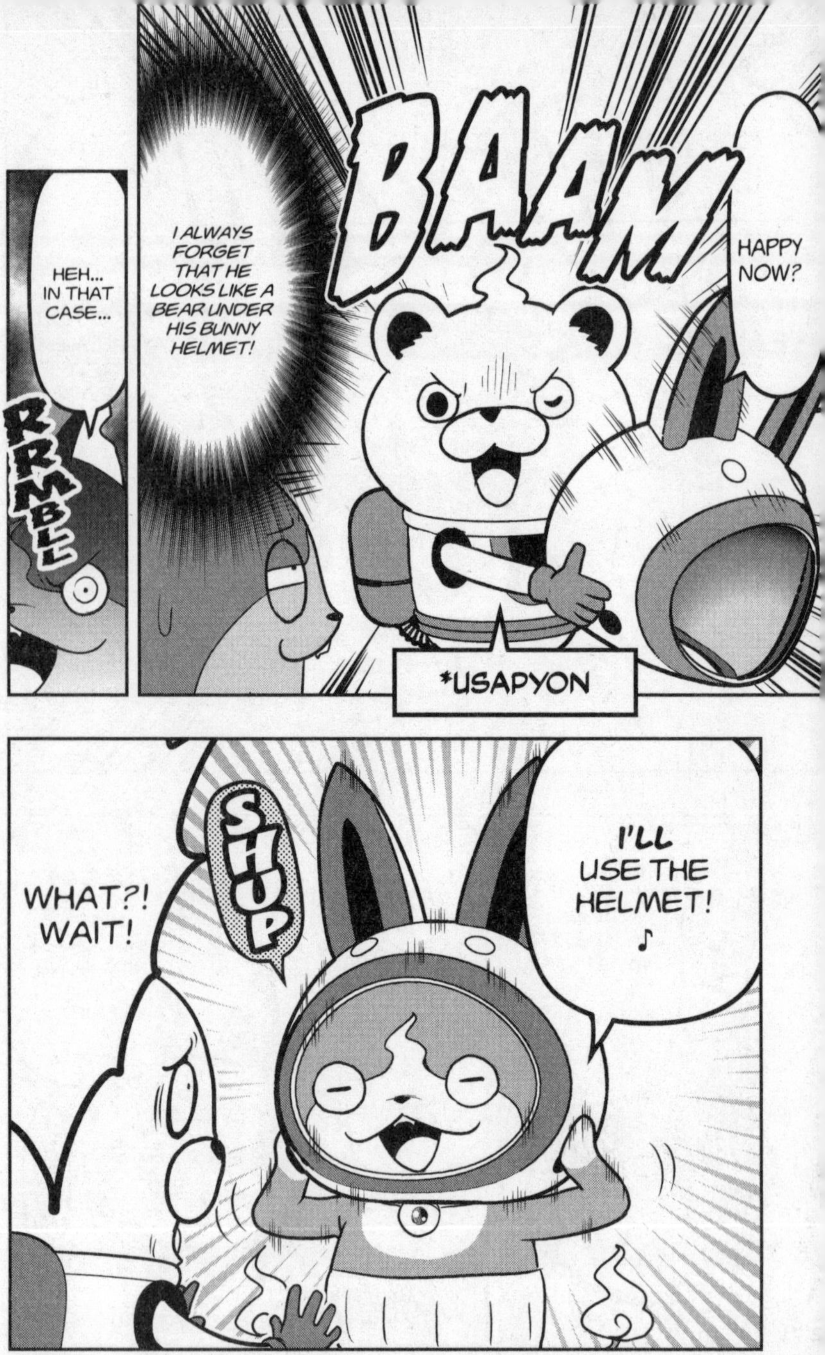
BAAM
HAPPY NOW?
I ALWAYS FORGET THAT HE LOOKS LIKE A BEAR UNDER HIS BUNNY HELMET!
*USAPYON
HEH... IN THAT CASE...
RRMBLE
I'LL USE THE HELMET! ♪
SHUP
WHAT?! WAIT!

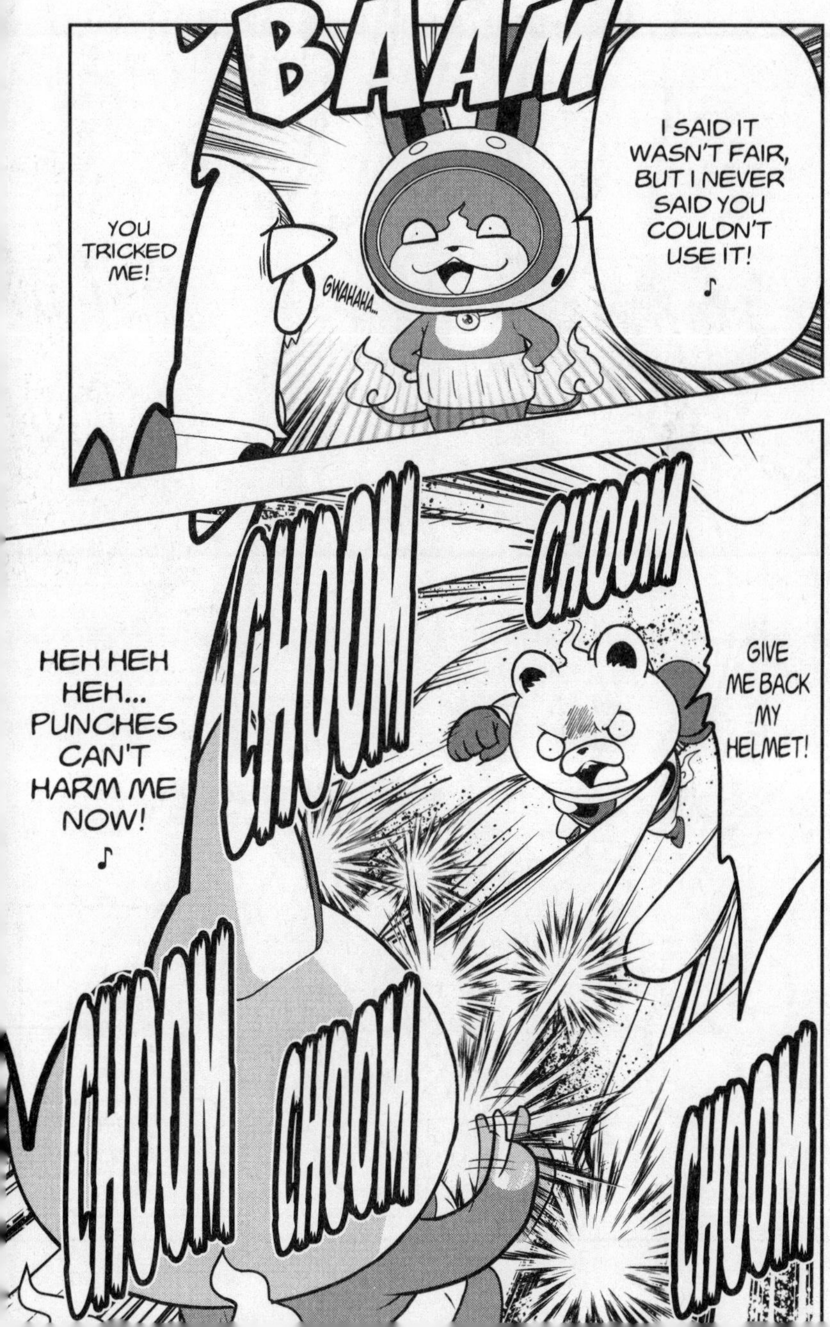
BAAM
I SAID IT WASN'T FAIR, BUT I NEVER SAID YOU COULDN'T USE IT! ♪
GWAHAHA...
YOU TRICKED ME!
CHOOM
GIVE ME BACK MY HELMET!
CHOOM
HEH HEH HEH... PUNCHES CAN'T HARM ME NOW! ♪
CHOOM
CHOOM
CHOOM

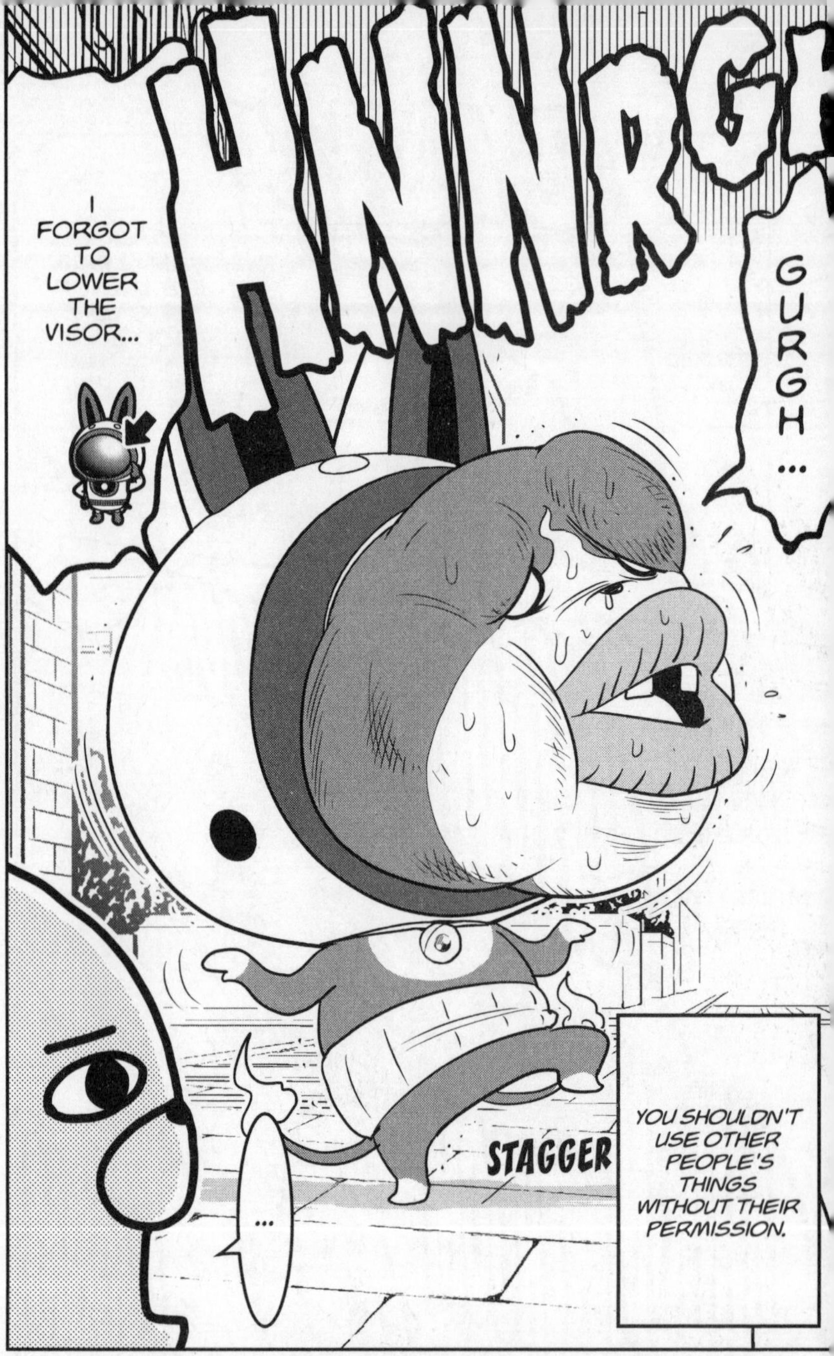
HNNRG
GURGH...
I FORGOT TO LOWER THE VISOR...
YOU SHOULDN'T USE OTHER PEOPLE'S THINGS WITHOUT THEIR PERMISSION.
STAGGER
...

CHAPTER 250
FLURRY YO-KAI CEREAL SPILLER

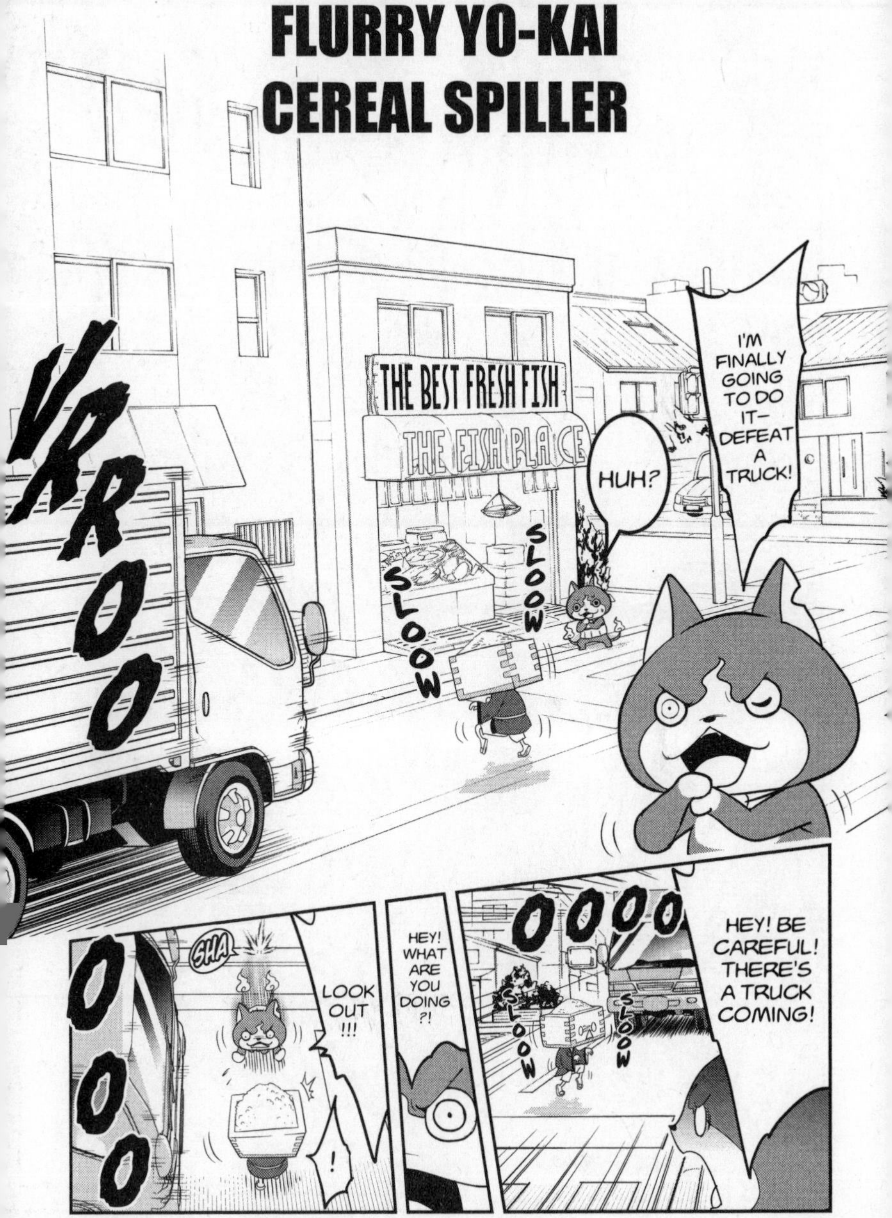
I'M FINALLY GOING TO DO IT— DEFEAT A TRUCK!
HUH?
THE BEST FRESH FISH
THE FISH PLACE
SLOOW
SLOOW
VRROOO
HEY! BE CAREFUL! THERE'S A TRUCK COMING!
OOOO
SLOOW
SLOOW
HEY! WHAT ARE YOU DOING?!
LOOK OUT!!!
SHA
OOOO
!

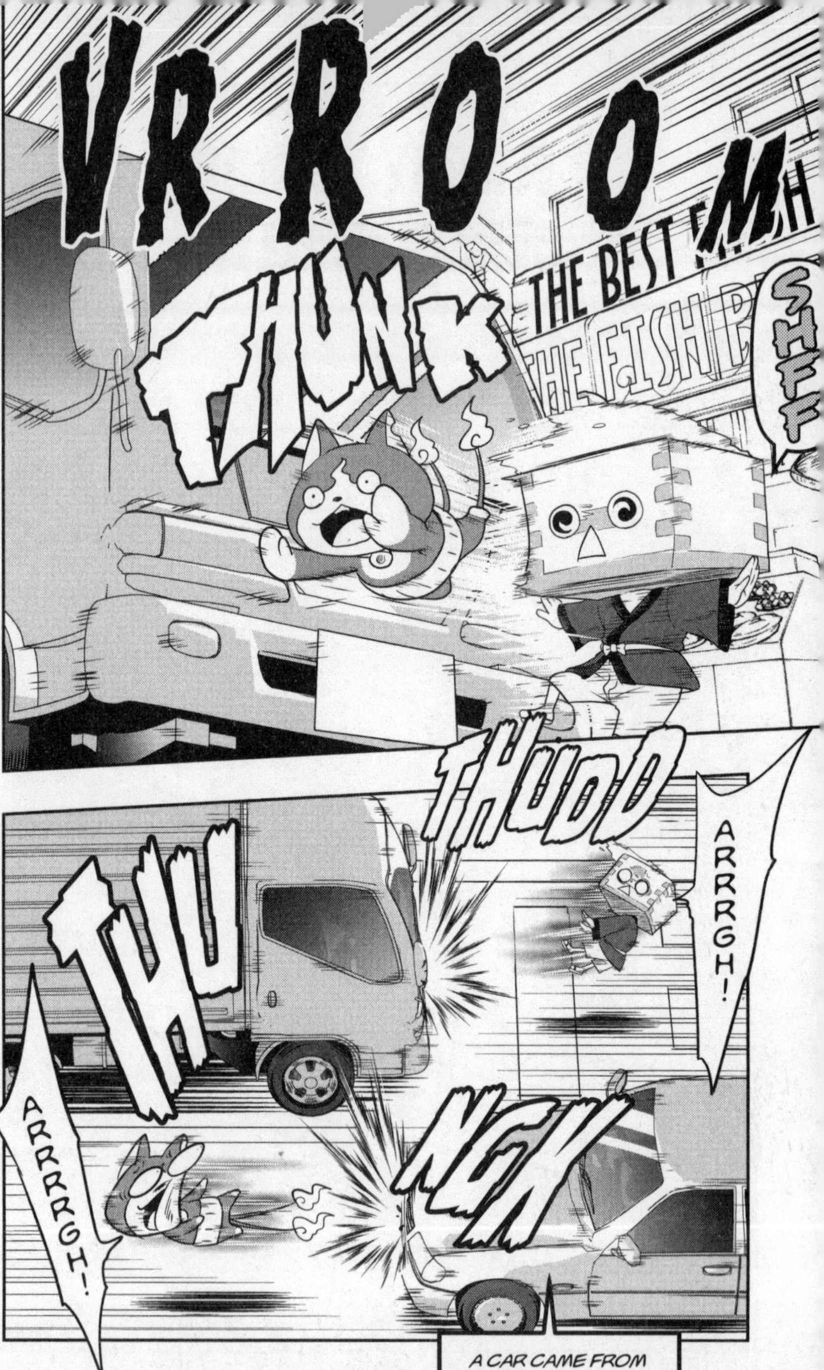
VRROOM
THE BEST
THE FISH
SHFF
THUNK
THUDD
ARRRGH!
THUNCK
ARRRRGH!
A CAR CAME FROM THE OTHER WAY TOO...

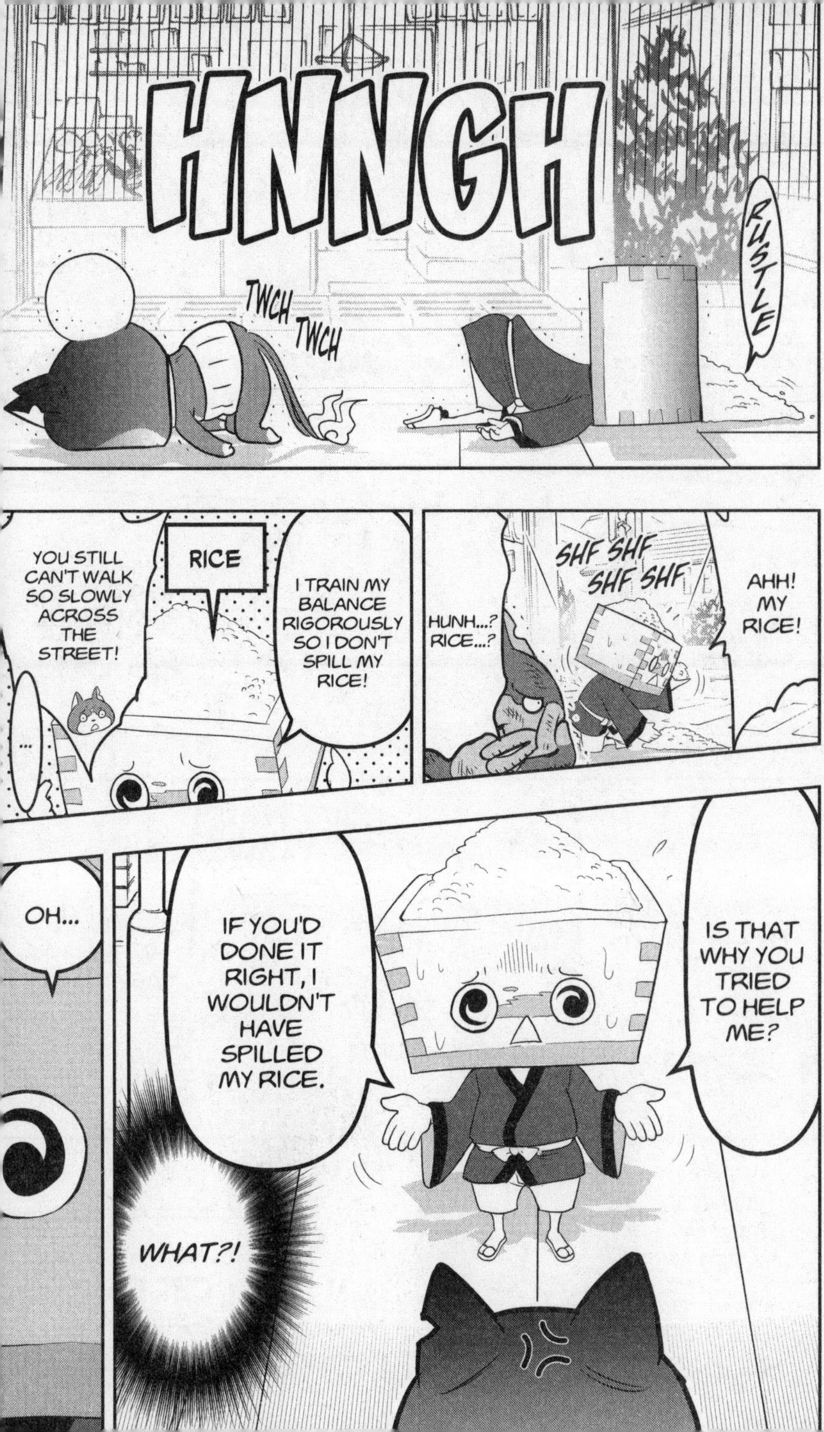
RUSTLE
HNNGH
TWCH TWCH
AHH! MY RICE!
SHF SHF SHF SHF
HUNH...? RICE...?
I TRAIN MY BALANCE RIGOROUSLY SO I DON'T SPILL MY RICE!
RICE
YOU STILL CAN'T WALK SO SLOWLY ACROSS THE STREET!
...
IS THAT WHY YOU TRIED TO HELP ME?
IF YOU'D DONE IT RIGHT, I WOULDN'T HAVE SPILLED MY RICE.
OH...
WHAT?!

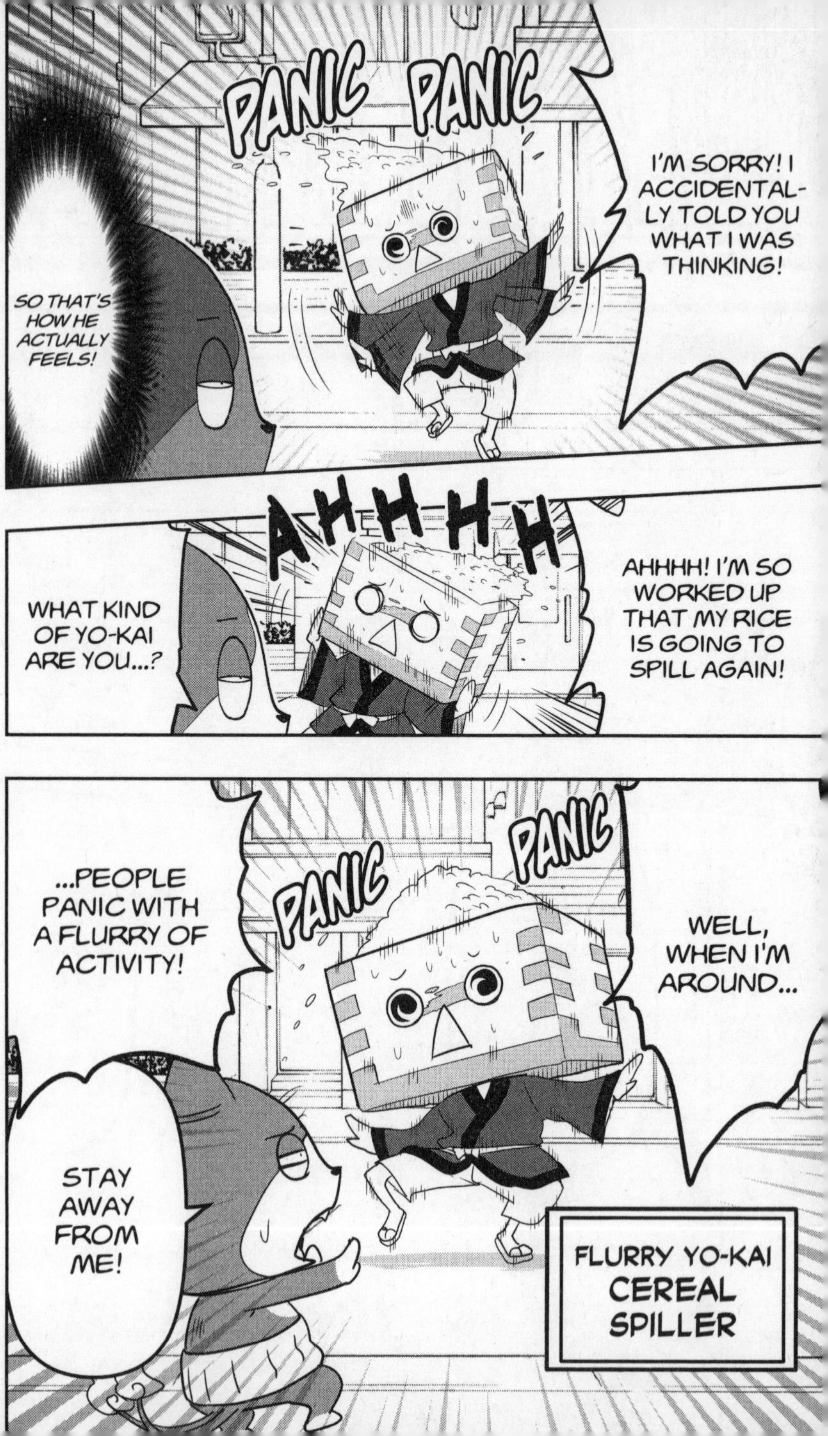
PANIC PANIC
I'M SORRY! I ACCIDENTAL-LY TOLD YOU WHAT I WAS THINKING!
SO THAT'S HOW HE ACTUALLY FEELS!
AHHHHH
AHHHH! I'M SO WORKED UP THAT MY RICE IS GOING TO SPILL AGAIN!
WHAT KIND OF YO-KAI ARE YOU...?
WELL, WHEN I'M AROUND...
PANIC PANIC
...PEOPLE PANIC WITH A FLURRY OF ACTIVITY!
FLURRY YO-KAI CEREAL SPILLER
STAY AWAY FROM ME!

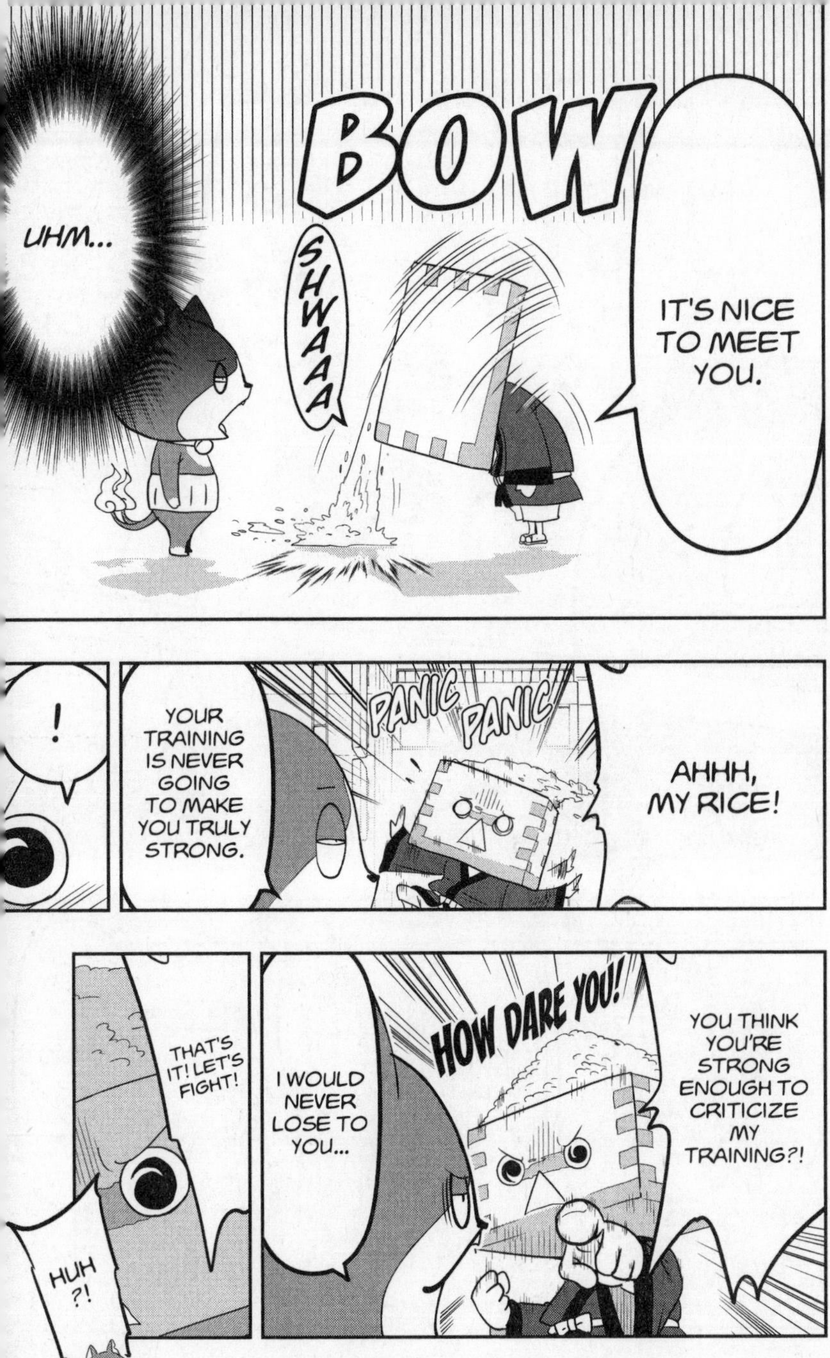
IT'S NICE TO MEET YOU.
BOW
SHWAAA
UHM...
AHHH, MY RICE!
PANIC PANIC
YOUR TRAINING IS NEVER GOING TO MAKE YOU TRULY STRONG.
!
YOU THINK YOU'RE STRONG ENOUGH TO CRITICIZE MY TRAINING?!
HOW DARE YOU!
I WOULD NEVER LOSE TO YOU...
THAT'S IT! LET'S FIGHT!
HUH ?!

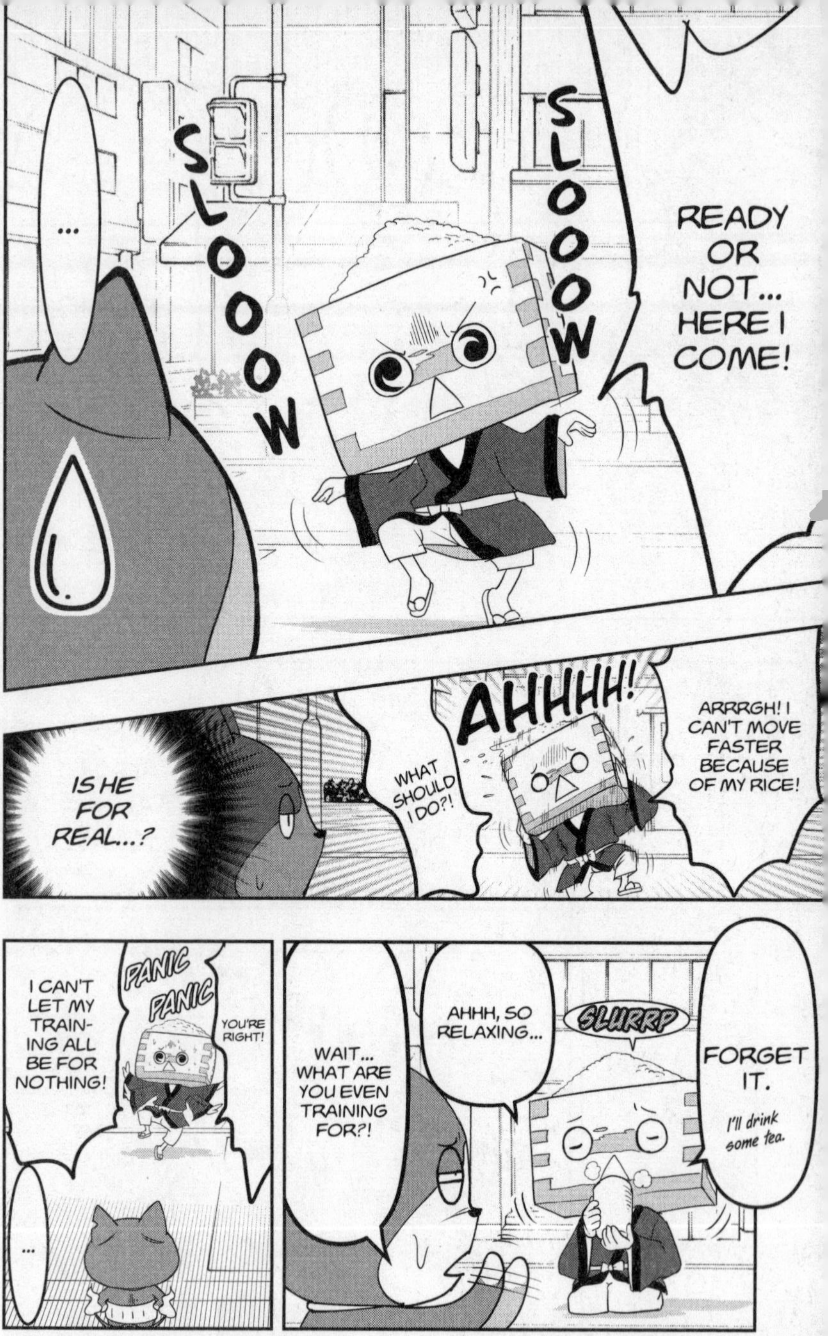
READY OR NOT... HERE I COME!
SLOOOW
SLOOOW
...
ARRRGH! I CAN'T MOVE FASTER BECAUSE OF MY RICE!
AHHHH!
WHAT SHOULD I DO?!
IS HE FOR REAL...?
FORGET IT.
I'll drink some tea.
SLURRP
AHHH, SO RELAXING...
WAIT... WHAT ARE YOU EVEN TRAINING FOR?!
PANIC
PANIC
YOU'RE RIGHT!
I CAN'T LET MY TRAIN-ING ALL BE FOR NOTHING!
...

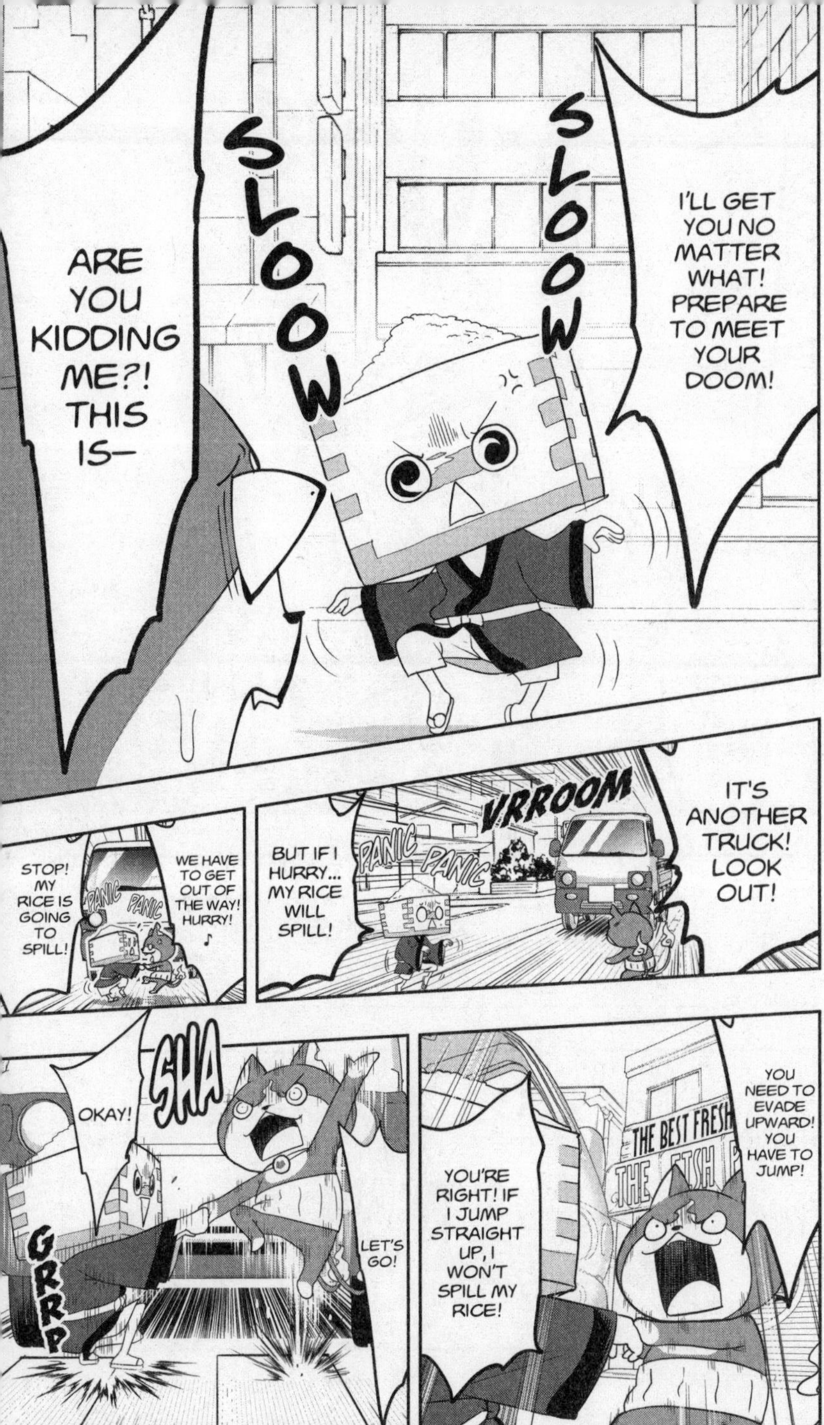
I'LL GET YOU NO MATTER WHAT! PREPARE TO MEET YOUR DOOM!
SLOOW
SLOOW
ARE YOU KIDDING ME?! THIS IS—
IT'S ANOTHER TRUCK! LOOK OUT!
VRROOM
PANIC PANIC
BUT IF I HURRY... MY RICE WILL SPILL!
WE HAVE TO GET OUT OF THE WAY! HURRY!
PANIC PANIC
STOP! MY RICE IS GOING TO SPILL!
YOU NEED TO EVADE UPWARD! YOU HAVE TO JUMP!
THE BEST FRESH
THE FISH
YOU'RE RIGHT! IF I JUMP STRAIGHT UP, I WON'T SPILL MY RICE!
LET'S GO!
SHA
OKAY!
GRRP

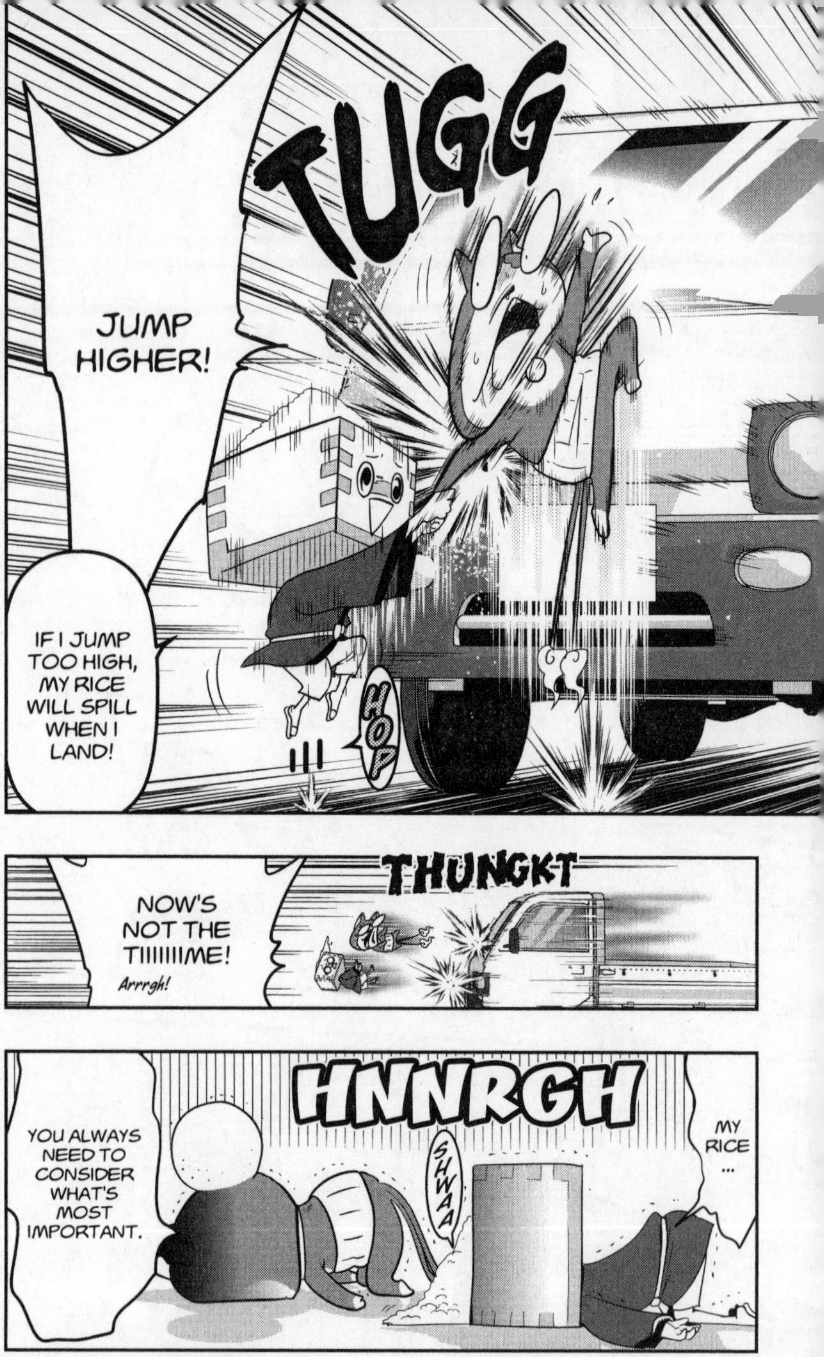
TUGG
JUMP HIGHER!
HOP
IF I JUMP TOO HIGH, MY RICE WILL SPILL WHEN I LAND!
THUNGKT
NOW'S NOT THE TIIIIIIIME!
Arrrgh!
HNNRGH
MY RICE ...
SHWAA
YOU ALWAYS NEED TO CONSIDER WHAT'S MOST IMPORTANT.

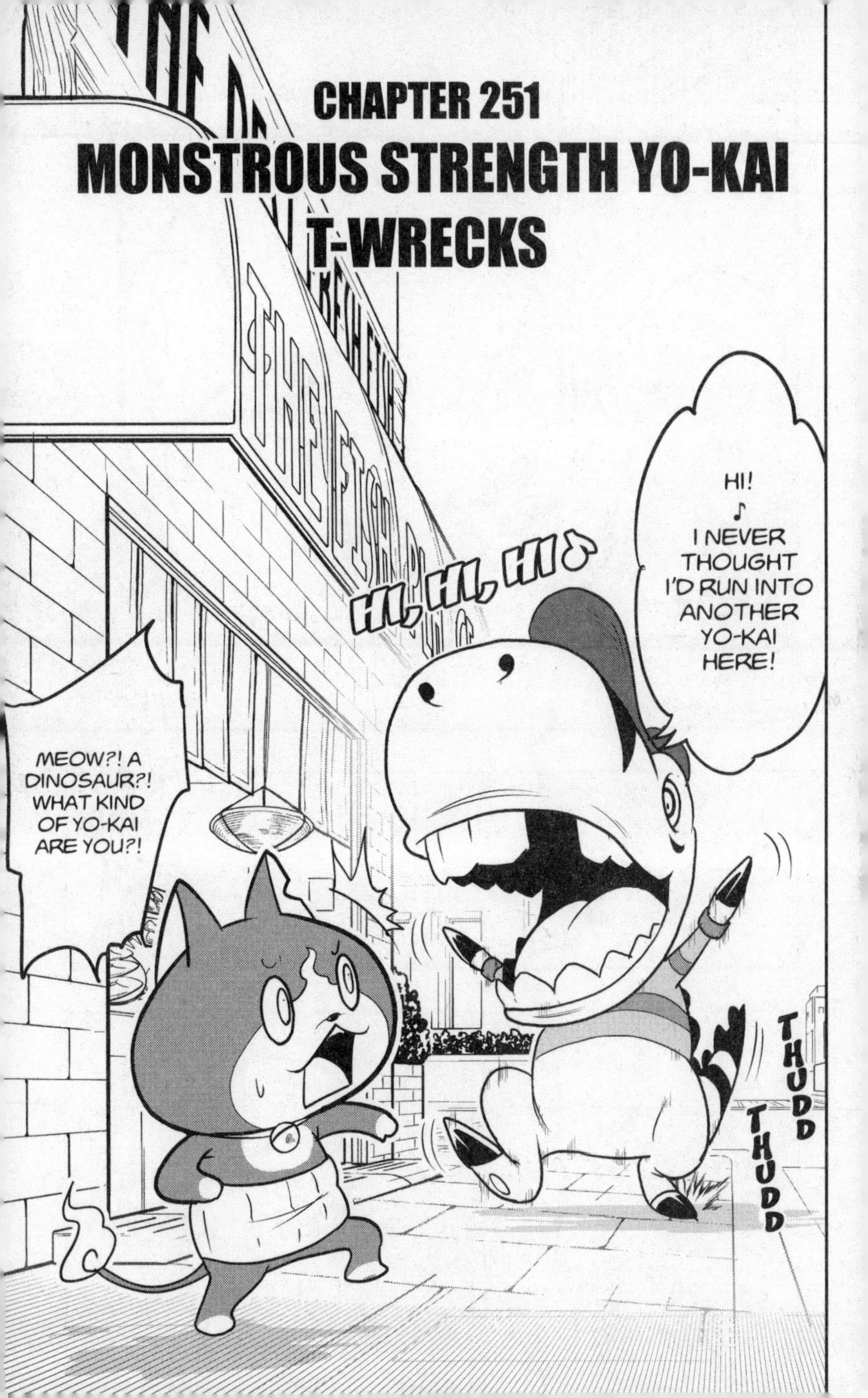
CHAPTER 251
MONSTROUS STRENGTH YO-KAI T-WRECKS
HI! ♪ I NEVER THOUGHT I'D RUN INTO ANOTHER YO-KAI HERE!
HI, HI, HI♪
MEOW?! A DINOSAUR?! WHAT KIND OF YO-KAI ARE YOU?!
THUDD
THUDD

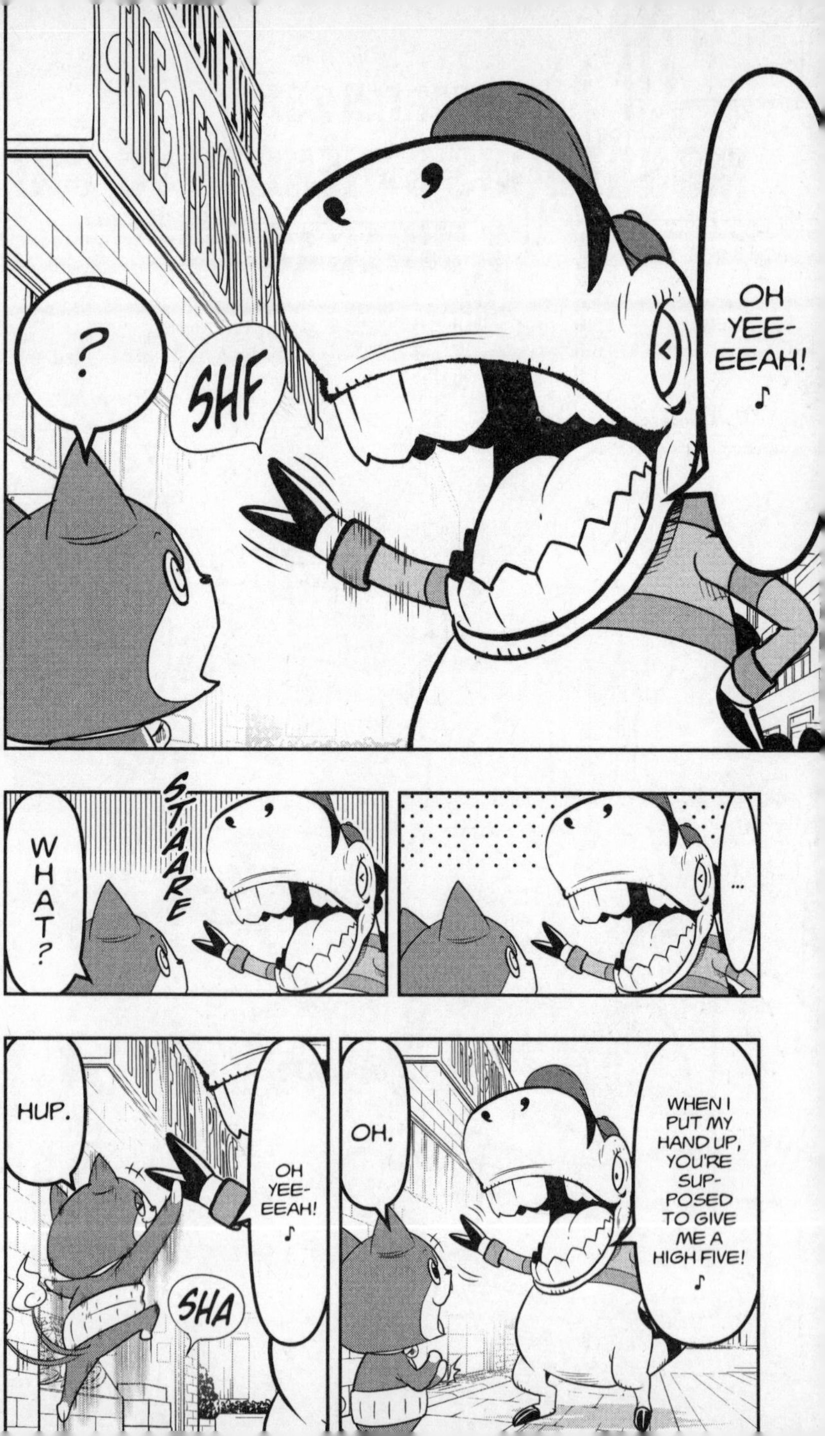
OH YEE-EEAH! ♪
SHF
?
...
STAARE
WHAT?
WHEN I PUT MY HAND UP, YOU'RE SUP-POSED TO GIVE ME A HIGH FIVE! ♪
OH.
OH YEE-EEAH! ♪
HUP.
SHA

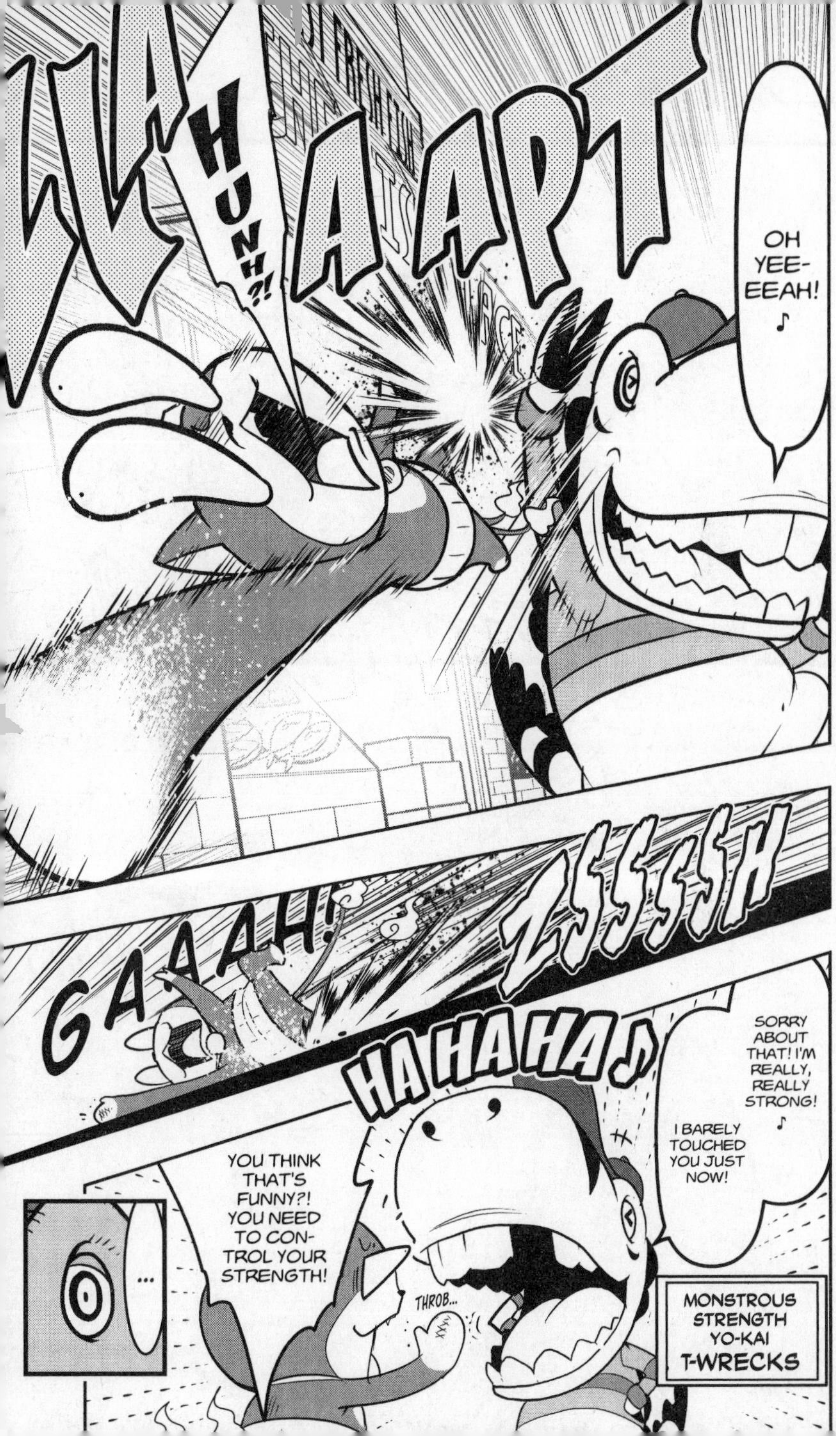
OH YEEEEAH! ♪
SLAAAPT
HUNH?!
ZSSSSSH
GAAAAH!
HA HA HA ♪
SORRY ABOUT THAT! I'M REALLY, REALLY STRONG! ♪
I BARELY TOUCHED YOU JUST NOW!
MONSTROUS STRENGTH YO-KAI T-WRECKS
THROB...
YOU THINK THAT'S FUNNY?! YOU NEED TO CONTROL YOUR STRENGTH!
...

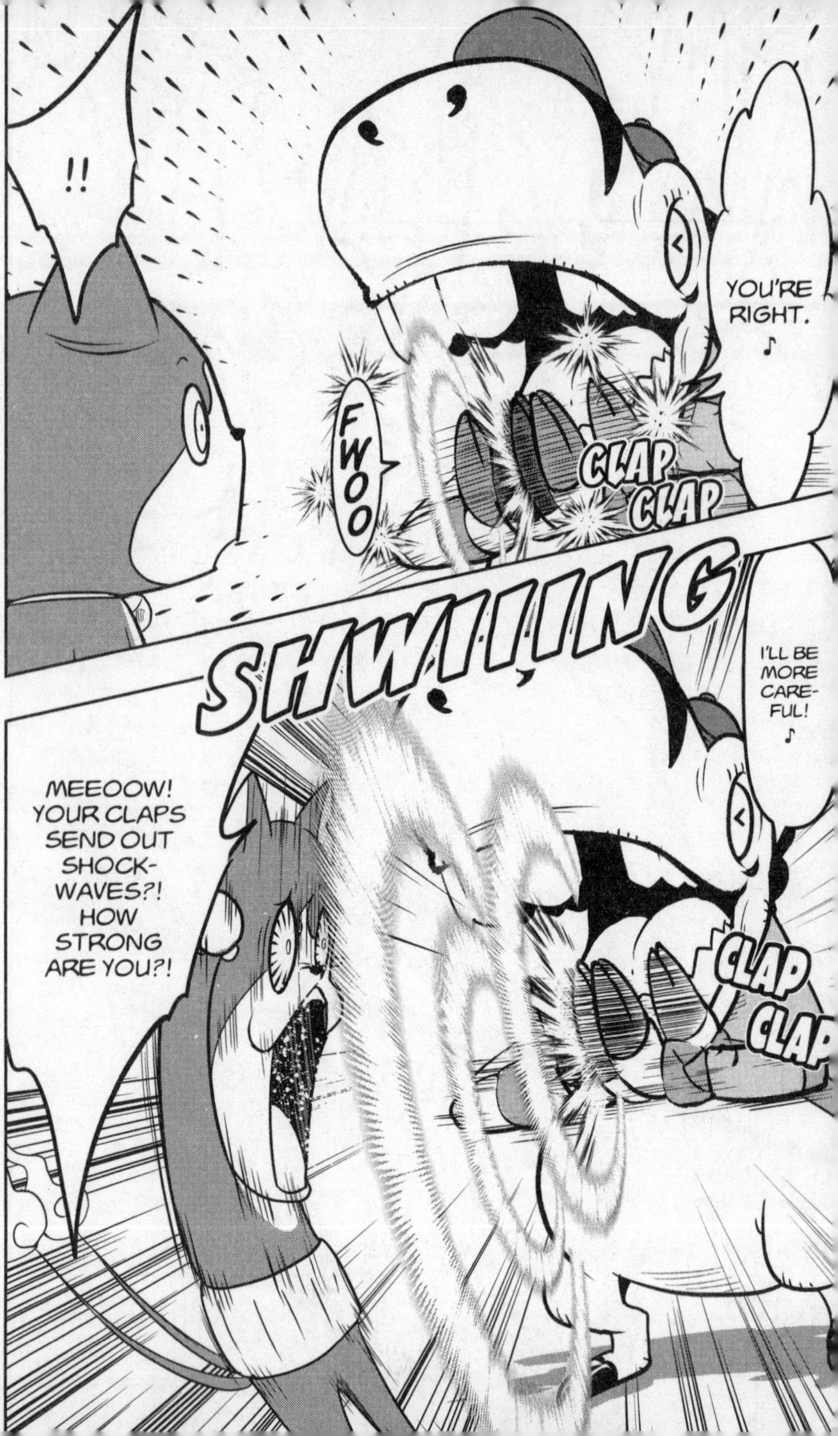
YOU'RE RIGHT. ♪
CLAP CLAP
FWOO
!!
SHWIIING
I'LL BE MORE CAREFUL! ♪
CLAP CLAP
MEEOOW! YOUR CLAPS SEND OUT SHOCKWAVES?! HOW STRONG ARE YOU?!

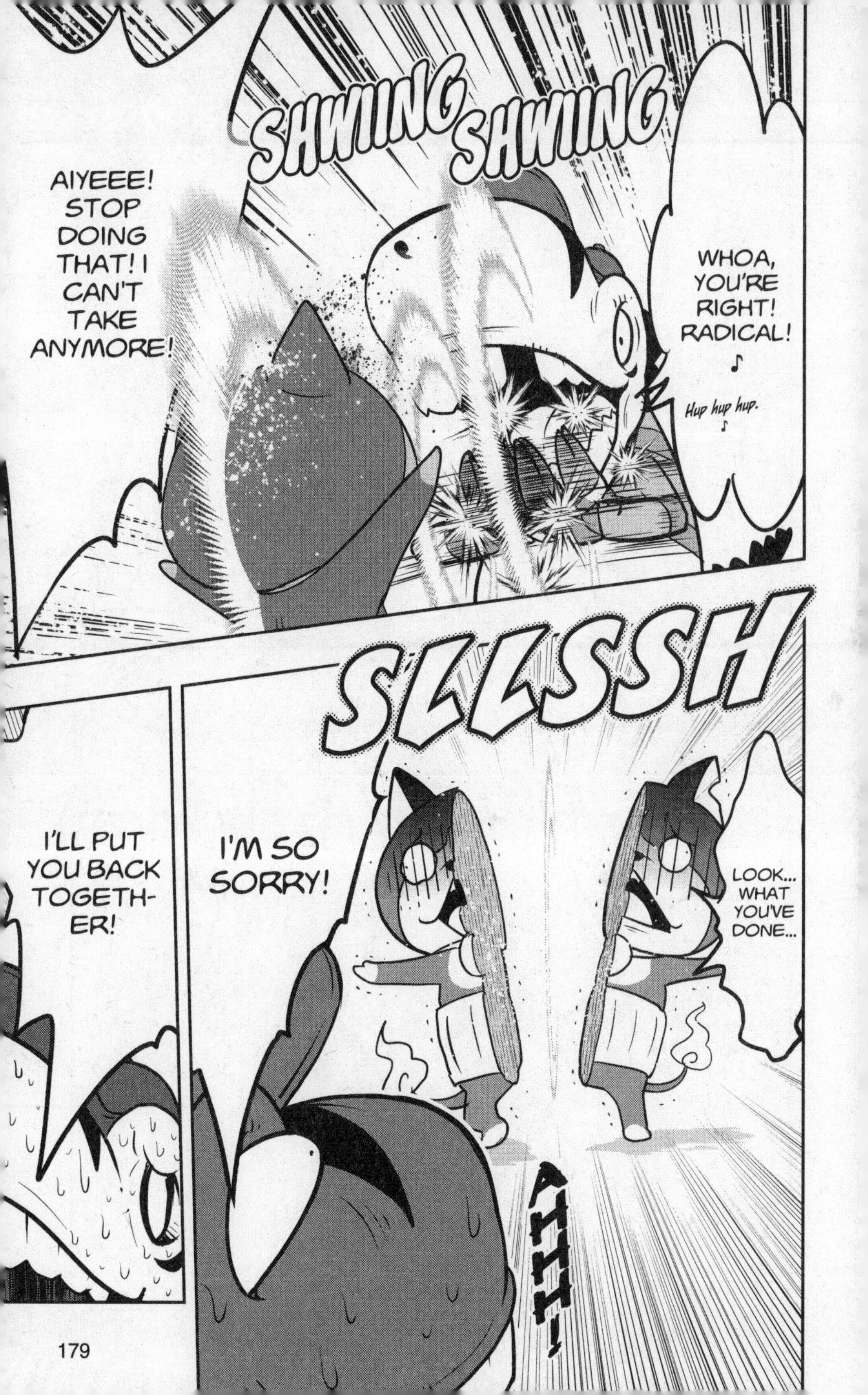
SHWIING SHWIING
WHOA, YOU'RE RIGHT! RADICAL! ♪
Hup hup hup. ♪
AIYEEE! STOP DOING THAT! I CAN'T TAKE ANYMORE!
SLLSSH
LOOK... WHAT YOU'VE DONE...
AHHH!
I'M SO SORRY!
I'LL PUT YOU BACK TOGETH-ER!

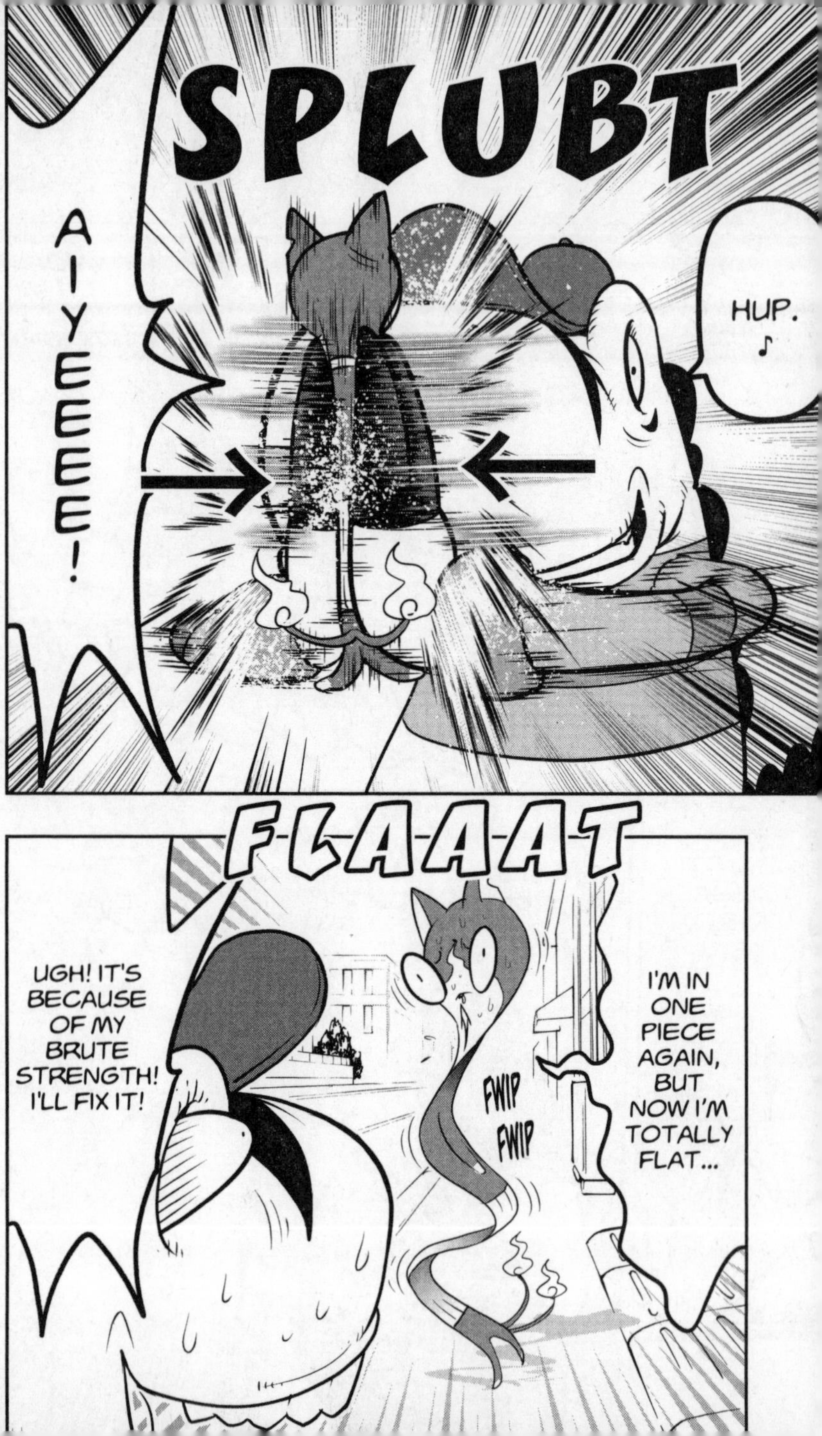
SPLUBT
HUP. ♪
AIYEEEEE!
FLAAAT
I'M IN ONE PIECE AGAIN, BUT NOW I'M TOTALLY FLAT...
FWIP FWIP
UGH! IT'S BECAUSE OF MY BRUTE STRENGTH! I'LL FIX IT!

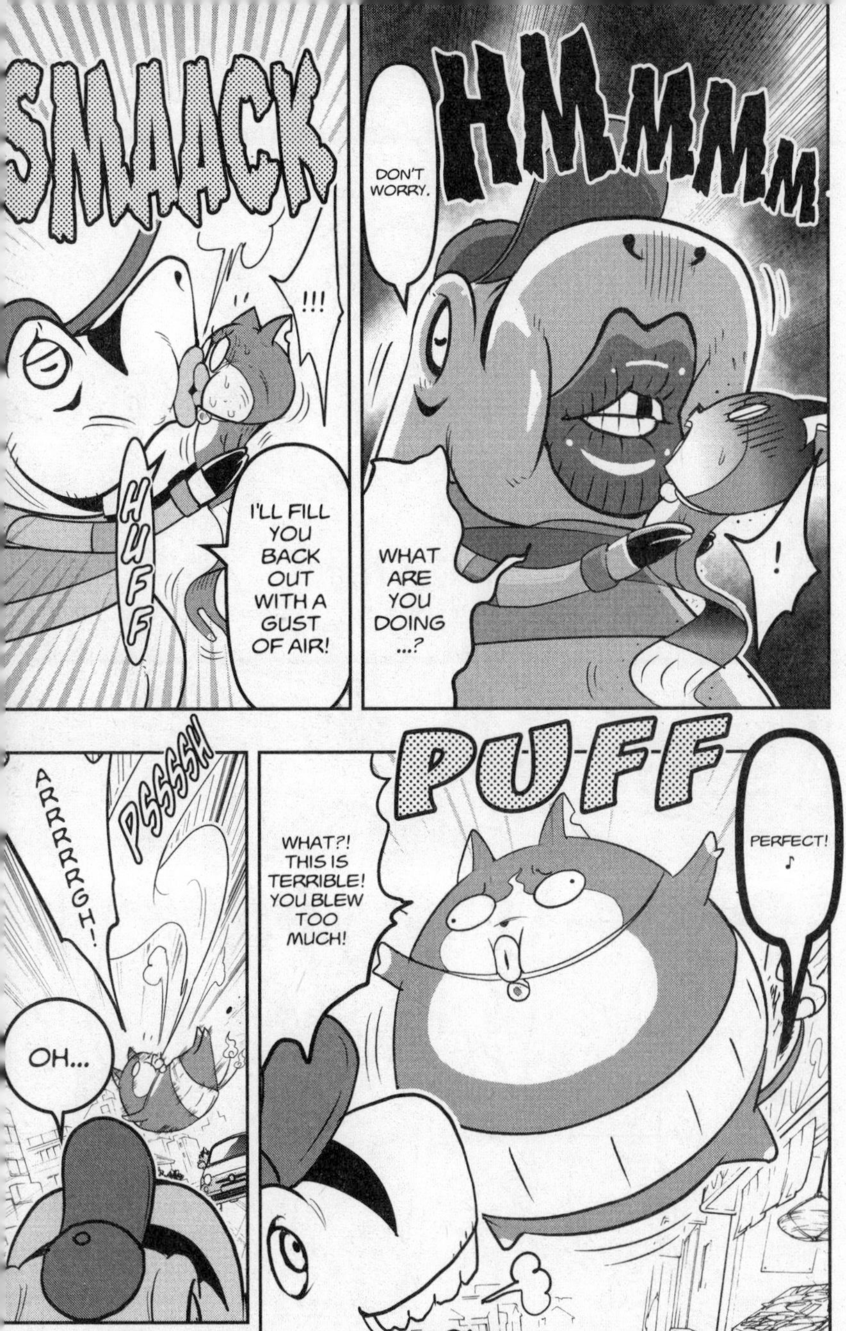
HMMMMM
DON'T WORRY.
!
WHAT ARE YOU DOING ...?
SMACK
!!!
I'LL FILL YOU BACK OUT WITH A GUST OF AIR!
HUFF
PUFF
PERFECT! ♪
WHAT?! THIS IS TERRIBLE! YOU BLEW TOO MUCH!
PSSSSH
ARRRRRGH!
OH...

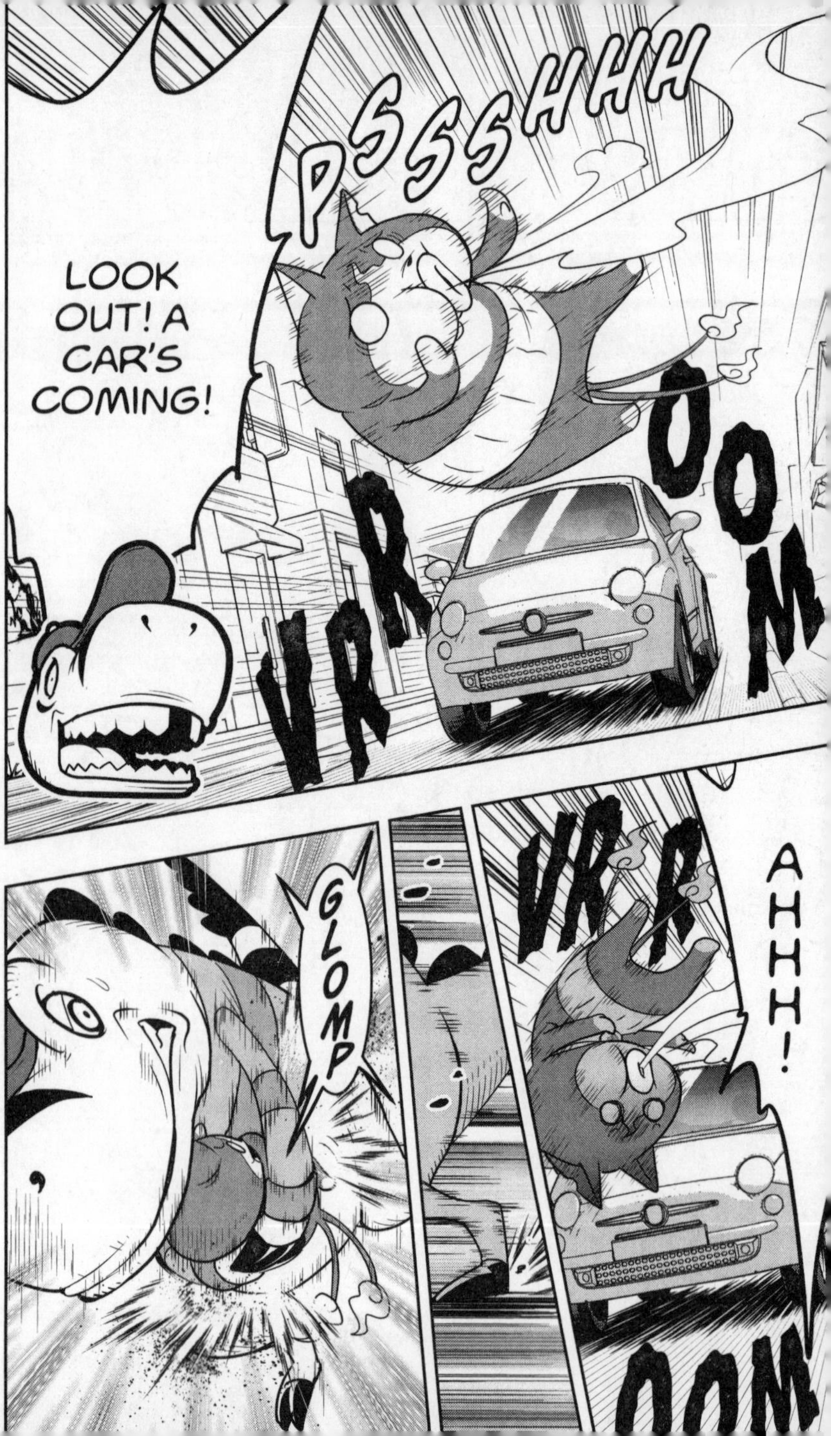
PSSSHHH
LOOK OUT! A CAR'S COMING!
VROOM
VRR
AHHH!
OOM
GLOMP

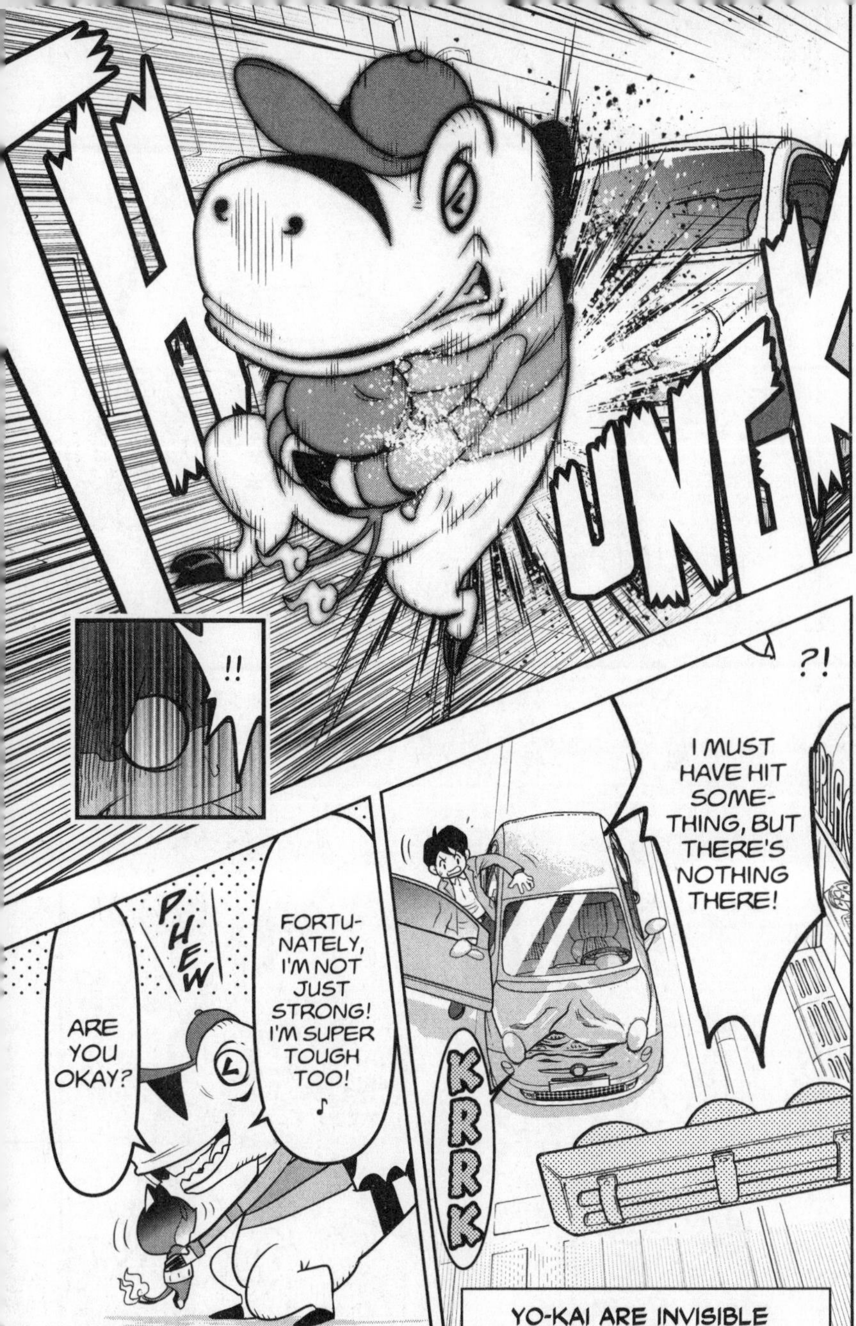

?!
I MUST HAVE HIT SOME-THING, BUT THERE'S NOTHING THERE!
KRRK
YO-KAI ARE INVISIBLE TO THE HUMAN EYE.
!!
PHEW
FORTU-NATELY, I'M NOT JUST STRONG! I'M SUPER TOUGH TOO! ♪
ARE YOU OKAY?

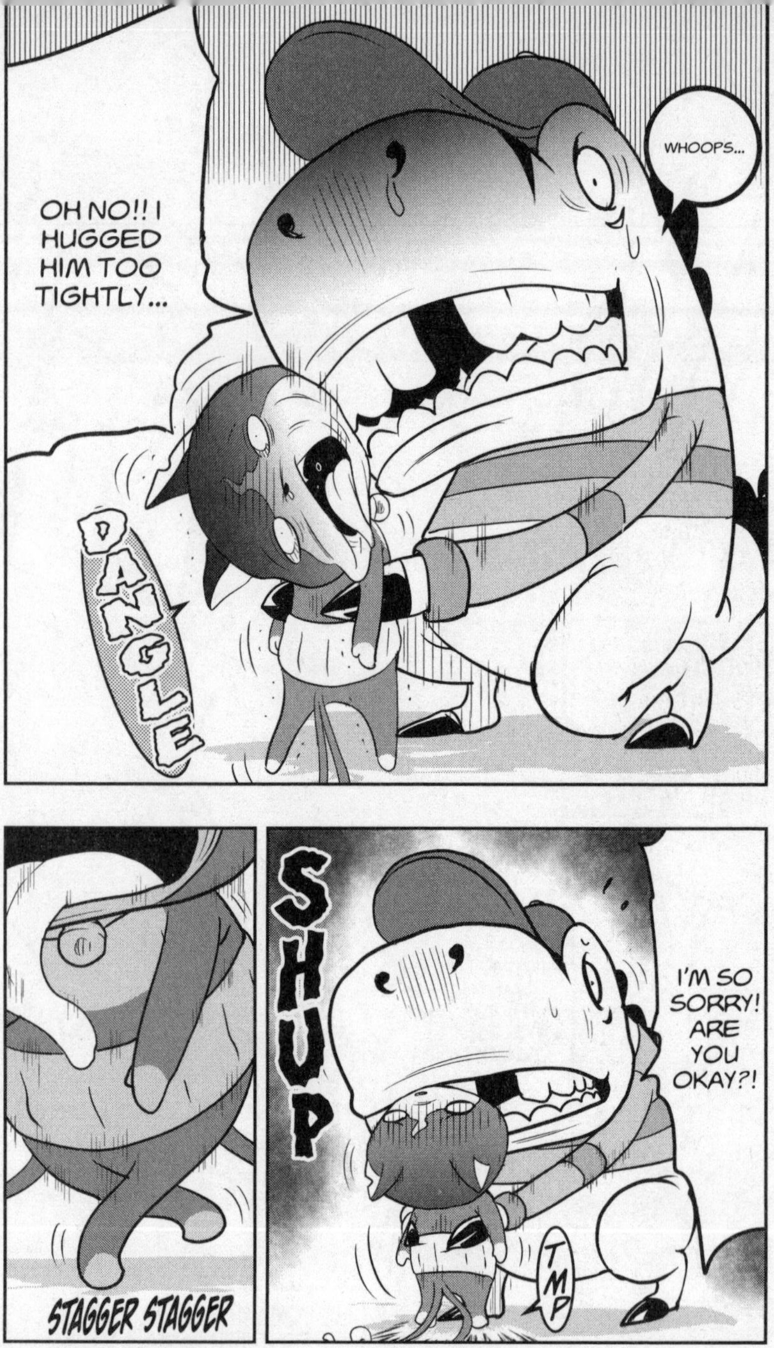
WHOOPS...
OH NO!! I HUGGED HIM TOO TIGHTLY...
DANGLE
I'M SO SORRY! ARE YOU OKAY?!
SHUP
TMP
STAGGER STAGGER

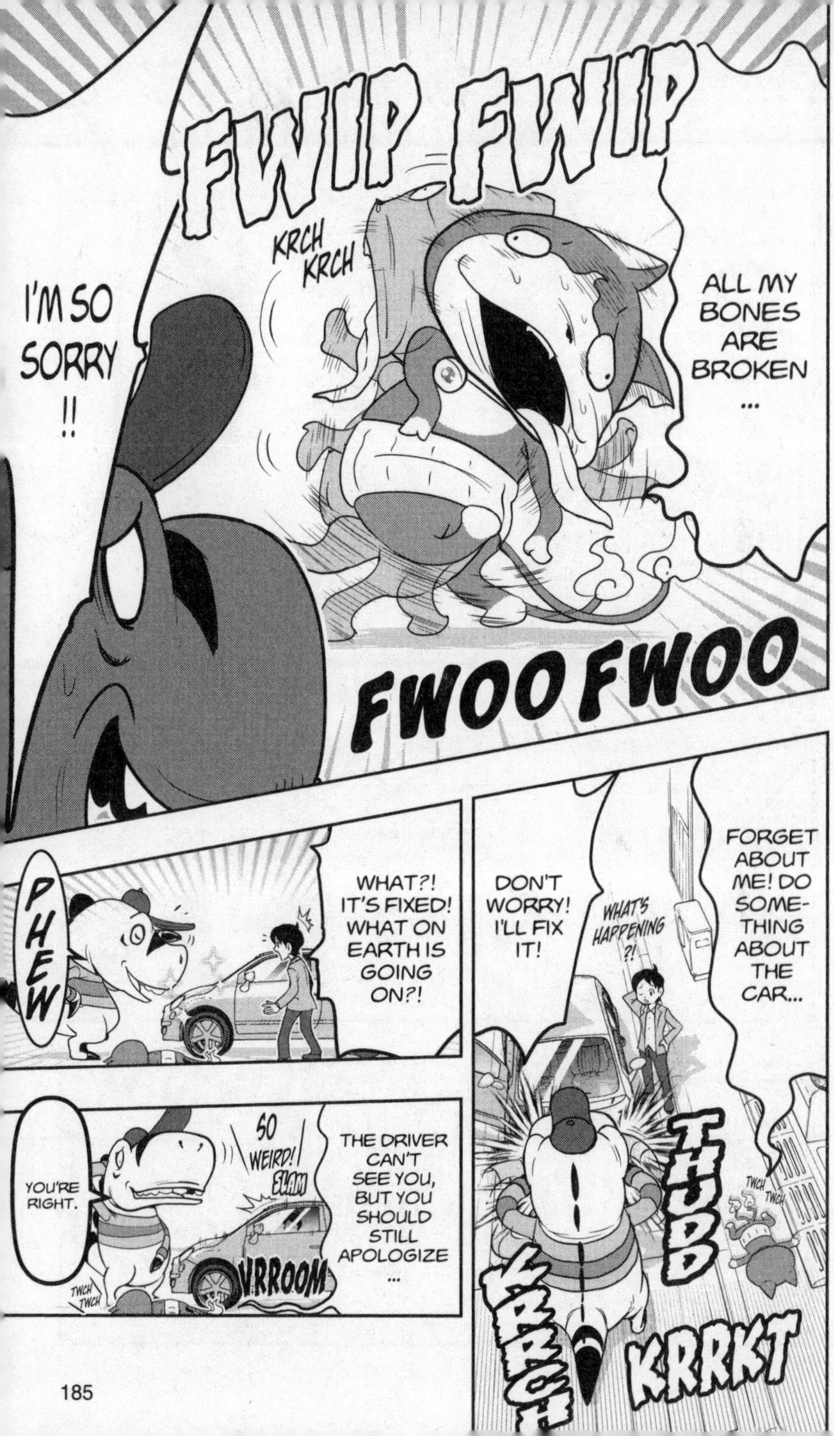
FWIP FWIP
ALL MY BONES ARE BROKEN...
KRCH KRCH
I'M SO SORRY!!
FWOO FWOO
FORGET ABOUT ME! DO SOME-THING ABOUT THE CAR...
WHAT'S HAPPENING?!
DON'T WORRY! I'LL FIX IT!
THUD
TWCH TWCH
KRRKT
WHAT?! IT'S FIXED! WHAT ON EARTH IS GOING ON?!
PHEW
THE DRIVER CAN'T SEE YOU, BUT YOU SHOULD STILL APOLOGIZE...
SO WEIRD!
SLAM
YOU'RE RIGHT.
VRROOM
TWCH TWCH

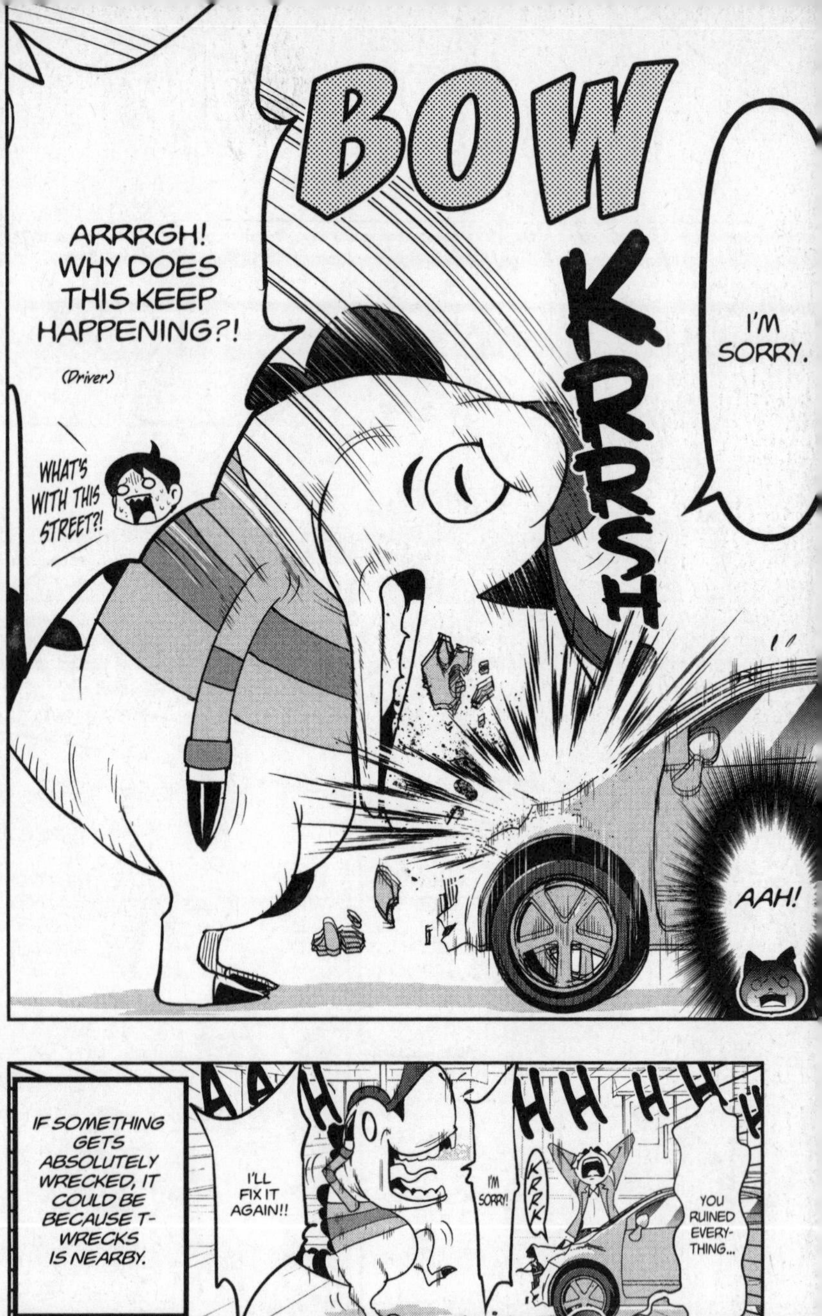
BOW
I'M SORRY.
KRRRSH
ARRRGH! WHY DOES THIS KEEP HAPPENING?!
(Driver)
WHAT'S WITH THIS STREET?!
AAH!
AAH HHHHH
YOU RUINED EVERY-THING...
KRRK
I'M SORRY!
I'LL FIX IT AGAIN!!
IF SOMETHING GETS ABSOLUTELY WRECKED, IT COULD BE BECAUSE T-WRECKS IS NEARBY.

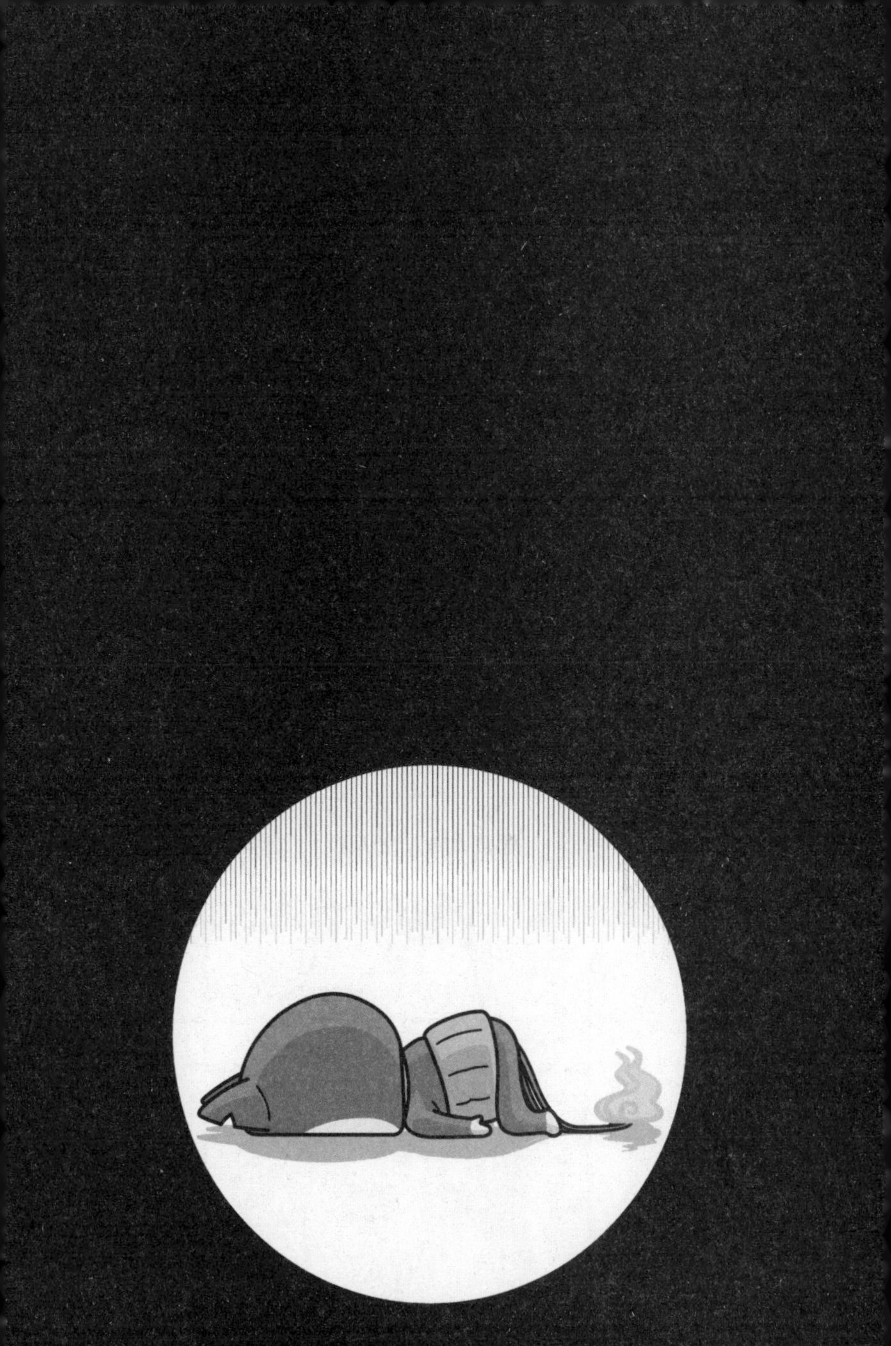

YO-KAI WATCH VOLUME 22 END! / CONTINUED IN VOLUME 23

TENTH ANNIVERSARY!

THIS MANGA SERIES BEGAN IN 2012.
ANNOUNCEMENT♪
THE VIDEO GAME CAME OUT IN 2013 AND THE ANIME STARTED IN 2014.
THAT MEANS THE *YO-KAI WATCH* MANGA REACHED ITS TENTH ANNIVERSARY IN DECEMBER OF 2022!
HURRAY!
THANK YOU VERY MUCH. ♪
A LOT HAPPENED DURING THESE TEN YEARS...
EMOTIONAL
YES, WE FOUGHT AGAINST MANY YO-KAI AND ALSO BE-FRIENDED MANY. ♪
...LIKE ALL THOSE SPIN-OFFS INCLUDING *SHADOW-SIDE*, *Y-SCHOOL HEROES*, AND SO ON...
OH, THAT'S WHAT YOU MEANT BY A LOT HAP-PENED.

AUTHOR BIO

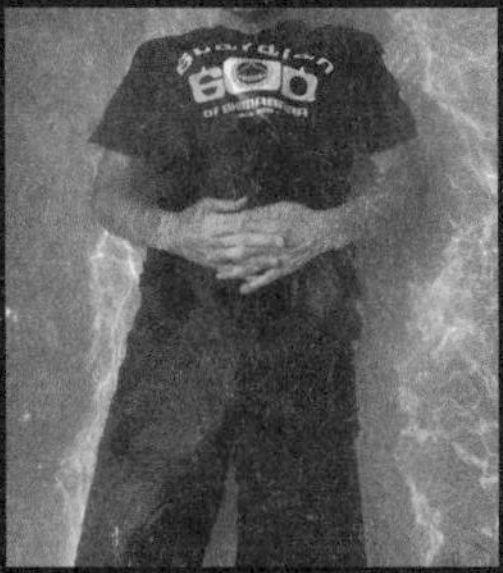

Guardian

December 22, the day volume 22 was published in Japan, marked the tenth anniversary of the series. There are also many spin-off manga titles based on the *Yo-kai Watch* movies, such as *Shadowside* and *Y School Heroes*. Including all of that, more than 30 titles have been published. I would like to thank all the fans who have supported me for ten years.

Cover Illustration: Noriyuki Konishi

Noriyuki Konishi hails from Shimabara City in Nagasaki Prefecture, Japan. He debuted with the one-shot *E-CUFF* in *Monthly Shonen Jump Original* in 1997. He is known in Japan for writing manga adaptations of *AM Driver* and *Mushiking: King of the Beetles*, along with *Saiyuki Hiro Go-Kū Den!*, *Chōhenshin Gag Gaiden!! Card Warrior Kamen Riders*, *Go-Go-Go Saiyuki: Shin Gokūden*, and more. Konishi was the recipient of the 38th Kodansha manga award in 2014 and the 60th Shogakukan manga award in 2015.